THINGS GO BUMP IN THE NIGHT

A Treasury of Classic Weird

Selected by
Douglas Draa and David A. Riley

Parallel Universe Publications

First Published in the UK in 2015
Collection © Douglas Draa and David A. Riley 2015

All rights reserved. No part of this publication may be reproduced, stored in a retrieval system, rebound or transmitted in any form or by any means, electronic, mechanical, photocopying, recording or otherwise, without the prior written permission of the author and publisher. This book is sold subject to the condition that it shall not by way of trade or otherwise be lent, resold, hired out or otherwise circulated without the publisher's prior consent in any form of binding or cover other than that in which it is published.

ISBN: 978-0-9574535-6-2
Parallel Universe Publications, 130 Union Road, Oswaldtwistle, Lancashire, BB5 3DR, UK

CONTENTS

Introduction	5
Douglas Draa	
The Ghoul	9
Sir Hugh Clifford	
The House of the Nightmare	25
Edward Lucas White	
The Voice in the Night	37
William Hope Hodgson	
The Thing from Outside	53
George Allan England	
For the Blood is the Life	77
F. Marion Crawford	
The White Wolf of the Hartz Mountains	97
Frederick Marryat	
The Room in the Tower	127
E. F. Benson	
His Unconquered Enemy	143
W. C. Morrow	
The Late Mrs. Fowke	155
Amyas Northcote	
Xélucha	167
M. P. Shiel	
A Narrow Escape	179
Lord Dunsany	
Thurnley Abbey	183
Perceval Landon	
The Black Stone	203
Robert E, Howard	
Werewolf of the Sahara	225
G. G. Pendarves	

The Devil of the Marsh	265
Henry Brereton Marriott Watson	
Fishhead	271
Irvin S. Cobb	
The Black Statue	283
Huan Mee	
The Pool of the Stone God	295
Abraham Merritt	
The Sea-Witch	301
Nictzin Dyalhis	
The Lady's Maid's Bell	341
Edith Wharton	

INTRODUCTION

*From ghoulies and ghosties
And long-leggedy beasties
And things that go bump in the night,
Good Lord, deliver us!*
                      Traditional Scottish Prayer

What you are holding in your hands, or should I say what you are reading on the device that you are holding in your hands, is the first in a series of anthologies from Parallel Universe Publications. The concept behind *Things that go Bump* is a simple one; to reintroduce readers to classic weird fiction that hasn't seen print in many a year. Now a cynic might believe that this is nothing more than a ploy to cash in on the public domain. I'll admit that it's true that the tales that you are reading here are from the public domain. But to think that the stories included here are nothing more than cheaply available material is doing these stories a grave injustice.

These stories are so much more than purely "up for grabs".

What we are attempting to do here is to reintroduce old school weird to a new generation of readers, before these stories disappear into that abyss known as obscurity.

Until the early 1980s almost all weird fiction anthologies were made up of reprinted material from the pulps and other pre WWII publications. It was only after the 1981 paperback publication of Kirby McCauley's *Dark Forces* that the "original anthology" became the norm. This change in format was both a blessing and a curse for genre fans. While these original anthologies expanded the market for new writers, they also insured that many wonderful classics became relics of the past; only to be read and enjoyed by collectors, who made the effort to seek out these forgotten anthologies.

It has to be mentioned that it was exactly such long forgotten anthologies that kept classic weird fiction alive during the years between the middle 1950s and early 1980s. There is many an exceptional story that has never again seen print after the rise of the original anthology format. *Things that go Bump* plans on changing all of this. Each collection will feature only the best of classic weird fiction. And hopefully we will be introducing you to a whole new world of reading pleasure. The stories that we will be sharing are from a time when fiction was the main form of entertainment available to the public. And entertainment is the key word here. These tales were written to be read and enjoyed.

You won't be finding any urban elves or sparkly vampires in the pages of *Things that go Bump*. Nor will you find gratuitous sex and gore. The chills that we are offering are of the more fiendishly subtle kind. And even when our offerings are lacking in bare breasts and buckets of blood, the theater of the mind is amply capable in painting a canvas that more than compensates for this lack of simple titillation. And it is this vividly morbid canvas that is the backdrop used by *Things that go Bump*.

Our first volume is a treasury of what awaits you in later releases. Here you will relive the oppressive rural horror of Edward Lucas White's "House of Nightmare", the slowly building dread of William Hope Hodgson's maritime classic "The Voice in the Night". We're even delivering a large dose of unexplainable cosmic horror in the proto-Lovecraftian "The Thing from Outside" by George Allan England. Robert E. Howard, the man who gave us Conan the Cimmerian and the puritan avenger Solomon Kane, supplies us with a tale of eldritch horror from beyond time in "The Black Stone". And E. F. Benson, the master of the slow burn, will keep you awake with his "The Room in the Tower", which is an extremely subtle horror story, that once read will make it impossible to stay in a guest room with out asking yourself "what horrid events might have taken place during previous occupancies?"

I personally hope that David and I can live up to the collections put together by the great anthologists of the past such as August Derleth, Peter Haining, Lin Carter, Donald A. Wohlheim, Groff Conklin, Mary Danby, Kurt Singer, Roger Elwood, Vic Ghidalia, Leo Margulies, Sam Moskowitz, Christine Campbell Thomson, Hugh Lamb, and Herbert Van Thal.

All of these wonderful assemblers of the weird have left some huge footprints that it will be extremely hard to fill. But I can assure that we are up to the challenge. These anthologists inspired the creation of *Things that go Bump* and it's to their collective memories that this anthology is dedicated. Through their combined efforts, many a great story teller has become a household name and many a wonderful tale has been rescued from oblivion.

David and I hope that you enjoy these stories as much as we have. It is our hope that they'll make your sleep this evening just a wee bit more uneasy than it would have been if you hadn't had this treasury of classic weird in your hands.

Enjoy!
Douglas Draa

THE GHOUL
Sir Hugh Clifford

We had been sitting late upon the veranda of my bungalow at Kuala Lipis, which, from the top of a low hill covered with coarse grass, overlooked the long, narrow reach formed by the combined waters of the Lipis and the Jelai.

The moon had risen some hours earlier, and the river ran white between the black masses of forest, which seemed to shut it in on all sides, giving to it the appearance of an isolated tarn. The roughly cleared compound, with the tennis ground which had never got beyond the stage of being dug over and weeded, and the rank growths beyond the bamboo fence, were flooded by the soft light, every tattered detail of their ugliness standing revealed as relentlessly as though it were noon. The night was very still, but the heavy, scented air was cool after the fierce heat of the day.

I had been holding forth to the handful of men who had been dining with me on the subject of Malay superstitions, while they manfully stifled their yawns. When a man has a working knowledge of anything which is not commonly known to his neighbours, he is apt to presuppose their interest in it when a chance to descant upon it occurs, and in those days it was only at long intervals that I had an opportunity of forgathering with other white men. Therefore, 1 had made the most of it, and looking back, I fear that I had occupied the rostrum during the greater part of that evening. I had told my audience of the penanggal, "the "Undone One", that horrible wraith of a woman who has died in childbirth, who comes to torment and prey upon small children in the guise of a ghastly face and bust, with a comet's tail of blood-stained entrails flying in her wake; of the mdti-dnalc, the weird little white animal which makes beast noises round the graves of children, and is supposed to have absorbed their souls; and of the polong, or familiar spirits, which men bind to their service by raising them up from the corpses of babies that have been stillborn, the tips of whose tongues they bite off and swallow after the infant has been brought to life by magic agencies. It was at this point that young Middleton began to pluck up his ears; and I, finding that one of my hearers was at last showing signs of being interested, launched out with renewed vigour, until my sorely tried companions, one by one, went off to bed, each to his own quarters.

Middleton was staying with me at the time, and he and I sat for a while in silence, after the others had gone, looking at the moonlight on the river. Middleton was the first to speak.

"That was a curious myth you were telling us about the polong," he said. "There is an incident connected with it which I have never spoken of before, and have always sworn that I would keep to myself; but I have a good mind to tell you about it, because you are the only man I know who will not write me down a liar if I do."

"That's all right. Fire away," I said.

"Well," said Middleton. "It was like this. You remember Juggins, of course? He was a naturalist, you know, dead nuts upon becoming an F. R. S. and all that sort of thing, and he came to stay with me during the close season last year. He was hunting for bugs and orchids and things, and spoke of himself as an anthropologist and a botanist and a zoologist, and Heaven knows what besides; and he used to fill his bedroom with all sorts of creeping, crawling things, kept in very indifferent custody, and my veranda with all kinds of trash and rotting green trade that he brought in from the jungle. He stopped with me for about ten days, and when he heard that duty was taking me upriver into the Sakai country, he asked me to let him come, too. I was rather bored, for the tribesmen are mighty shy of strangers and were only just getting used to me; but he was awfully keen, and a decent beggar enough, in spite of his dirty ways, so I couldn't very well say 'No.' When we had poled upstream for about a week, and had got well up into the Sakai country, we had to leave our boats behind at the foot of the big rapids, and leg it for the rest of the time. It was very rough going, wading up and down streams when one wasn't clambering up a hillside or sliding down and the leeches were worse than I have ever seen them, thousands of them, swarming up your back, and fastening in clusters on to your neck, even when you had defeated those which made a frontal attack.

"I had not enough men with me to do more than hump the camp-kit and a few clothes, so we had to live on the country, which doesn't yield much up among the Sakai except yams and tapioca roots and a little Indian corn, and soft stuff of that sort. It was all new to Juggins, and gave him fits; but he stuck to it like a man.

"Well, one evening when the night was shutting down pretty fast and rain was beginning to fall, Juggins and I struck a fairly large Sakai camp in the middle of a clearing. As soon as we came out of the jungle, and began tight roping along the felled timber, the Sakai sighted us and bolted for covert en masse.

"By the time we reached the huts it was pelting in earnest, and as my men were pretty well fagged out, I decided to spend the night in the camp, and not to make them put up temporary shelters for us. Sakai huts are uncleanly places at best, and any port has to do in a storm.

"We went into the largest of the hovels, and there we found a woman lying by the side of her dead child. She had apparently felt too sick to bolt with the rest of her tribe. The kid was as stiff as Herod, and had not been born many hours,

I should say.

"The mother seemed pretty bad, and I went to her, thinking I might be able to do something for her; but she did not seem to see it, and bit and snarled at me like a wounded animal, clutching at the dead child the while, as though she feared I should take it from her. I therefore left her alone; and Juggins and I took up our quarters in a smaller hut nearby, which was fairly new and not so filthy dirty as most Sakai lairs.

"Presently, when the beggars who had run away found out that I was the intruder, they began to come back again. You know their way. First a couple of men came and peeped at us, and vanished as soon as they saw they were observed. Then they came a trifle nearer, bobbed up suddenly, and peeped at us again. I called to them in Se-noi, which always reassures them, and when they at last summoned up courage to approach, gave them each a handful of tobacco. Then they went back into the jungle and fetched the others, and very soon the place was crawling with Sakai of both sexes and all ages.

"We got a meal of sorts, and settled down for the night as best we could; but it wasn't a restful business. Juggins swore with eloquence at the uneven flooring, made of very roughly trimmed boughs, which is an infernally uncomfortable thing to lie down upon, and makes one's bones ache as though they were coming out at the joints, and the Sakai are abominably restless bedfellows as you know.

"I suppose one ought to realize that they have as yet only partially emerged from the animal, and that, like the beasts, they are still naturally nocturnal. Anyway, they never sleep for long at a stretch, though from time to time they snuggle down and snore among the piles of warm wood ashes round the central fireplace, and whenever you wake, you will always see half a dozen of them squatting near the blazing logs, half hidden by the smoke, and jabbering like monkeys. It is a marvel to me what they find to yarn about: food, or rather the patent impossibility of ever getting enough to eat, and the stony heartedness of Providence and of the neighbouring Malays must furnish the principal topics, I should fancy, with an occasional respectful mention of beasts of prey and forest demons. That night they were more than ordinarily restless. The dead baby was enough to make them uneasy, and besides, they had got wet while hiding in the jungle after our arrival, and that always sets the skin disease, with which all Sakai are smothered, itching like mad. Whenever I woke I could hear their nails going on their dirty hides; but I had had a hard day and was used to my hosts' little ways, so I contrived to sleep fairly sound.

"Juggins told me next morning that he had had *une mat blanche*, and he nearly caused another stampede among the Sakai by trying to get a specimen of the fungus or bacillus, or whatever it is, that occasions the skin disease. I do not know whether he succeeded. For my own part, I think it is probably due to chronic anaemia the poor devils have never had more than a very occasional full meal for hundreds of generations. I have seen little brats, hardly able to stand, white with it, the skin peeling off in flakes, and I used to frighten Juggins out of his senses by telling him he had contracted it when his nose was flayed by the sun.

"Next morning I woke just in time to see the still-born baby put into a hole in the ground. They fitted its body into a piece of bark, and stuck it in the grave they had dug for it at the edge of the clearing. They buried a flint and steel and a woodknife and some food, and a few other things with it, though no living baby could have had any use for most of them, let alone a dead one. Then the old medicine man of the tribe recited the ritual over the grave. I took the trouble to translate it once. It goes something like this: "O Thou, who hast gone forth from among those who dwell upon the surface of the earth, and hast taken for thy dwelling-place the land which is beneath the earth, flint and steel have we given thee to kindle thy fire, raiment to clothe thy nakedness, food to fill thy belly, and a woodknife to clear thy path. Go, then, and make unto thyself friends among those who dwell beneath the earth, and come back no more to trouble or molest those who dwell upon the surface of the earth.'

"It was short and to the point; and then they trampled down the soil, while the mother, who had got upon her feet by now, whimpered about the place like a cat that had lost its kittens. A mangy, half-starved dog came and smelt hungrily about the grave, until it was sent howling away by kicks from every human animal that could reach it; and a poor little brat, who chanced to set up a piping song a few minutes later, was kicked and cuffed and knocked about by all who could conveniently get at him with foot, hand, or missile. Abstinence from song and dance for a period of nine days is the Sakai way of mourning the dead, and any breach of this is held to give great offence to the spirit of the departed and to bring bad luck upon the tribe. It was considered necessary, therefore, to give the urchin who had done the wrong a fairly bad time of it in order to propitiate the implacable dead baby.

"Next the Sakai set to work to pack all their household goods - not a very laborious business; and in about half an hour the last of the laden women, who was carrying so many cooking-pots, and babies and rattan bags and carved bamboo-boxes and things, that she looked like the outside of a gypsy's cart at home, had filed out of the clearing and disappeared in the forest. The Sakai always shift camp, like that, when a death occurs, because they think the ghost of the dead haunts the place where the body died. When an epidemic breaks out among them they are so busy changing quarters, building new huts, and planting fresh catch crops that they have no time to procure proper food, and half those who are not used up by the disease die of semi-starvation. They are a queer lot.

"Well, Juggins and I were left alone, but the men needed a rest, so I decided to trek no farther that day, and Juggins and I spent our time trying to get a shot at a selddang[1], but though we came upon great ploughed-up runs, which the herds had made going down to water, we saw neither hoof nor horn, and returned at night to the deserted Sakai camp, two of my Malays fairly staggering under the piles of rubbish which Juggins called his botanical specimens. The men we had left behind had contrived to catch some fish, and with that and yams we got a pretty decent meal, and I was lying on my mat reading by the aid of a torch, and thinking how lucky it was that the Sakai had cleared out, when suddenly old Juggins sat up, with his eyes fairly snapping at me through his gig-lamps in his excitement.

"'I say,' he said. 'I must have that baby. It would make a unique and invaluable ethnological specimen.'

"'Rot,' I said. 'Go to sleep, old man. I want to read.'

"'No, but I'm serious,' said Juggins. 'You do not realize the unprecedented character of the opportunity. The Sakai have gone away, so their susceptibilities would not be outraged. The potential gain to science is immense simply immense. It would be criminal to neglect such a chance. I regard the thing in the light of a duty which I owe to human knowledge. I tell you straight, I mean to have that baby whether you like it or not, and that is flat.'

"Juggins was forever talking about human knowledge, as though he and it were partners in a business firm. 'It is not only the Sakai one has to consider,' I said. 'My Malays are

---

[1] 'Siladang The gaur or wild buffalo. It is the same as the Indian variety, but ii\ the Malay Peninsula attains to a grease size than in any other part of Asia.

sensitive about body snatching, too. One has to think about the effect upon them.'

"'I can't help that,' said Juggins resolutely. 'I am going out to dig it up now.'

"He had already put his boots on, and was sorting out his botanical tools in search of a trowel. I saw that there was no holding him.

"'Juggins,' I said sharply. 'Sit down. You are a lunatic, of course, but I was another when I allowed you to come up here with me, knowing as I did that you are the particular species of crank you are. However, I've done you as well as circumstances permitted, and as a mere matter of gratitude and decency, I think you might do what I wish.'

"'I am sorry,' said Juggins stiffly. 'I am extremely sorry not to be able to oblige you. My duty as a man of science, however, compels me to avail myself of this god-sent opportunity of enlarging our ethnological knowledge of a little-known people.'

"'I thought you did not believe in God,' I said sourly; for Juggins added a militant agnosticism to his other attractive qualities.

"'I believe in my duty to human knowledge,' he replied sententiously. 'And if you will not help me to perform it, I must discharge it unaided.'

"He had found his trowel, and again rose to his feet.

"'Don't be an ass, Juggins,' I said. 'Listen to me. I have forgotten more about the people and the country here than you will ever learn. If you go and dig up that dead baby, and my Malays see you, there will be the devil to pay. They do not hold with exhumed corpses, and have no liking for or sympathy with people who go fooling about with such things. They have not yet been educated up to the pitch of interest in the secrets of science which has made of you a potential criminal, and if they could understand our talk, they would be convinced that you needed the kid's body for some devilry or witchcraft business, and ten to one they would clear out and leave us in the lurch. Then who would carry your precious botanical specimens back to the boats for you, and just think how the loss of them would knock the bottom out of human knowledge for good and all.'

"'The skeleton of the child is more valuable still,' replied Juggins. 'It is well that you should understand that in this matter, which for me is a question of my duty, I am not to be moved from my purpose either by arguments or threats.'

"He was as obstinate as a mule, and I was pretty sick with him; but I saw that if I left him to himself he would do the tiling so clumsily that my fellows would get wind of it, and if that happened I was afraid that they might desert us. The tracks in that Sakai country are abominably confusing, and quite apart from the fear of losing all our camp-kit, which we could not hump for ourselves, I was by no means certain that I could find my own way back to civilization unaided. Making a virtue of necessity, therefore, I decided that I would let Juggins have his beastly specimen, provided that he would consent to be guided entirely by me in all details connected with the exhumation.

"'You are a rotter of the first water,' I said frankly. 'And if I ever get you back to my station, I'll have nothing more to do with you as long as I live. All the same, I am to blame for having brought you up here, and I suppose I must see you through.'

"'You're a brick,' said Juggins, quite unmoved by my insults. 'Come on.'

"'Wait,' I replied repressively. 'This thing cannot be done until my people are all asleep. Lie down on your mat and keep quiet. When it is safe, I'll give you the word.'

"Juggins groaned, and tried to persuade me to let him go at once; but I swore that nothing would induce me to move before midnight, and with that I rolled over on my side and lay reading and smoking, while Juggins fumed and fretted as he watched the slow hands of his watch creeping round the dial.

"I always take books with me into the jungle, and the more completely incongruous they are to my immediate surroundings the more refreshing I find them. That evening, I remember, I happened to be rereading Miss Florence Montgomery's 'Misunderstood' with tears running down my nose; and by the time my Malays were all asleep, this incidental wallowing in sentimentality had made me more sick with Juggins and his disgusting project than ever.

"I never felt so like a criminal as I did that night, as Juggins and I gingerly picked our way out of the hut across the prostrate forms of my sleeping Malays; nor had I realized before what a difficult job it is to walk without noise on an openwork flooring of uneven boughs. We got out of the place and down the crazy stair-ladder at last, without waking any of my fellows, and we then began to creep along the edge of the jungle that hedged the clearing about. Why did we think it necessary to creep? I don't know. Partly we did not want to be seen by the Malays, if any of them happened to wake; but besides that, the long wait and the uncanny sort of work we were after had set our nerves going a bit, I expect.

"The night was as still as most nights are in real, pukka jungle. That is to say, that it was as full of noises little, quiet, half-heard beast and tree noises as an egg is full of meat; and every occasional louder sound made me jump almost out of my skin. There was not a breath astir in the clearing, but miles up above our heads the clouds were racing across the moon, which looked as though it were scudding through them in the opposite direction at a tremendous rate, like a great white fire balloon. It was pitch dark along the edge of the clearing, for the jungle threw a heavy shadow; and Juggins kept knocking those great clumsy feet of his against the stumps, and swearing softly under his breath.

"Just as we were getting near the child's grave the clouds obscuring the moon became a trifle thinner, and the slightly increased light showed me something that caused me to clutch Juggins by the arm.

"'Hold hard!' I whispered, squatting down instinctively in the shadow, and dragging him after me. 'What's that on the grave?'

"Juggins hauled out his six-shooter with a tug, and looking at his face, I saw that he was as pale as death and more than a little shaky. He was pressing up against me, too, as he squatted, a bit closer, I fancied, than he would have thought necessary at any other time, and it seemed to me that he was trembling. I whispered to him, telling him not to shoot; and we sat there for nearly a minute, I should think, peering through the uncertain light, and trying to make out what the creature might be which was crouching above the grave and making a strange scratching noise.

"Then the moon came out suddenly into a patch of open sky, and we could see clearly at last, and what it revealed did not make me, for one, feel any better. The thing we had been looking at was kneeling on the grave, facing us. It, or rather she, was an old, old Sakai hag. She was stark naked, and in the brilliant light of the moon I could see her long, pendulous, breasts swaying about like an ox's dewlap, and the creases and wrinkles with which her withered hide was criss-crossed, and the discoloured patches of foul skin disease. Her hair hung about her face in great matted locks, falling forward as she bent above the grave, and her eyes glinted through the tangle like those of some unclean and shaggy animal. Her long fingers, which had nails like claws, were tearing at the dirt of the grave, and her body was drenched with sweat, so that it glistened in the moonlight.

"'It looks as though some one else wanted your precious baby for a specimen, Juggins,' I whispered; and a spirit of emulation set him floundering on to his feet, till I pulled him back. 'Keep still, man,' I added. 'Let us see what the old hag is up to. It isn't the brat's mother, is it?'

"'No,' panted Juggins. 'This is a much older woman. Great God! What a ghoul it is!'

"Then we were silent again. Where we squatted we were hidden from the hag by a few tufts of rank Idlang grass, and the shadow of the jungle also covered us. Even if we had been in the open, however, I question whether the old woman would have seen us, she was so eagerly intent upon her work. For full five minutes, as near as I can guess, we squatted there watching her scrape and tear and scratch at the earth of the grave, with a sort of frenzy of energy; and all the while her lips kept going like a shivering man's teeth, though no sound that I could hear came from them.

"At length she got down to the corpse, and I saw her lift the bark wrapper out of the grave, and draw the baby's body from it. Then she sat back upon her heels, threw up her head, just like a dog, and bayed at the moon. She did this three times, and I do not know what there was about those long-drawn howls that jangled up one's nerves, but each time the sound became more insistent and intolerable, and as I listened, my hair fairly lifted. Then, very carefully, she laid the child's body down in a position that seemed to have some connection with the points of the compass, for she took a long time, and consulted the moon and the shadows repeatedly before she was satisfied with the orientation of the thing's head and feet.

"Then she got up, and began very slowly to dance round and round the grave. It was not a reassuring sight, out there in the awful loneliness of the night, miles away from every one and everything, to watch that abominable old beldam capering uncleanly in the moonlight, while those restless lips of hers called noiselessly upon all the devils in hell, with words that we could not hear. Juggins pressed up against me harder than ever, and his hand on my arm gripped tighter and tighter. He was shaking like a leaf, and I do not fancy that I was much steadier. It does not sound very terrible, as I tell it to you here in comparatively civilized surroundings; but at the time, the sight of that obscure figure dancing silently in the moonlight with its ungainly shadow scared me badly.

"She capered like that for some minutes, setting to the dead baby as though she were inviting it to join her, and the intent purposefulness of her made me feel sick. If anybody had told me that morning that I was capable of being frightened out of my wits by an old woman, I should have laughed; but I saw nothing outlandish in the idea while that grotesque dancing lasted.

"Her movements, which had been very slow at first, became gradually faster and faster, till every atom of her was in violent motion, and her body and limbs were swaying this way and that, like the boughs of a tree in a tornado. Then, all of a sudden, she collapsed on the ground, with her back toward us, and seized the baby's body. She seemed to nurse it, as a mother might nurse her child; and as she swayed from side to side, I could see first the curve of the creature's head, resting on her thin left arm, and then its feet near the crook of her right elbow. And now she was crooning to it in a cracked falsetto chant that might have been a lullaby or perhaps some incantation.

"She rocked the child slowly at first, but very rapidly the pace quickened, until her body was .swaying to and fro from the hips, and from side to side, at such a rate that, to me, she looked as though she were falling all ways at once. And simultaneously her shrill chanting became faster and faster, and every instant more nerve-sawing.

"Next she suddenly changed the motion. She gripped the thing she was nursing by its arms, and began to dance it up and down, still moving with incredible agility, and crooning more damnably than ever. I could see the small, puckered face of the thing above her head every time she danced it up, and then, as she brought it down again, I lost sight of it for a second, until she danced it up once more. I kept my eyes fixed upon the thing's face every time it came into view, and I swear it was not an optical illusion it began to be alive. Its eyes were open and moving, and its mouth was working, like that of a child which tries to laugh but is too young to do it properly. Its face ceased to be like that of a newborn baby at all. It was distorted by a horrible animation. It was the most unearthly sight.

"Juggins saw it, too, for I could hear him drawing his breath harder and shorter than a healthy man should.

"Then, all in a moment, the hag did something. I did not see clearly precisely what it was; but it looked to me as though she bent forward and kissed it; and at that very instant a cry went up like the wail of a lost soul. It may have been something in the jungle, but I know my Malayan forests pretty thoroughly, and I have never heard any cry like it before nor since. The next thing we knew was that the old hag had thrown the body back into the grave, and was dumping down the earth and jumping on it, while that strange cry grew fainter and fainter. 1t all happened so quickly that I had not had time to think or move before I was startled back into full consciousness by the sharp crack of Juggins's revolver fired close to my ear.

"'She's burying it alive!' he cried.

"It was a queer thing for a man to say, who had seen the child lying stark and dead more than thirty hours earlier; but the same thought was in my mind, too, as we both started forward at a run. The hag had vanished into the jungle as silently as a shadow. Juggins had missed her, of course. He was always a rotten bad shot. However, we had no thought for her. We just flung ourselves upon the grave, and dug at the earth with our hands, until the baby lay in my arms. It was cold and stiff, and putrefaction had already begun its work. I forced open its mouth, and saw something that I had expected. The tip of its tongue was missing. It looked as though it had been bitten off by a set of shocking bad teeth, for the edge left behind was like a saw.

"'The thing's quite dead,' I said to Juggins.

"'But it cried it cried!' whimpered Juggins. 'I can hear it now. To think that we let that horrible creature murder it.'

"He sat down with his head in his hands. He was utterly unmanned.

"Now that the fright was over, I was beginning to be quite brave again. It is a way I have.

"'Rot,' I said. 'The thing's been dead for hours, and anyway, here's your precious specimen if you want it.'

"I had put it down, and now pointed at it from a distance. Its proximity was not pleasant. Juggins, however, only shuddered. ''Bury it, in Heaven's name,' he said, his voice broken by sobs. 'I would not have it for the world. Besides, it was alive. I saw and heard it.'

"Well, I put it back in its grave, and next day we left the Sakai country. Juggins had a whacking dose of fever, and anyway we had had about enough of the Sakai and of all their engaging habits to last us for a bit.

"We swore one another to secrecy as Juggins, when he got his nerve back, said that the accuracy of our observations was not susceptible of scientific proof, which, I understand, was the rock his religion had gone to pieces on; and I did not fancy being told that I was drunk or that I was lying. You, however, know something of the uncanny things of the East, so to-night

I have broken our vow. Now I'm going to turn in. Don't give me away."

Young Middleton died of fever and dysentery, somewhere upcountry, a year or two later. His name was not Middleton, of course; so I am not really "giving him away," as he called it, even now. As for his companion, though when I last heard of him he was still alive and a shining light in the scientific world, I have named him Juggins, and as the family is a large one, he will run no great risk of being identified.

THE HOUSE OF THE NIGHTMARE
Edward Lucas White

I first caught sight of the house from the brow of the mountain as I cleared the woods and looked across the broad valley several hundred feet below me, to the low sun sinking toward the far blue hills. From that momentary viewpoint I had an exaggerated sense of looking almost vertically down. I seemed to be hanging over the checker-board of roads and fields, dotted with farm buildings, and felt the familiar deception that I could almost throw a stone upon the house. I barely glimpsed its slate roof.

What caught my eyes was the bit of road in front of it, between the mass of dark-green trees about the house and the orchard opposite. Perfectly straight it was, bordered by an even row of trees, through which I made out a cinder side path and a low stone wall.

Conspicuous on the orchard side between two of the flanking trees was a white object, which I took to be a tall stone, a vertical splinter of one of the tilted lime-stone reefs with which the fields of the region are scarred.

The road itself I saw plain as a box-wood ruler on a green baize table. It gave me a pleasurable anticipation of a chance for a burst of speed. I had been painfully traversing closely forested, semi-mountainous hills. Not a farmhouse had I passed, only wretched cabins by the road, more than twenty miles of which I had found very bad and hindering. Now, when I was not many miles from my expected stopping-place, I looked forward to better going, and to that straight, level bit in particular.

As I sped cautiously down the sharp beginning of the long

descent the trees engulfed me again, and I lost sight of the valley. I dipped into a hollow, rose on the crest of the next hill, and again saw the house, nearer, and not so far below.

The tall stone caught my eye with a shock of surprise. Had I not thought it was opposite the house next the orchard? Clearly it was on the left-hand side of the road toward the house. My self-questioning lasted only the moment as I passed the crest. Then the outlook was cut off again; but I found myself gazing ahead, watching for the next chance at the same view.

At the end of the second hill I only saw the bit of road obliquely and could not be sure, but, as at first, the tall stone seemed on the right of the road.

At the top of the third and last hill I looked down the stretch of road under the over-arching trees, almost as one would look through a tube. There was a line of whiteness which I took for the tall stone. It was on the right.

I dipped into the last hollow. As I mounted the farther slope I kept my eyes on the top of the road ahead of me. When my line of sight surmounted the rise I marked the tall stone on my right hand among the serried maples. I leaned over, first on one side, then on the other, to inspect my tyres, then I threw the lever.

As I flew forward, I looked ahead. There was the tall stone - on the left of the road! I was really scared and almost dazed. I meant to stop dead, take a good look at the stone, and make up my mind beyond peradventure whether it was on the right or the left - if not, indeed, in the middle of the road.

In my bewilderment I put on the highest speed. The machine leaped forward; everything I touched went wrong; I steered wildly, slewed to the left, and crashed into a big maple.

When I came to my senses, I was flat on my back in the dry ditch. The last rays of the sun sent shafts of golden-green light through the maple boughs overhead. My first thought was an odd mixture of appreciation of the beauties of nature and disapproval of my own conduct in touring without a companion - a fad I had regretted more than once. Then my mind cleared and I sat up. I felt myself from the head down. I was not bleeding; no bones were broken; and, while much shaken, I had suffered no serious bruises.

Then I saw the boy. He was standing at the edge of the cinder path, near the ditch. He was so stocky and solidly built; barefoot, with his trousers rolled up to his knees; wore a sort of butternut shirt, open at the throat; and was coatless and hatless. He was tow-headed, with a shock of tousled hair; was much freckled, and had a hideous harelip. He shifted from one foot to the other, twiddled his toes, and said nothing whatever, though he stared at me intently.

I scrambled to my feet and proceeded to survey the wreck. It seemed distressingly complete. It had not blown up, nor even caught fire; but otherwise the ruin appeared hopelessly thorough. Everything I examined seemed worse smashed than the rest. My two hampers, alone, by one of those cynical jokes of chance, had escaped - both had pitched clear of the wreckage and were unhurt, not even a bottle broken.

During my investigations the boy's faded eyes followed me continuously, but he uttered no word. When I had convinced myself of my helplessness I straightened up and addressed him:

"How far is it to a blacksmith's shop?"

"Eight mile," he answered. He had a distressing case of cleft palate and was scarcely intelligible.

"Can you drive me there?" I inquired.

"Nary team on the place," he replied; "nary horse, nary cow."

"How far to the next house?" I continued.

"Six mile," he responded.

I glanced at the sky. The sun had set already. I looked at my watch: it was going - seven thirty-six.

"May I sleep in your house tonight?" I asked.

"You can come in if you want to," he said, "and sleep if you can. House all messy; ma's been dead three year, and dad's away. Nothin' to eat but buckwheat flour and rusty bacon."

"I've plenty to eat," I answered, picking up a hamper. "Just take that hamper, will you?"

"You can come in if you've a mind to," he said, "but you got to carry your own stuff." He did not speak gruffly or rudely, but appeared mildly stating an inoffensive fact.

"All right," I said, picking up the other hamper; "lead the way." The yard in front of the house was dark under a dozen or more immense ailanthus trees. Below them many smaller trees had grown up, and beneath these a dank underwood of tall, rank suckers out of the deep, shaggy, matted grass. What had once been, apparently, a carriage-drive, left a narrow, curved track, disused and grass-grown, leading to the house. Even here were some shoots of the ailanthus, and the air was unpleasant with the vile smell of the roots and suckers and the insistent odour of their flowers.

The house was of grey stone, with green shutters faded almost as grey as the stone. Along its front was a veranda, not much raised from the ground, and with no balustrade or railing. On it were several hickory splint rockers. There were eight shuttered windows toward the porch, and midway of them a wide door, with small violet panes on either side of it and a fanlight above.

"Open the door," I said to the boy.

"Open it yourself," he replied, not unpleasantly nor disagreeably, but in such a cone that one could not but take the suggestion as a matter of course.

I put down the two hampers and tried the door. It was

latched but not locked, and opened with a rusty grind of its hinges, on which it sagged crazily, scraping the floor as it turned. The passage smelt mouldy and damp. There were several doors on either side; the boy pointed to the first on the right.

"You can have that room," he said.

I opened the door. What with the dusk, he interlacing trees outside, the piazza roof, and the closed shutters, I could make out little.

"Better get a lamp," I said to the boy.

"Nary lamp," he declared cheerfully. "Nary candle. Mostly I get abed before dark."

I returned to the remains of my conveyance. All four of my lamps were merely scrap metal and splintered glass. My lantern was mashed flat. I always, however, carried candles in my valise. This I found split and crushed, but still holding together. I carried it to the porch, opened it, and took out three candles.

Entering the room, where I found the boy standing just where I had left him. I lit the candle. The walls were whitewashed, the floor bare. There was a mildewed, chilly smell, but the bed looked freshly made up and clean, although it felt clammy.

With a few drops of its own grease I stuck the candle on the corner of a mean, rickety little bureau. There was nothing else in the room save two rush-bottomed chairs and a small table. I went out on the porch, brought in my valise, and put it on the bed. I raised the sash of each window and pushed open the shutter. Then I asked the boy, who had not moved or spoken, to show me the way to the kitchen. He led me straight through the hall to the back of the house. The kitchen was large, and had no furniture save some pine chairs, a pine bench, and a pine table.

I stuck two candles on opposite corners of the table. There

was no stove or range in the kitchen, only a big hearth, the ashes in which smelt and looked a month old. The wood in the woodshed was dry enough, but even it had a cellary, stale smell. The axe and hatchet were both rusty and dull, but usable, and I quickly made a big fire. To my amazement, for the mid-June evening was hot and still, the boy, a wry smile on his ugly face, almost leaned over the flame, hands and arms spread out, and fairly roasted himself.

"Are you cold?" I inquired.

"I'm allus cold," he replied, hugging the fire closer than ever, till I thought he must scorch. I left him toasting himself while I went in search of water. I discovered the pump, which was in working order and not dry on the valves; but I had a furious struggle to fill the two leaky pails I had found. When I had put water to boil I fetched my hampers from the porch.

I brushed the table and set out my meal - cold fowl, cold ham, white and brown bread, olives, jam, and cake. When the can of soup was hot and the coffee made I drew up two chairs to the table and invited the boy to join me.

"I ain't hungry," he said; "I've had supper."

He was a new sort of boy to me; all the boys I knew were hearty eaters and always ready. I had felt hungry myself, but somehow when I came to eat I had little appetite and hardly relished the food. I soon made an end of my meal, covered the fire, blew out the candles, and returned to the porch, where I dropped into one of the hickory rockers to smoke. The boy followed me silently and seated himself on the porch floor, leaning against a pillar, his feet on the grass outside.

"What do you do," I asked, "when your father is away?"

"Just loaf 'round," he said. "Just fool 'round."

"How far off are your nearest neighbours?" I asked.

"Don't no neighbours never come here," he stated. "Say they're afeared of the ghosts." I was not at all startled; the place had all those aspects which lead to a house being called haunted. I was struck by his odd matter-of-fact way of speaking - it was as if he had said they were afraid of a cross dog.

"Do you ever see any ghosts around here?" I continued.

"Never see 'em," he answered, as if I had mentioned tramps or partridges. "Never hear 'em. Sort o' feel 'em 'round sometimes."

"Are you afraid of them?" I asked.

"Nope," he declared. "I ain't skeered o' ghosts; I'm skeered o' nightmares. Ever have nightmares?"

"Very seldom," I replied.

"I do," he returned. "Allus have the same nightmare—big sow, big as a steer, trying to eat me up. Wake up so skeered I could run to never. Nowheres to run to. Go to sleep, and have it again. Wake up worse skeered than ever. Dad says it's buckwheat cakes in summer."

"You must have teased a sow some time," I said.

"Yep," he answered. "Teased a big sow wunst, holding up one of her pigs by the hind leg. Teased her too long. Fell in the pen and got bit up some. Wisht I hadn't a' teased her. Have that nightmare three times a week sometimes. Worse'n being burnt out. Worse'n ghosts. Say, I sorter feel ghosts around now."

He was not trying to frighten me. He was as simply stating an opinion as if he had spoken of bats or mosquitoes. I made no reply, and found myself listening involuntarily. My pipe went out. I did not really want another, but felt disinclined for bed as yet, and was comfortable where I was, while the smell of the ailanthus blossoms was very disagreeable. I filled my pipe again, lit it, and then, as I puffed, somehow dozed off for a moment.

I awoke with a sensation of some light fabric trailed across my face. The boy's position was unchanged.

"Did you do that?" I asked sharply.

"Ain't done nary thing," he rejoined. "What was it?"

"It was like a piece of mosquito-netting brushed over my face."

"That ain't netting," he asserted; "that's a veil. That's one of the ghosts. Some blow on you; some touch you with their long, cold fingers. That one with the veil she drags acrosst your face -well, mostly I think it's ma."

He spoke with the unassailable conviction of the child in *We Are Seven*. I found no words to reply, and rose to go to bed.

"Good night," I said.

"Good night," he echoed. "I'll sit out here a spell yet."

I lit a match, found the candle I had stuck on the corner of the shabby little bureau, and undressed. The bed had a comfortable husk mattress, and I was soon asleep.

I had the sensation of having slept some time when I had a nightmare - the very nightmare the boy had described. A huge sow, big as a dray horse, was reared up with her forelegs over the foot-board of the bed, trying to scramble over to me. She grunted and puffed, and I felt I was the food she craved. I knew in the dream that it was only a dream, and strove to wake up.

Then the gigantic dream-beast floundered over the foot-board, fell across my shins, and I awoke.

I was in darkness as absolute as if I were sealed in a jet vault, yet the shudder of the nightmare instantly subsided, my nerves quieted; I realised where I was, and felt not the least panic. I turned over and was asleep again almost at once. Then I had a real nightmare, not recognisable as a dream, but appallingly real - an unutterable agony of reasonless horror.

There was a Thing in the room; not a sow, nor any other nameable creature, but a Thing. It was as big as an elephant, filled the room to the ceiling, was shaped like a wild boar, seated on its haunches, with its forelegs braced stiffly in front of it. It had a hot, slobbering, red mouth, full of big tusks, and its jaws worked hungrily. It shuffled and hunched itself forward, inch by inch, till its vast forelegs straddled the bed.

The bed crushed up like wet blotting-paper, and I felt the weight of the Thing on my feet, on my legs, on my body, on my chest. It was hungry, and I was what it was hungry for, and it meant to begin on my face. Its dripping mouth was nearer and nearer.

Then the dream-helplessness that made me unable to call or move suddenly gave way, and I yelled and awoke. This time my terror was positive and not to be shaken off.

It was near dawn: I could descry dimly the cracked, dirty window-panes. I got up, lit the stump of my candle and two fresh ones, dressed hastily, strapped my ruined valise, and put it on the porch against the wall near the door. Then I called the boy. I realised quite suddenly that I had not told him my name or asked his.

1 shouted. "Hello!" a few times, but won no answer. I had had enough of that house. I was still permeated with the panic of the nightmare. I desisted from shouting, made no search, but with two candles went out to the kitchen. I took a swallow of cold coffee and munched a biscuit as I hustled my belongings into my hampers. Then, leaving a silver dollar on the table, I carried the hampers out on the porch and dumped them by my valise.

It was now light enough to see the walk, and I went out to the road. Already the night-dew had rusted much of the wreck, making it look more hopeless than before. It was, however, entirely undisturbed. There was not so much as a wheel-track or a hoof-print on the road. The tall, white stone, uncertainty about which had caused my disaster, stood like a sentinel opposite where I had upset.

I set out to find that blacksmith shop. Before I had gone far the sun rose clear from the horizon, and was almost at once scorching. As I footed it along I grew very much heated, and it seemed more like ten miles than six before I reached the first house. It was a new frame house, neatly painted and close to the road, with a whitewashed fence along its garden front.

I was about to open the gate when a big black dog with a curly tail bounded out of the bushes. He did not bark but stood inside the gate wagging his tail and regarding me with a friendly eye; yet I hesitated with my hand on the latch and considered. The dog might not be as friendly as he looked, and the sight of him made me realise that except for the boy I had seen no creature about the house where I had spent the night; no dog or cat; not even a toad or bird. While I was ruminating upon this a man came from behind the house.

"Will your dog bite?" I asked.

"Naw," he answered; "he don't bite. Come in."

I told him I had had an accident to my automobile, and asked if he could drive me to the blacksmith shop and back to my wreckage.

"Cert," he said. "Happy to help you. I'll hitch up fore shortly. Wher'd you smash?"

"In front of the grey house about six miles back," I answered.

"That big stone-built house?" he queried.

"The same," I assented.

"Did you go a-past here?" he inquired astonished. "I didn't hear ye."

"No," I said; "I came from the other direction."

"Why," he meditated, "you must'a' smashed about sun-up. Did you come over them mountains in the dark?"

"No," I replied; "I came over them yesterday evening. I smashed up about sunset."

"Sundown!" he exclaimed. "Where in thunder've ye been all night?"

"I slept in the house where I broke down."

"In that big stone-built house in the trees?" he demanded.

"Yes," I agreed.

"Why," he answered excitedly, "that there house is haunted! They say if you have to drive past it after dark, you can't tell which side of the road the big white stone is on."

"I couldn't tell even before sunset," I said.

"There!" he exclaimed. "Look at that, now! And you slep' in that house! Did you sleep, honest?"

"I slept pretty well," I said. "Except for a nightmare, I slept all night."

"Well," he commented, "I wouldn't go in that there house for a farm, nor sleep in it for my salvation. And you slep'! How in thunder did you get in?"

"The boy took me in," I said.

"What sort of boy?" he queried, his eyes fixed on me with a queer, countrified look of absorbed interest.

"A thick-set, freckle-faced boy with a harelip," I said.

"Talk like his mouth was full of mush?" he demanded.

"Yes," I said; "bad case of cleft palate."

"Well!" he exclaimed. "I never did believe in ghosts, and I never did half believe that house was haunted, but I know it now. And you slep'!"

"I didn't see any ghosts," I retorted irritably.

"You seen a ghost for sure," he rejoined solemnly. "That there harelip boy's been dead six months."

THE VOICE IN THE NIGHT
William Hope Hodgson

It was a dark, starless night. We were becalmed in the northern Pacific. Our exact position I do not know; for the sun had been hidden during the course of a weary, breathless week by a thin haze which had seemed to float above us, about the height of our mastheads, at whiles descending and shrouding the surrounding sea.

With there being no wind, we had steadied the tiller, and I was the only man on deck. The crew, consisting of two men and a boy, were sleeping forward in their den, while Will - my friend, and the master of our little craft - was aft in his bunk on the port side of the little cabin.

Suddenly, from out of the surrounding darkness, there came a hail:

"Schooner, ahoy!"

The cry was so unexpected that I gave no immediate answer, because of my surprise.

It came again - a voice curiously throaty and inhuman, calling from somewhere upon the dark sea away on our port broadside:

"Schooner, ahoy!"

"Hullo!" I sang out, having gathered my wits somewhat. "What are you? What do you want?"

"You need not be afraid," answered the queer voice, having probably noticed some trace of confusion in my tone. "I am only an old - man."

The pause sounded odd, but it was only afterward that it came back to me with any significance.

"Why don't you come alongside, then?" I queried

somewhat snappishly, for I liked not his hinting at my having been a trifle shaken.

"I – I - can't. It wouldn't be safe. I -" The voice broke off, and there was silence.

"What do you mean?" I asked, growing more and more astonished. "What's not safe? Where are you?"

I listened for a moment, but there came no answer. And then, a sudden indefinite suspicion, of I knew not what, coming to me, I stepped swiftly to the binnacle and took out the lighted lamp. At the same time, I knocked on the deck with my heel to waken Will. Then I was back at the side, throwing the yellow funnel of light out into the silent immensity beyond our rail. As I did so, I heard a slight muffled cry, and then the sound of a splash, as though someone had dipped oars abruptly. Yet I cannot say with certainty that I saw anything; save, it seemed to me, that with the first flash of the light there had been something upon the waters, where now there was nothing.

"Hullo, there!" I called. "What foolery is this?"

But there came only the indistinct sounds of a boat being pulled away into the night.

Then I heard Will's voice from the direction of the after scuttle:

"What's up, George?"

"Come here, Will!" I said.

"What is it?" he asked, coming across the deck.

I told him the queer thing that had happened. He put several questions; then, after a moment's silence, he raised his hands to his lips and hailed:

"Boat, ahoy!"

From a long distance away there came back to us a faint reply, and my companion repeated his call. Presently, after a short period of silence, there grew on our hearing the muffled sound of oars, at which Will hailed again.

This time there was a reply: "Put away the light."

"I'm damned if I will," I muttered; but Will told me to do as the voice bade, and I shoved it down under the bulwarks.

"Come nearer," he said, and the oar strokes continued. Then, when apparently some half dozen fathoms distant, they again ceased.

"Come alongside!" exclaimed Will. "There's nothing to be frightened of aboard here."

"Promise that you will not show the light?"

"What's to do with you," I burst out, "that you're so infernally afraid of the light?"

"Because -" began the voice, and stopped short.

"Because what?" I asked quickly.

Will put his hand on my shoulder. "Shut up a minute, old man," he said in a low voice. "Let me tackle him."

He leaned more over the rail. "See here, mister," he said, "this is a pretty queer business, you coming upon us like this, right out in the middle of the blessed Pacific. How are we to know what sort of a hanky-panky trick you're up to? You say there's only one of you. How are we to know, unless we get a squint at you - eh? What's your objection to the light, anyway?"

As he finished, I heard the noise of the oars again, and then the voice came; but now from a greater distance, and sounding extremely hopeless and pathetic.

"I am sorry - sorry! I would not have troubled you, only I am hungry, and - so is she."

The voice died away, and the sound of the oars, dipping irregularly, was borne to us.

"Stop!" sang out Will. "I don't want to drive you away. Come back! We'll keep the light hidden if you don't like it."

He turned to me. "It's a damned queer rig, this; but I think there's nothing to be afraid of?"

There was a question in his tone, and I replied, "No, I

think the poor devil's been wrecked around here, and gone crazy."

The sound of the oars drew nearer.

"Shove that lamp back in the binnacle," said Will; then he leaned over the rail and listened. I replaced the lamp and came back to his side. The dipping of the oars ceased some dozen yards distant.

"Won't you come alongside now?" asked Will in an even voice. "I have had the lamp put back in the binnacle."

"I - I cannot," replied the voice. "I dare not come nearer. I dare not even pay you for the - the provisions."

"That's all right," said Will, and hesitated. "You're welcome to as much grub as you can take -" Again he hesitated.

"You are very good!" exclaimed the voice. "May God, who understands everything, reward you -" It broke off huskily.

"The - the lady?" said Will abruptly. "Is she - ?"

"I have left her behind upon the island," came the voice.

"What island?" I cut in.

"I know not its name," returned the voice. "I would to God-" it began, and checked itself as suddenly.

"Could we not send a boat for her?" asked Will at this point.

"No!" said the voice, with extraordinary emphasis. "My God! No!" There was a moment's pause; then it added, in a tone which seemed a merited reproach, "It was because of our want I ventured - because her agony tortured me."

"I am a forgetful brute!" exclaimed Will. "Just wait a minute, whoever you are, and I will bring you up something at once."

In a couple of minutes he was back again, and his arms were full of various edibles. He paused at the rail.

"Can't you come alongside for them?" he asked.

"No - I dare not," replied the voice, and it seemed to me that in its tones I detected a note of stifled craving, as though the owner hushed a mortal desire. It came to me then in a flash that the poor old creature out there in the darkness was suffering for actual need for that which Will held in his arms; and yet, because of some unintelligible dread, refraining from dashing to the side of our schooner and receiving it. And with the lightning-like conviction there came the knowledge that the Invisible was not mad, but sanely facing some intolerable horror.

"Damn it, Will!" I said, full of many feelings, over which predominated a vast sympathy. "Get a box. We must float off the stuff to him in it."

This we did, propelling it away from the vessel, out into the darkness, by means of a boat hook.

In a minute a slight cry from the Invisible came to us, and we knew that he had secured the box.

A little later he called out a farewell to us, and so heartful a blessing that I am sure we were the better for it. Then, without more ado, we heard the ply of oars across the darkness.

"Pretty soon off," remarked Will, with perhaps just a little sense of injury.

"Wait," I replied. "I think somehow he'll come back. He must have been badly needing that food."

"And the lady," said Will. For a moment he was silent; then he continued, "It's the queerest thing ever I've tumbled across since I've been fishing."

"Yes," I said, and fell to pondering.

And so the time slipped away - an hour, another, and still Will stayed with me; for the queer adventure had knocked all desire for sleep out of him.

The third hour was three parts through when we heard again the sound of oars across the silent ocean.

"Listen!" said Will, a low note of excitement in his voice.

"He's coming, just as I thought," I muttered.

The dipping of the oars grew nearer, and I noted that the strokes were firmer and longer. The food had been needed.

They came to a stop a little distance off the broadside, and the queer voice came again to us through the darkness:

"Schooner, ahoy!"

"That you?" asked Will.

"Yes," replied the voice. "I left you suddenly, but - but there was great need."

"The lady?" questioned Will.

"The - lady is grateful now on earth. She will be more grateful soon in - in heaven."

Will began to make some reply, in a puzzled voice, but became confused and broke off. I said nothing. I was wondering at the curious pauses, and apart from my wonder, I was full of a great sympathy.

The voice continued, "We - she and I, have talked, as we shared the result of God's tenderness and yours -"

Will interposed, but without coherence

"I beg of you not to - to belittle your deed of Christian charity this night," said the voice. "Be sure that it has not escaped His notice."

It stopped, and there was a full minute's silence. Then it came again. "We have spoken together upon that which - which has befallen us. We had thought to go out, without telling anyone of the terror which has come into our - lives. She is with me in believing that tonight's happenings are under a special ruling, and that it is God's wish that we should tell to you all that we have suffered since – since -"

"Yes?" said Will softly.

"Since the sinking of the Albatross."

"Ah!" I exclaimed involuntarily. "She left Newcastle for 'Frisco some six months ago, and hasn't been heard of since."

"Yes" answered the voice. "But some few degrees to the north of the line, she was caught in a terrible storm and dismasted. When the calm came, it was found that she was leaking badly, and presently, it falling to a calm, the sailors took to the boats, leaving - leaving a young lady - my fiancée - and myself upon the wreck.

"We were below, gathering together a few of our belongings, when they left. They were entirely callous, through fear, and when we came up upon the decks, we saw them only as small shapes afar off upon the horizon. Yet we did not despair, but set to work and constructed a small raft. Upon this we put such few matters as it would hold, including a quantity of water and some ship's biscuit. Then, the vessel being very deep in the water, we got ourselves onto the raft and pushed off.

"It was later that I observed we seemed to be in the way of some tide or current, which bore us from the ship at an angle, so that in the course of three hours, by my watch, her hull became invisible to our sight, her broken masts remaining in view for a somewhat longer period. Then, toward evening, it grew misty, and so through the night. The next day we were still encompassed by the mist, the weather remaining quiet.

"For four days we drifted through this strange haze, until, on the evening of the fourth day, there grew upon our ears the murmur of breakers at a distance. Gradually it became plainer, and somewhat after midnight, it appeared to sound upon either hand at no very great space. The raft was raised upon a swell several times, and then we were in smooth water, and the noise of the breakers was behind.

"When the morning came, we found that we were in a sort of great lagoon, but of this we noticed little at the time; for close before us, through the enshrouding mist, loomed the hull of a large sailing vessel. With one accord we fell upon our knees and thanked God, for we thought that here was an end to our perils. We had much to learn.

"The raft drew near to the ship, and we shouted on them to take us aboard; but none answered. Presently the raft touched against the side of the vessel, and seeing a rope hanging downward, I seized it and began to climb. Yet I had much ado to make my way up, because of a kind of grey, lichenous fungus that had seized upon the rope and blotched the side of the ship lividly.

"I reached the rail and clambered over it, onto the deck. Here I saw that the decks were covered in great patches with the grey masses, some of them rising into nodules several feet in height; but at the time I thought less of this matter than of the possibility of there being people aboard the ship. I shouted, but none answered. Then I went to the door below the poop deck. I opened it and peered in. There was a great smell of staleness, so that I knew in a moment that nothing living was within, and with the knowledge, I shut the door quickly, for I felt suddenly lonely.

"I went back to the side where I had scrambled up. My - my sweetheart was still sitting quietly upon the raft. Seeing me look down, she called up to know whether there were any aboard the ship. I replied that the vessel had the appearance of having been long deserted, but that if she would wait a little, I would see whether there was anything in the shape of a ladder by which she could ascend to the deck. Then we would make a search through the vessel together. A little later, on the opposite side of the decks, I found a rope side ladder. This I carried across, and a minute afterward she was beside me.

"Together we explored the cabins and apartments in the afterpart of the ship, but nowhere was there any sign of life. Here and there, within the cabins themselves, we came across odd patches of that queer fungus; but this, as my sweetheart said, could be cleansed away.

"In the end, having assured ourselves that the after portion of the vessel was empty, we picked our ways to the bows, between the ugly grey nodules of that strange growth; and here we made a further search, which told us that there was indeed none aboard but ourselves.

"This being now beyond any doubt, we returned to the stern of the ship and proceeded to make ourselves as comfortable as possible. Together we cleared out and cleaned two of the cabins, and after that I made examination whether there was anything eatable in the ship. This I soon found was so, and thanked God for His goodness. In addition to this I discovered a fresh-water pump, and having fixed it, I found the water drinkable, though somewhat unpleasant to the taste.

"For several days we stayed aboard the ship without attempting to get to the shore. We were busily engaged in making the place habitable. Yet even thus early we became aware that our lot was even less to be desired than might have been imagined; for though, as a first step, we scraped away the odd patches of growth that studded the floors and walls of the cabins and saloon, yet they returned almost to their original size within the space of twenty-four hours, which not only discouraged us but gave us a feeling of vague unease.

"Still we would nor admit ourselves beaten, so set to work afresh, and not only scraped away the fungus but soaked the places where it had been with carbolic, a canful of which I had found in the pantry. Yet by the end of the week the growth had returned in full strength, and in addition it had spread to other places, as though our touching it had allowed germs from it to travel elsewhere.

"On the seventh morning, my sweetheart woke to find a small patch of it growing on her pillow, close to her face. At that, she came to me, as soon as she could get her garments upon her. I was in the galley at the time, lighting the fire for breakfast."

"'Come here, John,' she said, and led me aft. When I saw the thing upon her pillow I shuddered, and then and there we agreed to go right out of the ship and see whether we could not fare to make ourselves more comfortable ashore.

"Hurriedly we gathered together our few belongings, and even among these I found that the fungus had been at work, for one of her shawls had a little lump of it growing near one edge. I threw the whole thing over the side without saying anything to her.

"The raft was still alongside, but it was too clumsy to guide, and I lowered down a small boat that hung across the stern, and in this we made our way to the shore. Yet as we drew near to it, I became gradually aware that here the vile fungus, which had driven us from the ship, was growing riot. In places it rose into horrible, fantastic mounds, which seemed almost to quiver, as with a quiet life, when the wind blew across them. Here and there it took on the forms of vast fingers, and in others it just spread out flat and smooth and treacherous. Odd places, it appeared as grotesque stunted trees, extraordinarily kinked and gnarled - the whole quaking vilely at times.

"At first it seemed to us that there was no single portion of the surrounding shore which was not hidden beneath the masses of the hideous lichen; yet in this I found we were mistaken, for somewhat later, coasting along the shore at a little distance, we descried a smooth white patch of what appeared to be fine sand, and there we landed. It was not sand. What it was I do not know.

"All that I have observed is that upon it the fungus will not grow; while everywhere else, save where the sandlike earth wanders oddly, pathwise, amid the grey desolation of the lichen, there is nothing but that loathsome greyness.

"It is difficult to make you understand how cheered we

were to find one place that was absolutely free from the growth, and here we deposited our belongings. Then we went back to the ship for such things as it seemed to us we should need. Among other matters, I managed to bring ashore with me one of the ship's sails. With it I constructed two small tents, which, though exceedingly rough-shaped, served the purposes for which they were intended. In these we lived and stored our various necessities, and thus for a matter of some four weeks all went smoothly and without particular unhappiness. Indeed, I may say with much happiness - for - we were together.

"It was on the thumb of her right hand that the growth first showed. It was only a small circular spot, much like a little grey mole My God! How the fear leaped to my heart when she showed me the place. We cleansed it, between us, washing it with carbolic and water. In the morning of the following day she showed her hand to me again. The grey warty thing had returned. For a little while we looked at one another in silence. Then, still wordless, we started again to remove it. In the midst of the operation she spoke suddenly.

"'What's that on the side of your face, dear?' Her voice was sharp with anxiety. I put my hand up to feel.

"'There! Under the hair by your ear. A little to the front a bit.' My finger rested upon the place, and then I knew.

"'Let us get your thumb done first,' I said. And she submitted, only because she was afraid to touch me until it was cleansed. I finished washing and disinfecting her thumb, and then she turned to my face. After it was finished we sat together and talked awhile of many things; for there had come into our lives sudden, very terrible thoughts. We were, all at once, afraid of something worse than death. We spoke of loading the boat with provisions and water and making our way out onto the sea; yet we were helpless, for many causes, and - and the growth had attacked us already. We decided to stay. God would do with us what was His will. We would wait.

"A month, two months, three months passed and the places grew somewhat, and there had come others. Yet we fought so strenuously with the fear that its headway was but slow, comparatively speaking.

"Occasionally we ventured off to the ship for such stores as we needed. There we found that the fungus grew persistently. One of the nodules on the main deck soon became as high as my head.

"We had now given up all thought or hope of leaving the island. We had realized that it would be unallowable to go among healthy humans with the thing from which we were suffering.

"With this determination and knowledge in our minds we knew that we should have to husband our food and water; for we did not know, at that time, but that we should possibly live for many years.

"This reminds me that I have told you that I am an old man. Judged by years this is not so. But – but -"

He broke off, then continued somewhat abruptly, "As I was saying, we knew that we should have to use care in the matter of food. But we had no idea then how little food there was left of which to take care. It was a week later that I made the discovery that all the other bread tanks - which I had supposed full - were empty, and that (beyond odd tins of vegetables and meat, and some other matters) we had nothing on which to depend but the bread in the tank which I had already opened.

"After learning this I bestirred myself to do what I could, and set to work at fishing in the lagoon; but with no success. At this I was somewhat inclined to feel desperate, until the thought came to me to try outside the lagoon, in the open sea.

"Here, at times, I caught odd fish, but so infrequently that they proved of but little help in keeping us from the hunger which threatened. It seemed to me that our deaths were likely to come by hunger, and not by the growth of the thing which had seized upon our bodies.

"We were in this state of mind when the fourth month wore out. Then I made a very horrible discovery. One morning, a little before midday, I came off from the ship with a portion of the biscuits which were left. In the mouth of her tent I saw my sweetheart sitting, eating something. 'What is it, my dear?' I called out as I leaped ashore. Yet, on hearing my voice, she seemed confused, and turning, slyly threw something toward the edge of the little clearing. It fell short, and a vague suspicion having arisen within me, I walked across and picked it up. It was a piece of the grey fungus.

"As I went to her with it in my hand, she turned deadly pale; then a rose red.

"I felt strangely dazed and frightened.

"'My dear! My dear!' I said, and could say no more. Yet at my words she broke down and cried bitterly. Gradually, as she calmed, I got from her the news that she had tried it the preceding day, and - and liked it. I got her to promise on her knees not to touch it again, however great our hunger. After she had promised, she told me that the desire for it had come suddenly, and that until the moment of desire, she had experienced nothing toward it but the most extreme repulsion.

"Later in the day, feeling strangely restless and much shaken with the thing which I had discovered, I made my way along one of the twisted paths - formed by the white, sandlike substance - which led among the fungoid growth. I had, once before, ventured along there, but not to any great distance. This time, being involved in perplexing thought, I went much farther than hitherto.

"Suddenly I was called to myself by a queer hoarse sound

on my left. Turning quickly, I saw that there was movement among an extraordinarily shaped mass of fungus close to my elbow. It was swaying uneasily, as though it possessed life of its own. Abruptly, as I stared, the thought came to me that the thing had a grotesque resemblance to the figure of a distorted human creature. Even as the fancy flashed into my brain, there was a slight, sickening noise of tearing, and I saw that one of the branchlike arms was detaching itself from the surrounding masses, and coming toward me. The head of the thing, a shapeless grey ball, inclined in my direction. I stood stupidly, and the vile arm brushed across my face. I gave out a frightened cry and ran back a few paces. There was a sweetish taste upon my lips where the thing had touched me. I licked them, and was immediately filled with an inhuman desire. I turned and seized a mass of the fungus.

Then more, and - more. I was insatiable. In the midst of devouring, the remembrance of the morning's discovery swept into my amazed brain. It was sent by God. I dashed the fragment I held to the ground. Then, utterly wretched and feeling a dreadful guiltiness, I made my way back to the encampment.

"I think she knew, by some marvellous intuition which love must have given, so soon as she set eyes on me. Her quiet sympathy made it easier for me, and I told her of my sudden weakness, yet omitted to mention the extraordinary thing which had gone before. I desired to spare her all unnecessary terror.

"But for myself I had added an intolerable knowledge, to breed an incessant terror in my brain; for I doubted not that I had seen the end of one of these men who had come to the island in the ship in the lagoon; and in that monstrous ending I had seen our own.

"Thereafter we kept from the abominable food, though the desire for it had entered into our blood. Yet our dreary punishment was upon us; for day by day, with monstrous rapidity, the fungoid growth took hold of our poor bodies. Nothing we could do would check it materially, and so - and so - we who had been human became - well, it matters less each day. Only - only we had been man and maid!

"And day by day the fight is more dreadful to withstand the hunger-lust for the terrible lichen.

"A week ago we ate the last of the biscuit, and since that time I have caught three fish. I was out here fishing tonight when your schooner drifted upon me out of the mist. I hailed you. You know the rest, and may God, out of His great heart, bless you for your goodness to a - a couple of poor outcast souls."

There was the dip of an oar - another. Then the voice came again, and for the last time, sounding through the slight surrounding mist, ghostly and mournful.

"God bless you! Good-by!"

"Good-by," we shouted together hoarsely, our hearts full of many emotions I glanced about me. I became aware that the dawn was upon us.

The sun flung a stray beam across the hidden sea, pierced the mist dully, and lit up the receding boat with a gloomy fire. Indistinctly I saw something nodding between the oars. I thought of a sponge - a great, grey nodding sponge. The oars continued to ply. They were grey - as was the boat - and my eyes searched a moment vainly for the conjunction of hand and oar. My gaze flashed back to the - head. It nodded forward as the oars went backward for the stroke. Then the oars were dipped, the boat shot out of the patch of light, and the - the thing went nodding into the mist.

THE THING FROM OUTSIDE
George Allan England

They sat about their camp-fire, that little party of Americans retreating southward from Hudson Bay before the on-coming menace of the great cold. Sat there, stolid under the awe of the North, under the uneasiness that the day's trek had laid upon their souls. The three men smoked. The two women huddled close to each other. Fireglow picked their faces from the gloom of night among the dwarf firs. A splashing murmur told of the Albany River's haste to escape from the wilderness, and reach the Bay.

"I don't see what there was in a mere circular print on a rock-ledge to make our guides desert," said Professor Thorburn. His voice was as dry as his whole personality. "Most extraordinary."

"They knew what it was, all right," answered Jandron, geologist of the party. "So do I." He rubbed his cropped moustache. His eyes glinted greyly. I've seen prints like that before. That was on the Labrador. And I've seen things happen, where they were."

"Something surely happened to our guides, before they'd got a mile into the bush," put in the Professor's wife; while Vivian, her sister, gazed into the fire that revealed her as a beauty, not to be spoiled even by a tam and a rough-knit sweater. "Men don't shoot wildly, and scream like that, unless -"

"They're all three dead now, anyhow," put in Jandron. "So they're out of harm's way. While we - well, we're two hundred and fifty wicked miles from the C. P. R. rails."

"Forget it, Jandy!" said Marr, the journalist. "We're just

suffering from an attack of nerves, that's all. Give me a fill of 'baccy. Thanks. We'll all be better in the morning. Ho-hum! Now, speaking of spooks and such -"

He launched into an account of how he had once exposed a fraudulent spiritualist, thus proving - to his own satisfaction - that nothing existed beyond the scope of mankind's everyday life. But nobody gave him much heed. And silence fell upon the little night-encampment in the wilds; a silence that was ominous.

Pale, cold stars watched down from spaces infinitely far beyond man's trivial world.

Next day, stopping for chow on a ledge miles upstream, Jandron discovered another of the prints. He cautiously summoned the other two men. They examined the print, while the women-folk were busy by the fire. A harmless thing the marking seemed; only a ring about four inches in diameter, a kind of cup-shaped depression with a raised centre. A sort of glaze coated it, as if the granite had been fused by heat.

Jandron knelt, a well-knit figure in bright mackinaw and canvas leggings, and with a shaking finger explored the smooth curve of the print in the rock. His brows contracted as he studied it.

"We'd better get along out of this as quick as we can," said he in an unnatural voice. "You've got your wife to protect, Thorburn, and I, - well, I've got Vivian. And -"

"You have?" nipped Marr. The light of an evil jealously gleamed in his heavy-lidded look. "What you need is an alienist."

"Really, Jandron," the Professor admonished, "you mustn't let your imagination run away with you."

"I suppose it's imagination that keeps this print cold!" the geologist retorted. His breath made faint, swirling coils of vapour above it.

"Nothing but a pot-hole," judged Thorburn, bending his spare, angular body to examine the print. The Professor's vitality all seemed centred in his big-bulged skull that sheltered a marvellous thinking machine. Now he put his lean hand to the base of his brain, rubbing the back of his head as if it ached. Then, under what seemed some powerful compulsion, he ran his bony finger around the print in the rock.

"By Jove, but it is cold!" he admitted. "And looks as if it had been stamped right out of the stone. Extraordinary!"

"Dissolved out, you mean," corrected the geologist. "By cold."

The journalist laughed mockingly.

"Wait till I write this up!" he sneered. "'Noted Geologist Declares Frigid Ghost Dissolves Granite!'"

Jandron ignored him. He fetched a little water from the river and poured it into the print.

"Ice!" ejaculated the Professor. "Solid ice!"

"Frozen in a second," added Jandron, while Marr frankly stared. "And it'll never melt, either. I tell you, I've seen some of these rings before; and every time, horrible things have happened. Incredible things! Something burned this ring out of the stone - burned it out with the cold interstellar space. Something that can import cold as a permanent quality of matter. Something that can kill matter, and totally remove it."

"Of course that's all sheer poppycock," the journalist tried to laugh, but his brain felt numb.

"This something, this Thing," continued Jandron, "is a Thing that can't be killed by bullets. It's what caught our guides on the barrens, as they ran away - poor fools!"

A shadow fell across the print in the rock. Mrs. Thorburn had come up, was standing there. She had overheard a little of what Jandron had been saying.

"Nonsense!" she tried to exclaim, but she was shivering so

she could hardly speak.

That night, after a long afternoon of paddling and portaging - labouring against inhibitions like those in a nightmare - they camped on shelving rocks that slanted to the river.

"After all," said the Professor, when supper was done, "we mustn't get into a panic. I know extraordinary things are reported from the wilderness, and more than one man has come out, raving. But we, by Jove! with our superior brains - we aren't going to let Nature play us any tricks!"

"And of course," added his wife, her arm about Vivian, "everything in the universe is a natural force. There's really no super-natural, at all."

"Admitted," Jandron replied. "But how about things outside the universe?"

"And they call you a scientist?" gibed Marr; but the Professor leaned forward, his brows knit.

"Hm!" he grunted. A little silence fell.

"You don't mean, really," asked Vivian, "that you think there's life and intelligence - Outside?"

Jandron looked at the girl. Her beauty, haloed with ruddy gold from the firelight, was a pain to him as he answered:

"Yes, I do. And dangerous life, too. I know what I've seen, in the North Country. I know what I've seen!"

Silence again, save for the crepitation of the flames, the fall of an ember, the murmur of the current. Darkness narrowed the wilderness to just that circle of flickering light ringed by the forest and the river, brooded over by the pale stars.

"Of course you can't expect a scientific man to take you seriously," commented the Professor. "I know what I've seen! I tell you there's Something entirely outside man's knowledge."

"Poor fellow!" scoffed the journalist; but even as he spoke his hand pressed his forehead.

"There are Things at work," Jandron affirmed, with dogged persistence. He lighted his pipe with a blazing twig. Its flame revealed his face drawn, lined. "Things. Things that reckon with us no more than we do with ants. Less, perhaps."

The flame of the twig died. Night stood closer, watching.

"Suppose there are?" the girl asked. "What's that got to do with these prints in the rock?"

"They," answered Jandron, "are marks left by one of those Things. Footprints, maybe. That Thing is near us, here and now!"

Marr's laugh broke a long stillness.

"And you," he exclaimed, "with an A. M. and a B. S. to write after your name,"

"If you knew more," retorted Jandron, "you'd know a devilish sight less. It's only ignorance that's cock-sure."

"But," dogmatised the Professor, "no scientist of any standing has ever admitted any outside interference with this planet."

"No, and for thousands of years nobody ever admitted that the world was round, either. What I've seen, I know."

"Well, what have you seen?" asked Mrs. Thorburn, shivering.

"You'll excuse me, please, for not going into that just now."

"You mean," the Professor demanded, dryly, "if the - hm! - this suppositious Thing wants to - ?"

"It'll do any infernal thing it takes a fancy to, yes! If it happens to want us -"

"But what could Things like that want of us? Why should They come here, at all?"

"Oh, for various reasons. For inanimate objects, at times, and then again for living beings. They've come here lots of times, I tell you," Jandron asserted with strange irritation, "and got what They wanted, and then gone away to -

Somewhere. If one of Them happens to want us, for any reason, It will take us, that's all. If It doesn't want us, It will ignore us, as we'd ignore gorillas in Africa if we were looking for gold. But if it was gorilla-fur we wanted, that would be different for the gorillas, wouldn't it?"

"What in the world," asked Vivian, "could a - well, a Thing from Outside want of us?"

"What do men want, say, of guinea-pigs? Men experiment with 'em, of course. Superior beings use inferior, for their own ends. To assume that man is the supreme product of evolution is gross self-conceit. Might not some superior Thing want to experiment with human beings?

"But how?" demanded Marr,

"The human brain is the most highly-organized form of matter known to this planet. Suppose, now -"

"Nonsense!" interrupted the Professor. "All hands to the sleeping-bags, and no more of this. I've got a wretched headache. Let's anchor in Blanket Bay!"

He, and both the women, turned in. Jandron and Marr sat a while longer by the fire. They kept plenty of wood piled on it, too, for an unnatural chill transfixed the night-air. The fire burned strangely blue, with greenish flicks of flame.

At length, after vast acerbities of disagreement, the geologist and the newspaperman sought their sleeping-bags. The fire was a comfort. Not that a fire could avail a pin's weight against a Thing from interstellar space, but subjectively it was a comfort. The instincts of a million years, centring around protection by fire, cannot be obliterated.

After a time - worn out by a day of nerve-strain and of battling with swift currents, of flight from Something invisible, intangible - they all slept.

The depths of space, star-sprinkled, hung above them with vastness immeasurable, cold beyond all understanding of the human mind.

Jandron woke first, in a red dawn.

He blinked at the fire, as he crawled from his sleeping-bag. The fire was dead; and yet it had not burned out. Much wood remained unconsumed, charred over, as if some gigantic extinguisher had in the night been lowered over it.

"Hmmm!" growled Jandron. He glanced about him, on the ledge. "Prints, too. I might have known!"

He aroused Marr. Despite all the journalist's mocking hostility, Jandron felt more in common with this man of his own age than with the Professor, who was close on sixty.

"Look here, now!" said he. "It has been all around here. See? It put out our fire - maybe the fire annoyed It, some way - and It walked round us, everywhere." His grey eyes smouldered. "I guess, by gad, you've got to admit facts, now!"

The journalist could only shiver and stare.

"Lord, what a head I've got on me, this morning!" he chattered. He rubbed his forehead with a shaking hand, and started for the river. Most of his assurance had vanished. He looked badly done up.

"Well, what say?" demanded Jandron. "See these fresh prints?"

"Damn the prints!" retorted Marr, and fell to grumbling some unintelligible thing. He washed unsteadily, and remained crouching at the river's lip, inert, numbed.

Jandron, despite a gnawing at the base of his, brain, carefully examined the ledge. He found prints scattered everywhere, and some even on the river-bottom near the shore. Wherever water had collected in the prints on the rock, it had frozen hard. Each print in the river-bed, too, was white with ice. Ice that the rushing current could not melt.

"Well, by gad!" he exclaimed. He lighted his pipe and tried to think. Horribly afraid - yes, he felt horribly afraid, but determined. Presently, as a little power of concentration came back, he noticed that all the prints were in straight lines, each mark about two feet from the next.

"It was observing us while we slept," said Jandron.

"What nonsense are you talking, eh?" demanded Marr. His dark, heavy face sagged. "Fire, now, and grub!"

He got up and shuffled unsteadily away from the river. Then he stopped with a jerk, staring.

"Look! Look a' that axe!" he gulped, pointing.

Jandron picked up the axe, by the handle, taking good care not to touch the steel. The blade was white-furred with frost. And deep into it, punching out part of the edge, one of the prints was stamped.

"This metal," said he, "is clean gone. It's been absorbed. The Thing doesn't recognize any difference in materials. Water and steel and rock are all the same to It."

"You're crazy!" snarled the journalist. "How could a Thing travel on one leg, hopping along, making marks like that?"

"It could roll, if it was disk-shaped. And -"

A cry from the Professor turned them. Thorburn was stumbling toward them, hands out and tremulous.

"My wife -!" he choked.

Vivian was kneeling beside her sister, frightened, dazed.

"Something's happened!" stammered the Professor. "Here - come here -!"

Mrs. Thorburn was beyond any power of theirs, to help. She was still breathing; but her respirations were stertorous, and a complete paralysla had stricken her. Her eyes, half-open and expressionless, showed pupils startlingly dilated. No resources of the party's drug-kit produced the slightest effect on the woman.

The next half-hour was a confused panic, breaking camp, getting Mrs. Thorburn into a canoe, and leaving that accursed place, with a furious energy of terror that could no longer reason. Up-stream, ever up against the swirl of the current the party fought, driven by horror. With no thought of food or drink, paying no heed to landmarks, lashed forward only by the mad desire to be gone, the three men and the girl flung every ounce of their energy into the paddles. Their panting breath mingled with the sound of swirling eddies. A mist-blurred sun brooded over the northern wilds. Unheeded, hosts of black-flies sang high-pitched keenings all about the fugitives. On either hand the forest waited, watched.

Only after two hours of sweating toil had brought exhaustion did they stop, in the shelter of a cove where black waters circled, foam-flecked. There they found the Professor's wife - she was dead.

Nothing remained to do but bury her. At first Thorburn would not hear of it. Like a madman he insisted that through all hazards he would fetch the body out. But no - impossible. So, after a terrible time, he yielded.

In spite of her grief, Vivian was admirable. She understood what must be done. It was her voice that said the prayers; her hand that - lacking flowers - laid the fir boughs on the cairn. The Professor was dazed past doing anything, saying anything.

Toward mid-afternoon, the party landed again, many miles up-river. Necessity forced them to eat. Firs would not burn. Every time they lighted it, it smouldered and went out with a heavy, greasy smoke. The fugitives ate cold food and drank water, then shoved off in two canoes and once more fled.

In the third canoe, hauled to the edge of the forest, lay all the rock-specimens, data and curios, scientific instruments. The party kept only Marr's diary, a compass, supplies, fire-arms and medicine-kit.

"We can find the things we've left - sometime," said Jandron, noting the place well. "Sometime - after - It has gone,"

"And bring the body out," added Thorburn. Tears, for the

first time, wet his eyes. Vivian said nothing. Marr tried to light his pipe. He seemed to forget that nothing, not even tobacco, would burn now.

Vivian and Jandron occupied one canoe. The other carried the Professor and Marr. Thus the power of the two canoes was about the same. They kept well together, up-stream.

The fugitives paddled and portaged with a dumb, desperate energy. Toward evening they struck into what they believed to be the Mamattawan. A mile up this, as the blurred sun faded beyond a wilderness of ominous silence, they camped. Here they made determined efforts to kindle fire. Not even alcohol from the drug-kit would start it. Cold, they mumbled a little food; cold, they huddled into their sleeping-bags, there to lie with darkness leaden on their fear. After a long time, up over a world void of all sound save the river-flow, slid an amber moon notched by the ragged tops of the conifers. Even the wail of a timber-wolf would have come as welcome relief; but no wolf howled.

Silence and night enfolded them. And everywhere they felt that It was watching.

Foolishly enough, as a man will do foolish things in a crisis, Jandron laid his revolver outside his sleeping-bag, in easy reach. His thought - blurred by a strange, drawing headache - was:

"If It touches Vivian, I'll shoot!"

He realized the complete absurdity of trying to shoot a visitant from interstellar space; from the Fourth Dimension, maybe. But Jandron's ideas seemed tangled. Nothing would come right. He lay there, absorbed in a kind of waking nightmare. Now and then, rising on an elbow, he hearkened; all in vain. Nothing so much as stirred.

His thought drifted to better days, when all had been health, sanity, optimism; when nothing except jealousy of Marr, as concerned Vivian, had troubled him. Days when the sizzle of the frying-pan over friendly coals had made friendly wilderness music; when the wind and the northern star, the whirr of the reel, the whispering vortex of the paddle in clear water had all been things of joy. Yes, and when a certain happy moment had, through some word or look of the girl, seemed to promise his heart's desire. But now -

"Damn it, I'll save her, anyhow!" he swore with savage intensity, knowing all the while that what was to be, would be, unmitigably. Do ants, by any waving of antenna, stay the down-crushing foot of man?

Next morning, and the next, no sign of the Thing appeared. Hope revived that possibly It might have flitted away elsewhere; back, perhaps, to outer space. Many were the miles the urging paddles spurned behind. The fugitives calculated that a week more would bring them to the railroad. Fire burned again. Hot food and drink helped, wonderfully. But where were the fish?

"Most extraordinary," all at once said the Professor, at noonday camp. He had become quite rational again. "Do you realize, Jandron, we've seen no traces of life in some time?"

The geologist nodded. Only too clearly he had noted just that, but he had been keeping still about it.

"That's so, too!" chimed in Marr, enjoying the smoke that some incomprehensible turn of events was letting him have. "Not a muskrat or beaver. Not even a squirrel or bird."

"Not so much as a gnat or black-fly!" the Professor added. Jandron suddenly realized that he would have welcomed even those.

That afternoon, Marr fell into a suddenly vile temper. He mumbled curses against the guides, the current, the portages, everything. The Professor seemed more cheerful. Vivian complained of an oppressive headache. Jandron gave her the last of the aspirin tablets; and as he gave them, took her hand in his.

"I'll see you through, anyhow," said he, "I don't count, now. Nobody counts, only you!"

She gave him a long, silent look. He saw the sudden glint of tears in her eyes; felt the pressure of her hand, and knew they two had never been so near each other as in that moment under the shadow of the Unknown.

Next day - or it may have been two days later, for none of them could be quite sure about the passage of time - they came to a deserted lumber-camp. Even more than two days might have passed; because now their bacon was all gone, and only coffee, tobacco, beef-cubes and pilot-bread remained. The lack of fish and game had cut alarmingly into the duffle-bag. That day - whatever day it may have been - all four of them suffered terribly from headache of an odd, ring-shaped kind, as if something circular were being pressed down about their heads. The Professor said it was the sun that made his head ache. Vivian laid it to the wind and the gleam of the swift water, while Marr claimed it was the heat. Jandron wondered at all this, inasmuch as he plainly saw that the river had almost stopped flowing, and the day had become still and overcast.

They dragged their canoes upon a rotting stage of fir-poles and explored the lumber-camp; a mournful place set back in an old "slash," now partly overgrown with scrub poplar, maple and birch. The log buildings, covered with tar-paper partly torn from the pole roofs, were of the usual North Country type. Obviously the place had not been used for years. Even the landing-stage where once logs had been rolled into the stream had sagged to decay.

"I don't quite get the idea of this," Marr exclaimed. "Where did the logs go to? Downstream, of course. But that would take 'em to Hudson Bay, and there's no market for spruce timber or pulpwood at Hudson Bay." He pointed down the current.

"You're entirely mistaken," put in the Professor. "Any fool could see this river runs the other way. A log thrown in here would go down toward the St. Lawrence!"

"But then," asked the girl, "why can't we drift back to civilization?" The Professor retorted:

"Just what we have been doing, all along! Extraordinary, that I have to explain the obvious!' He walked away in a huff,

"I don't know but he's right, at that," half admitted the journalist. "I've been thinking almost the same thing, myself, the past day or two - that is, ever since the sun shifted."

"What do you mean, shifted?" from Jandron, "You haven't noticed it?"

"But there's been no sun at all, for at least two days!"

"Hanged if I'll waste time arguing with a lunatic!" Marr growled. He vouchsafed no explanation of what he meant by the sun's having "shifted," but wandered off, grumbling.

"What are we going to do?" the girl appealed to Jandron. The sight of her solemn, frightened eyes, of her palm-outward hands and (at last) her very feminine fear, constricted Jandron's heart.

"We're going through, you and I," he answered simply. "We've got to save them from themselves, you and I have."

Their hands met again, and for a moment held. Despite the dead calm, a fir-tip at the edge of the clearing suddenly flicked aside, shrivelled as if frozen. But neither of them saw it.

The fugitives, badly spent, established themselves in the "bar-room" or sleeping-shack of the camp. They wanted to feel a roof over them again, if only a broken one. The traces of men comforted them: a couple of broken peavies, a pair of snowshoes with the thongs all gnawed off, a cracked bit of mirror, a yellowed almanac dated 1899.

Jandron called the Professor's attention to this almanac, but the Professor thrust it aside.

"What do I want of a Canadian census-report?" he demanded, and fell to counting the bunks, over and over again. His big bulge of his forehead, that housed the massive brain of him, was oozing sweat. Marr cursed what he claimed was sunshine through the holes in the roof, though Jandron could see none; claimed the sunshine made his head ache.

"But it's not a bad place," he added. "We can make a blaze in that fireplace and be comfy. I don't like that window, though."

"What window?" asked Jandron. "Where?"

Marr laughed, and ignored him. Jandron turned to Vivian, who had sunk down on the "deacon-seat" and was staring at the stove.

"Is there a window here?" he demanded. "Don't ask me," she whispered. "I - I don't know."

With a very thriving fear in his heart, Jandron peered at her a moment. He fell to muttering:

"I'm Wallace Jandron. Wallace Jandron, 37 Ware Street, Cambridge, Massachusetts. I'm quite sane. And I'm going to stay so. I'm going to save her! I know perfectly well what I'm doing. And I'm sane. Quite, quite sane!"

After a time of confused and purposeless wrangling, they got a fire going and made coffee. This, and cube bouillon with hardtack, helped considerably. The camp helped, too. A house, even a poor and broken one, is a wonderful barrier against a Thing from—Outside.

Presently darkness folded down. The men smoked, thankful that tobacco still held out. Vivian lay in a bunk that Jandron had piled with spruce boughs for her, and seemed to sleep. The Professor fretted like a child, over the blisters his paddle had made upon his hands. Marr laughed, now and then; though what he might be laughing at was not apparent. Suddenly he broke out:

"After all, what should It want of us?"

"Our brains, of course," the Professor answered, sharply.

"That lets Jandron out," the journalist mocked.

"But," added the Professor, "I can't imagine a, Thing callously destroying human beings. And yet -"

He stopped short, with surging memories of his dead wife.

"What was it," Jandron asked, "that destroyed all those people in Valladolid, Spain, that time so many of 'em died in a few minutes after having been touched by an invisible Something that left a slight red mark on each? The newspapers were full of it."

"Piffle!" yawned Marr.

"I tell you," insisted Jandron, "there are forms of life as superior to us as we are to ants. We can't see 'em. No ant ever saw a man. And did any ant ever form the least conception of a man? These Things have left thousands of traces, all over the world. If I had my reference-books -"

"Tell that to the marines!"

"Charles Fort, the greatest authority in the world on unexplained phenomena," persisted Jandron, "gives innumerable cases of happenings that science can't explain, in his 'Book of the Damned.' He claims this earth was once a No-Man's land where all kinds of Things explored and colonized and fought for possession. And he says that now everybody's warned off, except the Owners. I happen to remember a few sentences of his: 'In the past, inhabitants of a host of worlds have dropped here, hopped here, wafted here, sailed, flown, motored, walked here; have come singly, have come in enormous numbers; have visited for hunting, trading, mining. They have been unable to stay here, have made colonies here, have been lost here.'"

"Poor fish, to believe that!" mocked the journalist, while the Professor blinked and rubbed his bulging forehead.

"I do believe it!" insisted Jandron. "The world is covered

with relics of dead civilizations, that have mysteriously vanished, leaving nothing but their temples and monuments."

"Rubbish!"

"How about Easter Island? How about all the gigantic works there and in a thousand other places! — Peru, Yucatan and so on - which certainly no primitive race ever built?"

"That's thousands of years ago," said Marr, "and I'm sleepy. For heaven's sake, can it!"

"Oh, all right. But how explain things, then!"

"What the devil could one of those Things want of our brains?" suddenly put in the Professor. "After all, what?"

"Well, what do we want of lower forms of life? Sometimes food. Again, some product or other. Or just information. Maybe It is just experimenting with us, the way we poke an ant-hill. There's always this to remember, that the human brain-tissue is the most highly-organized form of matter in this world."

"Yes," admitted the Professor, "but what -?"

"It might want brain-tissue for food, for experimental purposes, for lubricant - how do I know?"

Jandron fancied he was still explaining things; but all at once he found himself waking up in one of the bunks. He felt terribly cold, stiff, sore. A sift of snow lay here and there on the camp floor, where it had fallen through holes in the roof.

"Vivian!" he croaked hoarsely. "Thorburn! Marr!"

Nobody answered. There was nobody to answer. Jandron crawled with immense pain out of his bunk, and blinked round with bleary eyes. All of a sudden he saw the Professor, and gulped.

The Professor was lying stiff and straight in another bunk, on his back. His waxen face made a mask of horror. The open, staring eyes, with pupils immensely dilated, sent Jandron shuddering back. A livid ring marked the forehead, that now sagged inward as if empty.

"Vivian!" croaked Jandron, staggering away from the body. He fumbled to the bunk where the girl had lain. The bunk was quite deserted.

On the stove, in which lay half-charred wood - wood smothered out as if by some noxious gas - still stood the coffee-pot. The liquid in it was frozen solid. Of Vivian and the journalist, no trace remained.

Along one of the sagging beams that supported the roof, Jandron's horror-blasted gaze perceived a straight line of frosted prints, ring-shaped, bitten deep.

"Vivian! Vivian!"

No answer.

Shaking, sick, grey, half-blind with a horror not of this world, Jandron peered slowly around. The duffle-bag and supplies were gone. Nothing was left but that coffee-pot and the revolver at Jandron's hip.

Jandron turned, then. A-stare, his skull feeling empty as a burst drum, he crept lamely to the door and out - out into the snow.

Snow. It came slanting down. From a grey sky it steadily filtered. The trees showed no leaf. Birches, poplars, rock-maples all stood naked. Only the conifers drooped sickly-green. In a little shallow across the river snow lay white on thin ice.

Ice? Snow? Rapt with terror, Jandron stared. Why, then, he must have been unconscious three or four weeks? But how -?

Suddenly, all along the upper branches of trees that edged the clearing, puffs of snow flicked down. The geologist shuffled after two half-obliterated sets of footprints that wavered toward the landing.

His body was leaden. He wheezed, as he reached the river. The light, dim as it was, hurt his eyes. He blinked in a confusion that could just perceive one canoe was gone. He pressed a hand to his head, where an iron band seemed screwed up tight, tighter.

"Vivian! Marr! Halloooo!"

Not even an echo. Silence clamped the world; silence, and a cold that gnawed. Everything had gone a sinister grey.

After a certain time - though time now possessed neither reality nor duration - Jandron dragged himself back to the camp and stumbled in. Heedless of the staring corpse he crumpled down by the stove and tried to think, but his brain had been emptied of power. Everything blent to a grey blur. Snow kept slithering in through the roof.

"Well, why don't you come and get me. Thing?" suddenly snarled Jandron. "Here I am. Damn you, come and get me!"

Voices. Suddenly he heard voices. Yes, somebody was outside, there. Singularly aggrieved, he got up and limped to the door. He squinted out into the grey; saw two figures down by the landing. With numb indifference he recognized the girl and Marr.

"Why should they bother me again?" he nebulously wondered. "Can't they go away and leave me alone?" He felt peevish irritation.

Then, a modicum of reason returning, he sensed that they were arguing. Vivian, beside a canoe freshly dragged from thin ice, was pointing; Marr was gesticulating. All at once Marr snarled, turned from her, plodded with bent back toward the camp.

"But listen!" she called, her rough-knit sweater all powdered with snow. "That's the way!" She gestured downstream.

"I'm not going either way!" Marr retorted. "I'm going to stay right here!" He came on, bareheaded. Snow greyed his stubble of beard; but on his head it melted as it fell, as if some fever there had raised the brain-stuff to improbable temperatures. "I'm going to stay right here, all summer." His heavy lids sagged. Puffy and evil, his lips showed a glint of teeth. "Let me alone!"

Vivian lagged after him, kicking up the ash-like snow. With indifference, Jandron watched them. Trivial human creatures!

Suddenly Marr saw him in the doorway and stopped short. He drew his gun; he aimed at Jandron.

"You get out!" he mouthed. "Why in - - - - can't you stay dead?"

"Put that gun down, you idiot!" Jandron managed to retort. The girl stopped and seemed trying to understand. "We can get away yet, if we all stick together."

"Are you going to get out and leave me alone?" demanded the journalist, holding his gun steadily enough.

Jandron, wholly indifferent, watched the muzzle. Vague curiosity possessed him. Just what, he wondered, did it feel like to be shot?

Mart pulled trigger.

Snap!

The cartridge missed fire. Not even powder would bum.

Marr laughed, horribly, and shambled forward. "Serves him right!" he mouthed, "He'd better not come back again!"

Jandron understood that Marr had seen him fall. But still he felt himself standing there, alive. He shuffled away from the door. No matter whether he was alive or dead, there was always Vivian to be saved.

The journalist came to the door, paused, looked down, grunted and passed into the camp. He shut the door. Jandron heard the rotten wooden bar of the latch drop. From within echoed a laugh, monstrous in its brutality.

Then quivering, the geologist felt a touch on his arm.

"Why did you desert us like that?" he heard Vivian's reproach. "Why?"

He turned, hardly able to see her at all.

"Listen," he said, thickly. "I'll admit anything. It's all right. But just forget it, for now. We've got to get out o' here. The Professor is dead, in there, and Marr's gone mad and barricaded himself in there. So there's no use staying. There's a chance for us yet. Come along!"

He took her by the arm and tried to draw her toward the river, but she held back. The hate in her face sickened him. He shook in the grip of a mighty chill.

"Go, with - you?" she demanded.

"Yes, by God!" he retorted, in a swift blaze of anger, "or I'll kill you where you stand. It shan't get you, anyhow!"

Swiftly piercing, a greater cold smote to his inner marrows. A long row of the cup-shaped prints had just appeared in the snow beside the camp. And from these marks wafted a faint, bluish vapour of unthinkable cold.

"What are you staring at?" the girl demanded. "Those prints! In the snow, there - see?" He pointed a shaking finger.

"How can there be snow at this season?"

He could have wept for the pity of her, the love of her. On her red tam, her tangle of rebel hair, her sweater, the snow came steadily drifting; yet there she stood before him and prated of summer. Jandron heaved himself out of a very slough of down-dragging lassitudes. He whipped himself into action.

"Summer, winter - no matter!" he flung at her. "You're coming along with me!" He seized her arm with the brutality of desperation that must hurt, to save. And murder, too, lay in his soul. He knew that he would strangle her with his naked hands, if need were, before he would ever leave her there, for It to work Its horrible will upon.

"You come with me," he mouthed, "or by the Almighty -!"

Marr's scream in the camp, whirled him toward the door. That scream rose higher, higher, even more and more piercing, just like the screams of the runaway Indian guides in what now appeared the infinitely long ago. It seemed to last hours; and always it rose, rose, as if being wrung out of a human body by some kind of agony not conceivable in this world. Higher, higher -

Then it stopped.

Jandron hurled himself against the plank door. The bar smashed; the door shivered inward.

With a cry, Jandron recoiled. He covered his eyes with a hand that quivered, claw-like.

"Go away, Vivian! Don't come here - don't look -"

He stumbled away, babbling.

Out of the door crept something like a man. A queer, broken, bent over thing; a thing crippled, shrunken and flabby, that whined.

This thing - yes, it was still Marr - crouched down at one side, quivering, whimpering. It moved its hands as a crushed ant moves its antennæ, jerkily, without significance.

All at once Jandron no longer felt afraid. He walked quite steadily to Marr, who was breathing in little gasps. From the camp issued an odour unlike anything terrestrial. A thin, greyish grease covered the sill.

Jandron caught hold of the crumpling journalist's arm. Marr's eyes leered, filmed, unseeing. He gave the impression of a creature whose back has been broken, whose whole essence and energy have been wrenched asunder, yet in which life somehow clings, palpitant. A creature vivisected.

Away through the snow Jandron dragged him. Marr made no resistance; just let himself be led, whining a little, palsied, rickety, shattered. The girl, her face whitely cold as the snow that fell on it, came after.

Thus they reached the landing at the river.

"Come, now, let's get away!" Jandron made shift to articulate. Marr said nothing. But when Jandron tried to bundle him into a canoe, something in the journalist revived with swift, mad hatefulness. That something lashed him into a spasm of wiry, incredibly venomous resistance. Slavers of blood and foam streaked Marr's lips. He made horrid noises, like an animal. He howled dismally, and bit, clawed, writhed and grovelled! he tried to sink his teeth into Jandron's leg. He fought appallingly, as men must have fought in the inconceivably remote days even before the Stone Age. And Vivian helped him. Her fury was a tiger-cat's.

Between the pair of them, they almost did him in. They almost dragged Jandron down - and themselves, too - into the black river that ran swiftly sucking under the ice. Not till Jandron had quite flung off all vague notions and restraints of gallantry; not until he struck from the shoulder - to kill, if need were - did he best them.

He beat the pair of them unconscious, trussed them hand and foot with the painters of the canoes, rolled them into the larger canoe, and shoved off. After that, the blankness of a measureless oblivion descended.

Only from what he was told, weeks after, in the Royal Victoria Hospital at Montreal, did Jandron ever learn how and when a field-squad of Dominion Foresters had found them drifting in Lake Mooaswamkeag. And that knowledge filtered slowly into his brain during a period inchoate as Iceland fogs.

That Marr was dead and the girl alive - that much, at all events, was solid. He could hold to that; he could climb back, with that, to the real world again.

Jandron climbed back, came back. Time healed him, as it healed the girl. After a long, long while, they had speech together. Cautiously he sounded her wells of memory. He saw that she recalled nothing. So he told her white lies about capsized canoes and the sad death - in realistically-described rapids - of all the party except herself and him.

Vivian believed. Fate, Jandron knew, was being very kind to both of them.

But Vivian could never understand in the least why, her husband, not very long after marriage, asked her not to wear a wedding-ring or any ring whatever.

"Men are so queer!" covers a multitude of psychic agonies.

Life, for Jandron - life, softened by Vivian - knit itself up into some reasonable semblance of a normal pattern. But when, at lengthening intervals, memories even now awake - memories crawling amid the slime of cosmic mysteries that it is madness to approach - or when at certain times Jandron sees a ring of any sort, his heart chills with a cold that reeks of the horrors of Infinity.

And from shadows past the boundaries of our universe seem to beckon Things that, God grant, can never till the end of time be known on earth.

FOR THE BLOOD IS THE LIFE
F. Marion Crawford

We had dined at sunset on the broad roof of the old tower, because it was cooler there during the great heat of summer. Besides, the little kitchen was built at one corner of the great square platform, which made it more convenient than if the dishes had to be carried down the steep stone steps broken in places and everywhere worn with age. The tower was one of those built all down the west coast of Calabria by the Emperor Charles V early in the sixteenth century, to keep off the Barbary pirates, when the unbelievers were allied with Francis I against the Emperor and the Church. They have gone to ruin, a few still stand intact, and mine is one of the largest. How it came into my possession ten years ago, and why I spend a part of each year in it, are matters which do not concern this tale. The tower stands in one of the loneliest spots in Southern Italy, at the extremity of a curving, rocky promontory, which forms a small but safe natural harbour at the southern extremity of the Gulf of Policastro, and just north of Cape Scalea, the birthplace of Judas Iscariot, according to the old local legend. The tower stands alone on this hooked spur of the rock, and there is not a house to be seen within three miles of it. When I go there I take a couple of sailors, one of whom is a fair cook, and when I am away it is in charge of a gnome-like little being who was once a miner and who attached himself to me long ago.

My friend, who sometimes visits me in my summer solitude, is an artist by profession, a Scandinavian by birth, and a cosmopolitan by force of circumstances. We had dined at sunset; the sunset glow had reddened and faded again, and the evening purple steeped the vast chain of the mountains that embrace the deep gulf to eastward and rear themselves higher and higher towards the south. It was hot, and we sat at the landward corner of the platform, waiting for the night breeze to come down from the lower hills. The colour sank out of the air, there was a little interval of deep-grey twilight, and a lamp sent a yellow streak from the open door of the kitchen, where the men were getting their supper. Then the moon rose suddenly above the crest of the promontory, flooding the platform and lighting up every little spur of rock and knoll of grass below us, down to the edge of the motionless water. My friend lighted his pipe and sat looking at a spot on the hillside. I knew that he was looking at it, and for a long time past I had wondered whether he would ever see anything there that would fix his attention. I knew that spot well. It was clear that he was interested at last, though it was a long time before he spoke. Like most painters, he trusts to his own eyesight, as a lion trusts his strength and a stag his speed, and he is always disturbed when he cannot reconcile what he sees with what he believes that he ought to see.

"It's strange," he said. "Do you see that little mound just on this side of the boulder?"

"Yes," I said, and I guessed what was coming.

"It looks like a grave," observed Holger.

"Very true. It does look like a grave."

"Yes," continued my friend, his eyes still fixed on the spot.

"But the strange thing is that I see the body lying on the top of it. Of course," continued Holger, turning his head on one side as artists do, "it must be an effect of light. In the first place, it is not a grave at all. Secondly, if it were, the body would be inside and not outside. Therefore, it's an effect of the moonlight. Don't you see it?"

"Perfectly; I always see it on moonlight nights."

"It doesn't seem to interest you much," said Holger.

"On the contrary, it does interest me, though I am used to it. You're not so far wrong, either. The mound is really a grave."

"Nonsense!" cried Holger incredulously. "I suppose you'll tell me that what I see lying on it is really a corpse!"

"No," I answered, "it's not. I know, because I have taken the trouble to go down and see."

"Then what is it?" asked Holger.

"It's nothing."

"You mean that it's an effect of light, I suppose?"

"Perhaps it is. But the inexplicable part of the matter is that it makes no difference whether the moon is rising or setting, or waxing or waning. If there's any moonlight at all, from east or west or overhead, so long as it shines on the grave you can see the outline of the body on top."

Holger stirred up his pipe with the point of his knife, and then used his finger for a stopper. When the tobacco burned well, he rose from his chair.

"If you don't mind," he said, "I'll go down and take a look at it."

He left me, crossed the roof, and disappeared down the dark steps. I did not move, but sat looking down until he came out of the tower below. I heard him humming an old Danish song as he crossed the open space in the bright moonlight, going straight to the mysterious mound. When he was ten paces from it, Holger stopped short, made two steps forward, and then three or four backward, and then stopped again. I know what that meant. He had reached the spot where the Thing ceased to be visible - where, as he would have said, the effect of light changed.

Then he went on till he reached the mound and stood upon it. I could see the Thing still, but it was no longer lying down; it was on its knees now, winding its white arms round Holger's body and looking up into his face. A cool breeze stirred my hair at that moment, as the night wind began to come down from the hills, but it felt like a breath from another world.

The Thing seemed to be trying to climb to its feet helping itself up by Holger's body while he stood upright, quite unconscious of it and apparently looking toward the tower, which is very picturesque when the moonlight falls upon it on that side.

"Come along!" I shouted. "Don't stay there all night!"

It seemed to me that he moved reluctantly as he stepped from the mound, or else with difficulty. That was it. The Thing's arms were still round his waist, but its feet could not leave the grave. As he came slowly forward it was drawn and lengthened like a wreath of mist, thin and white, till I saw distinctly that Holger shook himself, as a man does who feels a chill. At the same instant a little wail of pain came to me on the breeze - it might have been the cry of the small owl that lives amongst the rocks - and the misty presence floated swiftly back from Holger's advancing figure and lay once more at its length upon the mound.

Again I felt the cool breeze in my hair, and this time an icy thrill of dread ran down my spine. I remembered very well that I had once gone down there alone in the moonlight; that presently, being near, I had seen nothing; that, like Holger, I had gone and had stood upon the mound; and I remembered how when I came back, sure that there was nothing there, I had felt the sudden conviction that there was something after all if I would only look back, a temptation I had resisted as unworthy of a man of sense, until, to get rid of it, I had shaken myself just as Holger did.

And now I knew that those white, misty arms had been round me, too; I knew it in a flash, and I shuddered as I remembered that I had heard the night owl then, too. But it had not been the night owl. It was the cry of the Thing.

I refilled my pipe and poured out a cup of strong southern wine; in less than a minute Holger was seated beside me again.

"Of course there's nothing there," he said, "but it's creepy, all the same. Do you know, when I was coming back I was so sure that there was something behind me that I wanted to turn around and look? It was an effort not to."

He laughed a little, knocked the ashes out of his pipe, and poured himself out some wine. For a while neither of us spoke, and the moon rose higher and we both looked at the Thing that lay on the mound.

"You might make a story about that," said Holger after a long time.

"There is one," I answered. "If you're not sleepy, I'll tell it to you."

"Go ahead," said Holger, who likes stories.

Old Aderio was dying up there in the village beyond the hill. You remember him, I have no doubt. They say that he made his money by selling sham jewellery in South America, and escaped with his gains when he was found out. Like all those fellows, if they bring anything back with them, he at once set to work to enlarge his house, and as there are no masons here, he sent all the way to Paola for two workmen. They were a rough-looking pair of scoundrels - a Neapolitan who had lost one eye and a Sicilian with an old scar half an inch deep across his left cheek. I often saw them, for on Sundays they used to come down here and fish off the rocks. When Alario caught the fever that killed him the masons were still at work. As he had agreed that part of their pay should be their board and lodging, he made them sleep in the house. His wife was dead, and he had an only son called Angelo, who was a much better sort than himself. Angelo was to marry the daughter of the richest man in the village, and, strange to say, though the marriage was arranged by their parents, the young people were said to be in love with each other.

For that matter, the whole village was in love with Angelo, and among the rest a wild, good-looking creature called Cristina, who was more like a gipsy than any girl I ever saw about here. She had very red lips and very black eyes, she was built like a greyhound, and had the tongue of the devil. But Angelo did not care a straw for her. He was rather a simpleminded fellow, quite different from his old scoundrel of a father, and under what I should call normal circumstances I really believe that he would never have looked at any girl except the nice plump little creature, with a fat dowry, whom his father meant him to marry. But things turned up which were neither normal nor natural.

On the other hand, a very handsome young shepherd from the hills above Maratea was in love with Cristina, who seems to have been quite indifferent to him. Cristina had no regular means of subsistence, but she was a good girl and willing to do any work or go on errands to any distance for the sake of a loaf of bread or a mess of beans, and permission to sleep under cover. She was especially glad when she could get something to do about the house of Angelo's father. There is no doctor in the village, and when the neighbours saw that old Alario was dying they sent Cristina to Scalea to fetch one. That was late in the afternoon, and if they had waited so long it was because the dying miser refused to allow any such extravagance while he was able to speak. But while Cristina was gone matters grew rapidly worse, the priest was brought to the bedside, and when he had done what he could he gave it as his opinion to the bystanders that the old man was dead, and left the house.

You know these people. They have a physical horror of

death. Until the priest spoke, the room had been full of people. The words were hardly out of his mouth before it was empty. It was night now. They hurried down the dark steps and out into the street.

Angelo, as I have said, was away, Cristina had not come back - the simple woman-servant who had nursed the sick man fled with the rest, and the body was left alone in the flickering light of the earthen oil lamp.

Five minutes later two men looked in cautiously and crept forward toward the bed. They were the one-eyed Neapolitan mason and his Sicilian companion. They knew what they wanted. In a moment they had dragged from under the bed a small but heavy iron-bound box, and long before anyone thought of coming back to the dead man they had left the house and the village under cover of darkness. It was easy enough, for Alario's house is the last toward the gorge which leads down here, and the thieves merely went out by the back door, got over the stone wall, and had nothing to risk after that except that possibility of meeting some belated countryman, which was very small indeed, since few of the people use that path. They had a mattock and shovel, and they made their way without accident.

I am telling you this story as it must have happened, for, of course, there were no witnesses to this part of it. The men brought the box down by the gorge, intending to bury it on the beach in the wet sand, where it would have been much safer. But the paper would have rotted if they had been obliged to leave it there long so they dug their hole down there, close to that boulder. Yes, just where the mound is now.

Cristina did not find the doctor in Scalea, for he had been sent for from a place up the valley, half-way to San Domenico. If she had found him we would have come on his mule by the upper road, which is smoother but much longer. But Cristina took the short cut by the rocks, which passes about fifty feet above the mound, and goes round that corner. The men were digging when she passed, and she heard them at work. It would not have been like her to go by without finding out what the noise was, for she was never afraid of anything in her life, and, besides, the fishermen sometimes come ashore here at night to get a stone for an anchor or to gather sticks to make a little fire. The night was dark and Cristina probably came close to the two men before she could see what they were doing. She knew them, of course, and they knew her, and understood instantly that they were in her power. There was only one thing to be done for their safety, and they did it. They knocked her on the head, they dug the hole deep, and they buried her quickly with the iron-bound chest. They must have understood that their only chance of escaping suspicion lay in getting back to the village before their absence was noticed, for they returned immediately, and were found half and hour later gossiping quietly with the man who was making Alario's coffin. He was a crony of theirs, and had been working at the repairs in the old man's house. So far as I have been able to make out, the only persons who were supposed to know where Alario kept his treasure were Angelo and the one woman-servant I have mentioned. Angelo was away; it was the woman who discovered the theft.

It was easy enough to understand why no one else knew where the money was. The old man kept his door locked and the key in his pocket when he was out, and did not let the woman enter to clean the place unless he was there himself. The whole village knew that he had money somewhere, however, and the masons had probably discovered the whereabouts of the chest by climbing in at the window in his absence. If the old man had not been delirious until he lost consciousness he would have been in frightful agony of mind for his riches. The faithful woman-servant forgot their existence only for a few moments when she fled with the rest, overcome by the horror of death. Twenty minutes had not passed before she returned with the two hideous old hags who are always called in to prepare the dead for burial. Even then she had not at first the courage to go near the bed with them, but she made a pretence of dropping something, went down on her knees as if to find it, and looked under the bedstead. The walls of the room were newly whitewashed down to the floor and she saw at a glance that the chest was gone. It had been there in the afternoon, it had therefore been stolen in the short interval since she had left the room.

There are no carabineers stationed in the village; there is not so much as a municipal watchman, for there is no municipality. There never was such a place, I believe. Scalea is supposed to look after it in some mysterious way, and it takes a couple of hours to get anybody from there. As the old woman had lived in the village all her life, it did not even occur to her to apply to any civil authority for help. She simply set up a howl and ran through the village in the dark, screaming out that her dead master's house had been robbed. Many of the people looked out, but at first no one seemed inclined to help her. Most of them, judging her by themselves, whispered to each other that she had probably stolen the money herself. The first man to move was the father of the girl whom Angelo was to marry; having collected his household, all of whom felt a personal interest in the wealth which was to have come into the family, he declared it to be his opinion that the chest had been stolen by the two journeymen masons who lodged in the house. He headed a search for them, which naturally began in Alario's house and ended in the carpenter's workshop, where the thieves were found discussing a measure of wine with the carpenter over the half-finished coffin, by the light of one earthen lamp filled with oil and tallow. The search-party at once accused the delinquents of the crime, and threatened to lock them up in the cellar till the carabineers could be fetched from Scalea. The two men looked at each other for one moment, and then without the slightest hesitation they put out the single light, seized the unfinished coffin between them, and using it as a sort of battering ram, dashed upon their assailants in the dark. In a few moments they were beyond pursuit.

That is the end of the first part of the story. The treasure had disappeared, and as no trace of it could be found the people supposed that the thieves had succeeded in carrying it off. The old man was buried, and when Angelo came back at last he had to borrow money to pay for the miserable funeral, and had some difficulty in doing so. He hardly needed to be told that in losing his inheritance he had lost his bride. In this part of the world marriages are made on strictly business principles, and if the promised cash is not forthcoming on the appointed day, the bride or the bridegroom whose parents have failed to produce it may as well take themselves off, for there will be no wedding. Poor Angelo knew that well enough. His father had been possessed of hardly any land, and now that the hard cash which he had brought from South America was gone, there was nothing left but debts for the building materials that were to have been used for enlarging and improving the old house. Angelo was beggared, and the nice plump little creature who was to have been his, turned up her nose at him in the most approved fashion. As for Cristina, it was several days before she was missed, for no one remembered that she had been sent to Scalea for the doctor, who had never come. She often disappeared in the same way for days together, when she could find a little work here and there at the distant farms among the hills. But when she did not come back at all, people began to wonder, and at last made up their minds that she had connived with the masons and had escaped with them.

I paused and emptied my glass.

"That sort of thing could not happen anywhere else," observed Holger, filling his everlasting pipe again. "It is wonderful what a natural charm there is about murder and sudden death in a romantic country like this. Deeds that would be simply brutal and disgusting anywhere else become dramatic and mysterious because this is Italy, and we are living in a genuine tower of Charles V built against Barbary pirates."

"There's something in that," I admitted. Holger is the most romantic man in the world inside of himself, but he always thinks it necessary to explain why he feels anything.

"I suppose they found the poor girl's body with the box," he said presently.

"As it seems to interest you," I answered, "I'll tell you the rest of the story."

The mood had risen by this time; the outline of the Thing on the mound was clearer to our eyes than before.

The village very soon settled down to its small dull life. No one missed old Alario, who had been away so much on his voyages to South America that he had never been a familiar figure in his native place. Angelo lived in the half-finished house, and because he had no money to pay the old woman-servant, she would not stay with him, but once in a long time she would come and wash a shirt for him for old acquaintance' sake. Besides the house, he had inherited a small patch of ground at some distance from the village; he tried to cultivate it, but he had no heart in the work, for he knew he could never pay the taxes on it and on the house, which would certainly be confiscated by the Government, or seized for the debt of the building material, which the man who had supplied it refused to take back.

Angelo was very unhappy. So long as his father had been

alive and rich, every girl in the village had been in love with him; but that was all changed now. It had been pleasant to be admired and courted, and invited to drink wine by fathers who had girls to marry. It was hard to be stared at coldly, and sometimes laughed at because he had been robbed of his inheritance. He cooked his miserable meals for himself, and from being sad became melancholy and morose.

At twilight, when the day's work was done, instead of hanging about in the open space before the church with young fellows of his own age, he took to wandering in lonely places on the outskirts of the village till it was quite dark. Then he slunk home and went to bed to save the expense of a light. But in those lonely twilight hours he began to have strange waking dreams. He was not always alone, for often when he sat on the stump of a tree, where the narrow path turns down the gorge, he was sure that a woman came up noiselessly over the rough stones, as if her feet were bare; and she stood under a clump of chestnut trees only half a dozen yards down the path, and beckoned to him without speaking. Though she was in the shadow he knew that her lips were red, and that when they parted a little and smiled at him she showed two small sharp teeth. He knew this at first rather than saw it, and he knew that it was Cristina, and that she was dead. Yet he was not afraid; he only wondered whether it was a dream, for he thought that if he had been awake he should have been frightened.

Besides, the dead woman had red lips, and that could only happen in a dream. Whenever he went near the gorge after sunset she was already there waiting for him, or else she very soon appeared, and he began to be sure of her blood-red mouth, but now each feature grew distinct, and the pale face looked at him with deep and hungry eyes.

It was the eyes that grew dim. Little by little he came to know that someday the dream would not end when he turned away to go home, but would lead him down the gorge out of which the vision rose. She was nearer now when she beckoned to him. Her cheeks were not livid like those of the dead, but pale with starvation, with the furious and unappeased physical hunger of her eyes that devoured him. They feasted on his soul and cast a spell over him, and at last they were close to his own and held him. He could not tell whether her breath was as hot as fire, or as cold as ice; he could not tell whether her red lips burned his or froze them, or whether her five fingers on his wrists seared scorching scars or bit his flesh like frost; he could not tell whether he was awake or asleep, whether she was alive or dead, but he knew that she loved him, she alone of all creatures, earthly or unearthly, and her spell had power over him.

When the moon rose high that night the shadow of that Thing was not alone down there upon the mound.

Angelo awoke in the cool dawn, drenched with dew and chilled through flesh, and blood, and bone. He opened his eyes to the faint grey light, and saw the stars were still shining overhead. He was very weak, and his heart was beating so slowly that he was almost like a man fainting. Slowly he turned his head on the mound, as on a pillow, but the other face was not there. Fear seized him suddenly, a fear unspeakable and unknown; he sprang to his feet and fled up the gorge, and he never looked behind him until he reached the door of the house on the outskirts of the village. Drearily he went to his work that day, and wearily the hours dragged themselves after the sun, till at last it touched the sea and sank, and the great sharp hills above Maratea turned purple against the dove-coloured eastern sky.

Angelo shouldered his heavy hoe and left the field. He felt less tired now than in the morning when he had begun to work, but he promised himself that he would go home without lingering by the gorge, and eat the best supper he could get himself, and sleep all night in his bed like a Christian man. Not again would he be tempted down the narrow way by a shadow with red lips and icy breath; not again would he dream that dream of terror and delight. He was near the village now; it was half an hour since the sun had set, and the cracked church bell sent little discordant echoes across the rocks and ravines to tell all good people that the day was done. Angelo stood still a moment where the path forked, where it led toward the village on the left, and down to the gorge on the right, where a clump of chestnut trees overhung the narrow way. He stood still a minute, lifting his battered hat from his head and gazing at the fast-fading sea westward, and his lips moved as he silently repeated the familiar evening prayer. His lips moved, but the words that followed them in his brain lost their meaning and turned into others, and ended in a name that he spoke aloud - Cristina! With the name, the tension of his will relaxed suddenly, reality went out and the dream took him again, and bore him on swiftly and surely like a man walking in his sleep, down, down, by the steep path in the gathering darkness. And as she glided beside him, Cristina whispered strange, sweet things in his ear, which somehow, if he had been awake, he knew that he could not quite have understood; but now they were the most wonderful words he had ever heard in his life. And she kissed him also, but not upon his mouth. He felt her sharp kisses upon his white throat, and he knew that her lips were red. So the wild dream sped on through twilight and darkness and moonrise, and all the glory of the summer's night. But in the chilly dawn he lay as one half dead upon the mound down there, recalling and not recalling, drained of his blood, yet strangely longing to give those red lips more. Then came the fear, the awful nameless panic, the mortal horror that guards the confines of the world we see not, neither know of as we know of other things, but which we feel when its icy chill freezes our bones and stirs our hair with the touch of a ghostly hand. Once more Angelo sprang from the mound and fled up the gorge in the breaking day, but his step was less sure this time, and he panted for breath as he ran; and when he came to the bright spring of water that rises half way up the hillside, he dropped upon his knees and hands and plunged his whole face in and drank as he had never drunk before - for it was the thirst of the wounded man who has lain bleeding all night upon the battle-field.

She had him fast now, and he could not escape her, but would come to her every evening at dusk until she had drained him of his last drop of blood. It was in vain that when the day was done he tried to take another turning and to go home by a path that did not lead near the gorge. It was in vain that he made promises to himself each morning at dawn when he climbed the lonely way up from the shore to the village. It was all in vain, for when the sun sank burning into the sea, and the coolness of the evening stole out as from a hiding-place to delight the weary world, his feet turned toward the old way, and she was waiting for him in the shadow under the chestnut trees; and then all happened as before, and she fell to kissing his white throat even as she flitted lightly down the way, winding one arm about him. And as his blood failed, she grew more hungry and more thirsty every day, and every day when he awoke in the early dawn it was harder to rouse himself to the effort of climbing the steep path to the village; and when he went to his work his feet dragged painfully, and there was hardly strength in his arms to wield the heavy hoe. He scarcely spoke to anyone now, but the people said he was "consuming himself" for love of the girl he was to have married when he lost his inheritance; and they laughed heartily at the thought, for this is not a very romantic country. At this time Antonio, the man who stays here to look after the tower, returned from a visit to his people, who live near Salerno. He had been away all the time since before Alario's death and knew nothing of what had happened. He has told me that he came back late in the afternoon and shut himself up in the tower to eat and sleep, for he was very tired. It was past midnight when he awoke, and when he looked out toward the mound, and he saw something, and he did not sleep again that night. When he went out again in the morning it was broad daylight, and there was nothing to be seen on the mound but loose stones and driven sand. Yet he did not go very near it; he went straight up the path to the village and directly to the house of the old priest.

"I have seen an evil thing this night," he said; "I have seen how the dead drink the blood of the living. And the blood is the life."

"Tell me what you have seen," said the priest in reply.

Antonio told him everything he had seen.

"You must bring your book and your holy water tonight," he added. "I will be here before sunset to go down with you, and if it pleases your reverence to sup with me while we wait, I will make ready."

"I will come," the priest answered, "for I have read in old books of these strange beings which are neither quick nor dead, and which lie ever fresh in their graves, stealing out in the dusk to taste life and blood."

Antonio cannot read, but he was glad to see that the priest understood the business; for, of course, the books must have been instructed him as to the best means of quieting the half-living Thing for ever.

So Antonio went away to his work, which consists largely in sitting on the shady side of the tower, when he is not perched upon a rock with a fishing-line catching nothing. But on that day he went twice to look at the mound in the bright sunlight, and he searched round and round it for some hole through which the being might get in and out; but he found none. When the sun began to sink and the air was cooler in the shadows, he went up to fetch the old priest, carrying a little wicker basket with him; and in this they placed a bottle of holy water, and the basin, and sprinkler, and the stole which the priest would need; and they came down and waited in the door of the tower till it should be dark. But while the light still lingered very grey and faint, they saw something moving, just there, two figures, a man's that walked, and a woman's that flitted beside him, and while her head lay on his shoulder she kissed his throat. The priest has told me that, too, and that his teeth chattered and he grasped Antonio's arm. The vision passed and disappeared into the shadow. Then Antonio got the leathern flask of strong liquor, which he kept for great occasions, and poured such a draught as made the old man feel almost young again; and gave the priest his stole to put on and the holy water to carry, and they went out together toward the spot where the work was to be done. Antonio says that in spite of the rum his own knees shook together, and the priest stumbled over his Latin. For when they were yet a few yards from the mound the flickering light of the lantern fell upon Angelo's white face, unconscious as if in sleep, and on his upturned throat, over which a very thin red line of blood trickled down into his collar; and the flickering light of the lantern played upon another face that looked up from the feast, upon two deep, dead eyes that saw in spite of death - upon parted lips, redder than life itself - upon two gleaming teeth on which glistened a rosy drop. Then the priest, good old man, shut his eyes tight and showered holy water before him, and his cracked voice rose almost to a scream; and then Antonio, who is no coward after all, raised his pick in one hand and the lantern in the other, as he sprang forward, not knowing what the end should be; and then he swears that he heard a woman's cry, and the Thing was gone, and Angelo lay alone on the mound unconscious, with the red line on his throat and the beads of deathly sweat on his cold forehead. They lifted him, half-dead as he was, and laid him on the ground close by; then Antonio went to work, and the priest helped him, though he was old and could not do much; and they dug deep, and at last Antonio, standing in the grave, stooped down with his lantern to see what he might see.

His hair used to be dark brown, with grizzled streaks about the temples; in less than a month from that day he was as grey as a badger. He was a miner when he was young, and most of these fellows have seen ugly sights now and then, when accidents have happened, but he had never seen what he saw that night - that Thing which is neither alive nor dead, that Thing that will abide neither above ground nor in the grave. Antonio had brought something with him which the priest had not noticed - a sharp stake shaped from a piece of tough old driftwood. He had it with him now, and he had his heavy pick, and he had taken the lantern down into the grave. I don't think any power on earth could make him speak of what happened then, and the old priest was too frightened to look in. He says he heard Antonio breathing like a wild beast, and moving as if he were fighting with something almost as strong as himself; and he heard an evil sound also, with blows, as of something violently driven through flesh and bone; and then, the most awful sound of all - a woman's shriek, the unearthly scream of a woman neither dead nor alive, but buried deep for many days. And he, the poor old priest, could only rock himself as he knelt there in the sand, crying aloud his prayers and exorcisms to drown these dreadful sounds. Then suddenly a small iron-bound chest was thrown up and rolled over against the old man's knee, and in a moment more Antonio was beside him, his face as white as tallow in the flickering light of the lantern, shovelling the sand and pebbles into the grave with furious haste, and looking over the edge till the pit was half full; and the priest said that there was much fresh blood on Antonio's hands and on his clothes.

I had come to the end of my story. Holger finished his wine and leaned back in his chair.

"So Angelo got his own again." he said. "Did he marry the prim and plump young person to whom he had been betrothed?"

"No; he had been badly frightened. He went to South America, and has not been heard of since."

"And that poor thing's body is there still, I suppose," said Holger. "Is it quite dead yet, I wonder?"

I wonder, too. But whether it be dead or alive, I should hardly care to see it, even in broad daylight. Antonio is as grey as a badger, and he has never been quite the same man since that night.

THE WHITE WOLF OF THE HARTZ MOUNTAINS
Frederick Marryat

Scarcely had the soldiers performed their task, and thrown down their shovels, when they commenced an altercation. It appeared that this money was to be again the cause of slaughter and bloodshed. Philip and Krantz determined to sail immediately in one of the peroquas, and leave them to settle their disputes as they pleased. He asked permission of the soldiers to take from the provisions and water, of which there was ample supply, a larger proportion than was their share; stating, that he and Krantz had a long voyage and would require it, and pointing out to them that there were plenty of cocoa-nuts for their support. The soldiers, who thought of nothing but their newly-acquired wealth, allowed him to do as he pleased; and, having hastily collected as many cocoa-nuts as they could, to add to their stock of provisions, before noon, Philip and Krantz had embarked and made sail in the peroqua, leaving the soldiers with their knives again drawn, and so busy in their angry altercation as to be heedless of their departure.

"There will be the same scene over again, I expect," observed Krantz, as the vessel parted swiftly from the shore.

"I have little doubt of it; observe, even now they are at blows and stabs."

"If I were to name that spot, it should be the 'Accursed Isle.'"

"Would not any other be the same, with so much to inflame the passions of men?"

"Assuredly: what a curse is gold!"

"And what a blessing!" replied Krantz. "I am sorry Pedro is left with them."

"It is their destiny," replied Philip; "so let's think no more of them. Now what do you propose? With this vessel, small as she is, we may sail over these seas in safety, and we have, I imagine, provisions sufficient for more than a month."

"My idea is, to run into the track of the vessels going to the westward, and obtain a passage to Goa."

"And if we do not meet with any, we can, at all events, proceed up the Straits, as far as Pulo Penang without risk. There we may safely remain until a vessel passes."

"I agree with you; it is our best, nay our only, place; unless, indeed, we were to proceed to Cochin, where junks are always leaving for Goa."

"But that would be out of our way, and the junks cannot well pass us in the Straits, without their being seen by us."

They had no difficulty in steering their course; the islands by day, and the clear stars by night, were their compass. It is true that they did not follow the more direct track, but they followed the more secure, working up the smooth waters, and gaining to the northward more than to the west. Many times they were chased by the Malay proas which infested the islands, but the swiftness of their little peroqua was their security; indeed, the chase was, generally speaking, abandoned as soon as the smallness of the vessel was made out by the pirates, who expected that little or no booty was to be gained.

That Amine and Philip's mission was the constant theme of their discourse, may easily be imagined. One morning, as they were sailing between the isles, with less wind than usual, Philip observed:

"Krantz, you said that there were events in your own life, or connected with it, which would corroborate the mysterious tale I confided to you. Will you now tell me to what you referred?"

"Certainly," replied Krantz; "I've often thought of doing so, but one circumstance or another has hitherto prevented me; this is, however, a fitting opportunity. Prepare, therefore, to listen to a strange story, quite as strange, perhaps, as your own:

"I take it for granted, that you have heard people speak of the Hartz Mountains," observed Krantz.

"I have never heard people speak of them, that I can recollect," replied Philip; "but I have read of them in some book, and of the strange things which have occurred there."

"It is indeed a wild region," rejoined Krantz, "and many strange tales are told of it; but strange as they are, I have good reason for believing them to be true. I have told you, Philip, that I fully believe in your communion with the other world - that I credit the history of your father, and the lawfulness of your mission; for that we are surrounded, impelled, and worked upon by beings different in their nature from ourselves, I have had full evidence, as you will acknowledge, when I state what has occurred in my own family. Why such malevolent beings as I am about to speak of, should be permitted to interfere with us, and punish, I may say, comparatively unoffending mortals, is beyond my comprehension; but that they are so permitted is most certain."

"The great principle of all evil fulfils his work of evil; why, then, not the other minor spirits of the same class?" inquired Philip. "What matters it to us, whether we are tried by, and have to suffer from, the enmity of our fellow-mortals, or whether we are persecuted by beings more powerful and more malevolent than ourselves? We know that we have to work out our salvation, and that we shall be judged according to our strength; if then there be evil spirits who delight to oppress man, there surely must be, as Amine asserts, good spirits, whose delight is to do him service. Whether, then, we have to struggle against our passions only, or whether we have to struggle not only against our passions, but also the dire influence of unseen enemies, we ever struggle with the same odds in our favour, as the good are stronger than the evil which we combat. In either case we are on the 'vantage ground, whether, as in the first, we fight the good cause single-handed, or as in the second, although opposed, we have the host of Heaven ranged on our side. Thus are the scales of Divine justice evenly balanced, and man is still a free agent, as his own virtuous or vicious propensities must ever decide whether he shall gain or lose the victory."

"Most true," replied Krantz, "and now to my history:

"My father was not born, or originally a resident, in the Hartz Mountains; he was the serf of an Hungarian nobleman, of great possessions, in Transylvania; but, although a serf, he was not by any means a poor or illiterate man. In fact, he was rich and his intelligence and respectability were such, that he had been raised by his lord to the stewardship; but, whoever may happen to be born a serf, a serf must he remain, even though he become a wealthy man: and such was the condition of my father. My father had been married for about five years; and by his marriage had three children - my eldest brother Caesar, myself (Hermann), and a sister named Marcella. You know, Philip, that Latin is still the language spoken in that country; and that will account for our high-sounding names. My mother was a very beautiful woman, unfortunately more beautiful than virtuous: she was seen and admired by the lord of the soil; my father was sent away upon some mission; and, during his absence, my mother, flattered by the attentions, and won by the assiduities, of this nobleman, yielded to his wishes. It so happened that my father returned very unexpectedly, and discovered the intrigue. The evidence of my mother's shame was positive; he surprised her in the company of her seducer! Carried away by the impetuosity of his feelings, he watched the opportunity of a meeting taking place between them, and murdered both his wife and her seducer. Conscious that, as a serf, not even the provocation which he had received would be allowed as a justification of his conduct, he hastily collected together what money he could lay his hands upon, and, as we were then in the depth of winter, he put his horses to the sleigh, and taking his children with him, he set off in the middle of the night, and was far away before the tragical circumstance had transpired. Aware that he would be pursued, and that he had no chance of escape if he remained in any portion of his native country (in which the authorities could lay hold of him), he continued his flight without intermission until he had buried himself in the intricacies and seclusion of the Hartz Mountains.

Of course, all that I have now told you I learned afterwards. My oldest recollections are knit to a rude, yet comfortable cottage, in which I lived with my father, brother, and sister. It was on the confines of one of those vast forests which cover the northern part of Germany; around it were a few acres of ground, which, during the summer months, my father cultivated, and which, though they yielded a doubtful harvest, were sufficient for our support. In the winter we remained much indoors, for, as my father followed the chase, we were left alone, and the wolves, during that season, incessantly prowled about. My father had purchased the cottage, and land about it, of one of the rude foresters, who gain their livelihood partly by hunting, and partly by burning charcoal, for the purpose of smelting the ore from the neighbouring mines; it was distant about two miles from any other habitation. I can call to mind the whole landscape now: the tall pines which rose up on the mountain above us, and the wide expanse of forest beneath, on the topmost boughs and heads of whose trees we looked down from our cottage, as the mountain below us rapidly descended into the distant valley. In summer-time the prospect was beautiful: but during the severe winter, a more desolate scene could not well be imagined.

"I said that, in the winter, my father occupied himself with the chase; every day he left us, and often would he lock the door, that we might not leave the cottage. He had no one to assist him, or to take care of us - indeed, it was not easy to find a female servant who would live in such a solitude; but could he have found one, my father would not have received her, for he had imbibed a horror of the sex, as the difference of his conduct towards us, his two boys, and my poor little sister, Marcella evidently proved. You may suppose we were sadly neglected; indeed, we suffered much, for my father, fearful that we might come to some harm, would not allow us fuel, when he left the cottage; and we were obliged, therefore, to creep under the heaps of bears' skins, and there to keep ourselves as warm as we could until he returned in the evening, when a blazing fire was our delight. That my father chose this restless sort of life may appear strange, but the fact was, that he could not remain quiet; whether from the remorse for having committed murder, or from the misery consequent on his change of situation, or from both combined, he was never happy unless he was in a state of activity. Children, however, when left much to themselves, acquire a thoughtfulness not common to their age. So it was with us; and during the short cold days of winter, we would sit silent, longing for the happy hours when the snow would melt and the leaves would burst out, and the birds begin their songs, and when we should again be set at liberty.

"Such was our peculiar and savage sort of life until my brother Caesar was nine, myself seven, and my sister five years old, when the circumstances occurred on which is based the extraordinary narrative which I am about to relate.

"One evening my father returned home rather later than usual; he had been unsuccessful, and, as the weather was very severe, and many feet of snow were upon the ground, he was not only very cold, but in a very bad humour. He had brought in wood, and we were all three gladly assisting each other in blowing on the embers to create the blaze, when he caught poor little Marcella by the arm and threw her aside; the child fell, struck her mouth, and bled very much. My brother ran to raise her up. Accustomed to ill-usage and afraid of my father, she did not dare to cry, but looked up in his face very piteously. My father drew his stool nearer to the hearth, muttered something in abuse of women, and busied himself with the fire, which both my brother and I had deserted when our sister was so unkindly treated. A cheerful blaze was soon the result of his exertions; but we did not, as usual, crowd round it. Marcella, still bleeding, retired to a corner, and my brother and I took our seats beside her, while my father hung over the fire gloomily and alone. Such had been our position for about half an hour, when the howl of a wolf, close under the window of the cottage, fell on our ears. My father started up, and seized his gun: the howl was repeated, he examined the priming, and then hastily left the cottage, shutting the door after him. We all waited (anxiously listening), for we thought that if he succeeded in shooting the wolf, he would return in a better humour; and, although he was harsh to all of us, and particularly so to our little sister, still we loved our father, and loved to see him cheerful and happy, for what else had we to look up to? And I may here observe, that perhaps there never were three children who were fonder of each other; we did not, like other children, fight and dispute together; and if, by chance, any disagreement did arise between my elder brother and me, little Marcella would run to us, and kissing us both, seal, through her entreaties, the peace between us. Marcella was a lovely, amiable child; I can recall her beautiful features even now - Alas! poor little Marcella."

"She is dead, then?" observed Philip.

"*Dead! yes, dead!* - but how did she die? - But I must not anticipate, Philip; let me tell my story.

"We waited for some time, but the report of the gun did not reach us, and my elder brother then said, 'Our father has followed the wolf, and will not be back for some time. Marcella, let us wash the blood from your mouth, and then we will leave this corner, and go to the fire and warm ourselves.'

"We did so, and remained there until near midnight, every minute wondering, as it grew later, why our father did not return. We had no idea that he was in any danger, but we thought that he must have chased the wolf for a very long time. 'I will look out and see if father is coming,' said my brother Caesar, going to the door. 'Take care,' said Marcella, 'the wolves must be about now, and we cannot kill them, brother.' My brother opened the door very cautiously, and but a few inches: he peeped out. 'I see nothing,' said he, after a time, and once more he joined us at the fire. 'We have had no supper,' said I, for my father usually cooked the meat as soon as he came home; and during his absence we had nothing but the fragments of the preceding day.

"'And if our father comes home after his hunt, Caesar,' said Marcella, 'he will be pleased to have some supper; let us cook it for him and for ourselves.' Caesar climbed upon the stool, and reached down some meat - I forget now whether it was venison or bear's meat; but we cut off the usual quantity, and proceeded to dress it, as we used to do under our father's superintendence. We were all busy putting it into the platters before the fire, to await his coming, when we heard the sound of a horn. We listened - there was a noise outside, and a minute afterwards my father entered, ushering in a young female, and a large dark man in a hunter's dress.

"Perhaps I had better now relate what was only known to me many years afterwards. When my father had left the cottage, he perceived a large white wolf about thirty yards from him; as soon as the animal saw my father, it retreated slowly, growling and snarling. My father followed; the animal did not run, but always kept at some distance; and my father did not like to fire until he was pretty certain that his ball would take effect; thus they went on for some time, the wolf now leaving my father far behind, and then stopping and snarling defiance at him, and then, again, on his approach, setting off at speed.

"Anxious to shoot the animal (for the white wolf is very rare) my father continued the pursuit for several hours, during which he continually ascended the mountain.

"You must know, Philip, that there are peculiar spots on those mountains which are supposed, and, as my story will prove, truly supposed, to be inhabited by the evil influences: they are well known to the huntsmen, who invariably avoid them. Now, one of these spots, an open space in the pine forests above us, had been pointed out to my father as dangerous on that account. But, whether he disbelieved these wild stories, or whether, in his eager pursuit of the chase, he disregarded them, I know not; certain, however, it is, that he was decoyed by the white wolf to this open space, when the animal appeared to slacken her speed. My father approached, came close up to her, raised his gun to his shoulder, and was about to fire, when the wolf suddenly disappeared. He thought that the snow on the ground must have dazzled his sight, and he let down his gun to look for the beast - but she was gone; how she could have escaped over the clearance, without his seeing her, was beyond his comprehension. Mortified at the ill success of his chase, he was about to retrace his steps, when he heard the distant sound of a horn. Astonishment at such a sound - at such an hour - in such a wilderness, made him forget for the moment his disappointment, and he remained riveted to the spot. In a minute the horn was blown a second time, and at no great distance; my father stood still, and listened: a third time it was blown. I forget the term used to express it, but it was the signal which, my father well knew, implied that the party was lost in the woods. In a few minutes more my father beheld a man on horseback, with a female seated on the crupper, enter the cleared space, and ride up to him. At first, my father called to mind the strange stories which he had heard of the supernatural beings who were said to frequent these mountains; but the nearer approach of the parties satisfied him that they were mortals like himself. As soon as they came up to him, the man who guided the horse accosted him. 'Friend Hunter, you are out late, the better fortune for us; we have ridden far, and are in fear of our lives which are eagerly sought after. These mountains have enabled us to elude our pursuers; but if we find not shelter and refreshment, that will avail us little, as we must perish from hunger and the inclemency of the night. My daughter, who rides behind me, is now more dead than alive - say, can you assist us in our difficulty?'

"'My cottage is some few miles distant,' replied my father, 'but I have little to offer you besides a shelter from the weather; to the little I have you are welcome. May I ask whence you come?'

"'Yes, friend, it is no secret now; we have escaped from Transylvania, where my daughter's honour and my life were equally in jeopardy!'

"This information was quite enough to raise an interest in my father's heart, he remembered his own escape; he remembered the loss of his wife's honour, and the tragedy by which it was wound up. He immediately, and warmly, offered all the assistance which he could afford them.

"'There is no time to be lost then, good sir,' observed the horseman; 'my daughter is chilled with the frost, and cannot hold out much longer against the severity of the weather.'

"'Follow me,' replied my father, leading the way towards his home.

"'I was lured away in pursuit of a large white wolf,' observed my father; 'it came to the very window of my hut, or I should not have been out at this time of night.'

"'The creature passed by us just as we came out of the wood,' said the female, in a silvery tone.

"'I was nearly discharging my piece at it,' observed the hunter; 'but since it did us such good service, I am glad I allowed it to escape.'

"In about an hour and a half, during which my father walked at a rapid pace, the party arrived at the cottage, and, as I said before, came in.

"'We are in good time, apparently,' observed the dark hunter, catching the smell of the roasted meat, as he walked to the fire and surveyed my brother and sister, and myself. 'You have young cooks here, Meinheer.' 'I am glad that we shall not have to wait,' replied my father. 'Come, mistress, seat yourself by the fire; you require warmth after your cold ride.' 'And where can I put up my horse, Meinheer?' observed the huntsman. 'I will take care of him,' replied my father, going out of the cottage door.

"The female must, however, be particularly described. She was young, and apparently twenty years of age. She was dressed in a travelling-dress, deeply bordered with white fur, and wore a cap of white ermine on her head. Her features were very beautiful, at least I thought so, and so my father has since declared. Her hair was flaxen, glossy, and shining, and bright as a mirror; and her mouth, although somewhat large when it was open, showed the most brilliant teeth I have ever beheld. But there was something about her eyes, bright as they were, which made us children afraid; they were so restless, so furtive; I could not at that time tell why, but I felt as if there was cruelty in her eye; and when she beckoned us to come to her, we approached her with fear and trembling. Still she was beautiful, very beautiful. She spoke kindly to my brother and myself, patted our heads and caressed us; but Marcella would not come near her; on the contrary, she slunk away, and hid herself in the bed, and would not wait for the supper, which half an hour before she had been so anxious for.

"My father, having put the horse into a close shed, soon returned, and supper was placed upon the table. When it was over, my father requested that the young lady would take possession of his bed, and he would remain at the fire, and sit up with her father. After some hesitation on her part, this arrangement was agreed to, and I and my brother crept into the other bed with Marcella, for we had as yet always slept together.

"But we could not sleep; there was something so unusual, not only in seeing strange people, but in having those people sleep at the cottage, that we were bewildered. As for poor little Marcella, she was quiet, but I perceived that she trembled during the whole night, and sometimes I thought that she was checking a sob. My father had brought out some spirits, which he rarely used, and he and the strange hunter remained drinking and talking before the fire. Our ears were ready to catch the slightest whisper - so much was our curiosity excited.

"'You said you came from Transylvania?' observed my father.

"'Even so, Meinheer,' replied the hunter. 'I was a serf to the noble house of ---; my master would insist upon my surrendering up my fair girl to his wishes: it ended in my giving him a few inches of my hunting-knife.'

"'We are countrymen, and brothers in misfortune,' replied my father, taking the huntsman's hand, and pressing it warmly.

"'Indeed! Are you then from that country?'

"'Yes; and I too have fled for my life. But mine is a melancholy tale.'

"'Your name?' inquired the hunter.

"'Krantz.'

"'What! Krantz of---? I have heard your tale; you need not renew your grief by repeating it now. Welcome, most welcome, Meinheer, and, I may say, my worthy kinsman. I am your second cousin, Wilfred of Barnsdorf,' cried the hunter, rising up and embracing my father.

"They filled their horn-mugs to the brim, and drank to one another after the German fashion. The conversation was then carried on in a low tone; all that we could collect from it was that our new relative and his daughter were to take up their abode in our cottage, at least for the present. In about an hour they both fell back in their chairs and appeared to sleep.

"'Marcella, dear, did you hear?' said my brother, in a low tone.

"'Yes,' replied Marcella in a whisper, 'I heard all. Oh! brother, I cannot bear to look upon that woman - I feel so frightened.'

"My brother made no reply, and shortly afterwards we were all three fast asleep.

"When we awoke the next morning, we found that the hunter's daughter had risen before us. I thought she looked more beautiful than ever. She came up to little Marcella and caressed her: the child burst into tears, and sobbed as if her heart would break.

"But, not to detain you with too long a story, the

huntsman and his daughter were accommodated in the cottage. My father and he went out hunting daily, leaving Christina with us. She performed all the household duties; was very kind to us children; and, gradually, the dislike even of little Marcella wore away. But a great change took place in my father; he appeared to have conquered his aversion to the sex, and was most attentive to Christina. Often, after her father and we were in bed would he sit up with her, conversing in a low tone by the fire. I ought to have mentioned that my father and the huntsman Wilfred, slept in another portion of the cottage, and that the bed which he formerly occupied, and which was in the same room as ours, had been given up to the use of Christina. These visitors had been about three weeks at the cottage, when, one night, after we children had been sent to bed, a consultation was held. My father had asked Christina in marriage, and had obtained both her own consent and that of Wilfred; after this, a conversation took place, which was, as nearly as I can recollect, as follows.

"'You may take my child, Meinheer Krantz, and my blessing with her, and I shall then leave you and seek some other habitation - it matters little where.'

"'Why not remain here, Wilfred?'

"'No, no, I am called elsewhere; let that suffice, and ask no more questions. You have my child.'

"'I thank you for her, and will duly value her; but there is one difficulty.'

"'I know what you would say; there is no priest here in this wild country: true; neither is there any law to bind; still must some ceremony pass between you, to satisfy a father. Will you consent to marry her after my fashion? If so, I will marry you directly.'

"'I will,' replied my father.

"'Then take her by the hand. Now, Meinheer, swear.'

"'I swear,' repeated my father.

"'By all the spirits of the Hartz Mountains -'

"'Nay, why not by Heaven?' interrupted my father.

"'Because it is not my humour,' rejoined Wilfred; 'if I prefer that oath, less binding perhaps, than another, surely you will not thwart me.'

"'Well be it so then; have your humour. Will you make me swear by that in which I do not believe?'

"'Yet many do so, who in outward appearance are Christians,' rejoined Wilfred; 'say, will you be married, or shall I take my daughter away with me?'

"'Proceed,' replied my father, impatiently.

"'I swear by all the spirits of the Hartz mountains, by all their power for good or for evil, that I take Christina for my wedded wife; that I will ever protect her, cherish her, and love her; that my hand shall never be raised against her to harm her.'

"My father repeated the words after Wilfred.

"'And if I fail in this my vow, may all the vengeance of the spirits fall upon me and upon my children; may they perish by the vulture, by the wolf, or other beasts of the forest; may their flesh be torn from their limbs, and their bones blanch in the wilderness: all this I swear.'

"My father hesitated, as he repeated the last words; little Marcella could not restrain herself, and as my father repeated the last sentence, she burst into tears. This sudden interruption appeared to discompose the party, particularly my father; he spoke harshly to the child, who controlled her sobs, burying her face under the bed-clothes.

"Such was the second marriage of my father. The next morning, the hunter Wilfred mounted his horse, and rode away.

"My father resumed his bed, which was in the same room as ours; and things went on much as before the marriage, except that our new mother-in-law did not show any kindness towards us; indeed during my father's absence, she would often beat us, particularly little Marcella, and her eyes would flash fire, as she looked eagerly upon the fair and lovely child.

"One night, my sister awoke me and my brother.

"'What is the matter?' said Caesar.

"'She has gone out,' whispered Marcella.

"'Gone out!'

"'Yes, gone out at the door, in her night-clothes,' replied the child; 'I saw her get out of bed, look at my father to see if he slept, and then she went out at the door.'

"What could induce her to leave her bed, and all undressed to go out, in such bitter wintry weather, with the snow deep on the ground was to us incomprehensible; we lay awake, and in about an hour we heard the growl of a wolf, close under the window.

"'There is a wolf,' said Caesar. 'She will be torn to pieces.'

"'Oh no!' cried Marcella.

"In a few minutes afterwards our mother-in-law appeared; she was in her night-dress, as Marcella had stated. She let down the latch of the door, so as to make no noise, went to a pail of water, and washed her face and hands, and then slipped into the bed where my father lay.

"We all three trembled - we hardly knew why; but we resolved to watch the next night: we did so; and not only on the ensuing night, but on many others, and always at about the same hour, would our mother-in-law rise from her bed and leave the cottage; and after she was gone we invariably heard the growl of a wolf under our window, and always saw her, on her return, wash herself before she retired to bed. We observed also that she seldom sat down to meals, and that when she did she appeared to eat with dislike; but when the meat was taken down to be prepared for dinner, she would often furtively put a raw piece into her mouth.

"My brother Caesar was a courageous boy; he did not like to speak to my father until he knew more. He resolved that he would follow her out, and ascertain what she did. Marcella and I endeavoured to dissuade him from this project; but he would not be controlled; and the very next night he lay down in his clothes, and as soon as our mother-in-law had left the cottage he jumped up, took down my father's gun, and followed her.

"You may imagine in what a state of suspense Marcella and I remained during his absence. After a few minutes we heard the report of a gun. It did not awaken my father; and we lay trembling with anxiety. In a minute afterwards we saw our mother-in-law enter the cottage - her dress was bloody. I put my hand to Marcella's mouth to prevent her crying out, although I was myself in great alarm. Our mother-in-law approached my father's bed, looked to see if he was asleep, and then went to the chimney and blew up the embers into a blaze.

"'Who is there?' said my father, waking up.

"'Lie still, dearest,' replied my mother-in-law; 'it is only me; I have lighted the fire to warm some water; I am not quite well.'

"My father turned round, and was soon asleep; but we watched our mother-in-law. She changed her linen, and threw the garments she had worn into the fire; and we then perceived that her right leg was bleeding profusely, as if from a gun-shot wound. She bandaged it up, and then dressing herself, remained before the fire until the break of day.

"Poor little Marcella, her heart beat quick as she pressed me to her side - so indeed did mine. Where was our brother Caesar? How did my mother-in-law receive the wound unless from his gun? At last my father rose, and then for the first time I spoke, saying, 'Father, where is my brother Caesar?'

"'Your brother!' exclaimed he; 'why, where can he be?'

"'*Merciful Heaven!* I thought, as I lay very restless last night,' observed our mother-in-law, 'that I heard somebody open the latch of the door; and, dear me, husband, what has become of your gun?'

"My father cast his eyes up above the chimney, and perceived that his gun was missing. For a moment he looked perplexed; then, seizing a broad axe, he went out of the cottage without saying another word.

"He did not remain away from us long; in a few minutes he returned, bearing in his arms the mangled body of my poor brother; he laid it down, and covered up his face.

"My mother-in-law rose up, and looked at the body, while Marcella and I threw ourselves by its side, wailing and sobbing bitterly.

"'Go to bed again, children,' said she, sharply. 'Husband,' continued she, 'your boy must have taken the gun down, to shoot a wolf, and the animal has been too powerful for him. Poor boy! He has paid dearly for his rashness.'

"My father made no reply. I wished to speak - to tell all - but Marcella who perceived my intention, held me by the arm, and looked at me so imploringly, that I desisted.

"My father, therefore, was left in his error; but Marcella and I, although we could not comprehend it, were conscious that our mother-in-law was in some way connected with my brother's death.

"That day my father went out and dug a grave; and when he hid the body in the earth, he piled up stones over it so that the wolves should not be able to dig it up. The shock of this catastrophe was to my poor father very severe; for several days he never went to the chase, although at times he would utter bitter anathemas and vengeance against the wolves.

"But during this time of mourning on his part, my mother-in-law's nocturnal wanderings continued with the same regularity as before.

"At last my father took down his gun to repair to the forest; but he soon returned, and appeared much annoyed.

"'Would you believe it, Christina, that the wolves - perdition to the whole race - have actually contrived to dig up the body of my poor boy, and now there is nothing left of him but his bones?'

"'Indeed!' replied my mother-in-law. Marcella looked at me; and I saw in her intelligent eye all she would have uttered.

"'A wolf growls under our window every night, father,' said I.

"'Ay, indeed! Why did you not tell me, boy? Wake me the next time you hear it.'

"I saw my mother-in-law turn away; her eyes flashed fire, and she gnashed her teeth.

"My father went out again, and covered up with a larger pile of stones the little remnants of my poor brother which the wolves had spared. Such was the first act of the tragedy.

"The spring now came on; the snow disappeared, and we were permitted to leave the cottage; but never would I quit for one moment my dear little sister, to whom since the death of my brother, I was more ardently attached than ever; indeed, I was afraid to leave her alone with my mother-in-law, who appeared to have a particular pleasure in ill-treating the child. My father was now employed upon his little farm, and I was able to render him some assistance.

"Marcella used to sit by us while we were at work, leaving my mother-in-law alone in the cottage. I ought to observe that, as the spring advanced, so did my mother-in-law decrease her nocturnal rambles, and that we never heard the growl of the wolf under the window after I had spoken of it to my father.

"One day, when my father and I were in the field, Marcella being with us, my mother-in-law came out, saying that she was going into the forest to collect some herbs my father wanted, and that Marcella must go to the cottage and watch the dinner. Marcella went; and my mother-in-law soon disappeared in the forest, taking a direction quite contrary to that in which the cottage stood, and leaving my father and I, as it were, between her and Marcella.

"About an hour afterwards we were startled by shrieks from the cottage - evidently the shrieks of little Marcella. 'Marcella has burnt herself, father,' said I, throwing down my spade. My father threw down his, and we both hastened to the cottage. Before we could gain the door, out darted a large white wolf, which fled with the utmost celerity. My father had no weapon; he rushed into the cottage, and there saw poor little Marcella expiring. Her body was dreadfully mangled, and the blood pouring from it had formed a large pool on the cottage floor. My father's first intention had been to seize his gun and pursue; but he was checked by this horrid spectacle; he knelt down by his dying child, and burst into tears. Marcella could just look kindly on us for a few seconds, and then her eyes were closed in death.

"My father and I were still hanging over my poor sister's body, when my mother-in-law came in. At the dreadful sight she expressed much concern; but she did not appear to recoil from the sight of blood, as most women do.

"'Poor child!' said she, 'it must have been that great white wolf which passed me just now, and frightened me so. She's quite dead, Krantz.'

"'I know it - I know it!' cried my father, in agony.

"I thought my father would never recover from the effects of this second tragedy; he mourned bitterly over the body of his sweet child, and for several days would not consign it to its grave, although frequently requested by my mother-in-law to do so. At last he yielded, and dug a grave for her close by that of my poor brother, and took every precaution that the wolves should not violate her remains.

"I was now really miserable, as I lay alone in the bed which I had formerly shared with my brother and sister. I could not help thinking that my mother-in-law was implicated in both their deaths, although I could not account for the manner; but I no longer felt afraid of her; my little heart was full of hatred and revenge.

"The night after my sister had been buried, as I lay awake, I perceived my mother-in-law get up and go out of the cottage. I waited some time, then dressed myself, and looked out through the door, which I half opened. The moon shone bright and I could see the spot where my brother and my sister had been buried; and what was my horror when I perceived my mother-in-law busily removing the stones from Marcella's grave!

"She was in her white night-dress and the moon shone full upon her. She was digging with her hands, and throwing away the stones behind her with all the ferocity of a wild beast. It was some time before I could collect my senses, and decide what I should do. At last I perceived that she had arrived at the body, and raised it up to the side of the grave. I could bear it no longer, I ran to my father and awoke him.

"'Father, father!' cried I, 'dress yourself, and get your gun.'

"'What!' cried my father, 'the wolves are there, are they?'

"He jumped out of bed, threw on his clothes, and, in his anxiety, did not appear to perceive the absence of his wife. As soon as he was ready I opened the door; he went out, and I followed him.

"Imagine his horror, when (unprepared as he was for such a sight) he beheld, as he advanced towards the grave not a wolf, but his wife, in her night-dress, on her hands and knees, crouching by the body of my sister, and tearing off large pieces of the flesh, and devouring them with all the avidity of a wolf. She was too busy to be aware of our approach. My father dropped his gun; his hair stood on end, so did mine; he breathed heavily, and then his breath for a time stopped. I picked up the gun and put it into his hand. Suddenly he appeared as if concentrated rage had restored him to double vigour; he levelled his piece, fired, and with a loud shriek down fell the wretch whom he had fostered in his bosom.

"'God of Heaven!' cried my father, sinking down upon the earth in a swoon, as soon as he had discharged his gun.

"I remained some time by his side before he recovered. 'Where am I?' said he, 'what has happened? Oh - yes, yes! I recollect now. Heaven forgive me!'

"He rose and we walked up to the grave; what again was our astonishment and horror to find that, instead of the dead body of my mother-in-law, as we expected, there was lying over the remains of my poor sister, a large white she-wolf.

"'The white wolf!' exclaimed my father, 'the white wolf which decoyed me into the forest - I see it all now - I have dealt with the spirits of the Hartz Mountains.'.

"For some time my father remained in silence and deep thought. He then carefully lifted up the body of my sister, replaced it in the grave, and covered it over as before, having struck the head of the dead animal with the heel of his boot, and raving like a madman. He walked back to the cottage, shut the door, and threw himself on the bed; I did the same, for I was in a stupor of amazement.

"Early in the morning we were both roused by a loud knocking at the door, and in rushed the hunter Wilfred.

"'*My daughter – man - my daughter! - where is my daughter?*' cried he in a rage.

"'Where the wretch, the fiend, should be, I trust,' replied my father, starting up, and displaying equal choler; 'where she should be - in hell! Leave this cottage, or you may fare worse.'

"'Ha ha!' replied the hunter, 'would you harm a potent

spirit of the Hartz Mountains. Poor mortal, who must needs wed a werewolf.'

"'Out, demon! I defy thee and thy power.'

"'Yet shall you feel it; remember your oath - your solemn oath - never to raise your hand against her to harm her.'

"'I made no compact with evil spirits.'

"'You did, and if you failed in your vow, you were to meet the vengeance of the spirits. Your children were to perish by the vulture, the wolf - '

"'Out, out, demon!'

"'And their bones blanch in the wilderness. Ha! - ha!'

"My father, frantic with rage, seized his axe, and raised it over Wilfred's head to strike.

"'All this I swear,' continued the huntsman, mockingly.

"The axe descended; but it passed through the form of the hunter, and my father lost his balance, and fell heavily on the floor.

"'Mortal!' said the hunter, striding over my father's body, 'we have power over those only who have committed murder. You have been guilty of a double murder: you shall pay the penalty attached to your marriage vow. Two of your children are gone, the third is yet to follow - and follow them he will, for your oath is registered. Go - it were kindness to kill thee - your punishment is, that you live!'

"With these words the spirit disappeared. My father rose from the floor, embraced me tenderly, and knelt down in prayer.

"The next morning he quitted the cottage for ever. He took me with him, and bent his steps to Holland, where we safely arrived. He had some little money with him; but he had not been many days in Amsterdam before he was seized with a brain fever, and died raving mad. I was put into the asylum, and afterwards was sent to sea before the mast. You now know all my history. The question is, whether I am to pay the penalty of my father's oath? I am myself perfectly convinced that, in some way or another, I shall."

On the twenty-second day the high land of the south of Sumatra was in view: as there were no vessels in sight, they resolved to keep their course through the Straits, and run for Pulo Penang, which they expected, as their vessel lay so close to the wind, to reach in seven or eight days. By constant exposure Philip and Krantz were now so bronzed that with their long beards and Mussulman dresses, they might easily have passed off for natives. They had steered the whole of the days exposed to a burning sun; they had lain down and slept in the dew of the night; but their health had not suffered. But for several days, since he had confided the history of his family to Philip, Krantz had become silent and melancholy: his usual flow of spirits had vanished and Philip had often questioned him as to the cause. As they entered the Straits, Philip talked of what they should do upon their arrival at Goa; when Krantz gravely replied, "For some days, Philip, I have had a presentiment that I shall never see that city."

"You are out of health, Krantz," replied Philip.

"No, I am in sound health, body and mind. I have endeavoured to shake off the presentiment, but in vain; there is a warning voice that continually tells me that I shall not be long with you. Philip, will you oblige me by making me content on one point? I have gold about my person which may be useful to you; oblige me by taking it, and securing it on your own."

"What nonsense, Krantz."

"It is no nonsense, Philip. Have you not had your warnings? Why should I not have mine? You know that I have little fear in my composition, and that I care not about death; but I feel the presentiment which I speak of more strongly every hour. It is some kind spirit who would warn me to prepare for another world. Be it so. I have lived long enough in this world to leave it without regret; although to part with you and Amine, the only two now dear to me, is painful, I acknowledge."

"May not this arise from over-exertion and fatigue, Krantz? Consider how much excitement you have laboured under within these last four months. Is not that enough to create a corresponding depression? Depend upon it, my dear friend, such is the fact."

"I wish it were; but I feel otherwise, and there is a feeling of gladness connected with the idea that I am to leave this world, arising from another presentiment, which equally occupies my mind."

"I hardly can tell you - but Amine and you are connected with it. In my dreams I have seen you meet again; but it has appeared to me as if a portion of your trial was purposely shut from my sight in dark clouds; and I have asked, 'May not I see what is there concealed?' - and an invisible has answered, 'No! 'twould make you wretched. Before these trials take place, you will be summoned away:' and then I have thanked Heaven, and felt resigned."

"These are the imaginings of a disturbed brain, Krantz; that I am destined to suffering may be true; but why Amine should suffer, or why you, young, in full health and vigour should not pass your days in peace, and live to a good old age, there is no cause for believing. You will be better tomorrow."

"Perhaps so," replied Krantz; "but still you must yield to my whim, and take the gold. If I am wrong, and we do arrive safe, you know, Philip, you can let me have it back," observed Krantz, with a faint smile - "but you forget, our water is nearly out, and we must look out for a rill on the coast to obtain a fresh supply."

"I was thinking of that when you commenced this unwelcome topic. We had better look out for the water before dark, and as soon as we have replenished our jars, we will make sail again."

At the time that this conversation took place, they were on the eastern side of the strait, about forty miles to the northward. The interior of the coast was rocky and mountainous; but it slowly descended to low land of alternate forest and jungles, which continued to the beach: the country appeared to be uninhabited. Keeping close in to the shore, they discovered, after two hours' run, a fresh stream which burst in a cascade from the mountains, and swept its devious course through the jungle, until it poured its tribute into the waters of the strait.

They ran close in to the mouth of the stream, lowered the sails, and pulled the peroqua against the current, until they had advanced far enough to assure them that the water was quite fresh. The jars were soon filled, and they were again thinking of pushing off; when, enticed by the beauty of the spot, the coolness of the fresh water, and wearied with their long confinement on board of the peroqua, they proposed to bathe - a luxury hardly to be appreciated by those who have not been in a similar situation. They threw off their Mussulman dresses, and plunged into the stream, where they remained for some time. Krantz was the first to get out: he complained of feeling chilled, and he walked on to the banks where their clothes had been laid. Philip also approached nearer to the beach, intending to follow him.

"And now, Philip," said Krantz, "this will be a good opportunity for me to give you the money. I will open my sash and pour it out, and you can put it into your own before you put it on."

Philip was standing in the water, which was about level with his waist.

"Well, Krantz," said he, "I suppose if it must be so, it must - but it appears to me an idea so ridiculous - however, you shall have your own way."

Philip quitted the run, and sat down by Krantz, who was already busy in shaking the doubloons out of the folds of his sash - at last he said:

"I believe, Philip, you have got them all now? I feel satisfied."

"What danger there can be to you, which I am not equally exposed to, I cannot conceive," replied Philip; "however -"

Hardly had he said these words, when there was a tremendous roar - a rush like a mighty wind through the air - a blow which threw him on his back - a loud cry - and a contention. Philip recovered himself, and perceived the naked form of Krantz carried off with the speed of an arrow by an enormous tiger through the jungle. He watched with distended eyeballs; in a few seconds the animal and Krantz had disappeared!

"God of Heaven! Would that thou hadst spared me this," cried Philip, throwing himself down in agony on his face. "Oh! Krantz, my friend - my brother - too sure was your presentiment. Merciful God! have pity - but thy will be done;" and Philip burst into a flood of tears.

For more than an hour did he remain fixed upon the spot, careless and indifferent to the danger by which he was surrounded. At last, somewhat recovered, he rose, dressed himself, and then again sat down - his eyes fixed upon the clothes of Krantz, and the gold which still lay on the sand.

"He would give me that gold. He foretold his doom. Yes! yes! it was his destiny, and it has been fulfilled. His bones will bleach in the wilderness, and the spirit-hunter and his wolfish daughter are avenged."

The shades of evening now set in, and the low growling of the beasts of the forest recalled Philip to a sense of his own danger. He thought of Amine; and hastily making the clothes of Krantz and the doubloons into a package, he stepped into the peroqua, with difficulty shoved it off, and with a melancholy heart, and in silence, hoisted the sail, and pursued his course.

"Yes, Amine," thought Philip, as he watched the stars twinkling and coruscating; "yes, you are right, when you assert that the destinies of men are foreknown, and may by some be read. My destiny is, alas! that I should be severed from all I value upon earth, and die friendless and alone. Then welcome death, if such is to be the case; welcome - a thousand welcomes! what a relief wilt thou be to me! what joy to find myself summoned to where the weary are at rest! I have my task to fulfil. God grant that it may soon be accomplished, and let not my life be embittered by any more trials such as this."

Again did Philip weep, for Krantz had been his long-tried, valued friend, his partner in all his dangers and privations, from the period that they had met when the Dutch fleet attempted the passage round Cape Horn.

After seven days of painful watching and brooding over bitter thoughts, Philip arrived at Pulo Penang, where he found a vessel about to sail for the city to which he was destined. He ran his peroqua alongside of her, and found that she was a brig under the Portuguese flag, having, however, but two Portuguese on board, the rest of the crew being natives. Representing himself as an Englishman in the Portuguese service, who had been wrecked, and offering to pay for his passage, he was willingly received, and in a few days the vessel sailed.

Their voyage was prosperous; in six weeks they anchored in the roads of Goa; the next day they went up the river. The Portuguese captain informed Philip where he might obtain lodging; and passing him off as one of his crew, there was no difficulty raised as to his landing. Having located himself at his new lodging, Philip commenced some inquiries of his host relative to Amine, designating her merely as a young woman who had arrived there in a vessel some weeks before, but he could obtain no information concerning her. "Signor," said the host, "to-morrow is the grand auto-da-fe; we can do nothing until that is over; afterwards, I will put you in the way to find out what you wish. In the meantime, you can walk about the town; to-morrow I will take you to where you can behold the grand procession, and then we will try what we can do to assist you in your search."

Philip went out, procured a suit of clothes, removed his beard, and then walked about the town, looking up at every window to see if he could perceive Amine. At a corner of one of the streets, he thought he recognised Father Mathias, and ran up to him; but the monk had drawn his cowl over his head, and when addressed by that name, made no reply.

"I was deceived," thought Philip; "but I really thought it was him." And Philip was right; it was Father Mathias, who thus screened himself from Philip's recognition.

Tired, at last he returned to his hotel, just before it was dark. The company there were numerous; everybody for miles distant had come to Goa to witness the auto-da-fe - and everybody was discussing the ceremony.

"I will see this grand procession," said Philip to himself, as he threw himself on his bed. "It will drive thought from me for a time; and God knows how painful my thoughts have now become. Amine, dear Amine, may angels guard thee!"

THE ROOM IN THE TOWER
E. F. Benson

It is probable that everybody who is at all a constant dreamer has had at least one experience of an event or a sequence of circumstances which have come to his mind in sleep being subsequently realized in the material world. But, in my opinion, so far from this being a strange thing, it would be far odder if this fulfilment did not occasionally happen, since our dreams are, as a rule, concerned with people whom we know and places with which we are familiar, such as might very naturally occur in the awake and daylit world. True, these dreams are often broken into by some absurd and fantastic incident, which puts them out of court in regard to their subsequent fulfilment, but on the mere calculation of chances, it does not appear in the least unlikely that a dream imagined by anyone who dreams constantly should occasionally come true. Not long ago, for instance, I experienced such a fulfilment of a dream which seems to me in no way remarkable and to have no kind of psychical significance. The manner of it was as follows.

A certain friend of mine, living abroad, is amiable enough to write to me about once in a fortnight. Thus, when fourteen days or thereabouts have elapsed since I last heard from him, my mind, probably, either consciously or subconsciously, is expectant of a letter from him. One night last week I dreamed that as I was going upstairs to dress for dinner I heard, as I often heard, the sound of the postman's knock on my front door, and diverted my direction downstairs instead. There, among other correspondence, was a letter from him. Thereafter the fantastic entered, for on opening it I found inside the ace of diamonds, and scribbled across it in his well-known handwriting, "I am sending you this for safe custody, as you know it is running an unreasonable risk to keep aces in Italy." The next evening I was just preparing to go upstairs to dress when I heard the postman's knock, and did precisely as I had done in my dream. There, among other letters, was one from my friend. Only it did not contain the ace of diamonds. Had it done so, I should have attached more weight to the matter, which, as it stands, seems to me a perfectly ordinary coincidence. No doubt I consciously or subconsciously expected a letter from him, and this suggested to me my dream. Similarly, the fact that my friend had not written to me for a fortnight suggested to him that he should do so. But occasionally it is not so easy to find such an explanation, and for the following story I can find no explanation at all. It came out of the dark, and into the dark it has gone again.

All my life I have been a habitual dreamer: the nights are few, that is to say, when I do not find on awaking in the morning that some mental experience has been mine, and sometimes, all night long, apparently, a series of the most dazzling adventures befall me. Almost without exception these adventures are pleasant, though often merely trivial. It is of an exception that I am going to speak.

It was when I was about sixteen that a certain dream first came to me, and this is how it befell. It opened with my being set down at the door of a big red-brick house, where, I understood, I was going to stay. The servant who opened the door told me that tea was being served in the garden, and led me through a low dark-panelled hall, with a large open fireplace, on to a cheerful green lawn set round with flower beds. There were grouped about the tea-table a small party of people, but they were all strangers to me except one, who was a schoolfellow called Jack Stone, clearly the son of the house, and he introduced me to his mother and father and a couple of sisters. I was, I remember, somewhat astonished to find myself here, for the boy in question was scarcely known to me, and I rather disliked what I knew of him; moreover, he had left school nearly a year before. The afternoon was very hot, and an intolerable oppression reigned. On the far side of the lawn ran a red-brick wall, with an iron gate in its centre, outside which stood a walnut tree. We sat in the shadow of the house opposite a row of long windows, inside which I could see a table with cloth laid, glimmering with glass and silver. This garden front of the house was very long, and at one end of it stood a tower of three stories, which looked to me much older than the rest of the building.

Before long, Mrs. Stone, who, like the rest of the party, had sat in absolute silence, said to me, "Jack will show you your room: I have given you the room in the tower."

Quite inexplicably my heart sank at her words. I felt as if I had known that I should have the room in the tower, and that it contained something dreadful and significant. Jack instantly got up, and I understood that I had to follow him. In silence we passed through the hall, and mounted a great oak staircase with many corners, and arrived at a small landing with two doors set in it. He pushed one of these open for me to enter, and without coming in himself, closed it after me. Then I knew that my conjecture had been right: there was something awful in the room, and with the terror of nightmare growing swiftly and enveloping me, I awoke in a spasm of terror.

Now that dream or variations on it occurred to me intermittently for fifteen years. Most often it came in exactly this form, the arrival, the tea laid out on the lawn, the deadly silence succeeded by that one deadly sentence, the mounting with Jack Stone up to the room in the tower where horror dwelt, and it always came to a close in the nightmare of terror at that which was in the room, though I never saw what it was. At other times I experienced variations on this same theme. Occasionally, for instance, we would be sitting at dinner in the dining-room, into the windows of which I had looked on the first night when the dream of this house visited me, but wherever we were, there was the same silence, the same sense of dreadful oppression and foreboding. And the silence I knew would always be broken by Mrs. Stone saying to me, "Jack will show you your room: I have given you the room in the tower." Upon which (this was invariable) I had to follow him up the oak staircase with many corners, and enter the place that I dreaded more and more each time that I visited it in sleep. Or, again, I would find myself playing cards still in silence in a drawing-room lit with immense chandeliers, that gave a blinding illumination. What the game was I have no idea; what I remember, with a sense of miserable anticipation, was that soon Mrs. Stone would get up and say to me, "Jack will show you your room: I have given you the room in the tower." This drawing-room where we played cards was next to the dining-room, and, as I have said, was always brilliantly illuminated, whereas the rest of the house was full of dusk and shadows. And yet, how often, in spite of those bouquets of lights, have I not pored over the cards that were dealt me, scarcely able for some reason to see them. Their designs, too, were strange: there were no red suits, but all were black, and among them there were certain cards which were black all over. I hated and dreaded those.

As this dream continued to recur, I got to know the greater part of the house. There was a smoking-room beyond the drawing-room, at the end of a passage with a green baize door. It was always very dark there, and as often as I went there I passed somebody whom I could not see in the doorway coming out. Curious developments, too, took place in the characters that peopled the dream as might happen to living persons. Mrs. Stone, for instance, who, when I first saw her, had been black-haired, became grey, and instead of rising briskly, as she had done at first when she said, "Jack will show you your room: I have given you the room in the tower," got up very feebly, as if the strength was leaving her limbs. Jack also grew up, and became a rather ill-looking young man, with a brown moustache, while one of the sisters ceased to appear, and I understood she was married.

Then it so happened that I was not visited by this dream for six months or more, and I began to hope, in such inexplicable dread did I hold it, that it had passed away for good. But one night after this interval I again found myself being shown out onto the lawn for tea, and Mrs. Stone was not there, while the others were all dressed in black. At once I guessed the reason, and my heart leaped at the thought that perhaps this time I should not have to sleep in the room in the tower, and though we usually all sat in silence, on this occasion the sense of relief made me talk and laugh as I had never yet done. But even then matters were not altogether comfortable, for no one else spoke, but they all looked secretly at each other. And soon the foolish stream of my talk ran dry, and gradually an apprehension worse than anything I had previously known gained on me as the light slowly faded.

Suddenly a voice which I knew well broke the stillness, the voice of Mrs. Stone, saying, "Jack will show you your room: I have given you the room in the tower." It seemed to come from near the gate in the red-brick wall that bounded the lawn, and looking up, I saw that the grass outside was sown thick with gravestones. A curious greyish light shone from them, and I could read the lettering on the grave nearest me, and it was, "In evil memory of Julia Stone." And as usual Jack got up, and again I followed him through the hall and up the staircase with many corners. On this occasion it was darker than usual, and when I passed into the room in the tower I could only just see the furniture, the position of which was already familiar to me. Also there was a dreadful odour of decay in the room, and I woke screaming.

The dream, with such variations and developments as I have mentioned, went on at intervals for fifteen years. Sometimes I would dream it two or three nights in succession; once, as I have said, there was an intermission of six months, but taking a reasonable average, I should say that I dreamed it quite as often as once in a month. It had, as is plain, something of nightmare about it, since it always ended in the same appalling terror, which so far from getting less, seemed to me to gather fresh fear every time that I experienced it. There was, too, a strange and dreadful consistency about it. The characters in it, as I have mentioned, got regularly older, death and marriage visited this silent family, and I never in the dream, after Mrs. Stone had died, set eyes on her again. But it was always her voice that told me that the room in the tower was prepared for me, and whether we had tea out on the lawn, or the scene was laid in one of the rooms overlooking it, I could always see her gravestone standing just outside the iron gate. It was the same, too, with the married daughter; usually she was not present, but once or twice she returned again, in company with a man, whom I took to be her husband. He, too, like the rest of them, was always silent. But, owing to the constant repetition of the dream, I had ceased to attach, in my waking hours, any significance to it. I never met Jack Stone again during all those years, nor did I ever see a house that resembled this dark house of my dream. And then something happened.

I had been in London in this year, up till the end of the July, and during the first week in August went down to stay with a friend in a house he had taken for the summer months, in the Ashdown Forest district of Sussex. I left London early, for John Clinton was to meet me at Forest Row Station, and we were going to spend the day golfing, and go to his house in the evening. He had his motor with him, and we set off, about five of the afternoon, after a thoroughly delightful day, for the drive, the distance being some ten miles. As it was still so early we did not have tea at the club house, but waited till we should get home. As we drove, the weather, which up till then had been, though hot, deliciously fresh, seemed to me to alter in quality, and become very stagnant and oppressive, and I felt that indefinable sense of ominous apprehension that I am accustomed to before thunder. John, however, did not share my views, attributing my loss of lightness to the fact that I had lost both my matches. Events proved, however, that I was right, though I do not think that the thunderstorm that broke that night was the sole cause of my depression.

Our way lay through deep high-banked lanes, and before we had gone very far I fell asleep, and was only awakened by the stopping of the motor. And with a sudden thrill, partly of fear but chiefly of curiosity, I found myself standing in the doorway of my house of dream. We went, I half wondering whether or not I was dreaming still, through a low oak-panelled hall, and out onto the lawn, where tea was laid in the shadow of the house. It was set in flower beds, a red-brick wall, with a gate in it, bounded one side, and out beyond that was a space of rough grass with a walnut tree. The facade of the house was very long, and at one end stood a three-storied tower, markedly older than the rest.

Here for the moment all resemblance to the repeated dream ceased. There was no silent and somehow terrible family, but a large assembly of exceedingly cheerful persons, all of whom were known to me. And in spite of the horror with which the dream itself had always filled me, I felt nothing of it now that the scene of it was thus reproduced before me. But I felt intensest curiosity as to what was going to happen.

Tea pursued its cheerful course, and before long Mrs. Clinton got up. And at that moment I think I knew what she was going to say. She spoke to me, and what she said was:

"Jack will show you your room: I have given you the room in the tower."

At that, for half a second, the horror of the dream took hold of me again. But it quickly passed, and again I felt nothing more than the most intense curiosity. It was not very long before it was amply satisfied.

John turned to me.

"Right up at the top of the house," he said, "but I think you'll be comfortable. We're absolutely full up. Would you like to go and see it now? By Jove, I believe that you are right, and that we are going to have a thunderstorm. How dark it has become."

I got up and followed him. We passed through the hall, and up the perfectly familiar staircase. Then he opened the door, and I went in. And at that moment sheer unreasoning terror again possessed me. I did not know what I feared: I simply feared. Then like a sudden recollection, when one remembers a name which has long escaped the memory, I knew what I feared. I feared Mrs. Stone, whose grave with the sinister inscription, "In evil memory," I had so often seen in my dream, just beyond the lawn which lay below my window. And then once more the fear passed so completely that I wondered what there was to fear, and I found myself, sober and quiet and sane, in the room in the tower, the name of which I had so often heard in my dream, and the scene of which was so familiar.

I looked around it with a certain sense of proprietorship, and found that nothing had been changed from the dreaming nights in which I knew it so well. Just to the left of the door was the bed, lengthways along the wall, with the head of it in the angle. In a line with it was the fireplace and a small bookcase; opposite the door the outer wall was pierced by two lattice-paned windows, between which stood the dressing-table, while ranged along the fourth wall was the washing-stand and a big cupboard. My luggage had already been unpacked, for the furniture of dressing and undressing lay orderly on the wash-stand and toilet-table, while my dinner clothes were spread out on the coverlet of the bed. And then, with a sudden start of unexplained dismay, I saw that there were two rather conspicuous objects which I had not seen before in my dreams: one a life-sized oil painting of Mrs. Stone, the other a black-and-white sketch of Jack Stone, representing him as he had appeared to me only a week before in the last of the series of these repeated dreams, a rather secret and evil-looking man of about thirty. His picture hung between the windows, looking straight across the room to the other portrait, which hung at the side of the bed. At that I looked next, and as I looked I felt once more the horror of nightmare seize me.

It represented Mrs. Stone as I had seen her last in my dreams: old and withered and white-haired. But in spite of the evident feebleness of body, a dreadful exuberance and vitality shone through the envelope of flesh, an exuberance wholly malign, a vitality that foamed and frothed with unimaginable evil. Evil beamed from the narrow, leering eyes; it laughed in the demon-like mouth. The whole face was instinct with some secret and appalling mirth; the hands, clasped together on the knee, seemed shaking with suppressed and nameless glee. Then I saw also that it was signed in the left-hand bottom corner, and wondering who the artist could be, I looked more closely, and read the inscription, "Julia Stone by Julia Stone."

There came a tap at the door, and John Clinton entered.

"Got everything you want?" he asked.

"Rather more than I want," said I, pointing to the picture.

He laughed.

"Hard-featured old lady," he said. "By herself, too, I

remember. Anyhow she can't have flattered herself much."

"But don't you see?" said I. "It's scarcely a human face at all. It's the face of some witch, of some devil."

He looked at it more closely.

"Yes; it isn't very pleasant," he said. "Scarcely a bedside manner, eh? Yes; I can imagine getting the nightmare if I went to sleep with that close by my bed. I'll have it taken down if you like."

"I really wish you would," I said. He rang the bell, and with the help of a servant we detached the picture and carried it out onto the landing, and put it with its face to the wall.

"By Jove, the old lady is a weight," said John, mopping his forehead. "I wonder if she had something on her mind."

The extraordinary weight of the picture had struck me too. I was about to reply, when I caught sight of my own hand. There was blood on it, in considerable quantities, covering the whole palm.

"I've cut myself somehow," said I.

John gave a little startled exclamation.

"Why, I have too," he said.

Simultaneously the footman took out his handkerchief and wiped his hand with it. I saw that there was blood also on his handkerchief.

John and I went back into the tower room and washed the blood off; but neither on his hand nor on mine was there the slightest trace of a scratch or cut. It seemed to me that, having ascertained this, we both, by a sort of tacit consent, did not allude to it again. Something in my case had dimly occurred to me that I did not wish to think about. It was but a conjecture, but I fancied that I knew the same thing had occurred to him.

The heat and oppression of the air, for the storm we had expected was still undischarged, increased very much after dinner, and for some time most of the party, among whom were John Clinton and myself, sat outside on the path bounding the lawn, where we had had tea. The night was absolutely dark, and no twinkle of star or moon ray could penetrate the pall of cloud that overset the sky. By degrees our assembly thinned, the women went up to bed, men dispersed to the smoking or billiard room, and by eleven o'clock my host and I were the only two left. All the evening I thought that he had something on his mind, and as soon as we were alone he spoke.

"The man who helped us with the picture had blood on his hand, too, did you notice?" he said.

"I asked him just now if he had cut himself, and he said he supposed he had, but that he could find no mark of it. Now where did that blood come from?"

By dint of telling myself that I was not going to think about it, I had succeeded in not doing so, and I did not want, especially just at bedtime, to be reminded of it.

"I don't know," said I, "and I don't really care so long as the picture of Mrs. Stone is not by my bed."

He got up.

"But it's odd," he said. "*Ha!* Now you'll see another odd thing."

A dog of his, an Irish terrier by breed, had come out of the house as we talked. The door behind us into the hall was open, and a bright oblong of light shone across the lawn to the iron gate which led on to the rough grass outside, where the walnut tree stood. I saw that the dog had all his hackles up, bristling with rage and fright; his lips were curled back from his teeth, as if he was ready to spring at something, and he was growling to himself. He took not the slightest notice of his master or me, but stiffly and tensely walked across the grass to the iron gate. There he stood for a moment, looking through the bars and still growling. Then of a sudden his courage seemed to desert him: he gave one long howl, and scuttled back to the house with a curious crouching sort of movement.

"He does that half-a-dozen times a day." said John. "He sees something which he both hates and fears."

I walked to the gate and looked over it. Something was moving on the grass outside, and soon a sound which I could not instantly identify came to my ears. Then I remembered what it was: it was the purring of a cat. I lit a match, and saw the purrer, a big blue Persian, walking round and round in a little circle just outside the gate, stepping high and ecstatically, with tail carried aloft like a banner. Its eyes were bright and shining, and every now and then it put its head down and sniffed at the grass.

I laughed.

"The end of that mystery, I am afraid." I said. "Here's a large cat having Walpurgis night all alone."

"Yes, that's Darius," said John. "He spends half the day and all night there. But that's not the end of the dog mystery, for Toby and he are the best of friends, but the beginning of the cat mystery. What's the cat doing there? And why is Darius pleased, while Toby is terror-stricken?"

At that moment I remembered the rather horrible detail of my dreams when I saw through the gate, just where the cat was now, the white tombstone with the sinister inscription. But before I could answer the rain began, as suddenly and heavily as if a tap had been turned on, and simultaneously the big cat squeezed through the bars of the gate, and came leaping across the lawn to the house for shelter. Then it sat in the doorway, looking out eagerly into the dark. It spat and struck at John with its paw, as he pushed it in, in order to close the door.

Somehow, with the portrait of Julia Stone in the passage outside, the room in the tower had absolutely no alarm for me, and as I went to bed, feeling very sleepy and heavy, I had nothing more than interest for the curious incident about our bleeding hands, and the conduct of the cat and dog. The last thing I looked at before I put out my light was the square empty space by my bed where the portrait had been. Here the paper was of its original full tint of dark red: over the rest of the walls it had faded. Then I blew out my candle and instantly fell asleep.

My awaking was equally instantaneous, and I sat bolt upright in bed under the impression that some bright light had been flashed in my face, though it was now absolutely pitch dark. I knew exactly where I was, in the room which I had dreaded in dreams, but no horror that I ever felt when asleep approached the fear that now invaded and froze my brain. Immediately after a peal of thunder crackled just above the house, but the probability that it was only a flash of lightning which awoke me gave no reassurance to my galloping heart. Something I knew was in the room with me, and instinctively I put out my right hand, which was nearest the wall, to keep it away. And my hand touched the edge of a picture-frame hanging close to me.

I sprang out of bed, upsetting the small table that stood by it, and I heard my watch, candle, and matches clatter onto the floor. But for the moment there was no need of light, for a blinding flash leaped out of the clouds, and showed me that by my bed again hung the picture of Mrs. Stone. And instantly the room went into blackness again. But in that flash I saw another thing also, namely a figure that leaned over the end of my bed, watching me. It was dressed in some close-clinging white garment, spotted and stained with mould, and the face was that of the portrait.

Overhead the thunder cracked and roared, and when it ceased and the deathly stillness succeeded, I heard the rustle of movement coming nearer me, and, more horrible yet, perceived an odour of corruption and decay. And then a hand was laid on the side of my neck, and close beside my ear I heard quick-taken, eager breathing. Yet I knew that this thing, though it could be perceived by touch, by smell, by eye and by ear, was still not of this earth, but something that had passed out of the body and had power to make itself manifest. Then a voice, already familiar to me, spoke.

"I knew you would come to the room in the tower," it said. "I have been long waiting for you. At last you have come. Tonight I shall feast; before long we will feast together."

And the quick breathing came closer to me; I could feel it on my neck.

At that the terror, which I think had paralysed me for the moment, gave way to the wild instinct of self-preservation. I hit wildly with both arms, kicking out at the same moment, and heard a little animal-squeal, and something soft dropped with a thud beside me. I took a couple of steps forward, nearly tripping up over whatever it was that lay there, and by the merest good-luck found the handle of the door. In another second I ran out on the landing, and had banged the door behind me. Almost at the same moment I heard a door open somewhere below, and John Clinton, candle in hand, came running upstairs.

"What is it?" he said. "I sleep just below you, and heard a noise as if - Good heavens, there's blood on your shoulder."

I stood there, so he told me afterwards, swaying from side to side, white as a sheet, with the mark on my shoulder as if a hand covered with blood had been laid there.

"It's in there," I said, pointing. "She, you know. The portrait is in there, too, hanging up on the place we took it from."

At that he laughed.

"My dear fellow, this is mere nightmare," he said.

He pushed by me, and opened the door, I standing there

simply inert with terror, unable to stop him, unable to move.

"Phew! What an awful smell," he said.

Then there was silence; he had passed out of my sight behind the open door. Next moment he came out again, as white as myself, and instantly shut it.

"Yes, the portrait's there," he said, "and on the floor is a thing - a thing spotted with earth, like what they bury people in. Come away, quick, come away."

How I got downstairs I hardly know. An awful shuddering and nausea of the spirit rather than of the flesh had seized me, and more than once he had to place my feet upon the steps, while every now and then he cast glances of terror and apprehension up the stairs. But in time we came to his dressing-room on the floor below, and there I told him what I have here described.

The sequel can be made short; indeed, some of my readers have perhaps already guessed what it was, if they remember that inexplicable affair of the churchyard at West Fawley, some eight years ago, where an attempt was made three times to bury the body of a certain woman who had committed suicide. On each occasion the coffin was found in the course of a few days again protruding from the ground. After the third attempt, in order that the thing should not be talked about, the body was buried elsewhere in unconsecrated ground. Where it was buried was just outside the iron gate of the garden belonging to the house where this woman had lived. She had committed suicide in a room at the top of the tower in that house. Her name was Julia Stone.

Subsequently the body was again secretly dug up, and the coffin was found to be full of blood.

HIS UNCONQUERABLE ENEMY
W.C. Morrow

I was summoned from Calcutta to the heart of India to perform a difficult surgical operation on one of the women of a great rajah's household. I found the rajah a man of a noble character, but possessed, as I afterwards discovered, of a sense of cruelty purely Oriental and in contrast to the indolence of his disposition. He was so grateful for the success that attended my mission that he urged me to remain a guest at the palace as long as it might please me to stay, and I thankfully accepted the invitation.

One of the male servants early attracted my notice for his marvellous capacity of malice. His name was Neranya, and I am certain that there must have been a large proportion of Malay blood in his veins, for, unlike the Indians (from whom he differed also in complexion), he was extremely alert, active, nervous, and sensitive. A redeeming circumstance was his love for his master. Once his violent temper led him to the commission of an atrocious crime - the fatal stabbing of a dwarf. In punishment for this the rajah ordered that Neranya's right arm (the offending one) be severed from his body. The sentence was executed in a bungling fashion by a stupid fellow armed with an axe, and I, being a surgeon, was compelled, in order to save Neranya's life, to perform an amputation of the stump, leaving not a vestige of the limb remaining.

After this he developed an augmented fiendishness. His love for the rajah was changed to hate, and in his mad anger he flung discretion to the winds. Driven once to frenzy by the rajah's scornful treatment, he sprang upon the rajah with a knife, but, fortunately, was seized and disarmed. To his unspeakable dismay the rajah sentenced him for this offence to suffer amputation of the remaining arm. It was done as in the former instance. This had the effect of putting a temporary curb on Neranya's spirit, or, rather, of changing the outward manifestations of his diabolism. Being armless, he was at first largely at the mercy of those who ministered to his needs - a duty which I undertook to see was properly discharged, for I felt an interest in this strangely distorted nature. His sense of helplessness, combined with a damnable scheme for revenge which he had secretly formed, caused Neranya to change his fierce, impetuous, and unruly conduct into a smooth, quiet, insinuating bearing, which he carried so artfully as to deceive those with whom he was brought in contact, including the rajah himself.

Neranya, being exceedingly quick, intelligent, and dexterous, and having an unconquerable will, turned his attention to the cultivating of an enlarged usefulness of his legs, feet, and toes, with so excellent effect that in time he was able to perform wonderful feats with those members. Thus his capability, especially for destructive mischief, was considerably restored.

One morning the rajah's only son, a young man of an uncommonly amiable and noble disposition, was found dead in bed. His murder was a most atrocious one, his body being mutilated in a shocking manner, but in my eyes the most significant of all the mutilations was the entire removal and disappearance of the young prince's arms.

The death of the young man nearly brought the rajah to the grave. It was not, therefore, until I had nursed him back to health that I began a systematic inquiry into the murder. I said nothing of my own discoveries and conclusions until after the rajah and his officers had failed and my work had been done; then I submitted to him a written report, making a close analysis of all the circumstances and closing by charging the crime to Neranya. The rajah, convinced by my proof and argument, at once ordered Neranya to be put to death, this to be accomplished slowly and with frightful tortures. The sentence was so cruel and revolting that it filled me with horror, and I implored that the wretch be shot. Finally, through a sense of gratitude to me, the rajah relaxed. When Neranya was charged with the crime he denied it, of course, but, seeing that the rajah was convinced, he threw aside all restraint, and, dancing, laughing, and shrieking in the most horrible manner, confessed his guilt, gloated over it, and reviled the rajah to his teeth - this, knowing that some fearful death awaited him.

The rajah decided upon the details of the matter that night, and in the morning he informed me of his decision. It was that Neranya's life should be spared, but that both of his legs should be broken with hammers, and that then I should amputate the limbs at the trunk! Appended to this horrible sentence was a provision that the maimed wretch should be kept and tortured at regular intervals by such means as afterwards might be devised.

Sickened to the heart by the awful duty set out for me, I nevertheless performed it with success, and I care to say nothing more about that part of the tragedy. Neranya escaped death very narrowly and was a long time in recovering his wonted vitality. During all these weeks the rajah neither saw him nor made inquiries concerning him, but when, as in duty bound, I made official report that the man had recovered his strength, the rajah's eyes brightened, and he emerged with deadly activity from the stupor into which he so long had been plunged.

The rajah's palace was a noble structure, but it is necessary here to describe only the grand hall. It was an immense chamber, with a floor of polished, inlaid stone and a lofty, arched ceiling. A soft light stole into it through stained glass set in the roof and in high windows on one side. In the middle of the room was a rich fountain, which threw up a tall, slender column of water, with smaller and shorter jets grouped around it. Across one end of the hall, half-way to the ceiling, was a balcony, which communicated with the upper story of a wing, and from which a flight of stone stairs descended to the floor of the hall. During the hot summers this room was delightfully cool; it was the rajah's favourite lounging-place, and when the nights were hot he had his cot taken thither, and there he slept.

This hall was chosen for Neranya's permanent prison; here was he to stay so long as he might live, with never a glimpse of the shining world or the glorious heavens. To one of his nervous, discontented nature such confinement was worse than death. At the rajah's order there was constructed for him a small pen of open iron-work, circular, and about four feet in diameter, elevated on four slender iron posts, ten feet above the floor, and placed between the balcony and the fountain. Such was Neranya's prison. The pen was about four feet in depth, and the pen-top was left open for the convenience of the servants whose duty it should be to care for him. These precautions for his safe confinement were taken at my suggestion, for, although the man was now deprived of all four of his limbs, I still feared that he might develop some extraordinary, unheard-of power for mischief. It was provided that the attendants should reach his cage by means of a movable ladder.

All these arrangements having been made and Neranya hoisted into his cage, the rajah emerged upon the balcony to see him for the first time since the last amputation. Neranya had been lying panting and helpless on the floor of his cage, but when his quick ear caught the sound of the rajah's footfall he squirmed about until he had brought the back of his head against the railing, elevating his eyes above his chest, and enabling him to peer through the open-work of the cage. Thus the two deadly enemies faced each other. The rajah's stern face paled at sight of the hideous, shapeless thing which met his gaze; but he soon recovered, and the old hard, cruel, sinister look returned. Neranya's black hair and beard had grown long, and they added to the natural ferocity of his aspect. His eyes blazed upon the rajah with a terrible light, his lips parted, and he gasped for breath; his face was ashen with rage and despair, and his thin, distended nostrils quivered.

The rajah folded his arms and gazed down from the balcony upon the frightful wreck that he had made. Oh, the dreadful pathos of that picture; the inhumanity of it; the deep and dismal tragedy of it! Who might look into the wild, despairing heart of the prisoner and see and understand the frightful turmoil there; the surging, choking passion; unbridled but impotent ferocity; frantic thirst for a vengeance that should be deeper than hell! Neranya gazed, his shapeless body heaving, his eyes aflame; and then, in a strong, clear voice, which rang throughout the great hall, with rapid speech he hurled at the rajah the most insulting defiance, the most awful curses. He cursed the womb that had conceived him, the food that should nourish him, the wealth that had brought him power; cursed him in the name of Buddha and all the wise men; cursed by the sun, the moon, and the stars; by the continents, mountains, oceans, and rivers; by all things living; cursed his head, his heart, his entrails; cursed in a whirlwind of unmentionable words; heaped unimaginable insults and contumely upon him; called him a knave, a beast, a fool, a liar, an infamous and unspeakable coward.

The rajah heard it all calmly, without the movement of a muscle, without the slightest change of countenance; and when the poor wretch had exhausted his strength and fallen helpless and silent to the floor, the rajah, with a grim, cold smile, turned and strode away.

The days passed. The rajah, not deterred by Neranya's curses often heaped upon him, spent even more time than formerly in the great hall, and slept there oftener at night; and finally Neranya wearied of cursing and defying him, and fell into a sullen silence. The man was a study for me, and I observed every change in his fleeting moods. Generally his condition was that of miserable despair, which he attempted bravely to conceal. Even the boon of suicide had been denied him, for when he would wriggle into an erect position the rail of his pen was a foot above his head, so that he could not clamber over and break his skull on the stone floor beneath; and when he had tried to starve himself the attendants forced food down his throat; so that he abandoned such attempts. At times his eyes would blaze and his breath would come in gasps, for imaginary vengeance was working within him; but steadily he became quieter and more tractable, and was pleasant and responsive when I would converse with him. Whatever might have been the tortures which the rajah had decided on, none as yet had been ordered; and although Neranya knew that they were in contemplation, he never referred to them or complained of his lot.

The awful climax of this situation was reached one night, and even after this lapse of years I cannot approach its description without a shudder.

It was a hot night, and the rajah had gone to sleep in the great hall, lying on a high cot placed on the main floor just underneath the edge of the balcony. I had been unable to sleep in my own apartment, and so I had stolen into the great hall through the heavily curtained entrance at the end farthest from the balcony. As I entered I heard a peculiar, soft sound above the patter of the fountain. Neranya's cage was partly concealed from my view by the spraying water, but I suspected that the unusual sound came from him. Stealing a little to one side, and crouching against the dark hangings of the wall, I could see him in the faint light which dimly illuminated the hall, and then I discovered that my surmise was correct - Neranya was quietly at work. Curious to learn more, and knowing that only mischief could have been inspiring him, I sank into a thick robe on the floor and watched him.

To my great astonishment Neranya was tearing off with his teeth the bag which served as his outer garment. He did it cautiously, casting sharp glances frequently at the rajah, who, sleeping soundly on his cot below, breathed heavily. After starting a strip with his teeth, Neranya, by the same means, would attach it to the railing of his cage and then wriggle away, much after the manner of a caterpillar's crawling, and this would cause the strip to be torn out the full length of his garment. He repeated this operation with incredible patience and skill until his entire garment had been torn into strips. Two or three of these he tied end to end with his teeth, lips, and tongue, tightening the knots by placing one end of the strip under his body and drawing the other taut with his teeth. In this way he made a line several feet long, one end of which he made fast to the rail with his mouth. It then began to dawn upon me that he was going to make an insane attempt - impossible of achievement without hands, feet, arms, or legs - to escape from his cage! For what purpose? The rajah was asleep in the hall--ah! I caught my breath. Oh, the desperate, insane thirst for revenge which could have unhinged so clear and firm a mind! Even though he should accomplish the impossible feat of climbing over the railing of his cage that he might fall to the floor below (for how could he slide down the rope?), he would be in all probability killed or stunned; and even if he should escape these dangers it would be impossible for him to clamber upon the cot without rousing the rajah, and impossible even though the rajah were dead! Amazed at the man's daring, and convinced that his sufferings and brooding had destroyed his reason, nevertheless I watched him with breathless interest.

With other strips tied together he made a short swing across one side of his cage. He caught the long line in his teeth at a point not far from the rail; then, wriggling with great effort to an upright position, his back braced against the rail, he put his chin over the swing and worked toward one end. He tightened the grasp of his chin on the swing, and with tremendous exertion, working the lower end of his spine against the railing, he began gradually to ascend the side of his cage. The labour was so great that he was compelled to pause at intervals, and his breathing was hard and painful; and even while thus resting he was in a position of terrible strain, and his pushing against the swing caused it to press hard against his windpipe and nearly strangle him.

After amazing effort he had elevated the lower end of his body until it protruded above the railing, the top of which was now across the lower end of his abdomen. Gradually he worked his body over, going backward, until there was sufficient excess of weight on the outer side of the rail; and then, with a quick lurch, he raised his head and shoulders and swung into a horizontal position on top of the rail. Of course, he would have fallen to the floor below had it not been for the line which he held in his teeth. With so great nicety had he estimated the distance between his mouth and the point where the rope was fastened to the rail, that the line tightened and checked him just as he reached the horizontal position on the rail. If one had told me beforehand that such a feat as I had just seen this man accomplish was possible, I should have thought him a fool.

Neranya was now balanced on his stomach across the top of the rail, and he eased his position by bending his spine and hanging down on either side as much as possible. Having rested thus for some minutes, he began cautiously to slide off backward, slowly paying out the line through his teeth, finding almost a fatal difficulty in passing the knots. Now, it is quite possible that the line would have escaped altogether from his teeth laterally when he would slightly relax his hold to let it slip, had it not been for a very ingenious plan to which he had resorted. This consisted in his having made a turn of the line around his neck before he attacked the swing, thus securing a threefold control of the line - one by his teeth, another by friction against his neck, and a third by his ability to compress it between his cheek and shoulder. It was quite evident now that the minutest details of a most elaborate plan had been carefully worked out by him before beginning the task, and that possibly weeks of difficult theoretical study had been consumed in the mental preparation. As I observed him I was reminded of certain hitherto unaccountable things which he had been doing for some weeks past - going through certain hitherto inexplicable motions, undoubtedly for the purpose of training his muscles for the immeasurably arduous labour which he was now performing.

A stupendous and seemingly impossible part of his task had been accomplished. Could he reach the floor in safety? Gradually he worked himself backward over the rail, in imminent danger of falling; but his nerve never wavered, and I could see a wonderful light in his eyes. With something of a lurch, his body fell against the outer side of the railing, to which he was hanging by his chin, the line still held firmly in his teeth. Slowly he slipped his chin from the rail, and then hung suspended by the line in his teeth. By almost imperceptible degrees, with infinite caution, he descended the line, and, finally, his unwieldy body rolled upon the floor, safe and unhurt!

What miracle would this superhuman monster next accomplish? I was quick and strong, and was ready and able to intercept any dangerous act; but not until danger appeared would I interfere with this extraordinary scene.

I must confess to astonishment upon having observed that Neranya, instead of proceeding directly toward the sleeping rajah, took quite another direction. Then it was only escape, after all, that the wretch contemplated, and not the murder of the rajah. But how could he escape? The only possible way to reach the outer air without great risk was by ascending the stairs to the balcony and leaving by the corridor which opened upon it, and thus fall into the hands of some British soldiers quartered thereabout, who might conceive the idea of hiding him; but surely it was impossible for Neranya to ascend that long flight of stairs! Nevertheless, he made directly for them, his method of progression this: He lay upon his back, with the lower end of his body toward the stairs; then bowed his spine upward, thus drawing his head and shoulders a little forward; straightened, and then pushed the lower end of his body forward a space equal to that through which he had drawn his head; repeating this again and again, each time, while bending his spine, preventing his head from slipping by pressing it against the floor. His progress was laborious and slow, but sensible; and, finally, he arrived at the foot of the stairs.

It was manifest that his insane purpose was to ascend them. The desire for freedom must have been strong within him! Wriggling to an upright position against the newel-post, he looked up at the great height which he had to climb and sighed; but there was no dimming of the light in his eyes. How could he accomplish the impossible task?

His solution of the problem was very simple, though daring and perilous as all the rest. While leaning against the newel-post he let himself fall diagonally upon the bottom step, where he lay partly hanging over, but safe, on his side. Turning upon his back, he wriggled forward along the step to the rail and raised himself to an upright position against it as he had against the newel-post, fell as before, and landed on the second step. In this manner, with inconceivable labour, he accomplished the ascent of the entire flight of stairs.

It being apparent to me that the rajah was not the object of Neranya's movements, the anxiety which I had felt on that account was now entirely dissipated. The things which already he had accomplished were entirely beyond the nimblest imagination. The sympathy which I had always felt for the wretched man was now greatly quickened; and as infinitesimally small as I knew his chances for escape to be, I nevertheless hoped that he would succeed. Any assistance from me, however, was out of the question; and it never should be known that I had witnessed the escape.

Neranya was now upon the balcony, and I could dimly see him wriggling along toward the door which led out upon the balcony. Finally he stopped and wriggled to an upright position against the rail, which had wide openings between the balusters. His back was toward me, but he slowly turned and faced me and the hall. At that great distance I could not distinguish his features, but the slowness with which he had worked, even before he had fully accomplished the ascent of the stairs, was evidence all too eloquent of his extreme exhaustion. Nothing but a most desperate resolution could have sustained him thus far, but he had drawn upon the last remnant of his strength. He looked around the hall with a sweeping glance, and then down upon the rajah, who was sleeping immediately beneath him, over twenty feet below. He looked long and earnestly, sinking lower, and lower, and lower upon the rail. Suddenly, to my inconceivable astonishment and dismay, he toppled through and shot downward from his lofty height! I held my breath, expecting to see him crushed upon the stone floor beneath; but instead of that he fell full upon the rajah's breast, driving him through the cot to the floor. I sprang forward with a loud cry for help, and was instantly at the scene of the catastrophe. With indescribable horror I saw that Neranya's teeth were buried in the rajah's throat! I tore the wretch away, but the blood was pouring from the rajah's arteries, his chest was crushed in, and he was gasping in the agony of death. People came running in, terrified. I turned to Neranya. He lay upon his back, his face hideously smeared with blood. Murder, and not escape, had been his intentions from the beginning; and he had employed the only method by which there was ever a possibility of accomplishing it. I knelt beside him, and saw that he too was dying; his back had been broken by the fall. He smiled sweetly into my face, and a triumphant look of accomplished revenge sat upon his face even in death.

THE LATE MRS. FOWKE
Amyas Northcote

The Reverend Barnabas Fowke, though he live to reach a century, will never forget the deathbed of his wife. Most widowers can probably say the same thing; though few, it may be hoped, have similar cause to recollect it.

Mr. Fowke, at the time of the event referred to, was a man of middle age, and the incumbent of G., a small agricultural town on the edge of one of our Northern moors. He was a hard-working, honest parson, of no great strength of character and of no particular ability, nor had he had any special experience with the more subtle side of life. He had been educated at a good second class public school and a small Oxford College, whence he had gone in due course to take up a curacy in one of our lesser manufacturing towns.

After serving some years in this capacity, he had been promoted, on the death of the Vicar, to take charge of the living, in which position he had remained till a few weeks before his marriage to Stella Farnleigh, at whose instigation he had exchanged his town living at R. for the country one at G. which he still occupied at the time of this story. The reverend gentleman's history is thus commonplace and uninteresting, as, I fear, are the histories of many of our clergy, which it resembled save that, unlike most of his cloth, he had remained unmarried till he fell a victim at the age of forty to the charms of Miss Stella Farnleigh.

This lady requires a closer study. She was the only child of a certain Mr. Farnleigh, who for many years was a merchant of and acted as British Consul in Z., a town in Hungary, where by hard work and close attention to business he amassed a fair-sized fortune. Somewhat late in life he had met a beautiful and attractive woman, whose nationality even was uncertain, but who boasted of a considerable admixture of gipsy blood in her veins. Exactly who she was or where she came from is at this distance of time impossible to ascertain. At the time she met Mr. Farnleigh she was giving music lessons, by which she gained a small pittance, and her marriage to the well-to-do English merchant may well be considered a very fortunate event for her.

However, her married life did not last long, for Mr. Farnleigh died very suddenly within six months of the wedding day, leaving his widow his sole executrix and legatee. It is not known whether Mrs. Farnleigh had any relatives; if she had she never kept up any connection with them, and after her husband's death she acquired a small and lonely estate on the banks of the River Theiss and removed thither to dwell in complete retirement. Here in due course Stella was born and here the child lived with her mother until about the age of twenty-five, when Mrs. Farnleigh died, leaving her fortune entirely to the girl.

The latter at first appeared to be inclined to remain on in her old home, but it would seem as if neither she nor her mother had been popular in the district, and apparently some pretty strong hints were conveyed to the young lady that she had best betake herself elsewhere. Mr. Fowke knew nothing of all this at the time he married Stella, and for reasons which will transpire he did not care to make any investigations into the matter later on. Therefore the history of mother and daughter in Hungary and the reasons why the latter left that country are buried in an obscurity which will never be lightened. Whatever they may have been, Stella no doubt felt that it would be difficult for her to settle down by herself in any new country, and she accordingly put herself into communication with the only relative she knew herself possessed of, a Miss Farnleigh, the elderly sister of her father, with a view to taking up her abode with her as a paying guest.

The elder Miss Farnleigh was a poor woman, living in solitude at R. She was a worthy soul, narrow-minded, unintelligent, devoted to clergymen and church work; in fact, an absolute type of thousands of middle-aged, middle-class English spinsters. The proposal of her niece, whom she had never seen and with whom she had but rarely corresponded, was a welcome one, as the young lady would certainly provide some much needed cash for the household, and would probably, as she fondly believed, provide a pleasant companion for herself also. Besides, she was sorry for the orphaned girl, and altogether it was with pleasure she made the preliminary arrangements and welcomed the arrival of the traveller.

However, these high hopes were doomed to disappointment. Stella and her aunt quickly found that they were uncongenial in nearly every respect. Miss Farnleigh I have described, and when I say that Stella was a young woman of considerable though rather peculiar literary accomplishments, and that she had a strong will which she frequently exercised in the pursuit of some highly unconventional purpose, I think it will be clear why the two ladies did not agree together. Stella had brought with her from Hungary a considerable library of foreign books, none of which her aunt could understand, but which actually dealt largely with occult subjects, and she also brought with her a habit of going away alone every few weeks for a night on the moors not far from R., a custom which she said she found necessary for her health and happiness. To these occasional expeditions Miss Farnleigh at first took great exception, but after a stormy scene with her niece the elder lady felt herself worsted and, as she had ceased to take any affectionate interest in the younger woman, she also ceased to care greatly as to what she did or thought. Stella, therefore, went on her own way undisturbed but conscious of perpetual criticism, and no doubt was eager to escape from an atmosphere so uncongenial to her. At the same time she realized the conventions that bound her and that her best hope for the future lay in marrying some man, weaker than herself, whom she could bend to her will. This, no doubt, actuated her in encouraging the somewhat timid suit of Mr. Fowke, and in astonishing as well as delighting that gentleman when she accepted his rather diffident offer of marriage.

The young lady showed herself of an obliging disposition in the arrangements made prior to the wedding, her only stipulation being that Mr. Fowke should change his present living for one nearer the moors. In accordance with this Mr. Fowke negotiated an exchange with the Vicar of G., and after a short honeymoon took possession of his new cure. Here he settled down to what he anticipated would prove a peaceful and happy life. He was devoted to his new wife, and she, while less demonstratively happy, appeared to be contented both with her husband and her new surroundings.

The first flaw in their married life showed itself a few months after their arrival at G., when one day, Mr. Fowke, having occasion to speak to his wife, went upstairs to the room which she had selected as her private sitting-room and in which she had installed her voluminous library. On reaching it he heard from within a sound of low chanting in a language that he did not understand, and at the same time became aware of a singular smell as of the burning of some aromatic herb. He tried the door and, finding it locked, called to his wife. The chanting ceased immediately and his wife's voice told him to wait a few minutes and she would admit him. On the door being opened he found the room filled with a pungent smell emanating from some herbs, which were burning in a small brazier set upon the table.

"Whatever are you doing, my dear?" he asked.

Stella replied that she was suffering from a severe headache, which she was trying to cure by inhaling the smoke; it was a Hungarian remedy, she added, but she did not explain the singing. Mr. Fowke remained somewhat puzzled, and his astonishment was considerably increased when a little later his wife informed him that she intended to go to L- a tiny hamlet far up on the Fells - that afternoon and would spend the night there, returning the following day. It was the first time that Mr. Fowke had heard of Stella's solitary visits to the moorland and he not unnaturally sought an explanation of them, which his wife refused to give in any greater detail than the mere statement that she had for long been accustomed to make these periodical trips into solitude. He asked to be allowed to accompany her, but she positively refused to permit this, and it was with a heavy and worried heart that he watched her leave the house later in the day.

The following afternoon she returned, tired and with muddy clothes, but seeming exhilarated by her expedition. She refused all information about it, save that during these trips she was in the habit of staying at the Three Magpies, a small inn at I. and making thence expeditions on the higher Fells. With this slender explanation Mr. Fowke had to be satisfied.

A few weeks passed, when again one day Mr. Fowke detected the odour of burning herbs and again learnt that his wife was on the point of starting for I. She again declined his proffered company and left the house as before.

Mr. Fowke had never been to I., which is a remote hamlet, not distant as far as mileage is concerned from G., but only approachable by a branch line of railway with an infrequent service of trains. He was, however, acquainted with its Vicar, to whom he presently wrote to inquire as to the standing of the Three Magpies, since he was not over-pleased that his wife, a foreigner ignorant of our ways, should elect to stay alone at an absolutely unknown inn. The reply he received was not at all reassuring, for the Vicar of I. wrote that the Three Magpies was a public house of poor repute, kept by an old couple of more than doubtful respectability.

This letter decided Mr. Fowke and, when for the third time his wife announced her intention of proceeding to I. and for the third time refused his company, he determined to follow her there secretly and observe her movements and surroundings. It was not difficult for him to arrange to do this, since he could easily reach I. on his motor-cycle long before her slow train could land her there, even if he did not start until after she had left the parsonage. He carried out his programme and in due course reached I. and made his way to the Three Magpies. Here he found that the old man was very nearly bedridden and quite senile, whilst his wife regarded her clerical visitor with almost open hostility. However, the gift of a sovereign and the promise of another effected a great change and unlocked the old woman's tongue, so that she poured forth volubly all she knew.

Yes, she knew the lady quite well. She had been in the habit of coming to I. once every few weeks for a long time. No; she always came alone and had never spoken to anyone except herself, to her knowledge.

"What does she do?"

"Oh, she always goes straight up to her room and shuts herself in, then she sings to herself something I cannot make out and burns something that smells sweet and strong. About dark like, sometimes sooner, sometimes later, she comes down and goes out towards the Fells."

"Have you ever followed her?"

"No, never, nor anybody else as I know of. A shepherd once saw her walking all alone in a wild part of the moor but he did not follow her or speak to her."

"How long is she out?"

"Well, that depends, but generally till near morning. She takes the key of the house with her and lets herself in, but I hear her come in once in a while."

"What does she do then?"

"Why, goes up to her room and stays there quietly and has breakfast and then goes to the train."

This was about all that Mr. Fowke could find out, except the curious detail that his wife never wore a hat on her nocturnal rambles, but went draped in a hooded grey cloak.

By the time this catechism was finished it was nearly time for Mrs. Fowke to arrive, and the Reverend Barnabas accordingly ensconced himself in a room into which he was ushered by the old woman, which commanded the front door of the inn. In a short time he saw his wife arrive. After exchanging a few words with the old woman she went upstairs, and husband and wife remained in their respective seclusions till dusk fell.

Then Mr. Fowke heard Stella descending the stairs and in a few moments he saw her emerge from the house clad, as described, in a long hooded grey cloak, and walking swiftly and resolutely. Giving her a short start, he followed, and as he left the inn the well-known smell of burning, aromatic herbs was in his nostrils. His wife was by now a few hundred yards away and had nearly cleared the little hamlet, heading for the open moor. As she proceeded a singular episode occurred. Mr. Fowke thought little of it at the time, but much, later.

A sheep-dog was lying asleep by the roadside and as Mrs. Fowke drew near it suddenly started up and, with back upraised and tail depressed, uttered a melancholy howl and darted through the hedge.

Mrs. Fowke paid not the least attention to the dog, but pursued her way steadily through the rapidly falling dusk.

Her husband followed as steadily, and thus for a long time they wound their way upwards towards the loneliest and wildest part of the Fells. It was by now night, but the moon had risen and flooded the landscape with her rays. The couple, one about two hundred yards behind the other, were now mounting the side of a steep hill, and hitherto Mr. Fowke had remained in the pleasant belief that his presence was unsuspected by his wife. He was to be undeceived. The lady passed round a corner of the hill, thereby disappearing from sight; Mr. Fowke hastened after her and on passing the corner in his turn found himself confronted by his wife, who stood watching for his appearance with a sarcastic smile. She greeted him:

"Well, Mr. Spy, are you very much puzzled?"

He remained silent, dumb with astonishment and chagrin, and she went on:

"I have been wondering what to do with you ever since you left home, but I have decided at last. You shall see all there is to see; I don't think you can do any harm and you may be useful by and by. Follow me." And she turned and went on again.

Mr. Fowke followed silently and abashed. Presently he became aware of a rosy light shining in front of them, and after walking a few yards more he found himself standing by the side of his wife on the edge of a small, cup-shaped hollow in the hills. In the centre of this hollow a large fire was burning and near the fire Mr. Fowke could make out a pile of stones shaped like a rough altar. A group of about half a dozen people, all clad in the same grey, hooded cloaks, were sitting silently near the fire; and towards these his wife now began to descend, first telling him in a low, imperious voice to stay where he was. As Stella advanced down the declivity the group by the fire became aware of her approach and, rising, moved to meet her with gestures of greeting and respect.

Stella passed through them, haughtily returning their salutations and slowly ascending the stone altar seated herself on a rock near its summit. As soon as she had taken up her position, she gave a signal, and the others forming round the fire commenced a slow and stately dance to the accompaniment of their own low chanting.

Mr. Fowke watched absorbed. Gradually the dance grew quicker and wilder and the chanting louder, the whirling forms flung themselves into grotesque attitudes and shrieked ejaculations, the meaning of which Mr. Fowke began dimly to divine though the words were strange. Suddenly they were silent and still and at the same moment Stella rose from her seat and, throwing back her hood and turning towards the summit of the altar, began in her turn to take up the chant. As she sang and bowed towards the topmost stone, her face and figure seemed transformed. In the flickering firelight and pale moonshine she seemed to grow weirdly and horribly beautiful and to grow statelier and taller in her person. Slowly, too, as the song progressed the horrified watcher saw another change. A grey cloud formed on the summit of the altar, diminishing, thickening and turning into a Shape, a Shape of evil and fear. The silent group by the fire once more broke forth into wild gesticulations and cries, Stella prostrated herself, the Form on the altar grew clearer and with a cry of horror Mr. Fowke turned away and rushed madly across the moor.

He never knew where he went or what he did. When he once more recovered his senses it was broad day and he was alone and lost on the moors. It was late afternoon before, broken and exhausted, he reached his own home, where the first person to greet him was his wife, cool and collected as ever. She led him into his study.

"Well," she said, "and what are you going to do now? Are you going to go about telling a cock-and-bull story of the moors, or are you going to be a good little man and hold your tongue? Don't imagine I care," she went on, "the Great One can protect his servants and destroy his enemies."

Mr. Fowke groaned.

"It was true then," he said, "not a horrid dream."

"You had better call it that," she answered with a laugh and left him. Mr. Fowke was utterly perplexed and, like many men of weak character, could decide on nothing. So matters drifted on: he had little or no communication with his wife, who was, however, invariably civil and pleasant when they met with a kind of mocking courtesy, which maddened him. At last came the day when she announced her intention of again going to I.

"And perhaps you would like to go with me," she said. "You will be ready for the grey robe soon."

She went and he spent the night in an agony of prayer.

The next day Stella returned and came immediately to his study. This time, however, she had no look of exhilaration on her face, she was troubled and angry.

"How dare you interfere with us," she began, "with your paltry little prayers and tears? You disturbed us last night. The Great One was angry -" She stopped and then went on, "I shall have to find a means of silencing you; it was a mistake to show you what I did."

He looked at her.

"So it is not too late, is it?" he said. "I can perhaps save you and drag you away from -" She interrupted him.

"Silence," she cried violently, "or I will take steps to quiet you; I will blast you; I will call upon the Powers of the Air. I will -" she was going on madly in her excitement when suddenly she became rigid, her face blanched and she fell senseless to the floor in a fit.

Mr. Fowke raised the prostrate body, laid it on a sofa and summoned help. The unfortunate woman was carried to her bedroom, still unconscious, and the doctor sent for. He was an ordinary country practitioner and the case seemed to be clearly beyond his powers to deal with, but he emphasized the need of a trained nurse; and, one being fortunately available in the village, she was presently duly installed at the Parsonage.

After having seen all done that was possible, Mr. Fowke, utterly worn out, retired to rest. Towards midnight he was awakened by a knocking at his door and opening it found the nurse pale and trembling on the threshold. She instantly assured him that she must throw up the case and leave the house at once. She could or would give no clear reasons for her action, but repeated again and again that she would sacrifice her whole professional career rather than remain in that sick room. Things had happened there, she said, things she could not tell of, but the place was accursed. In vain Mr. Fowke tried to reassure her; she would not remain and so, bidding her go to her room till morning without disturbing the household, Mr. Fowke went to his wife's room to take up the vigil himself.

When he entered the sick room all was still. Stella was lying motionless, breathing gently and at intervals murmuring a few words in her native tongue. Mr. Fowke settled himself down in an arm-chair and gradually fell into a doze.

He woke suddenly as the clock struck three and glanced around him. The lamp had burnt low and the room was very cold. His wife still lay quietly in her bed, muttering softly to herself, but as Mr. Fowke watched her, by the dim light, he fancied he noticed a horrible change in her. Gone were the full rounded outlines of a woman's form, the figure on the bed had become angular and misshaped. Her hand and arm, which lay outside the coverlet, were also changed and looked like a claw. Her face, too, was changing. As he watched, her beauty faded, the features altered, they ran together, became distorted, misplaced and, with a shudder, he found himself gazing on the lineaments of an unknown, hideous beast. Paralysed with horror he could not stir.

All at once there was a movement. The figure on the bed shivered violently, lifted itself up and sat gazing out beyond the foot of the bed. Mr. Fowke followed the direction of its eyes and saw growing up slowly at the end of the room a grey, shapeless form, of which the burning eyes alone were distinct.

The creature on the bed moved and slipping back the bedclothes stepped suddenly to the floor. Mr. Fowke saw that the lower limbs and, in fact, every part of it save the face that he could see were covered with a thick, grey fur. It moved again and passed swiftly across the room towards the grim shape in the corner; he heard its hoofs tap on the bare floor as it passed. It reached the motionless watcher, whose eyes seemed to blaze as it approached, and with a swift movement the two forms met, intermingled and - Mr. Fowke could bear no more; he fainted.

It was daylight when he regained his senses. He glanced towards the bed; Mrs. Fowke lay there calm, beautiful and dead.

XÉLUCHA
M. P. Shiel

"He goeth after her...and knoweth not..."
(From a diary)

Three days ago! by heaven, it seems an age. But I am shaken - my reason is debauched. A while since, I fell into a momentary coma precisely resembling an attack of *petit mal*. "Tombs, and worms, and epitaphs" - that is my dream. At my age, with my physique, to walk staggery, like a man stricken! But all that will pass: I must collect myself - my reason is debauched. Three days ago! it seems an age! I sat on the floor before an old cista full of letters. I lighted upon a packet of Cosmo's. Why, I had forgotten them! they are turning sere! Truly, I can no more call myself a young man. I sat reading, listlessly, rapt back by memory. To muse is to be lost! of that evil habit I must wring the neck, or look to perish. Once more I threaded the mazy sphere-harmony of the minuet, reeled in the waltz, long pomps of candelabra, the noonday of the bacchanal, about me.

Cosmo was the very tsar and maharajah of the Sybarites! the Priap of the détraqués! In every unexpected alcove of the Roman Villa was a couch, raised high, with necessary footstool, flanked and canopied with mirrors of clarified gold. Consumption fastened upon him; reclining at last at table, he could, till warmed, scarce lift the wine! his eyes were like two fat glow-worms, coiled together! They seemed haloed with vaporous emanations of phosphorus! Desperate, one could see, was the secret struggle with the Devourer. But to the end the princely smile persisted calm; to the end - to the last day - he continued among that comic crew unchallenged choragus of all the rites, I will not say of Paphos, but of Chemos! and Baal-Peor! Warmed, he did not refuse the revel, the dance, the darkened chamber. It was utterly black, rayless; approached by a secret passage; in shape circular; the air hot, haunted always by odours of balms, bdellium, hints of dulcimer and flute; and radiated round with a hundred thick-strewn ottomans of Morocco.

Here Lucy Hill stabbed to the heart Caccofogo, mistaking the scar of his back for the scar of Soriac. In a bath of malachite the Princess Egla, waking late one morning, found Cosmo lying stiffly dead, the water covering him wholly.

"But in God's name, Mérimée!" (so he wrote), "to think of Xélucha dead! Xélucha! Can a moon-beam, then, perish of suppurations? Can the rainbow be eaten by worms? Ha! ha! ha! laugh with me, my friend: 'elle dérangera l'Enfer'! She will introduce the pas de tarantule into Tophet! Xélucha, the feminine Xélucha recalling the splendid harlots of history! Weep with me - manat rara meas lacrima per genas! expert as Thargelia; cultured as Aspatia; purple as Semiramis. She comprehended the human tabernacle, my friend, its secret springs and tempers, more intimately than any savant of Salamanca who breathes. Tarare - but Xélucha is not dead!

Vitality is not mortal; you cannot wrap flame in a shroud. Xélucha! where then is she? Translated, perhaps - rapt to a constellation like the daughter of Leda. She journeyed to Hindostan, accompanied by the train and appurtenance of a Begum, threatening descent upon the Emperor of Tartary. I spoke of the desolation of the West; she kissed me, and promised return.

Mentioned you, too, Mérimée - 'her Conqueror' - 'Mérimée, Destroyer of Woman.' A breath from the conservatory rioted among the ambery whiffs of her forelocks, sending it singly a-wave over that thulite tint you know. Costumed cap-à-pie, she had, my friend, the dainty little completeness of a daisy mirrored bright in the eye of the browsing ox.

A simile of Milton had for years, she said, inflamed the lust of her Eye: 'The barren plains of Sericana, where Chineses drive with sails and wind their cany wagons light.' I, and the Sabæans, she assured me, wrongly considered Flame the whole of being; the other half of things being Aristotle's quintessential light. In the Ourania Hierarchia and the Faust-book you meet a completeness: burning Seraph, Cherûb full of eyes. Xélucha combined them. She would reconquer the Orient for Dionysius, and return. I heard of her blazing at Delhi; drawn in a chariot by lions. Then this rumour - probably false. Indeed, it comes from a source somewhat turgid. Like Odin, Arthur, and the rest, Xélucha - will reappear.

Soon subsequently, Cosmo lay down in his balneum of malachite, and slept, having drawn over him the water as a coverlet. I, in England, heard little of Xélucha: first that she was alive, then dead, then alighted at old Tadmor in the Wilderness, Palmyra now. Nor did I greatly care, Xélucha having long since turned to apples of Sodom in my mouth. Till I sat by the cista of letters and re-read Cosmo, she had for some years passed from my active memories.

The habit is now confirmed in me of spending the greater part of the day in sleep, while by night I wander far and wide through the city under the sedative influence of a tincture which has become necessary to my life. Such an existence of shadow is not without charm; nor, I think, could many minds be steadily subjected to its conditions without elevation, deepened awe. To travel alone with the Primordial cannot but be solemn. The moon is of the hue of the glow-worm; and Night of the sepulchre. Nux bore not less Thanatos than Hupuos, and the bitter tears of Isis redundulate to a flood. At three, if a cab rolls by, the sound has the augustness of thunder. Once, at two, near a corner, I came upon a priest, seated, dead, leering, his legs bent.

One arm, supported on a knee, pointed with rigid accusing forefinger obliquely upward. By exact observation, I found that he indicated Betelgeux, the star "a" which shoulders the wet sword of Orion. He was hideously swollen, having perished of dropsy. Thus in all Supremes is a grotesquerie; and one of the sons of Night is - Buffo.

In a London square deserted, I should imagine, even in the day, I was aware of the metallic, silvery-clinking approach of little shoes. It was three in a heavy morning of winter, a day after my rediscovery of Cosmo. I had stood by the railing, regarding the clouds sail as under the sea-legged pilotage of a moon wrapped in cloaks of inclemency.

Turning, I saw a little lady, very gloriously dressed. She had walked straight to me. Her head was bare, and crisped with the amber stream which rolled lax to a globe, kneaded thick with jewels, at her nape.

In the redundance of her décolleté development, she resembled Parvati, mound-hipped love-goddess of the luscious fancy of the Brahmin.

She addressed to me the question:

"What are you doing there, darling?"

Her loveliness stirred me, and Night is bon camarade. I replied:

"Sunning myself by means of the moon."

"All that is borrowed lustre," she returned. "You have got it from old Drummond's Flowers of Sion."

Looking back, I cannot remember that this reply astonished me, though it should - of course - have done so. I said:

"On my soul, no; but you?"

"You might guess whence I come!"

"You are dazzling. You come from Paz."

"Oh, farther than that, my son! Say a subscription ball in Soho."

"Yes? ...and alone? in the cold? on foot...?"

"Why, I am old, and a philosopher. I can pick you out riding Andromeda yonder from the ridden Ram. They are in error, M'sieur, who suppose an atmosphere on the broad side of the moon. I have reason to believe that on Mars dwells a race whose lids are transparent like glass; so that the eyes are visible during sleep; and every varying dream moves imaged forth to the beholder in tiny panorama on the limpid iris. You cannot imagine me a mere fille! To be escorted is to admit yourself a woman, and that is improper in Nowhere. Young Eos drives an équipage à quatre, but Artemis 'walks' alone. Get out of my borrowed light in the name of Diogenes! I am going home."

"Near Piccadilly."

"But a cab?"

"No cabs for me, thank you. The distance is a mere nothing. Come."

We walked forward. My companion at once put an interval between us, quoting from the Spanish Curate that the open is an enemy to love. The Talmudists, she twice insisted, rightly held the hand the sacredest part of the person, and at that point also contact was for the moment interdict. Her walk was extremely rapid. I followed. Not a cat was anywhere visible. We reached at length the door of a mansion in St. James's. There was no light. It seemed tenantless, the windows all uncurtained, pasted across, some of them, with the words, To Let. My companion, however, flitted up the steps, and, beckoning, passed inward. I, following, slammed the door, and was in darkness. I heard her ascend, and presently a region of glimmer above revealed a stairway of marble, curving broadly up. On the floor where I stood was no carpet, nor furniture: the dust was very thick. I had begun to mount when, to my surprise, she stood by my side, returned; and whispered:

"To the very top, darling."

She soared nimbly up, anticipating me. Higher, I could no longer doubt that the house was empty but for us. All was a vacuum full of dust and echoes. But at the top, light streamed from a door, and I entered a good-sized oval saloon, at about the centre of the house. I was completely dazzled by the sudden resplendence of the apartment. In the midst was a spread table, square, opulent with gold plate, fruit dishes; three ponderous chandeliers of electric light above; and I noticed also (what was very bizarre) one little candlestick of common tin containing an old soiled curve of tallow, on the table. The impression of the whole chamber was one of gorgeousness not less than Assyrian. An ivory couch at the far end was made sun-like by a head-piece of chalcedony forming a sea for the sport of emerald ichthyotauri. Copper hangings, panelled with mirrors in iasperated crystal, corresponded with a dome of flame and copper; yet this latter, I now remember, produced upon my glance an impression of actual grime. My companion reclined on a small Sigma couch, raised high to the table-level in the Semitic manner, visible to her saffron slippers of satin. She pointed me a seat opposite. The incongruity of its presence in the middle of this arrogance of pomp so tickled me that no power could have kept me from a smile: it was a grimy chair, mean, all wood, nor was I long in discovering one leg somewhat shorter than its fellows.

She indicated wine in a black glass bottle, and a tumbler, but herself made no pretence of drinking or eating. She lay on hip and elbow, petite, resplendent, and looked gravely upward. I, however, drank.

"You are tired," I said, "one sees that."

"It is precious little than you see!" she returned, dreamy, hardly glancing.

"How! your mood is changed, then? You are morose."

"You never, I think, saw a Norse passage-grave?"

"And abrupt."

"Never?"

"A passage-grave? No."

"It is worth a journey! They are circular or oblong chambers of stone, covered by great earthmounds, with a 'passage' of slabs connecting them with the outer air. All round the chamber the dead sit with head resting upon the bent knees, and consult together in silence."

"Drink wine with me, and be less Tartarean."

"You certainly seem to be a fool," she replied with perfect sardonic iciness. "Is it not, then, highly romantic? They belong, you know, to the Neolithic age. As the teeth fall, one by one, from the lipless mouths - they are caught by the lap. When the lap thins - they roll to the floor of stone. Thereafter, every tooth that drops all round the chamber sharply breaks the silence."

"I Ia! ha! ha!"

"Yes. It is like a century-slow, circularly-successive dripping of slime in some cavern of the far subterrene."

"Ha! ha! This wine seems heady! They express themselves in a dialect largely dental."

"The Ape, on the other hand, in a language wholly guttural."

A town-clock tolled four. Our talk was holed with silences, and heavy-paced. The wine's yeasty exhalation reached my brain. I saw her through mist, dilating large, uncertain, shrinking again to dainty compactness. But amorousness had died within me.

"Do you know," she asked, "what has been discovered in one of the Danish Kjökkenmöddings by a little boy? It was ghastly. The skeleton of a huge fish with human -"

"You are most unhappy."

"Be silent."

"You are full of care."

"I think you a great fool."

"You are racked with misery."

"You are a child. You have not even an instinct of the meaning of the word."

"How! Am I not a man? I, too, miserable, careful?"

"You are not, really, anything - until you can create."

"Create what?"

"Matter."

"That is foppish. Matter cannot be created, nor destroyed."

"Truly, then, you must be a creature of unusually weak intellect. I see that now. Matter does not exist, then, there is no such thing, really - it is an appearance, a spectrum - every writer not imbecile from Plato to Fichte has, voluntary or involuntary, proved that for good. To create it is to produce an impression of its reality upon the senses of others; to destroy it is to wipe a wet rag across a scribbled slate."

"Perhaps. I do not care. Since no one can do it."

"No one? You are mere embryo -"

"Who then?"

"Anyone, whose power of Will is equivalent to the gravitating force of a star of the First Magnitude."

"Ha! ha! ha! By heaven, you choose to be facetious. Are there then wills of such equivalence?"

"There have been three, the founders of religions. There was a fourth: a cobbler of Herculaneum, whose mere volition induced the cataclysm of Vesuvius in '79 in direct opposition to the gravity of Sirius. There are more fames than you have ever sung, you know."

The greater number of disembodied spirits, too, I feel certain -

"By heaven, I cannot but think you full of sorrow! Poor wight! come, drink with me. The wine is thick and boon. Is it not Setian? It makes you sway and swell before me, I swear, like a purple cloud of evening -"

"But you are mere clayey ponderance! - I did not know that! - you are no companion! your little interest revolves round the lowest centres."

"Come - forget your agonies -"

"What, think you, is the portion of the buried body first sought by the worm?"

"The eyes! the eyes!"

"You are hideously wrong - you are so utterly at sea -"

"My God!"

She had bent forward with such rage of contradiction as to approach me closely. A loose gown of amber silk, wide-sleeved, had replaced her ball attire, though at what opportunity I could not guess; wondering, I noticed it as she now placed her palms far forth upon the table. A sudden wafture as of spice and orange-flowers, mingled with the abhorrent faint odour of mortality over-ready for the tomb, greeted my sense. A chill crept upon my flesh.

"You are so hopelessly at fault -"

"For God's sake -"

"You are so miserably deluded! Not the eyes at all!"

"Then, in heaven's name, what?"

Five tolled from a clock.

"The Uvula! the soft drop of mucous flesh, you know, suspended from the palate above the glottis. They eat through the face-cloth and cheek, or crawl by the lips through a broken tooth, filling the mouth. They make straight for it. It is the deliciæ of the vault."

At her horror of interest I grew sick, at her odour, and her words. Some unspeakable sense of insignificance, of debility, held me dumb.

"You say I am full of sorrows. You say I am racked with woe; that I gnash with anguish. Well, you are a mere child in intellect. You use words without realization of meaning like those minds in what Leibnitz calls 'symbolical consciousness.' But suppose it were so -"

"It is so."

"You know nothing."

"I see you twist and grind. Your eyes are very pale. I thought they were hazel. They are of the faint bluishness of phosphorus shimmerings seen in darkness."

"That proves nothing."

"But the 'white' of the sclerotic is dyed to yellow. And you look inward. Why do you look so palely inward, so woe-worn, upon your soul? Why can you speak of nothing but the sepulchre, and its rottenness? Your eyes seem to me wan with centuries of vigil, with mysteries and millenniums of pain."

"Pain! but you know so little of it! you are wind and words! of its philosophy and rationale nothing!"

"Who knows?"

"I will give you a hint. It is the sub-consciousness in conscious creatures of Eternity, and of eternal loss. The least prick of a pin not Pæan and Æsculapius and the powers of heaven and hell can utterly heal. Of an everlasting loss of pristine wholeness the conscious body is sub-conscious, and 'pain' is its sigh at the tragedy. So with all pain - greater, the greater the loss. The hugest of losses is, of course, the loss of Time. If you lose that, any of it, you plunge at once into the transcendentalisms, the infinitudes, of Loss; if you lose all of it -"

"But you so wildly exaggerate! Ha! ha! You rant, I tell you, of commonplaces with the woe -"

"Hell is where a clear, untrammelled Spirit is sub-conscious of lost Time; where it boils and writhes with envy of the living world; hating it for ever, and all the sons of Life!"

"But curb yourself! Drink - I implore - I implore - for God's sake - but once -"

"To hasten to the snare - that is woe! to drive your ship upon the lighthouse rock - that is Marah! To wake, and feel it irrevocably true that you went after her - and the dead were there - and her guests were in the depths of hell - and you did not know it! - though you might have. Look out upon the houses of the city this dawning day: not one, I tell you, but in it haunts some soul - walking up and down the old theatre of its little Day - goading imagination by a thousand childish tricks, vraisemblances - elaborately duping itself into the momentary fantasy that it still lives, that the chance of life is not for ever and for ever lost - yet riving all the time with under-memories of the wasted Summer, the lapsed brief light between the two eternal glooms - riving I say and shriek to you! - riving, Mérimée, you destroying fiend - She had sprung - tall now, she seemed to me - between couch and table.

"Mérimée!" I screamed, " - my name, harlot, in your maniac mouth! By God, woman, you terrify me to death!"

I too sprang, the hairs of my head catching stiff horror from my fancies.

"Your name? Can you imagine me ignorant of your name, or anything concerning you? Mérimée! Why, did you not sit yesterday and read of me in a letter of Cosmo's?"

"Ah-h ...," hysteria bursting high in sob and laughter from my arid lips--"Ah! ha! ha!"

"Xélucha! My memory grows palsied and grey, Xélucha! pity me - my walk is in the very valley of shadow! - senile and sere! - observe my hair, Xélucha, its grizzled growth - trepidant, Xélucha, clouded - I am not the man you knew, Xélucha, in the palaces - of Cosmo! You are Xélucha!"

"You rave, poor worm!" she cried, her face contorted by a species of malicious contempt. "Xélucha died of cholera ten years ago at Antioch. I wiped the froth from her lips. Her nose underwent a green decay before burial. So far sunken into the brain was the left eye -"

"You are - you are Xélucha!" I shrieked; "voices now of thunder howl it within my consciousness - and by the holy God, Xélucha, though you blight me with the breath of the hell you are, I shall clasp you, living or damned -"

I rushed toward her. The word "Madman!" hissed as by the tongues of ten thousand serpents through the chamber, I heard; a belch of pestilent corruption puffed poisonous upon the putrid air; for a moment to my wildered eyes there seemed to rear itself, swelling high to the roof, a formless tower of ragged cloud, and before my projected arms had closed upon the very emptiness of insanity, I was tossed by the operation of some Behemoth potency far-circling backward to the utmost circumference of the oval, where, my head colliding, I fell, shocked, into insensibility.

When the sun was low toward night, I lay awake, and listlessly observed the grimy roof, and the sordid chair, and the candlestick of tin, and the bottle of which I had drunk. The table was small, filthy, of common deal, uncovered. All bore the appearance of having stood there for years. But for them, the room was void, the vision of luxury thinned to air. Sudden memory flashed upon me. I scrambled to my feet, and plunged and tottered, bawling, through the twilight into the street.

A NARROW ESCAPE
Lord Dunsany

It was underground.

In that dank cavern down below Belgrave Square the walls were dripping. But what was that to the magician? It was secrecy that he needed, not dryness. There he pondered upon the trend of events, shaped destinies and concocted magical brews.

For the last few years the serenity of his ponderings had been disturbed by the noise of the motor-bus; while to his keen ears there came the earthquake-rumble, far off, of the train in the tube, going down Sloane Street; and when he heard of the world above his head was not to its credit.

He decided one evening over his evil pipe, down there in his dank chamber, that London had lived long enough, had abused its opportunities, had gone too far, in fine, with its civilisation. And so he decided to wreck it.

Therefore he beckoned up his acolyte from the weedy end of the cavern, and, "Bring me," he said, "the heart of the toad that dwelleth in Arabia and by the mountains of Bethany." The acolyte slipped away by the hidden door, leaving that grim old man with his frightful pipe, and whither he went who knows but the gipsy people, or by what path he returned; but within a year he stood in the cavern again, slipping secretly in by the trap while the old man smoked, and he brought with him a little fleshy thing that rotted in a casket of pure gold.

"What is it?" the old man croaked.

"It is," said the acolyte, "the heart of the toad that dwelt once in Arabia and by the mountains of Bethany."

The old man's crooked fingers closed on it, and he blessed

the acolyte with his rasping voice and claw-like hand uplifted; the motor-bus rumbled above on its endless journey; far off the train shook Sloane Street.

"Come," said the old magician, "it is time." And there and then they left the weedy cavern, the acolyte carrying cauldron, gold poker and all things needful, and went abroad in the light. And very wonderful the old man looked in his silks.

Their goal was the outskirts of London; the old man strode in front and the acolyte ran behind him, and there was something magical in the old man's stride alone, without his wonderful dress, the cauldron and wand, the hurrying acolyte and the small gold poker.

Little boys jeered till they caught the old man's eye. So there went on through London this strange procession of two, too swift for any to follow. Things seemed worse up there than they did in the cavern, and the further they got on their way towards London's outskirts the worse London got. "It is time," said the old man, "surely."

And so they came at last to London's edge and a small hill watching it with a mournful look. It was so mean that the acolyte longed for the cavern, dank though it was and full of terrible sayings that the old man said when he slept.

They climbed the hill and put the cauldron down, and put there in the necessary things, and lit a fire of herbs that no chemist will sell nor decent gardener grow, and stirred the cauldron with the golden poker. The magician retired a little apart and muttered, then he strode back to the cauldron and, all being ready, suddenly opened the casket and let the fleshy thing fall in to boil.

Then he made spells, then he flung up his arms; the fumes from the cauldron entering in at his mind he said raging things that he had not known before and runes that were dreadful (the acolyte screamed); there he cursed London from fog to loam-pit, from zenith to the abyss, motor-bus, factory, shop, parliament, people. "Let them all perish," he said, "and London pass away, tram lines and bricks and pavement, the usurpers too long of the fields, let them all pass away and the wild hares come back, blackberry and briar-rose."

"Let it pass," he said, "pass now, pass utterly."

In the momentary silence the old man coughed, then waited with eager eyes; and the long long hum of London hummed as it always has since first the reed-huts were set up by the river, changing its note at times but always humming, louder now than it was in years gone by, but humming night and day though its voice be cracked with age; so it hummed on.

And the old man turned him round to his trembling acolyte and terribly said as he sank into the earth: "YOU HAVE NOT BROUGHT ME THE HEART OF THE TOAD THAT DWELLETH IN ARABIA NOR BY THE MOUNTAINS OF BETHANY!"

THURNLEY ABBEY
Perceval Landon

Three years ago I was on my way out to the East, and as an extra day in London was of some importance, I took the Friday evening mail-train to Brindisi instead of the usual Thursday morning Marseilles express. Many people shrink from the long forty-eight-hour train journey through Europe, and the subsequent rush across the Mediterranean on the nineteen-knot Isis or Osiris; but there is really very little discomfort on either the train or the mail-boat, and unless there is actually nothing for me to do, I always like to save the extra day and a half in London before I say goodbye to her for one of my longer tramps. This time - it was early, I remember, in the shipping season, probably about the beginning of September - there were few passengers, and I had a compartment in the P. & O. Indian express to myself all the way from Calais. All Sunday I watched the blue waves dimpling the Adriatic, and the pale rosemary along the cuttings; the plain white towns, with their flat roofs and their bold "duomos," and the grey-green gnarled olive orchards of Apulia. The journey was just like any other. We ate in the dining-car as often and as long as we decently could. We slept after luncheon; we dawdled the afternoon away with yellow-backed novels; sometimes we exchanged platitudes in the smoking-room, and it was there that I met Alastair Colvin.

Colvin was a man of middle height, with a resolute, well-cut jaw; his hair was turning grey; his moustache was sun-whitened, otherwise he was clean-shaven - obviously a gentleman, and obviously also a pre-occupied man. He had no great wit. When spoken to, he made the usual remarks in the right way, and I dare say he refrained from banalities only because he spoke less than the rest of us; most of the time he buried himself in the Wagon-lit Company's time-table, but seemed unable to concentrate his attention on any one page of it. He found that I had been over the Siberian railway, and for a quarter of an hour he discussed it with me. Then he lost interest in it, and rose to go to his compartment. But he came back again very soon, and seemed glad to pick up the conversation again.

Of course this did not seem to me to be of any importance. Most travellers by train become a trifle infirm of purpose after thirty-six hours' rattling. But Colvin's restless way I noticed in somewhat marked contrast with the man's personal importance and dignity; especially ill suited was it to his finely made large hand with strong, broad, regular nails and its few lines. As I looked at his hand I noticed a long, deep, and recent scar of ragged shape. However, it is absurd to pretend that I thought anything was unusual. I went off at five o'clock on Sunday afternoon to sleep away the hour or two that had still to be got through before we arrived at Brindisi.

Once there, we few passengers transhipped our hand baggage, verified our berths - there were only a score of us in all - and then, after an aimless ramble of half an hour in Brindisi, we returned to dinner at the Hotel International, not wholly surprised that the town had been the death of Virgil. If I remember rightly, there is a gaily painted hall at the International - I do not wish to advertise anything, but there is no other place in Brindisi at which to await the coming of the mails - and after dinner I was looking with awe at a trellis overgrown with blue vines, when Colvin moved across the room to my table. He picked up Il Secolo, but almost immediately gave up the pretence of reading it. He turned squarely to me and said:

"Would you do me a favour?"

One doesn't do favours to stray acquaintances on Continental expresses without knowing something more of them than I knew of Colvin. But I smiled in a noncommittal way, and asked him what he wanted. I wasn't wrong in part of my estimate of him; he said bluntly:

"Will you let me sleep in your cabin on the Osiris?" And he coloured a little as he said it.

Now, there is nothing more tiresome than having to put up with a stable-companion at sea, and I asked him rather pointedly:

"Surely there is room for all of us?" I thought that perhaps he had been partnered off with some mangy Levantine, and wanted to escape from him at all hazards.

Colvin, still somewhat confused, said: "Yes; I am in a cabin by myself. But you would do me the greatest favour if you would allow me to share yours."

This was all very well, but, besides the fact that I always sleep better when alone, there had been some recent thefts on board English liners, and I hesitated, frank and honest and self-conscious as Colvin was. Just then the mail-train came in with a clatter and a rush of escaping steam, and I asked him to see me again about it on the boat when we started. He answered me curtly - I suppose he saw the mistrust in my manner -"I am a member of White's." I smiled to myself as he said it, but I remembered in a moment that the man - if he were really what he claimed to be, and I make no doubt that he was - must have been sorely put to it before he urged the fact as a guarantee of his respectability to a total stranger at a Brindisi hotel.

That evening, as we cleared the red and green harbour-lights of Brindisi, Colvin explained. This is his story in his own words.

"When I was travelling in India some years ago, I made the

acquaintance of a youngish man in the Woods and Forests. We camped out together for a week, and I found him a pleasant companion. John Broughton was a light-hearted soul when off duty, but a steady and capable man in any of the small emergencies that continually arise in that department. He was liked and trusted by the natives, and though a trifle over-pleased with himself when he escaped to civilisation at Simla or Calcutta, Broughton's future was well assured in Government service, when a fair-sized estate was unexpectedly left to him, and he joyfully shook the dust of the Indian plains from his feet and returned to England. For five years he drifted about London. I saw him now and then. We dined together about every eighteen months, and I could trace pretty exactly the gradual sickening of Broughton with a merely idle life. He then set out on a couple of long voyages, returned as restless as before, and at last told me that he had decided to marry and settle down at his place, Thurnley Abbey, which had long been empty. He spoke about looking after the property and standing for his constituency in the usual way. Vivien Wilde, his fiancée, had, I suppose, begun to take him in hand. She was a pretty girl with a deal of fair hair and rather an exclusive manner; deeply religious in a narrow school, she was still kindly and high-spirited, and I thought that Broughton was in luck. He was quite happy and full of information about his future.

"Among other things, I asked him about Thurnley Abbey. He confessed that he hardly knew the place. The last tenant, a man called Clarke, had lived in one wing for fifteen years and seen no one. He had been a miser and a hermit. It was the rarest thing for a light to be seen at the Abbey after dark. Only the barest necessities of life were ordered, and the tenant himself received them at the side-door. His one half-caste manservant, after a month's stay in the house, had abruptly left without warning, and had returned to the Southern States.

One thing Broughton complained bitterly about: Clarke had wilfully spread the rumour among the villagers that the Abbey was haunted, and had even condescended to play childish tricks with spirit-lamps and salt in order to scare trespassers away at night. He had been detected in the act of this tomfoolery, but the story spread, and no one, said Broughton, would venture near the house except in broad daylight. The hauntedness of Thurnley Abbey was now, he said with a grin, part of the gospel of the countryside, but he and his young wife were going to change all that. Would I propose myself any time I liked? I, of course, said I would, and equally, of course, intended to do nothing of the sort without a definite invitation.

"The house was put in thorough repair, though not a stick of the old furniture and tapestry were removed. Floors and ceilings were relaid: the roof was made watertight again, and the dust of half a century was scoured out. He showed me some photographs of the place. It was called an Abbey, though as a matter of fact it had been only the infirmary of the long-vanished Abbey of Clouster some five miles away. The larger part of the building remained as it had been in pre-Reformation days, but a wing had been added in Jacobean times, and that part of the house had been kept in something like repair by Mr. Clarke. He had in both the ground and first floors set a heavy timber door, strongly barred with iron, in the passage between the earlier and the Jacobean parts of the house, and had entirely neglected the former. So there had been a good deal of work to be done.

"Broughton, whom I saw in London two or three times about this period, made a deal of fun over the positive refusal of the workmen to remain after sundown. Even after the electric light had been put into every room, nothing would induce them to remain, though, as Broughton observed, electric light was death on ghosts. The legend of the Abbey's ghosts had gone far and wide, and the men would take no risks. They went home in batches of five and six, and even during the daylight hours there was an inordinate amount of talking between one and another, if either happened to be out of sight of his companion. On the whole, though nothing of any sort or kind had been conjured up even by their heated imaginations during their five months' work upon the Abbey, the belief in the ghosts was rather strengthened than otherwise in Thurnley because of the men's confessed nervousness, and local tradition declared itself in favour of the ghost of an immured nun.

"'Good old nun!' said Broughton.

"I asked him whether in general he believed in the possibility of ghosts, and, rather to my surprise, he said that he couldn't say he entirely disbelieved in them. A man in India had told him one morning in camp that he believed that his mother was dead in England, as her vision had come to his tent the night before. He had not been alarmed, but had said nothing, and the figure vanished again. As a matter of fact, the next possible dak-walla brought on a telegram announcing the mother's death. 'There the thing was,' said Broughton. But at Thurnley he was practical enough. He roundly cursed the idiotic selfishness of Clarke, whose silly antics had caused all the inconvenience. At the same time, he couldn't refuse to sympathise to some extent with the ignorant workmen. 'My own idea,' said he, 'is that if a ghost ever does come in one's way, one ought to speak to it.'

"I agreed. Little as I knew of the ghost world and its conventions, I had always remembered that a spook was in honour bound to wait to be spoken to. It didn't seem much to do, and I felt that the sound of one's own voice would at any rate reassure oneself as to one's wakefulness. But there are few ghosts outside Europe - few, that is, that a white man can see - and I had never been troubled with any. However, as I have said, I told Broughton that I agreed.

"So the wedding took place, and I went to it in a tall hat which I bought for the occasion, and the new Mrs. Broughton smiled very nicely at me afterwards. As it had to happen, I took the Orient Express that evening and was not in England again for nearly six months. Just before I came back I got a letter from Broughton. He asked if I could see him in London or come to Thurnley, as he thought I should be better able to help him than anyone else he knew. His wife sent a nice message to me at the end, so I was reassured about at least one thing. I wrote from Budapest that I would come and see him at Thurnley two days after my arrival in London, and as I sauntered out of the Pannonia into the Kerepesi Utcza to post my letters, I wondered of what earthly service I could be to Broughton. I had been out with him after tiger on foot, and I could imagine few men better able at a pinch to manage their own business. However, I had nothing to do, so after dealing with some small accumulations of business during my absence, I packed a kit-bag and departed to Euston.

"I was met by Broughton's great limousine at Thurnley Road station, and after a drive of nearly seven miles we echoed through the sleepy streets of Thurnley village, into which the main gates of the park thrust themselves, splendid with pillars and spread-eagles and tom-cats rampant atop of them. I never was a herald, but I know that the Broughtons have the right to supporters - Heaven knows why! From the gates a quadruple avenue of beech-trees led inwards for a quarter of a mile. Beneath them a neat strip of fine turf edged the road and ran back until the poison of the dead beech-leaves killed it under the trees. There were many wheel-tracks on the road, and a comfortable little pony trap jogged past me laden with a country parson and his wife and daughter. Evidently there was some garden party going on at the Abbey. The road dropped away to the right at the end of the avenue, and I could see the Abbey across a wide pasturage and a broad lawn thickly dotted with guests.

"The end of the building was plain. It must have been almost mercilessly austere when it was first built, but time had crumbled the edges and toned the stone down to an orange-lichened grey wherever it showed behind its curtain of magnolia, jasmine, and ivy. Farther on was the three-storied Jacobean house, tall and handsome. There had not been the slightest attempt to adapt the one to the other, but the kindly ivy had glossed over the touching-point. There was a tall fleche in the middle of the building, surmounting a small bell tower. Behind the house there rose the mountainous verdure of Spanish chestnuts all the way up the hill.

"Broughton had seen me coming from afar, and walked across from his other guests to welcome me before turning me over to the butler's care. This man was sandy-haired and rather inclined to be talkative. He could, however, answer hardly any questions about the house; he had, he said, only been there three weeks. Mindful of what Broughton had told me, I made no inquiries about ghosts, though the room into which I was shown might have justified anything. It was a very large low room with oak beams projecting from the white ceiling. Every inch of the walls, including the doors, was covered with tapestry, and a remarkably fine Italian fourpost bedstead, heavily draped, added to the darkness and dignity of the place. All the furniture was old, well made, and dark. Underfoot there was a plain green pile carpet, the only new thing about the room except the electric light fittings and the jugs and basins. Even the looking-glass on the dressing-table was an old pyramidal Venetian glass set in heavy repoussi frame of tarnished silver.

"After a few minutes' cleaning up, I went downstairs and out upon the lawn, where I greeted my hostess. The people gathered there were of the usual country type, all anxious to be pleased and roundly curious as to the new master of the Abbey. Rather to my surprise, and quite to my pleasure, I rediscovered Glenham, whom I had known well in old days in Barotseland: he lived quite close, as, he remarked with a grin, I ought to have known. 'But,' he added, 'I don't live in a place like this.' He swept his hand to the long, low lines of the Abbey in obvious admiration, and then, to my intense interest, muttered beneath his breath, 'Thank God!' He saw that I had overheard him, and turning to me said decidedly, 'Yes, "thank God"' I said, and I meant it. I wouldn't live at the Abbey for all Broughton's money.'

"'But surely,' I demurred, 'you know that old Clarke was discovered in the very act of setting light on his bug-a-boos?'

"Glenham shrugged his shoulders. 'Yes, I know about that. But there is something wrong with the place still. All I can say is that Broughton is a different man since he has lived there. I don't believe that he will remain much longer. But - you're staying here? - well, you'll hear all about it to-night. There's a big dinner, I understand.' The conversation turned off to old reminiscences, and Glenham soon after had to go.

"Before I went to dress that evening I had twenty minutes' talk with Broughton in his library. There was no doubt that the man was altered, gravely altered. He was nervous and fidgety, and I found him looking at me only when my eye was off him. I naturally asked him what he wanted of me. I told him I would do anything I could, but that I couldn't conceive what he lacked that I could provide. He said with a lustreless smile that there was, however, something, and that he would tell me the following morning. It struck me that he was somehow ashamed of himself, and perhaps ashamed of the part he was asking me to play. However, I dismissed the subject from my mind and went up to dress in my palatial room. As I shut the door a draught blew out the Queen of Sheba from the wall, and I noticed that the tapestries were not fastened to the wall at the bottom. I have always held very practical views about spooks, and it has often seemed to me that the slow waving in firelight of loose tapestry upon a wall would account for ninety-nine percent of the stories one hears. Certainly the dignified undulation of this lady with her attendants and huntsmen - one of whom was untidily cutting the throat of a fallow deer upon the very steps on which King Solomon, a grey-faced Flemish nobleman with the order of the Golden Fleece, awaited his fair visitor - gave colour to my hypothesis.

"Nothing much happened at dinner. The people were very much like those of the garden party. A young woman next me seemed anxious to know what was being read in London. As she was far more familiar than I with the most recent magazines and literary supplements, I found salvation in being myself instructed in the tendencies of modern fiction. All true art, she said, was shot through and through with melancholy. How vulgar were the attempts at wit that marked so many modern books! From the beginning of literature it had always been tragedy that embodied the highest attainment of every age. To call such works morbid merely begged the question. No thoughtful man - she looked sternly at me through the steel rim of her glasses - could fail to agree with me. Of course, as one would, I immediately and properly said that I slept with Pett Ridge and Jacobs under my pillow at night, and that if Jorrocks weren't quite so large and cornery, I would add him to the company. She hadn't read any of them, so I was saved - for a time. But I remember grimly that she said that the dearest wish of her life was to be in some awful and soul-freezing situation of horror, and I remember that she dealt hardly with the hero of Nat Paynter's vampire story, between nibbles at her brown-bread ice. She was a cheerless soul, and I couldn't help thinking that if there were many such in the neighbourhood, it was not surprising that old Glenham had been stuffed with some nonsense or other about the Abbey. Yet nothing could well have been less creepy than the glitter of silver and glass, and the subdued lights and cackle of conversation all round the dinner-table.

"After the ladies had gone I found myself talking to the rural dean. He was a thin, earnest man, who at once turned the conversation to old Clarke's buffooneries. But, he said, Mr. Broughton had introduced such a new and cheerful spirit, not only into the Abbey, but, he might say, into the whole neighbourhood, that he had great hopes that the ignorant superstitions of the past were from henceforth destined to oblivion. Thereupon his other neighbour, a portly gentleman of independent means and position, audibly remarked 'Amen,' which damped the rural dean, and we talked to partridges past, partridges present, and pheasants to come. At the other end of the table Broughton sat with a couple of his friends, red-faced hunting men. Once I noticed that they were discussing me, but I paid no attention to it at the time. I remembered it a few hours later.

"By eleven all the guests were gone, and Broughton, his wife, and I were alone together under the fine plaster ceiling of the Jacobean drawing-room. Mrs. Broughton talked about one or two of the neighbours, and then, with a smile, said that she knew I would excuse her, shook hands with me, and went off to bed. I am not very good at analysing things, but I felt that she talked a little uncomfortably and with a suspicion of effort, smiled rather conventionally, and was obviously glad to go. These things seem trifling enough to repeat, but I had throughout the faint feeling that everything was not quite square. Under the circumstances, this was enough to set me wondering what on earth the service could be that I was to render - wondering also whether the whole business were not some ill-advised jest in order to make me come down from London for a mere shooting-party.

"Broughton said little after she had gone. But he was evidently labouring to bring the conversation round to the so-called haunting of the Abbey. As soon as I saw this, of course I asked him directly about it. He then seemed at once to lose interest in the matter. There was no doubt about it: Broughton was somehow a changed man, and to my mind he had changed in no way for the better. Mrs. Broughton seemed no sufficient cause. He was clearly very fond of her, and she of him. I reminded him that he was going to tell me what I could do for him in the morning, pleaded my journey, lighted a candle, and went upstairs with him. At the end of the passage leading into the old house he grinned weakly and said, 'Mind, if you see a ghost, do talk to it; you said you would.' He stood irresolutely a moment and then turned away. At the door of his dressing-room he paused once more: 'I'm here,' he called out, 'if you should want anything. Good night,' and he shut the door.

"I went along the passage to my room, undressed, switched on a lamp beside my bed, read a few pages of *The Jungle Book*, and then, more than ready for sleep, turned the light off and went fast asleep.

"Three hours later I woke up. There was not a breath of wind outside. There was not even a flicker of light from the fireplace. As I lay there, an ash tinkled slightly as it cooled, but there was hardly a gleam of the dullest red in the grate. An owl cried among the silent Spanish chestnuts on the slope outside. I idly reviewed the events of the day, hoping that I should fall off to sleep again before I reached dinner. But at the end I seemed as wakeful as ever. There was no help for it. I must read my Jungle Book again till I felt ready to go off, so I fumbled for the pear at the end of the cord that hung down inside the bed, and I switched on the bedside lamp. The sudden glory dazzled me for a moment. I felt under my pillow for my book with half-shut eyes. Then, growing used to the light, I happened to look down to the foot of my bed.

"I can never tell you really what happened then. Nothing I could ever confess in the most abject words could even faintly picture to you what I felt. I know that my heart stopped dead, and my throat shut automatically. In one instinctive movement I crouched back up against the head-boards of the bed, staring at the horror. The movement set my heart going again, and the sweat dripped from every pore. I am not a particularly religious man, but I had always believed that God would never allow any supernatural appearance to present itself to man in such a guise and in such circumstances that harm, either bodily or mental, could result to him. I can only tell you that at the moment both my life and my reason rocked unsteadily on their seats."

The other Osiris passengers had gone to bed. Only he and I remained leaning over the starboard railing, which rattled uneasily now and then under the fierce vibration of the over-engined mail-boat. Far over, there were the lights of a few fishing-smacks riding out the night, and a great rush of white combing and seething water fell out and away from us overside.

At last Colvin went on:

"Leaning over the foot of my bed, looking at me, was a figure swathed in a rotten and tattered veiling. This shroud passed over the head, but left both eyes and the right side of the face bare. It then followed the line of the arm down to where the hand grasped the bed-end. The face was not entirely that of a skull, though the eyes and the flesh of the face were totally gone. There was a thin, dry skin drawn tightly over the features, and there was some skin left on the hand. One wisp of hair crossed the forehead. It was perfectly still. I looked at it, and it looked at me, and my brains turned dry and hot in my head. I had still got the pear of the electric lamp in my hand, and I played idly with it; only I dared not turn the light out again. I shut my eyes, only to open them in a hideous terror the same second. The thing had not moved. My heart was thumping, and the sweat cooled me as it evaporated. Another cinder tinkled in the grate, and a panel creaked in the wall.

"My reason failed me. For twenty minutes, or twenty seconds, I was able to think of nothing else but this awful figure, till there came, hurtling through the empty channels of my senses, the remembrances that Broughton and his friends had discussed me furtively at dinner. The dim possibility of its being a hoax stole gratefully into my unhappy mind, and once there, one's pluck came creeping back along a thousand tiny veins. My first sensation was one of blind unreasoning thankfulness that my brain was going to stand the trial. I am not a timid man, but the best of us needs some human handle to steady him in time of extremity, and in this faint but growing hope that after all it might be only a brutal hoax, I found the fulcrum that I needed. At last I moved.

"How I managed to do it I cannot tell you, but with one spring towards the foot of the bed I got within arm's-length and struck out one fearful blow with my fist at the thing. It crumbled under it, and my hand was cut to the bone. With a sickening revulsion after my terror, I dropped half-fainting across the end of the bed. So it was merely a foul trick after all. No doubt the trick had been played many a time before: no doubt Broughton and his friends had had some large bet among themselves as to what I should do when I discovered the gruesome thing. From my state of abject terror I found myself transported into an insensate anger. I shouted curses upon Broughton. I dived rather than climbed over the bed-end of the sofa. I tore at the robed skeleton - how well the whole thing had been carried out, I thought - I broke the skull against the floor, and stamped upon its dry bones. I flung the head away under the bed, and rent the brittle bones of the trunk in pieces. I snapped the thin thigh-bones across my knee, and flung them in different directions. The shin-bones I set up against a stool and broke with my heel. I raged like a Berserker against the loathly thing, and stripped the ribs from the backbone and slung the breastbone against the cupboard. My fury increased as the work of destruction went on. I tore the frail rotten veil into twenty pieces, and the dust went up over everything, over the clean blotting-paper and the silver inkstand. At last my work was done. There was but a raffle of broken bones and strips of parchment and crumbling wool. Then, picking up a piece of the skull - it was the cheek and temple bone of the right side, I remember - I opened the door and went down the passage to Broughton's dressing-room. I remember still how my sweat-dripping pyjamas clung to me as I walked. At the door I kicked and entered.

"Broughton was in bed. He had already turned the light on and seemed shrunken and horrified. For a moment he could hardly pull himself together. Then I spoke. I don't know what I said. Only I know that from a heart full and over-full with hatred and contempt, spurred on by shame of my own recent cowardice, I let my tongue run on. He answered nothing. I was amazed at my own fluency. My hair still clung lankily to my wet temples, my hand was bleeding profusely, and I must have looked a strange sight. Broughton huddled himself up at the head of the bed just as I had. Still he made no answer, no defence. He seemed preoccupied with something besides my reproaches, and once or twice moistened his lips with his tongue. But he could say nothing though he moved his hands now and then, just as a baby who cannot speak moves its hands.

"At last the door into Mrs. Broughton's rooms opened and

she came in, white and terrified. 'What is it? What is it? Oh, in God's name! what is it?' she cried again and again, and then she went up to her husband and sat on the bed in her night-dress, and the two faced me. I told her what the matter was. I spared her husband not a word for her presence there. Yet he seemed hardly to understand. I told the pair that I had spoiled their cowardly joke for them. Broughton looked up.

"'I have smashed the foul thing into a hundred pieces,' I said. Broughton licked his lips again and his mouth worked. 'By God!' I shouted, 'it would serve you right if I thrashed you within an inch of your life. I will take care that not a decent man or woman of my acquaintance ever speaks to you again. And there,' I added, throwing the broken piece of the skull upon the floor beside his bed, 'there is a souvenir for you, of your damned work to-night!'

"Broughton saw the bone, and in a moment it was his turn to frighten me. He squealed like a hare caught in a trap. He screamed and screamed till Mrs. Broughton, almost as bewildered as myself, held on to him and coaxed him like a child to be quiet. But Broughton - and as he moved I thought that ten minutes ago I perhaps looked as terribly ill as he did - thrust her from him, and scrambled out of bed on to the floor, and still screaming put out his hand to the bone. It had blood on it from my hand. He paid no attention to me whatever. In truth I said nothing. This was a new turn indeed to the horrors of the evening. He rose from the floor with the bone in his hand and stood silent. He seemed to be listening. 'Time, time, perhaps,' he muttered, and almost at the same moment fell at full length on the carpet, cutting his head against the fender. The bone flew from his hand and came to rest near the door. I picked Broughton up, haggard and broken, with blood over his face. He whispered hoarsely and quickly, 'Listen, listen!' We listened.

"After ten seconds' utter quiet, I seemed to hear

something. I could not be sure, but at last there was no doubt. There was a quiet sound as one moving along the passage. Little regular steps came towards us over the hard oak flooring. Broughton moved to where his wife sat, white and speechless, on the bed, and pressed her face into his shoulder.

"Then, the last thing that I could see as he turned the light out, he fell forward with his own head pressed into the pillow of the bed. Something in their company, something in their cowardice, helped me, and I faced the open doorway of the room, which was outlined fairly clearly against the dimly lighted passage. I put out one hand and touched Mrs. Broughton's shoulder in the darkness. But at the last moment I too failed. I sank on my knees and put my face in the bed. Only we all heard. The footsteps came to the door and there they stopped. The piece of bone was lying a yard inside the door. There was a rustle of moving stuff, and the thing was in the room. Mrs. Broughton was silent: I could hear Broughton's voice praying, muffled in the pillow: I was cursing my own cowardice. Then the steps moved out again on the oak boards of the passage, and I heard the sounds dying away. In a flash of remorse I went to the door and looked out. At the end of the corridor I thought I saw something that moved away. A moment later the passage was empty. I stood with my forehead against the jamb of the door almost physically sick.

"'You can turn the light on,' I said, and there was an answering flare. There was no bone at my feet. Mrs. Broughton had fainted. Broughton was almost useless, and it took me ten minutes to bring her to. Broughton only said one thing worth remembering. For the most part he went on muttering prayers. But I was glad afterwards to recollect that he had said that thing. He said in a colourless voice, half as a question, half as a reproach, 'You didn't speak to her.'

"We spent the remainder of the night together. Mrs. Broughton actually fell off into a kind of sleep before dawn, but she suffered so horribly in her dreams that I shook her into consciousness again. Never was dawn so long in coming. Three or four times Broughton spoke to himself. Mrs. Broughton would then just tighten her hold on his arm, but she could say nothing. As for me, I can honestly say that I grew worse as the hours passed and the light strengthened. The two violent reactions had battered down my steadiness of view, and I felt that the foundations of my life had been built upon the sand. I said nothing, and after binding up my hand with a towel, I did not move. It was better so. They helped me and I helped them, and we all three knew that our reason had gone very near to ruin that night. At last, when the light came in pretty strongly, and the birds outside were chattering and singing, we felt that we must do something. Yet we never moved. You might have thought that we should particularly dislike being found as we were by the servants: yet nothing of that kind mattered a straw, and an overpowering listlessness bound us as we sat, until Chapman, Broughton's man, actually knocked and opened the door. None of us moved. Broughton, speaking hardly and stiffly, said, 'Chapman you can come back in five minutes.' Chapman was a discreet man, but it would have made no difference to us if he had carried his news to the 'room' at once.

"We looked at each other and I said I must go back. I meant to wait outside till Chapman returned. I simply dared not re-enter my bedroom alone. Broughton roused himself and said that he would come with me. Mrs. Broughton agreed to remain in her own room for five minutes if the blinds were drawn up and all the doors left open.

"So Broughton and I, leaning stiffly one against the other, went down to my room. By the morning light that filtered past the blinds we could see our way, and I released the blinds. There was nothing wrong with the room from end to end, except smears of my own blood on the end of the bed, on the sofa, and on the carpet where I had torn the thing to pieces."

Colvin had finished his story. There was nothing to say. Seven bells stuttered out from the fo'c'sle, and the answering cry wailed through the darkness. I took him downstairs.

"Of course I am much better now, but it is a kindness of you to let me sleep in your cabin.

THE BLACK STONE
Robert E. Howard

> *"They say foul things of Old Times still lurk*
> *In dark forgotten corners of the world.*
> *And Gates still gape to loose, on certain nights.*
> *Shapes pent in Hell."*
>
>   Justin Geoffrey

I read of it first in the strange book of Von Junzt, the German eccentric who lived so curiously and died in such grisly and mysterious fashion. It was my fortune to have access to his *Nameless Cults* in the original edition, the so-called *Black Book*, published in Dusseldorf in 1839, shortly before a hounding doom overtook the author. Collectors of rare literature were familiar with *Nameless Cults* mainly through the cheap and faulty translation which was pirated in London by Bridewall in 1845, and the carefully expurgated edition put out by the Golden Goblin Press of New York, 1909. But the volume I stumbled upon was one of the unexpurgated German copies, with heavy black leather covers and rusty iron hasps. I doubt if there are more than half a dozen such volumes in the entire world today, for the quantity issued was not great, and when the manner of the author's demise was bruited about, many possessors of the book burned their volumes in panic.

 Von Junzt spent his entire life (1795-1840) delving into forbidden subjects; he travelled in all parts of the world, gained entrance into innumerable secret societies, and read countless little-known and esoteric books and manuscripts in the original; and in the chapters of the *Black Book*, which range from startling clarity of exposition to murky ambiguity, there are statements and hints to freeze the blood of a thinking man.

Reading what Von Junzt dared put in print arouses uneasy speculations as to what it was that he dared not tell. What dark matters, for instance, were contained in those closely written pages that formed the unpublished manuscript on which he worked unceasingly for months before his death, and which lay torn and scattered all over the floor of the locked and bolted chamber in which Von Junzt was found dead with the marks of taloned fingers on his throat? It will never be known, for the author's closest friend, the Frenchman Alexis Ladeau, after having spent a whole night piecing the fragments together and reading what was written, burnt them to ashes and cut his own throat with a razor.

But the contents of the published matter are shuddersome enough, even if one accepts the general view that they but represent the ravings of a madman. There among many strange things I found mention of the Black Stone, that curious, sinister monolith that broods among the mountains of Hungary, and about which so many dark legends cluster. Van Junzt did not devote much space to it - the bulk of his grim work concerns cults and objects of dark worship which he maintained existed in his day, and it would seem that the Black Stone represents some order or being lost and forgotten centuries ago. But he spoke of it as one of the keys - a phrase used many times by him, in various relations, and constituting one of the obscurities of his work. And he hinted briefly at curious sights to be seen about the monolith on Midsummer's Night. He mentioned Otto Dostmann's theory that this monolith was a remnant of the Hunnish invasion and had been erected to commemorate a victory of Attila over the Goths. Von Junzt contradicted this assertion without giving any refutory facts, merely remarking that to attribute the origin of the Black Stone to the Huns was as logical as assuming that William the Conqueror reared Stonehenge.

This implication of enormous antiquity piqued my interest

immensely and after some difficulty I succeeded in locating a rat-eaten and mouldering copy of Dostmann's *Remnants of Lost Empires* (Berlin, 1809, "Der Drachenhaus" Press). I was disappointed to find that Dostmann referred to the Black Stone even more briefly than had Von Junzt, dismissing it with a few lines as an artefact comparatively modern in contrast with the Greco-Roman ruins of Asia Minor which were his pet theme. He admitted his inability to make out the defaced characters on the monolith but pronounced them unmistakably Mongoloid. However, little as I learned from Dostmann, he did mention the name of the village adjacent to the Black Stone – Stregoicavar - an ominous name, meaning something like Witch-Town.

A close scrutiny of guidebooks and travel articles gave me no further information - Stregoicavar, not on any map that I could find, lay in a wild, little-frequented region, out of the path of casual tourists. But I did find subject for thought in Dornly's *Magyar Folklore*. In his chapter on Dream Myths he mentions the Black Stone and tells of some curious superstitions regarding it - especially the belief that if anyone sleeps in the vicinity of the monolith, that person will be haunted by monstrous nightmares forever after; and he cited tales of the peasants regarding too-curious people who ventured to visit the Stone on Midsummer Night and who died raving mad because of something they saw there.

That was all I could gleam from Dornly, but my interest was even more intensely roused as I sensed a distinctly sinister aura about the Stone. The suggestion of dark antiquity, the recurrent hint of unnatural events on Midsummer Night, touched some slumbering instinct in my being, as one senses, rather than hears, the flowing of some dark subterranean river in the night.

And I suddenly saw a connection between this Stone and a certain weird and fantastic poem written by the mad poet,

Justin Geoffrey: *The People of the Monolith*. Inquiries led to the information that Geoffrey had indeed written that poem while travelling in Hungary, and I could not doubt that the Black Stone was the very monolith to which he referred in his strange verse. Reading his stanzas again, I felt once more the strange dim stirrings of subconscious promptings that I had noticed when first reading of the Stone.

I had been casting about for a place to spend a short vacation and I made up my mind. I went to Stregoicavar. A train of obsolete style carried me from Temesvar to within striking distance, at least, of my objective, and a three days' ride in a jouncing coach brought me to the little village which lay in a fertile valley high up in the fir-clad mountains. The journey itself was uneventful, but during the first day we passed the old battlefield of Schomvaal where the brave Polish-Hungarian knight, Count Boris Vladinoff, made his gallant and futile stand against the victorious hosts of Suleiman the Magnificent, when the Grand Turk swept over eastern Europe in 1526.

The driver of the coach pointed out to me a great heap of crumbling stones on a hill nearby, under which, he said, the bones of the brave Count lay. I remembered a passage from Larson's *Turkish Wars*. "After the skirmish" (in which the Count with his small army had beaten back the Turkish advance-guard) "the Count was standing beneath the half-ruined walls of the old castle on the hill, giving orders as to the disposition of his forces, when an aide brought to him a small lacquered case which had been taken from the body of the famous Turkish scribe and historian, Selim Bahadur, who had fallen in the fight. The Count took therefrom a roll of parchment and began to read, but he had not read far before he turned very pale and, without saying a word, replaced the parchment in the case and thrust the case into his cloak. At that very instant a hidden Turkish battery suddenly opened fire, and the balls striking the old castle, the Hungarians were horrified to see the walls crash down in ruin, completely covering the brave Count. Without a leader the gallant little army was cut to pieces, and in the war-swept years which followed, the bones of the noblemen were never recovered. Today the natives point out a huge and mouldering pile of ruins near Schomvaal beneath which, they say still rests all that the centuries have left of Count Boris Vladinoff."

I found the village of Stregoicavar a dreamy, drowsy little village that apparently belied its sinister cognomen - a forgotten back-eddy that Progress had passed by. The quaint houses and the quainter dress and manners of the people were those of an earlier century. They were friendly, mildly curious but not inquisitive, though visitors from the outside world were extremely rare.

"Ten years ago another American came here and stayed a few days in the village," said the owner of the tavern where I had put up, "a young fellow and queer-acting - mumbled to himself - a poet, I think."

I knew he must mean Justin Geoffrey.

"Yes, he was a poet," I answered, "and he wrote a poem about a bit of scenery near this very village."

"Indeed?" Mine host's interest was aroused. "Then, since all great poets are strange in their speech and actions, he must have achieved great fame, for his actions and conversations were the strangest of any man I ever I knew."

"As is usual with artists," I answered, "most of his recognition has come since his death."

"He is dead, then?"

"He died screaming in a madhouse five years ago."

"Too bad, too bad," sighed mine host sympathetically. "Poor lad - he looked too long at the Black Stone."

My heart gave a leap, but I masked my keen interest and said casually. "I have heard something of this Black Stone;

somewhere near this village, is it not?"

"Nearer than Christian folk wish," he responded. "Look!" He drew me to a latticed window and pointed up at the fir-clad slopes of the brooding blue mountains. "There beyond where you see the bare face of that jutting cliff stands that accursed Stone. Would that it were ground to powder and the powder flung into the Danube to be carried to the deepest ocean! Once men tried to destroy the thing, but each man who laid hammer or maul against it came to an evil end. So now the people shun it."

"What is there so evil about it?" I asked curiously.

"It is a demon-haunted thing," he answered uneasily and with the suggestion of a shudder. "In my childhood I knew a young man who came up from below and laughed at our traditions - in his foolhardiness he went to the Stone one Midsummer Night and at dawn stumbled into the village again, stricken dumb and mad. Something had shattered his brain and sealed his lips, for until the day of his death, which came soon after, he spoke only to utter terrible blasphemies or to slaver gibberish.

"My own nephew when very small was lost in the mountains and slept in the woods near the Stone, and now in his manhood he is tortured by foul dreams, so that at times he makes the night hideous with his screams and wakes with cold sweat upon him.

"But let us talk of something else, Herr; it is not good to dwell upon such things."

I remarked on the evident age of the tavern and he answered with pride. "The foundations are more than four hundred years old; the original house was the only one in the village which was not burned to the ground when Suleiman's devils swept through the mountains. Here, in the house that then stood on these same foundations, it is said, the scribe Selim Bahadur had his headquarters while ravaging the country hereabouts."

I learned then that the present inhabitants of Stregoicavar are not descendants of the people who dwelt there before the Turkish raid of 1526. The victorious Moslems left no living human in the village or the vicinity thereabouts when they passed over. Men, women and children they wiped out in one red holocaust of murder, leaving a vast stretch of country silent and utterly deserted. The present people of Stregoicavar are descended from hardy settlers from the lower valleys who came into the ruined village after the Turk was thrust back.

Mine host did not speak of the extermination of the original inhabitants with any great resentment and I learned that his ancestors in the lower levels had looked on the mountaineers with even more hatred and aversion than they regarded the Turks. He was rather vague regarding the causes of this feud, but said that the original inhabitants of Stregoicavar had been in the habit of making stealthy raids on the lowlands and stealing girls and children. Moreover, he said that they were not exactly of the same blood as his own people; the sturdy, original Magyar-Slavic stock had mixed and intermarried with a degraded aboriginal race until the breeds had blended, producing an unsavoury amalgamation. Who these aborigines were, he had not the slightest idea, but maintained that they were "pagans" and had dwelt in the mountains since time immemorial, before the coming of the conquering peoples.

I attached little importance to this tale; seeing in it merely a parallel to the amalgamation of Celtic tribes with Mediterranean aborigines in the Galloway hills, with the resultant mixed race which, as Picts, has such an extensive part in Scotch legendary. Time has a curious foreshortening effect on folklore, and just as tales of the Picts became intertwined with legends of an older Mongoloid race, so that eventually the Picts were ascribed the repulsive appearance of the squat primitives, whose individuality merged, in the telling, into Pictish tales, and was forgotten; so, I felt, the supposed inhuman attributes of the first villagers of Stregoicavar could be traced to older, outworn myths with invading Huns and Mongols.

The morning after my arrival I received directions from mine host, who gave them worriedly, and set out to find the Black Stone. A few hours' tramp up the fir-covered slopes brought me to the face of the rugged, solid stone cliff which jutted boldly from the mountainside. A narrow trail wound up it, and mounting this, I looked out over the peaceful valley of Stregoicavar, which seemed to drowse, guarded on either hand by the great blue mountains. No huts or any sign of human tenancy showed between the cliff whereon I stood and the village. I saw numbers of scattering farms in the valley but all lay on the other side of Stregoicavar, which itself seemed to shrink from the brooding slopes which masked the Black Stone.

The summit of the cliffs proved to be a sort of thickly wooded plateau. I made my way through the dense growth for a short distance and came into a wide glade; and in the centre of the glade reared a gaunt figure of black stone.

It was octagonal in shape, some sixteen feet in height and about a foot and a half thick. It had once evidently been highly polished, but now the surface was thickly dinted as if savage efforts had been made to demolish it; but the hammers had done little more than to flake off small bits of stone and mutilate the characters which once had evidently marched up in a spiralling line round and round the shaft to the top. Up to ten feet from the base these characters were almost completely blotted out, so that it was very difficult to trace their direction. Higher up they were plainer, and I managed to squirm part of the way up the shaft and scan them at close range. All were more or less defaced, but I was positive that they symbolized no language now remembered on the face of the earth. I am fairly familiar with all hieroglyphics known to researchers and philologists and I can say, with certainty that those characters were like nothing of which I have ever read or heard. The nearest approach to them that I ever saw were some crude scratches on a gigantic and strangely symmetrical rock in a lost valley of Yucatan. I remember that when I pointed out these marks to the archaeologist who was my companion, he maintained that they either represented natural weathering or the idle scratching of some Indian. To my theory that the rock was really the base of a long-vanished column, he merely laughed, calling my attention to the dimensions of it, which suggested, if it were built with any natural rules of architectural symmetry, a column a thousand feet high. But I was not convinced.

I will not say that the characters on the Black Stone were similar to those on that colossal rock in Yucatan; but one suggested the other. As to the substance of the monolith, again I was baffled. The stone of which it was composed was a dully gleaming black, whose surface, where it was not dinted and roughened, created a curious illusion of semi-transparency.

I spent most of the morning there and came away baffled. No connection of the Stone with any other artefact in the world suggested itself to me. It was as if the monolith had been reared by alien hands, in an age distant and apart from human ken.

I returned to the village with my interest in no way abated. Now that I had seen the curious thing, my desire was still more keenly whetted to investigate the matter further and seek to learn by what strange hands and for what strange purpose the Black Stone had been reared in the long ago.

I sought out the tavern-keeper's nephew and questioned him in regard to his dreams, but he was vague, though willing to oblige. He did not mind discussing them, but was unable to describe them with any clarity. Though he dreamed the same dreams repeatedly, and though they were hideously vivid at the time, they left no distinct impression on his waking mind. He remembered them only as chaotic nightmares through which huge whirling fires shot lurid tongues of flame and a black drum bellowed incessantly. One thing only he remembered clearly - in one dream he had seen the Black Stone, not on a mountain slope but set like a spire on a colossal black castle.

As for the rest of the villagers I found them not inclined to talk about the Stone, with the exception of the schoolmaster, a man of surprising education, who spent much more of his time out in the world than any of the rest.

He was much interested in what I told him of Von Junzt's remarks about the Stone, and warmly agreed with the German author in the alleged age of the monolith. He believed that a coven had once existed in the vicinity and that possibly all of the original villagers had been members of that fertility cult which once threatened to undermine European civilization and gave rise to the tales of witchcraft. He cited the very name of the village to prove his point; it had not been originally named Stregoicavar, he said; according to legends the builders had called it Xuthltan, which was the aboriginal name of the site on which the village had been built many centuries ago.

This fact roused again an indescribable feeling of uneasiness. The barbarous name did not suggest connection with any Scythic, Slavic or Mongolian race to which an aboriginal people of these mountains would, under natural circumstances, have belonged.

That the Magyars and Slavs of the lower valleys believed the original inhabitants of the village to be members of the witchcraft cult was evident, the schoolmaster said, by the name they gave it, which name continued to be used even after the older settlers had been massacred by the Turks, and the village rebuilt by a cleaner and more wholesome breed.

He did not believe that the members of the cult erected the monolith but he did believe that they used it as a centre of their activities, and repeating vague legends which had been handed down since before the Turkish invasion, he advanced the theory that the degenerate villagers had used it as a sort of altar on which they offered human sacrifices, using as victims the girls and babies stolen from his own ancestors in the lower valleys.

He discounted the myths of weird events on Midsummer Night, as well as a curious legend of a strange deity which the witch-people of Xuthltan were said to have invoked with chants and wild rituals of flagellation and slaughter.

He had never visited the Stone on Midsummer Night, he said, but he would not fear to do so; whatever had existed or taken place there in the past, had been long engulfed in the mists of time and oblivion, had lost its meaning save as a link to a dead and dusty past.

It was while returning from a visit with this schoolmaster one night about a week after my arrival at Stregoicavar that a sudden recollection struck me—it was Midsummer Night! The very time that the legends linked with grisly implications to the Black Stone. I turned away from the tavern and strode swiftly through the village. Stregoicavar lay silent; the villagers retired early. I saw no one as I passed rapidly out of the village and up into the firs which masked the mountain's slopes with whispering darkness. A broad silver moon hung above the valley, flooding the crags and slopes in a weird light and etching the shadows blackly. No wind blew through the firs, but a mysterious, intangible rustling and whispering was abroad. Surely on such nights in past centuries, my whimsical imagination told me, naked witches astride magic broomsticks had flown across the valley, pursued by jeering demoniac familiars.

I came to the cliffs and was somewhat disquieted to note that the illusive moonlight lent them a subtle appearance I had not noticed before - in the weird light they appeared less like natural cliffs and more like the ruins of cyclopean and Titan-reared battlements jutting from the mountain-slope.

Shaking off this hallucination with difficulty I came upon the plateau and hesitated a moment before I plunged into the brooding darkness of the woods. A sort of breathless tenseness hung over the shadows, like an unseen monster holding its breath lest it scare away its prey.

I shook off the sensation - a natural one, considering the eeriness of the place and its evil reputation - and made my way through the wood, experiencing a most unpleasant sensation that I was being followed, and halting once, sure that something clammy and unstable had brushed against my face in the darkness.

I came out into the glade and saw the tall monolith rearing its gaunt height above the sward. At the edge of the woods on the side toward the cliffs was a stone which formed a sort of natural seat. I sat down, reflecting that it was probably while there that the mad poet, Justin Geoffrey, had written his fantastic *People of the Monolith*. Mine host thought that it was the Stone which had caused Geoffrey's insanity, but the seeds of madness had been sown in the poet's brain long before he ever came to Stregoicavar.

A glance at my watch showed that the hour of midnight was close at hand. I leaned back, waiting whatever ghostly demonstration might appear. A thin night wind started up among the branches of the firs, with an uncanny suggestion of faint, unseen pipes whispering an eerie and evil tune. The monotony of the sound and my steady gazing at the monolith produced a sort of self-hypnosis upon me; I grew drowsy. I fought this feeling, but sleep stole on me in spite of myself; the monolith seemed to sway and dance, strangely distorted to my gaze, and then I slept.

I opened my eyes and sought to rise, but lay still, as if an icy hand gripped me helpless. Cold terror stole over me. The glade was no longer deserted. It was thronged by a silent crowd of strange people, and my distended eyes took in strange barbaric details of costume which my reason told me were archaic and forgotten even in this backward land. Surely, I thought, these are villagers who have come here to hold some fantastic conclave - but another glance told me that these people were not the folk of Stregoicavar. They were a shorter, more squat race, whose brows were lower, whose faces were broader and duller. Some had Slavic and Magyar features, but those features were degraded as from a mixture of some baser, alien strain I could not classify. Many wore the hides of wild beasts, and their whole appearance, both men and women, was one of sensual brutishness. They terrified and repelled me, but they gave me no heed. They formed in a vast half-circle in front of the monolith and began a sort of chant, flinging their arms in unison and weaving their bodies rhythmically from the waist upward. All eyes were fixed on the top of the Stone which they seemed to be invoking. But the strangest of all was the dimness of their voices; not fifty yards from me hundreds of men and women were unmistakably lifting their voices in a wild chant, yet those voices came to me as a faint indistinguishable murmur as if from across vast leagues of Space - or time.

Before the monolith stood a sort of brazier from which a vile, nauseous yellow smoke billowed upward, curling curiously in a swaying spiral around the black shaft, like a vast unstable snake.

On one side of this brazier lay two figures - a young girl, stark naked and bound hand and foot, and an infant, apparently only a few months old. On the other side of the brazier squatted a hideous old hag with a queer sort of black drum on her lap; this drum she beat with slow light blows of her open palms, but I could not hear the sound.

The rhythm of the swaying bodies grew faster and into the space between the people and the monolith sprang a naked young woman, her eyes blazing, her long black hair flying loose. Spinning dizzily on her toes, she whirled across the open space and fell prostrate before the Stone, where she lay motionless. The next instant a fantastic figure followed her - a man from whose waist hung a goatskin, and whose features were entirely hidden by a sort of mask made from a huge wolf's head, so that he looked like a monstrous, nightmare being, horribly compounded of elements both human and bestial. In his hand he held a bunch of long fir switches bound together at the larger ends, and the moonlight glinted on a chain of heavy gold looped about his neck. A smaller chain depending from it suggested a pendant of some sort, but this was missing.

The people tossed their arms violently and seemed to redouble their shouts as this grotesque creature loped across the open space with many a fantastic leap and caper. Coming to the woman who lay before the monolith, he began to lash her with the switches he bore, and she leaped up and spun into the wild mazes of the most incredible dance I have ever seen. And her tormentor danced with her, keeping the wild rhythm, matching her every whirl and bound, while incessantly raining cruel blows on her naked body. And at every blow he shouted a single word, over and over, and all the people shouted it back. I could see the working of their lips, and now the faint far-off murmur of their voices merged and blended into one distant shout, repeated over and over with slobbering ecstasy. But what the one word was, I could not make out.

In dizzy whirls spun the wild dancers, while the lookers-on, standing still in their tracks, followed the rhythm of their dance with swaying bodies and weaving arms. Madness grew in the eyes of the capering votaress and was reflected in the eyes of the watchers. Wilder and more extravagant grew the whirling frenzy of that mad dance - it became a bestial and obscene thing, while the old hag howled and battered the drum like a crazy woman, and the switches cracked out a devil's tune.

Blood trickled down the dancer's limbs but she seemed not to feel the lashing save as a stimulus for further enormities of outrageous motion; bounding into the midst of the yellow smoke which now spread out tenuous tentacles to embrace both flying figures, she seemed to merge with that foul fog and veil herself with it. Then emerging into plain view, closely followed by the beast-thing that flogged her, she shot into an indescribable, explosive burst of dynamic mad motion, and on the very crest of that mad wave, she dropped suddenly to the sward, quivering and panting as if completely overcome by her frenzied exertions. The lashing continued with unabated violence and intensity and she began to wriggle toward the monolith on her belly. The priest - or such I will call him - followed, lashing her unprotected body with all the power of his arm as she writhed along, leaving a heavy track of blood on the trampled earth. She reached the monolith, and gasping and panting, flung both arms about it and covered the cold stone with fierce hot kisses, as in frenzied and unholy adoration.

The fantastic priest bounded high in the air, flinging away the red-dabbled switches, and the worshippers, howling and foaming at the mouths, turned on each other with tooth and nail, rending one another's garments and flesh in a blind passion of bestiality. The priest swept up the infant with a long arm, and shouting again that Name, whirled the wailing babe high in the air and dashed its brains out against the monolith, leaving a ghastly stain on the black surface. Cold with horror I saw him rip the tiny body open with his bare brutish fingers and fling handfuls of blood on the shaft, then toss the red and torn shape into the brazier, extinguishing flame and smoke in a crimson rain, while the maddened brutes behind him howled over and over the Name. Then suddenly they all fell prostrate, writhing like snakes, while the priest flung wide his gory hands as in triumph. I opened my mouth to scream my horror and loathing, but only a dry rattle sounded; a huge monstrous toad-like thing squatted on the top of the monolith!

I saw its bloated, repulsive and unstable outline against the moonlight and set in what would have been the face of a natural creature, its huge, blinking eyes which reflected all the lust, abysmal greed, obscene cruelty and monstrous evil that has stalked the sons of men since their ancestors moved blind and hairless in the treetops. In those grisly eyes were mirrored all the unholy things and vile secrets that sleep in the cities under the sea, and that skulk from the light of day in the blackness of primordial caverns. And so that ghastly thing that the unhallowed ritual of cruelty and sadism and blood had evoked from the silence of the hills, leered and blinked down on its bestial worshippers, who grovelled in abhorrent abasement before it.

Now the beast-masked priest lifted the bound and weakly writhing girl in his brutish hands and held her up toward that horror on the monolith. And as that monstrosity sucked in its breath, lustfully and slobberingly, something snapped in my brain and I fell into a merciful faint.

I opened my eyes on a still white dawn. All the events of the night rushed back on me and I sprang up, then stared about me in amazement. The monolith brooded gaunt and silent above the sward which waved, green and untrampled, in the morning breeze. A few quick strides took me across the glade; here had the dancers leaped and bounded until the ground should have been trampled bare, and here had the votaress wriggled her painful way to the Stone, streaming blood on the earth. But no drop of crimson showed on the uncrushed sward. I looked, shudderingly, at the side of the monolith against which the bestial priest had brained the stolen baby - but no dark stain nor grisly clot showed there.

A dream! It had been a wild nightmare - or else - I shrugged my shoulders. What vivid clarity for a dream!

I returned quietly to the village and entered the inn without being seen. And there I sat meditating over the strange events of the night. More and more was I prone to discard the dream-theory. That what I had seen was illusion and without material substance, was evident. But I believed that I had looked on the mirrored shadow of a deed perpetrated in ghastly actuality in bygone days. But how was I to know? What proof to show that my vision had been a gathering of foul spectres rather than a nightmare originating in my brain?

As if for answer a name flashed into my mind—Selim Bahadur! According to legend this man, who had been a soldier as well as a scribe, had commanded that part of Suleiman's army which had devastated Stregoicavar; it seemed logical enough; and if so, he had gone straight from the blotted-out countryside to the bloody field of Schomvaal, and his doom. I sprang up with a sudden shout - that manuscript which was taken from the Turk's body, and which Count Boris shuddered over - might it not contain some narration of what the conquering Turks found in Stregoicavar? What else could have shaken the iron nerves of the Polish adventurer? And since the bones of the Count had never been recovered, what more certain than that the lacquered case, with its mysterious contents, still lay hidden beneath the ruins that covered Boris Vladinoff? I began packing my bag with fierce haste.

Three days later found me ensconced in a little village a few miles from the old battlefield, and when the moon rose I was working with savage intensity on the great pile of crumbling stone that crowned the hill. It was back-breaking toil - looking back now I cannot see how I accomplished it, though I laboured without a pause from moonrise to dawn. Just as the sun was coming up I tore aside the last tangle of stones and looked on all that was mortal of Count Boris Vladinoff - only a few pitiful fragments of crumbling bone - and among them, crushed out of all original shape, lay a case whose lacquered surface had kept it from complete decay through the centuries.

I seized it with frenzied eagerness, and piling back some of the stones on the bones I hurried away; for I did not care to be discovered by the suspicious peasants in an act of apparent desecration.

Back in my tavern chamber I opened the case and found the parchment comparatively intact; and there was something else in the case - a small squat object wrapped in silk. I was wild to plumb the secrets of those yellowed pages, but weariness forbade me. Since leaving Stregoicavar I had hardly slept at all, and the terrific exertions of the previous night combined to overcome me. In spite of myself I was forced to stretch myself on my bed, nor did I awake until sundown.

I snatched a hasty supper, and then in the light of a flickering candle, I set myself to read the neat Turkish characters that covered the parchment. It was difficult work, for I am not deeply versed in the language and the archaic style of the narrative baffled me. But as I toiled through it a word or a phrase here and there leaped at me and a dimly growing horror shook me in its grip. I bent my energies fiercely to the task, and as the tale grew clearer and took more tangible form my blood chilled in my veins, my hair stood up and my tongue clove to my mouth. All external things partook of the grisly madness of that infernal manuscript until the night sounds of insects and creatures in the woods took the form of ghastly murmurings and stealthy treadings of ghoulish horrors and the sighing of the night wind changed to tittering obscene gloating of evil over the souls of men.

At last when grey dawn was stealing through the latticed window, I laid down the manuscript and took up and unwrapped the thing in the bit of silk. Staring at it with haggard eyes I knew the truth of the matter was clinched, even had it been possible to doubt the veracity of that terrible manuscript.

And I replaced both obscene things in the case, nor did I rest nor sleep nor eat until that case containing them had been weighted with stones and flung into the deepest current of the Danube which, God grant, carried them back into the Hell from which they came.

It was no dream I dreamed on Midsummer Midnight in the hills above Stregoicavar. Well for Justin Geoffrey that he tarried there only in the sunlight and went his way, for had he gazed upon that ghastly conclave, his mad brain would have snapped before it did. How my own reason held, I do not know.

No - it was no dream - I gazed upon a foul rout of votaries long dead, come up from Hell to worship as of old; ghosts that bowed before a ghost. For Hell has long claimed their hideous god. Long, long he dwelt among the hills, a brain-shattering vestige of an outworn age, but no longer his obscene talons clutch for the souls of living men, and his kingdom is a dead kingdom, peopled only by the ghosts of those who served him in his lifetime and theirs.

By what foul alchemy or godless sorcery the Gates of Hell are opened on that one eerie night I do not know, but mine own eyes have seen. And I know I looked on no living thing that night, for the manuscript written in the careful hand of Selim Bahadur narrated at length what he and his raiders found in the valley of Stregoicavar; and I read, set down in detail, the blasphemous obscenities that torture wrung from the lips of screaming worshippers; and I read, too, of the lost, grim black cavern high in the hills where the horrified Turks hemmed a monstrous, bloated, wallowing toad-like being and slew it with flame and ancient steel blessed in old times by Muhammad, and with incantations that were old when Arabia was young. And even staunch old Selim's hand shook as he recorded the cataclysmic, earth-shaking death-howls of the monstrosity, which died not alone; for half-score of his slayers perished with him, in ways that Selim would not or could not describe.

And that squat idol carved of gold and wrapped in silk was an image of himself, and Selim tore it from the golden chain that looped the neck of the slain high priest of the mask.

Well that the Turks swept out that foul valley with torch and cleanly steel! Such sights as those brooding mountains have looked on belong to the darkness and abysses of lost eons. No - it is not fear of the toad-thing that makes me shudder in the night. He is made fast in Hell with his nauseous horde, freed only for an hour on the most weird night of the year, as I have seen. And of his worshippers, none remains.

But it is the realization that such things once crouched beast-like above the souls of men which brings cold sweat to my brow; and I fear to peer again into the leaves of Von Junzt's abomination. For now I understand his repeated phrase of keys! - *aye! Keys to Outer Doors* - links with an abhorrent past and - who knows? - of abhorrent spheres of the present. And I understand why the cliffs look like battlements in the moonlight and why the tavern-keeper's nightmare-haunted nephew saw in his dream, the Black Stone like a spire on a cyclopean black castle. If men ever excavate among those mountains they may find incredible things below those masking slopes. For the cave wherein the Turks trapped the – *thing* - was not truly a cavern, and I shudder to contemplate the gigantic gulf of eons which must stretch between this age and the time when the earth shook herself and reared up, like a wave, those blue mountains that, rising, enveloped unthinkable things. May no man ever seek to uproot that ghastly spire men call the Black Stone!

A Key! Aye, it is a Key, symbol of a forgotten horror. That horror has faded into the limbo from which it crawled, loathsomely, in the black dawn of the earth. But what of the other fiendish possibilities hinted at by Von Junzt - what of the monstrous hand which strangled out his life? Since reading what Selim Bahadur wrote, I can no longer doubt anything in the *Black Book*. Man was not always master of the earth - and is he now?

And the thought recurs to me - if such a monstrous entity as the Master of the Monolith somehow survived its own unspeakably distant epoch so long - what nameless shapes may even now lurk in the dark places of the world?

WEREWOLF OF THE SAHARA
G. G. Pendarves

The three of them were unusually silent that night over their after-dinner coffee. They were camping outside the little town of Sollum on the Libyan coast of North Africa. For three weeks they had been delayed here en route for the Siwa oasis. Two men and a girl.

"So we really start tomorrow," Merle Anthony blew a cloud of smoke toward the glittering night sky. "I'm almost sorry. Sollum's been fun. And I've done two of the best pictures I ever made here."

"Was that why you burned them up yesterday?" her cousin, Dale Fleming, inquired in his comfortable pleasant voice.

The girl's clear pallor slowly crimsoned. "Dale! What a -"

"It's all right, Merle," Gunnar Sven interrupted her. "Dale's quite right. Why pretend this delay has done you any good? And it's altogether my fault. I found that out today in the market. Overheard some Arabs discussing our expedition to Siwa."

"Your fault!" Merle's beautiful face, and eyes grey as a gull's wing, turned to him. "Why, you've simply slaved to get the caravan ready."

Gunnar got to his feet and walked out to the verge of the headland on which they were camped. Tall, straight as a pine he stood.

The cousins watched him; the girl with trouble and perplexity, the man more searchingly. His eyes, under straight upper lids, flatly contradicted the rest of his appearance. He was very fat, with fair hair and smooth unlined face despite his forty years. A sort of Pickwickian good humour radiated from him. Dale Fleming's really great intellectual power showed only in those three-cornered heavily-lidded eyes of his.

"Why did you give me away?" Merle demanded.

His round moon face beamed on her.

"Why bluff?" he responded.

"Snooping about as usual. Why don't you go and be a real detective?" she retorted crossly.

He gave a comfortable chuckle, but his eyes were sad. It was devilishly hard to watch her falling for this Icelander. Ever since his parents had adopted her - an orphan of six - she had come first in Dale's affections. His love was far from Platonic. Gunnar Sven was a fine creature, but there was something wrong. Some mystery shadowed his life. What it was, Dale was determined to discover.

"Truth will out, my child! The natives are in terror of him. You know it as well as I do! They're all against helping you and me because he's our friend."

"Stop being an idiot. No one could be afraid of Gunnar. And he's particularly good with natives."

"Yes. He handles them well. I've never seen a young 'un do it better."

"Well, then?"

"There's something queer about him. These Arabs know it. We know it. It's about two months now since he joined forces with us. Just after my mother decamped and left us in Cairo. The cable summoning her home to Aunt Sue's death-bed arrived Wednesday, May 3rd. She sailed May 5th. Gunnar Sven turned up May 6th."

"All right. I'm not contradicting you. It's never any use."

"You refused to wait for Mother's return in Cairo, according to her schedule."

"Well! Cairo! Everyone paints Cairo and the Nile. I

wanted subjects that every five-cent tourist hadn't raved over."

"You wanted Siwa Oasis. Of all God-forsaken dangerous filthy places! And in the summer -"

"You know you're dying to see the oasis too," she accused. "Just trying to save your face as my guardian and protector. Hypocrite!"

He roared with laughter. The Arab cook and several other servants stopped singing round their cooking-pots to grin at the infectious sound.

"*Touche!* I'd sacrifice my flowing raven locks to go to Siwa. But" - his face grew surprisingly stern - "about Gunnar. Why does he take such enormous pains not to tell us the name of the man he's been working for?"

"I've never asked him."

"I haven't in so many words, of course. But I've led him up to the fence over and over again. He's steadily refused it. With good reason."

"Well?"

"He works for an Arab. A sheykh. A man notorious from Morocco to Cairo. His nickname's Sheykh El Afrit. The Magician! His real name is Sheykh Zura El Shabur."

"And what's so earth-shaking about that?" asked Merle, patting a dark curl into place behind her ear.

"He's a very – bad - hat! Black Magic's no joke in this country. This Sheykh El Shabur's gone far. Too far."

"I'm going to talk to Gunnar. He'll tell me. It's fantastic. Gunnar and Black Magic indeed!"

Dale watched her, amused and touched. How she loathed subtleties and mysteries and tangled situations!

"She'd waltz up to a lion and pull its whiskers if anyone told her they were false. As good at concealment as a searchlight."

Gunnar turned from the sea as Merle walked purposefully in his direction. He stood beside her - mountain pine overshadowing a little silver birch.

"H-m-m!" Dale threw away a freshly lighted cigarette and took another. "Merle and I wouldn't suggest that. More like Friar Tuck and Maid Marian."

He was startled to see Gunnar suddenly leap and turn. The man looked as if he'd had a tremendous shock. He stood peering across the wastelands stretching eastward, frozen into an attitude of utmost horror.

Dale ran across to Merle. She broke from his detaining hand and rushed to Gunnar's side.

"What is it? What do you see? Gunnar! Answer me, Gunnar!"

His tense muscles relaxed. He sighed, and brushed a hand across his eyes and wet forehead.

"He's found me. He's coming. I had hoped never -"

"Who? What are you talking about?"

She shook his arm in terror at his wild look and words.

"He said I was free! *Free!* I wouldn't have come near you if I'd known he lied. Now I've brought him into your life. Merle! Forgive me!"

He took her hands, kissed them frantically, then turned to Dale with burning haste and fairly pushed him away.

"Go! Go! Go! Now - before he comes. Leave everything! Ride for your lives. He'll force me to... go! *Go!*"

"*Ma yarudd!* What means this, Gunnar - my servant?"

The deep guttural voice seemed to come up from the bowels of the earth. The three turned as if a bomb had exploded. A figure loomed up not ten feet away. Merle stared with wide startled eyes. A minute ago the level wasteland had shown bare, deserted. How had this tall Arab approached unseen?

Gunnar seemed to shrink and wither. His face was tragic.

The newcomer fixed him for a long moment in silence, staring him down.

"What means this, Gunnar, my servant?" Once more the words vibrated through the still night.

The Icelander made a broken ineffectual movement of his hands, and began to speak. His voice died away into low, vague murmurings.

"For this you shall account to me later," promised the tall Arab.

He strode forward. His black burnoose rippled and swayed about him. Its peaked hood was drawn close. A long face with pointed black beard, proud curving nose, and eyes dark and secret as forest pools gleamed beneath the hood.

Merle shrank back. Her fingers clutched Gunnar's. They were cold and limp in her grasp.

Dale leaned forward, peering into the Arab's face as a connoisseur examines an etching of rare interest.

"You speak very good English, my friend. Or is it enemy?"

The whole demeanour of the Arab changed. His white teeth flashed. He held out welcoming hands, clasped Dale's in his own, and bowed low to the girl. He turned last to the Icelander.

"Present me!" he ordered.

Gunnar performed the small ceremony with white lips. His voice sounded as if he'd been running hard.

"Zura El Shabur. Zura of the Mist," translated the sheykh. "I am your friend. I have many friends of your Western world. The language! All languages are one to me!"

Dale beamed. "Ah! Good linguist and all that! Jolly good name yours, what! Gave us quite a scare, popping up out of the atmosphere like Aladdin's djinnee!"

El Shabui's thin lips again showed his teeth.

"Those that dwell in the desert's solitude and silence learn to reflect its qualities."

"Quite! Quite!" Dale gurgled happy agreement. "Neat little accomplishment. Very convenient - for you!"

"Convenient on this occasion for you also, since my coming prevented the inhospitality of my servant from driving you away."

"No! You're wrong there. Gunnar's been our guardian angel for weeks past. Given us a wonderful time."

"Nevertheless, I heard that he urged you to go - to go quickly from Solium."

Dale burst into laughter; long, low gurgles that relieved tension all around. "I'm one of those fools that'd rather lose a pot of gold than alter my plans. One of the camel-drivers has made off with a few bits of loot. You heard the thrifty Gunnar imploring me to follow him."

Merle backed up the tale with quick wit. "Nothing of vast importance. My silver toilet things, a leather bag, and a camera. Annoying, but hardly worth wasting hours to retrieve."

She came forward, all anxiety to give Gunnar time to pull himself together.

El Shabur made her a second low obeisance and stared down into her upturned vivid face. "Such youth and beauty must be served. Shall I send Gunnar after the thief?"

The idea of separation gave her a shock. Intuition warned her to keep the Icelander at her side for his sake, and for her own. Together there seemed less danger.

Danger! From what? Why did the word drum through her brain like an S.O.S. signal? She glanced at Gunnar. His face was downbent.

"No." She met the Arab's eyes with effort and gave a valiant little smile. "No. Indeed not. We can't spare him. He's promised to come with us, to be our guide to the Siwa Oasis."

"Hope this won't clash with your plans for him. We've got

so dependent on his help now." Dale's cherubic face registered anxiety.

"So." The Arab put a hand on Gunnar's shoulder. "It is good. You have done well."

The young man shivered. His eyes met Merle's in warning.

El Shabur turned to reassure her and Dale.

"Now all goes well. I, too, will join your caravan. It is necessary for my - my work - that I should visit Siwa very soon. I go also."

Dale took the outstretched hand. "Fine! Fine! We'll make a record trip now."

In his tent, Dale slept after many hours of hard, concentrated thought and intellectual work - very pink, very tired, younger-looking than ever in his profound repose.

In her tent, Merle lay quiet too.

Native servants snored, shapeless cocoons in their blankets. Even the camels had stopped moaning and complaining, and couched peacefully, barracked in a semicircle. Great mounds of baggage within its wide curve lay ready for loading.

Moonlight silvered long miles of grass and rushes. Leagues of shining water swung in almost tideless rhythm half a mile from camp.

Gunnar looked out on the scene from his tent. What had roused him from sleep? Why was his heart thumping, and the blood drumming in his ears? He peered out into the hushed world.

Tents, men, camels and baggage showed still as things on a painted canvas. He left his tent, made a noiseless detour about the sleeping camp, then frowned and stared about in all directions.

A bird, rising on startled wing, made him look sharply at

an old Turkish fort. It stood, grim and battered sentinel, on a near-by promontory of Solium Bay. Through its gaping ruined walls he caught a glint of fire - green, livid, wicked names that stained the night most evilly.

"El Shabur! Already! The Pentacle of Fire!"

His whisper was harsh as the faint drag of pebbles on the shore. For several minutes he stood as if chained. Fear and anger warred with dawning resolution and a wild anxiety. Then he stumbled over to Merle's tent and tore open its flap. Flashlight in hand, he went in and stared down at the sleeping girl. She lay white and rigid as if in a trance. Gunnar touched her forehead, took up a limp hand in his own. She gave no sign of life.

He stood looking down at the still, waxen features. The rather square, resolute little face was uniformly white, even to the curved, just-parted lips. The hair seemed wrought in metal, so black and heavy and lifeless did it wave above the broad, intelligent brow. Gunnar looked in awe. The girl's animated, sparkling face was changed to something remote and strange and exquisite. Half child, half priestess.

"And in a few short weeks or months," he muttered, "El Shabur will initiate her. This is the first step. She will rot – perish - as I am doing!"

He bent, in passionate horror, over the still face.

"No! No! Not for you! Dear lovely child!"

He clenched his hands. "But if I disturb him now!"

For minutes he stood irresolute. Fear took him by the throat. He could not - he could not interfere! At last his will steadied. He mastered the sick terror that made him tremble and shiver like a beaten dog. As he left the tent, he glanced back once more.

"Good-bye! I'll do all I can," he promised softly. "I'd give my soul to save you - if I still had one."

He ran to the headland where the old fort stood. If El

Shabur's occupation was what he feared, he would neither hear nor see. Intensely concentrating on his rites, nothing in the visible world would reach him.

Gunnar's calculations were justified. He went boldly in through the arched entrance to an inner court where green fires burned in a great ring, five points of two interlacing triangles which showed black upon the grey dust of the floor. In the centre of this cabalistic symbol stood El Shabur, clothed in black. The rod he held was of black ebony.

Gunnar drew breath. He listened to the toneless continuous muttering of the sheykh. What point had El Shabur reached in his conjurations? How long since he had drawn Merle's soul from the lovely quiet body lying in her tent? It was of vital importance to know. If the devilish business was only begun, he might free her. If El Shabur had reached the last stage, closed the door behind the soul he was luring from its habitation, then it was fatally late.

He listened, head thrust forward, trying to distinguish the rapidly muttered words.

"Shekinah! Aralim! Ophanim! Assist me in the name of Melek Taos, Ruler of wind and stars and sea, who commands the four elements in the might of Adonai and the Ancient Ones!"

"A-h-h-h!" Gunnar gave a deep gasping sigh of relief. He was not too late. Sheykh El Shabur called on his allies. Merle's spirit was not yet cut off from its home. Her will resisted the Arab's compulsion.

He leaped forward, oversetting all five braziers. Their fire spilled and died out instantly. In the cold clear moonlight, El Shabur loomed tall, menacing. He stood glaring across the courtyard at the intruder. His black-clad figure overshadowed the Icelander's by many inches, like a cloud, like a bird of prey. Malignant, implacable he towered.

Gunnar's golden head sank. His strong, straight body seemed to shrink and crumple. Inch by inch he retreated, until he reached the wall. He tried to meet the Arab's unblinking stare and failed. Again his bright head sank. His eyes sought the dusty earth. But his whole frame trembled with a wild, fanatical excitement. He had succeeded so far - had brought El Shabur back from that void where Merle's spirit had so perilously wandered. She was free. Free to go back to that still white body lying in her tent.

"So! You love this girl. You would save her from me. You - who cannot save yourself!"

"You're right." The young man's voice shook. "Right as far as I'm concerned. But Miss Anthony's on a different plane. You're not going to play your filthy tricks on her."

"So! It would seem that, in spite of my teaching, you are not yet well disciplined. Have you forgotten your vow? Have you forgotten that a cabalist may never retreat one inch of the road he treads? Have you forgotten the punishment that overtakes the renegade?"

"I would die to save her from you."

The other showed white teeth in a mirthless sardonic grin.

"Die!" echoed his deep, mocking voice. "Death is not for us. Are you not initiated and under protection? What can bring death to such as you?"

"There must be a way of escape for me - and for her. I will defeat you yet, El Shabur!"

The Icelander's voice rose. His eyes were blazing. He stepped forward. Moonlight touched his shining hair, his passion-contorted features, his angry, bloodshot eyes. Control slipped from him. He strove in vain to recapture it, to use his reason. He knew that anger was delivering him bound and helpless into his enemy's hands. It had been so from their first encounter. Emotion versus reason. He knew his fatal weakness, and strove against it now - in vain. Long habit ruled. Anger made his will a thing of straw.

"You would defy me - the Power I serve - the Power that serves me?"

Gunnar felt the blood rushing to his head. His ears sang. Red mist obscured his sight.

"You are a devil! And you serve devils!" he shouted. "But you won't always win the game! Curse you, El Shabur! Curse you! Curse you!"

The Arab looked long into his angry eyes, and came closer. With an incredibly swift movement he clasped the shaking, furious figure.

Gunnar felt dry lips touch his ears and mouth and brow, heard a low quick mutter. Then El Shabur released him suddenly, and stood back.

"Ignorant and beast-like! Be what you are - slave to your own passion! You, yourself, create the devil that haunts you. Therefore are you mine - for all devils are subject to me. Be what you are! Out, beast! Howl and snarl with your own kind until the dawn."

For a moment something dark scuffled in the dust at El Shabur's feet. The courtyard rang with a long, desolate howl. A shadow, lean and swift, fled from the camp, far, far out across the empty wasteland.

At sunset, the next day, Dale Fleming and his caravan reached Bir Augerin, the first well on their march. They had delayed their start some hours. Merle had insisted in waiting for Gunnar, but he had not turned up.

"He will join us en route," the sheykh had assured her. "He is well used to desert travel, Mademoiselle!"

"But his camel?"

"We will take it. He can easily hire another."

"Have you no idea why he went off and left us without warning? It's so unlike him."

El Shabur gave his dark unmirthful smile.

"He is young. Young and careless and - undisciplined. He has - friends. Oh, he is popular! That golden hair of his - it has a fascination..."

Merle's face crimsoned and grew pale. Dale's round face concealed his thoughts. He glanced at the Arab's lean hands that twisted a stiff length of wire rope with such slow and vicious strength. He had learned how betraying hands may be.

Merle made no more objections, and at 3:30 p.m. the caravan set out. The natives were superstitious about a journey's start. Mondays, Thursdays and Saturdays were fortunate; and Saturday the luckiest of the week.

At Bir Augerin, camp was quickly made. The servants drew up water from the large rectangular tank in leather buckets. Merle sat disconsolate to watch, and smoke, and think of Gunnar. Dale joined her, leaving the sheykh to direct the men.

"I don't believe it!" Merle burst out.

"About our absent friend?"

"Gunnar's not that sort. I think they've had a quarrel. Dale!" She put a beseeching hand on his arm. "You don't think - he wouldn't kill Gunnar!"

"My prophetic bones tell me not." He patted the hand in brisk, business-like fashion. "He'll turn up and explain himself. Don't worry. This Sheykh of the Mist's a queer old josser. About as trustworthy as a black panther, but the boy's too useful to be killed off in a hurry. All the same - look here, Merle: keep this handy at night."

He put a small snub-nosed automatic in her hand.

"It's loaded. And I've taught you to use it. Listen! There are wolves on this trail. Heard 'em last night about the camp."

"Wolves? In the desert? Jackals, you mean."

"Don't speak out of turn. Wolves. You know - things that

go off like this."

He threw back his head and gave a blood-curdling howl that electrified the camp. El Shabur spun on his heel, long knife drawn. The servants grovelled, then ran to pluck brands from the fire.

Dale gave a rich, infectious gurgle. "Splendid! Must have done that jolly well. Now perhaps you'll recognize a wolf when you hear it. If you do - shoot!"

Soon after four a.m. the caravan set out again in the chill clear moonlight. In spite of grilling days, the nights remained cool and made travel easy. They reached their next halt, Bir Hamed, about eight o'clock. This cistern was the last before real desert began. They decided to give the camels a good day's grazing and watering and push off again in the small hours before dawn.

Cooking-pots were slung over crackling fires. Fragrance of wood smoke mingled with odour of frying sausages and onions. Dale went over and implored the cook to refrain from using last night's dish-water to brew coffee. El Shabur approached Merle and pointed to the east.

"He comes."

She dropped a camera and roll of films and jumped to her feet.

"Who? Gunnar? I see no one."

"He comes riding from over there."

Low rolling dunes to the east showed bare and smooth and empty of life. She stared, and frowned at the speaker. "I see nothing. Dale!" she called out. "The sheykh says Gunnar's coming from over there. Can you see him?"

Dale scrutinized the empty eastern horizon, then turned to El Shabur with a bland wide smile. "Ah, you wonderful Arabs! Putting one over on us, aren't you? You people have extra valve sets. Pick up things from the ether. It's enough to give me an inferiority complex."

He thrust an arm through Merle's. "If he says so, it is so! I'll tell cook to fry a few more sausages.

"Servants are all in a state of jim-jams this morning," he said as he returned from his hospitable errand. "Ilbrahaim's been handing out samples from the Thousand and One Nights' Entertainments, What d'you suppose he's started now?"

"They talk much," the sheykh's deep scornful voice replied. "And they say nothing."

"Ilbrahaim is a chatty little fellow. Be invaluable at a funeral, wouldn't he? Distract the mourners and all that! Unless he got on to vampires and ghouls. He's keen on cabalistic beliefs."

"Such things are childish; they have no interest for a cabalist."

"No - really! Well, you probably know. Is there a place called Bilad El Kelab?"

El Shabur's eyes glinted. His chin went up in a gesture of assent.

"There is? Ah, then Ilbrahaim tells the truth now and then. His brother went to this place. Country of the Dogs - suggestive name! The yarn is that all the men there turn to dogs at sunset. Like werewolves, you know."

"Bilad El Kelab is far away. South - far south in the Sudan. Ilbrahaim has no brother, moreover."

"No?"

"No. There are many foolish legends from the Sudan."

"Not so foolish. I'm interested in folklore and legend and primitive beliefs. That's why I'm going to Siwa, apart from looking after my little cousin here."

El Shabur's eyes smouldered. "It is unwise to be too curious about such things. That which feeds an eagle is no meat for a fish."

"Quite! Quite! Good that, isn't it, Merle? Meaning we Westerners are fish! Oh, definitely good! This Ilbrahaim, though - he swears our camp's being haunted. He thinks a weredog, or werewolf, has attached itself to us. Says he woke and saw it prowling about last night."

"A long trail from the Bilad El Kelab!"

"You're right, El Shabur. Still, what's a few hundred miles to a werewolf? And I suppose it travels on camel-back by day, if it's got its man's body in good repair. Have to be a new camel each morning - eh? Not likely a self-respecting mehari would trot hoof in paw with a wolf each night."

"Dale! Is it the same wolf you said was -"

A cousinly kick on the ankle, as Dale moved to replace a blazing branch on the fire, warned her.

"Is it the wolf-tale they talked about in Alexandria?" she switched off quickly.

"Dear child!" Dale beamed approval. "How your little wits do work! No! That wolf was a jackal that haunted the Valley of the Kings in Egypt."

El Shabur turned his head sharply. "The lost one arrives," he remarked.

In the distance, magnified and distorted by the hot desert air, a vast camel and rider loomed. Merle lighted a cigarette with slow, unsteady hands.

"It may be anyone. Impossible to tell yet."

The sheykh spread his hands. "Mademoiselle will soon discover."

In half an hour, Gunnar rode into Camp. A sorry figure, dishevelled, unshaven, he looked as if he'd been across Africa with a minimum of food and sleep. Merle had meant to be unrelenting at first, to await explanation, but her heart betrayed her at sight of this desperately weary man. She ran to meet him as he dismounted, and tried to lead him over to where Dale and the Arab sat smoking.

He stood swaying on his feet. "No. Not now." His cracked, parched lips could scarcely frame the words. "I must sleep. I-I could not help it. I was prevented - I was prevented," he croaked.

"Gunnar - of course!" She beckoned to a servant. "Take care of him. I'll send Dale effendi to give him medicine. He is ill."

In the late afternoon the camp was in more or less of an uproar. The camels were driven in from pasturage to drink once again. They would have preferred to go on grazing, and, being camels, they expressed disapproval noisily, and gave much trouble to the cursing, sweating men.

Dale sauntered off from their vicinity. The sun was casting shadows that lengthened steadily. He stopped in the shadow of a huge boulder and stared thoughtfully out across the barren desert.

"Got his goat all right about that legend and the cabalists. Now, just why did that strike home? The pattern's there, but all in little moving bits. I can't get the confounded mosaic right. Cabalists! Werewolves! Gunnar and the Sheykh of the Mist! Haunted camp and all the rest of it! A very, very pretty little mix-up. I wonder now... I wonder..."

His eyes, fixed in abstracted non-seeing gaze, suddenly became wary. His big body grew taut. Then, with the lightness of movement for which fat men are often remarkable, he vanished into a cleft of the great rock. His hearing was acute and voices carried far in the desert stillness.

"...until we reach Siwa. From sunrise to sunset I will be with her." Gunnar's bitterness was apparent. "If you interfere I will tell her what you are!"

"In return I will explain what you are - after sunset!" El Shabur's voice mocked. "Will the knowledge make her turn to you for protection?"

"You devil!"

"You fool! Do not meddle with power you cannot control. Until Siwa, then."

They passed out of earshot. Dale watched them return to camp.

"More bite of mosaic, nice lurid colour, too. Looks as though Siwa's going to be even more promising than I imagined. Evil old city, enough to make one write another *Book of Revelations*?"

The sun cast long shadows, stretching grotesquely over pink-stained leagues of sand. Dale was anxious to watch Gunnar when the sun actually did set; he felt that phrase of the young Icelander's had been significant: *From sunrise to sunset I will be with her*. Rather an odd poetic reference to time! Taken in conjunction with his unexplained disappearance last night, it was specially odd.

Dale ambled slowly in the direction of camp, empty pipe between his teeth. He had stayed a long hour. From his rocky crevice, he had watched Gunnar and the Arab return, seen Gunnar start off again with Merle into the desert. The two were returning now - dark against the reddening sky.

He was curious to see how the young man was going to behave; what explanation, if any, he had given to Merle. He was overwhelmingly anxious to discover just how far she returned the love that burned so steadfastly in Gunnar's eyes. If it was serious - really serious - with her, the whole queer dangerous situation was going to be deadly.

She would go her own way. If her heart was given, it was given, for good or evil. It seemed entirely evil, in his judgment, if she had decided to link her fate with this Icelander.

And El Shabur! How dangerous was this notorious Arab

magician? Men of his practises fairly haunted desert cities and oases. Mostly they were harmless, sometimes genuinely gifted in the matter of prophecy. Rarely, they were men of inexplicable and very terrible power; who were dedicated, brain and body, to the cause of evil - evil quite beyond the comprehension of normal people.

Dale's eyes were cold and implacable as he recollected one or two such men he had known: his pleasant face looked unbelievably austere and grim.

One way or another, Merle stood in imminent and pressing danger; from Gunnar, no less than from El Shabur; from Gunnar, not because he was of himself evil, but because he was a channel through which the Arab could reach her. She was vulnerable in proportion to her love. There were infinite sources of danger ahead. El Shabur had a definite plan regarding her, something that would mature at Siwa. Three days remained to discover the nature of that plan.

Three days! Perhaps not even that. Gunnar's relations with the Arab seemed dangerously explosive; a crisis might work up at any moment. Merle would then be implicated, for she would defend Gunnar with blind partisanship. All the odds were on El Shabur. It was his country; he could queer the expedition easily without any supernatural agency. And, if he were the deadly poisonous creature Dale began to suspect, then the lonely desert made a superb background for murder... he called it murder to himself, unwilling to give a far more terrible name to what he suspected El Shabur might do.

The lovers, walking slowly, reluctantly back to camp, were completely absorbed in each other.

"If only I'd known you earlier!" The man's sunken eyes looked down on the erect, slim, lovely girl beside him with immense regret.

"The only thing we can do about it is to make up for lost

time, darling."

He stopped, faced her, took both firm, lather square hands in his own. "Merle, you're being a miracle. But it's impossible. I oughtn't to have told you how much I cared."

"Poor dear! You hadn't any choice, really. I did the leap year stunt before you could stop me; and, being a little gent, you simply had to say you loved me, too!"

She rattled away, hardly knowing what she said. "I've got to alter that look in his eyes," she told herself. "I thought it was because of me, conceited little beast that I am. But it isn't - it isn't!

"Gunnar," she tackled him with characteristic impetuosity, "Is your fear of El Shabur the biggest thing in your life? Is it bigger than - than your love for me?"

The grip of his hands tightened. His face bent to hers. His haunted red-rimmed eyes looked into her candid grey ones, that shone with love and kindness and a steadfast unwavering trust that made him want to kiss her dusty shoes. Instead, he dropped her hands, pulled his hat down over his face, walked on with quickened stride toward the distant encampment.

"It's no use... I can't go on with it. I'm in a tangle that no one on earth can straighten out. It's revolting to think of you being caught up in such a beastly mess. I went into this thing because I was a young inquisitive fool! I'd no idea what it involved, no idea at all that there was something behind it stronger... stronger than death! I was blind, I was credulous, I was utterly ignorant; I walked into El Shabur's trap - and the door shut behind me!"

"Gunnar, darling, can't you explain? People don't have to go on serving masters they hate unless – unless -"

"Exactly! Unless they're slaves. Well, I am his slave."

"I don't understand you."

"Thank heaven for it, and don't try! It's because you must

never, never understand such things that I wanted you and Dale to go away that night at Sollum."

"If you owe the sheykh your time, can't you buy him off? Surely any contract can be broken."

"Not the one that binds me to him. Listen, Merle, my own! I can't - I daren't say more than this. Think of him as a poison - as something that blackens and burns like vitriol. Will you do what may seem a very childish thing, will you do it to please me?"

"What is it?"

"Tie this across the entrance of your sleeping-tent at night." He held out a little coloured plait, four threads of green, white, red, and black, from which a seal depended. "Once more, I daren't explain, but use it. Promise me!"

Taken aback by his tone and manner, she promised. What, she thought, had a bit of coloured string to do with all this mystery about him and the sheykh? A fleeting doubt as to his sanity came to her.

"No," he answered the look. "I was never more sane than now - when it's too late. Too late for myself, at least. You - nothing shall happen to you!"

"Won't you talk to Dale? He's such a queer wise old thing, I'm sure he could help if only you'd explain things to him."

"No. Not yet, at any rate. Not until we get to Siwa. I'll explain everything then. Silence is the price I've paid to be with you on this trip."

"But, really Dale is -"

"If you don't want him to die suddenly, say nothing to him. Anyone that interferes with El Shabur gets rubbed out like this!"

Gunnar stamped a small pebble deep into the sand.

"All right," she promised with a shiver. That quick vicious little movement had given her a sudden horrid fear of the sheykh - more than all Gunnar's words. "I'll say nothing. But Dale is pretty hard to deceive. There never seems any need to tell him things; he just knows them. I expect he's burrowing away underground about El Shabur already, just like an old ferret! I happen to know he loathes him."

"Nobody'd think so to see them chinwagging."

"He behaves like a garrulous moron when he's putting salt on anyone's tail, and I've seldom seen him wallowing quite so idiotically as now."

"Much more likely the sheykh's putting salt on his tail by pretending to believe Dale's a fool."

"You don't know Dale."

"You don't know El Shabur." Gunnar had the last word - it proved to be accurate.

They found the two in camp and deep in talk.

"Arguing about our pet werewolf." Dale was bland. "Will you sit up with me and try a pot shot at the beast, Gunnar?"

The tall Icelander stood in silence. His face was a grey mask, his sunken eyes stared hard and long into the other's blank smooth face. He turned to the sheykh at length.

"You suggested this?"

Merle shivered at his voice.

The Arab shrugged. "On the contrary. It would be wisdom to sleep before tomorrow's march. If the effendi desires to hunt it would be well to wait until we reach the hills of Siwa."

"Well," Dale seemed determined to prolong the discussion, "what do you vote for, old man? The werewolf tonight, or the Siwa hills later?"

"The hills - definitely, the hills," the young man's voice cracked on a laugh, "According to legend, you can't kill a werewolf. No use wasting our shots and a night's sleep too."

"Thwarted!" moaned Dale. "The hills of Siwa, then. You can promise good hunting there, Sheykh?"

"By my sacred wasm."

"Wasm?" Dale lighted a cigarette with casual air.

"My mark, my insignia, my tribal sign. It is like heraldry in your land."

"Heavens above! I must remember to call my little label a wasm in future. Intriguing word, that! And what is your mark?"

El Shabur leaned forward and traced it in the sand. Dale regarded it with a smile that masked deep uneasiness. He recognized the ghastly little sign; he was one of the very few who had the peculiar knowledge to do so. A smoke-screen from his eternal pipe shielded his face from the watchful Arab. Was El Shabur trying to trick him into exposing his very special and intimate knowledge of the occult; or did he make that deadly mark feeling sure that only an initiate would recognize it?

El Shabur was a Yezidee, a Satanist, and worshipped Melek Taos. The symbol was unmistakably the outspread tail of the Angel-Peacock. Dale recoiled inwardly at having his darkest fears confirmed; he knew of no tribe on earth more vicious and powerful than the Yezidees, Their name and their fame went back into mists of time. Seldom did one of them leave his hills and rock-dwelling up beyond Damascus. Once in a century or so, throughout the ages, a priest of the Yezidees would stalk the earth like a black destroying god to acquaint himself with the world and its conditions. He would return to teach his tribe. So they remained, a nucleus of evil power that never seemed to die out.

"Nice little design; looks like half a ray-fish," he commented. Impossible to fathom what was going on behind the sheykh's carven, immobile features. "Wasm - did you say? Wait, I must write that down."

The whites of the Arab's eyes glinted as he glanced at Merle. "Are you like your cousin in this - do you also suffer from loss of memory?"

"I – we - what do you mean?"

"You have a saying in your Book of Wisdom, "Thy much learning doth turn thee to madness.' The effendi is like to that man, Paul. For who, after years and years of study, could forget so simple a thing as a wasm?"

Dale didn't move a muscle. His bluff was called. All right! On with the next dance! Too late he realized why the Arab had started the absorbing wasm topic. It had been intended to shock and distract his own thoughts from Gunnar - to prevent his keeping an eye on him.

The Icelander had got up and gone over to his tent a minute ago with a murmur about tobacco. He had not returned. Dale was on his feet and peering into Gunnar's tent in a flash. No one there. He looked at the western horizon - the sun had dipped beyond it. He scanned the desert. It offered no shelter for Gunnar's six feet of height. He looked into every tent; saw that only the servants crouched before their fires, that only baggage lay heaped upon the ground.

Shadows were melting into dusk. But one long shadow seemed to move over there among the dunes not far away! Were his own dark thoughts inventing the thing that fled across the desert?

The darkest thought of all came as he went back to Merle and the silent watchful Arab. Was he a match for this man?

"You needn't worry about Gunnar. The Arab's at the back of these nightly disappearances, I'm quite certain, although the reasons he gave were of his own invention."

"Then you think he'll come back?" Merle looked tired and anxious in the light of her small lamp.

"He'll come back," asserted the man. "Good night, old lady. If you feel nervous or want anything, just give a yelp. I'll be awake - got to finish a bit of research work."

She caught a look that belied his cheerful voice. "Why

d'you look round my tent like that? Is there any special danger - that wolf?"

"Well, I don't mind telling you there is a spot of danger. You're not the sort that goes off like a repeating-rifle at being warned. But - have you got your doodah handy?"

She showed the automatic underneath her pillow. "Perhaps I ought to tell you that Gunnar warned me too. No. Not about the wolf, but El Shabur."

"Worse than a whole pack of wolves," he agreed. "Know where you are with those noisy brutes, but the sheykh's another cup of tea, entirely."

"He gave me this. Told me to tie up my tent with it. Queer, don't you think?"

He examined the plait of coloured string with profound interest.

"Jerusalem the Golden! If we ever reach dry land again, this will be an heirloom for you to hand on. That is, unless you're hard up and want to sell it to some Croesus for a sack of diamonds. This, my dear Black-eyed Susan, is a relic dating back thousands of years. The seal, of course, not the threads. It's an emerald. And that's the Eye of Horus cut in it."

"Emerald! It must be fearfully valuable. How on earth d'you think Gunnar got it?"

"From his master the sheykh. It's the sort of thing he'd need, poor fellow! It's a safeguard - oh, quite infallible."

"I never know when you're serious or when you're just being idiotic. Protection from what? What does it mean?"

"It means that El Shabur's a cabalist. And that Gunnar is an initiate and pretty far advanced too, to be in possession of this very significant thing. He's gone a long, long way on the road - poor lad!"

"He's in danger?"

"Extreme and imminent danger; there's scarcely a chance to cut him free now. Better face the thing, dear. Gunnar's not in a position to love or marry any woman; he's tied body and soul to El Shabur. It's a hideous, deplorable, ghastly mess, the whole affair." He sat down beside her on the little truckle bed and took her hand. "This is my fault. I knew well enough even at Solium that there was something abnormal about Gunnar."

"I love him," she answered very quietly, "and nothing can ever alter that. Whatever he's done, or is - I love him."

He stared at her a long minute. "And that's the damndest part of the whole show," he remarked with immense gravity.

He turned back at the tent opening. "About that thing Gunnar gave you. Fasten the tent-flap with it if you value your soul; wear it under your dress by day, never let the sheykh catch a glimpse of it. We reach Siwa the day after tomorrow. Try not to let El Shabur know we suspect anything, meantime. Sure you're all right - not afraid?"

"Not for myself. I don't understand what it's all about. But I'm afraid for my poor Gunnar. He's the sort that can't stand alone. Not like you and me, we're too hard-headed old things!"

"You're a wonder. Any other girl stranded here with a half-mad native sorcerer would go right up the pole. Tie up your tent, though, d'you hear?"

"The moment you've gone. Cross my heart!"

Night wore swiftly on. Dale sat smoking in his own tent, fully dressed, alert and expectant. He felt convinced that something was in the wind tonight. The sound of shots far off across the desert took him outside, rifle in hand. Sleep held the camp; not a man had stirred. The black Bedouin tent in which the sheykh slept was closed. No one seemed to have been disturbed except himself. Again came that queer little tug of his senses - a warning of danger near.

His grip tightened on his weapon. He went on more

slowly. A shadow seemed to move round the great mass of rock which had sheltered him a few hours ago. He halted half-way between rock and camp. Should he go back and rouse the men? Or should he go closer and inspect for himself? He walked on.

A high, piping wind blew clouds across the sky. A black mass obscured the moon. He halted once more, turned back to camp in a sudden certainty of peril. Too late. A rush. A scuffle. An arm of steel clasped him from behind, a hand like a vice was clamped across his lips before he could call out. His big body was enormously muscular and he fought like a tiger, threw off his assailant, shouted loudly. The strong wind shouted louder, tore his voice to shreds. It swept the black cloud from the moon too, and he saw a small band of natives, their faces veiled, knives glinting, burnooses bellying out like sails as they shouted and ran at him.

They were too close to take aim. He made for the rock. Unencumbered, and a good sprinter, he reached it safely, stood with his back to it and coolly picked out one after another of his enemies. It was only a momentary advantage; they were too many for him, and ran in again with savage yells.

To his amazement, a dark long swift body flung itself upon his attackers. A great wolf, huge, shaggy, thin and sudden as a torpedo. In vain the men plunged their knives into its rough pelt. Again and again Dale saw the wicked twisted blades drop as the brute caught the wrists of the raiders in its teeth.

The fight was short. Not a man was killed, but none escaped a wound. Some had faces slashed so that blood ran down and blinded them; some dragged a maimed foot; some a mangled arm. In terror of the swift, silent punishing creature that stood between them and their victim, the raiders turned and fled.

The wolf itself had been damaged in the savage encounter; an ear was torn, and it limped as it ran at the heels of the raiders, chasing them to their camels behind the huge rock pile.

The great panting beast looked full at Dale as it passed by. The man felt his heart beat, beat, beat in slow painful thuds against his chest. The creature's yellow, bloodshot eyes turned on him with a glance that cut deeper than any raider's knife. He leaned back. He felt very sick. The vast desert seemed to heave.

Slowly, soberly he made his way back to camp. He did not so much as glance back at the wolf. He knew now. He knew!

Siwa! Actually Siwa at last! The strange fort-like city loomed before the thin line of camels and their dusty weary riders. Like a vast house of cards Siwa had risen up and up from the plain. On its foundation of rock, one generation after another had built; father for son, father for son again; one story on another, the sun-baked mud and salt of its walls almost indistinguishable from the rock itself.

Tiny windows flecked the massive precipitous piles. Vast hives of life, these buildings. Layer upon layer, narrowing from their rocky base into turrets and towers and minarets.

Dale's eyes were for Merle, however. She rode beside him, her face so white and strained, her eyes so anxious that he was torn with doubt. Ought he to have told her Gunnar's secret? He had not turned up since the desert fight. Merle was sick with anxiety. Sheykh El Shabur smiled in his beard as he saw her quivering underlip, her glance that looked about with ever increasing fear.

"Where is he? Where is he?" She turned upon the sheykh. "You said he would be here at Siwa, waiting for us. Where is he?" she demanded.

Dale could have laughed had the situation been less grave

and horrible. She loved as she hated, with her whole strong vigorous soul and body. She tackled the sinister, haughty Arab, demanding of him the man she loved, with the fearlessness of untried youth.

She was worth dying for, his little Merle! And it looked as though he, and she too, would make a finish here in this old barbaric city. If he had to go, he would see to it that she was not left behind, to be a sacrifice on some blood-stained ancient altar hewn in the rock beneath the city, to die slowly and horribly that the lust of Melek Taos should be appeased, to die in body - to live on in soul, slave to Sheykh Zura El Shabur.

And Gunnar? It was unnerving to think what might be happening to him. Dale knew that Gunnar had saved his life as surely as that El Shabur had plotted to kill him two nights ago. It was not nice to consider how the cabalist might punish this second interference of his young disciple.

They rode on through an endless warren of twisting dark lanes. Dale dropped behind Merle and the Arab when only two could ride abreast; he liked to have El Shabur before his eyes when possible. He could see Merle talking earnestly. Her companion seemed interested, his hands moved in quick eloquent gestures, he seemed reassuring her on some point. Gunnar, surely! No other subject in common could exist between those two.

Past the date-markets, under the shadow of the square white tomb of Sidi Suliman, past palm-shaded gardens, until they reached a hill shaped like a sugar-loaf and honeycombed with tombs.

"The Hill of the Dead!" El Shabur waved a lean dark hand.

"Quite," replied Dale. "It looks like it."

The Arab pointed to the white Rest-House built on a level terrace cut in the hillside. "It is there that travellers stay - such as come to Siwa."

"Very appropriate. One does associate rest with tombs, after all."

Merle looked up at the remarkable hill with blank, uninterested gaze.

"Ilbrahaim will take your camels. If you will dismount here! The jonduk is on the other side of the city."

The sheykh dismounted as he spoke. He sent the servant off with the weary beasts, and left the cousins with a salaam to Dale and a deep mocking obeisance to the girl. They watched him out of sight. The hood of his black burnoose obscured head and face; its wide folds, dark and ominous as the sable wings of a bird of prey, swung to his proud free walk. They sighed with relief as the tall figure vanished in Siwa's gloomy narrow streets.

"What were you two chinning about on the way here?" Dale steered the exhausted girl up the steep rocky path. "You seemed to goad our friend to unusual eloquence."

"I was asking about Gunnar. What else is there to say to him? Oh, do look at that!"

Below stretched rolling sandy dunes, palm groves, distant ranges of ragged peaks, the silver glint of a salt lake, and a far-off village on the crest of a rocky summit in the east.

He looked, not at the extraordinary beauty of desert, hill and lake, but at Merle. She had switched the conversation abruptly. Also, she was gazing out over the desert with eyes that saw nothing before them. He was certain of that. She was keyed up - thinking, planning, anticipating something. What? He knew she'd made up her mind to action, and guessed it was concerned with Gunnar. Long experience had taught him the futility of questioning her.

They found the Rest-House surprisingly clean and cool. Ilbrahaim presently returned to look after them. No other guests were there.

It was getting on toward evening when Dale was

summoned to appear before the Egyptian authorities and report on his visit. He knew the easily offended, touchy character of local rulers and authorities, and that it was wise to obey the summons. But about Merle!

He glanced at her over the top of a map he was pretending to study.

"Would you care to come along with me across the city? Or will you stay here with Ilbrahaim and watch the sunset? Famous here, I've read."

"Yes," she replied, her eyes on a pencil sketch she was making of the huddled roofs seen from an open window where she sat.

"My fault, I'll start again! A - Will you come with me? B - Will you stay with Ilbrahaim?"

"B." She looked up for a moment, then returned to her sketch.

He got the impression of peculiar and sudden relief in her eyes, as if the problem had solved itself.

"Wants to get me off the scene!" he told himself.

She stopped further uneasy speculation on his part by bringing her sketch across and plunging into technical details about it. He was a sound critic and was beguiled into an enthusiastic discourse on architecture. She listened and argued and discussed points with flattering deference, until the sun was low and vast and crimson in the west.

Then she casually remarked, "You needn't go now, surely?"

He started up. "I'd completely forgotten my little call. Sorry, dear, to leave you even for an hour. Etiquette's extremely stiff on these small formalities; better go, I think. "Bye, old lady, don't go wandering about."

"Thank heaven, he's gone!" Merle thrust her drawings into a portfolio, put on a hat, scrutinized her pale face in her compact-mirror, applied lipstick and rouge with an artist's hand, and walked down the hill path.

At its junction with the dusty road, a tall black-clad figure joined her.

"You are punctual, Mademoiselle! That is well, for we must be there before sunset."

It seemed an interminable walk to her as they dived and twisted through a labyrinth of courtyards, flights of steps, and overshadowed narrow streets. She followed her silent guide closely. It would be unpleasant to lose even such a grim protector as El Shabur. She shrank from the filthy whining beggars with their rags and sores, from the bold evil faces of the young men who stood to stare at her. Even the children revolted her - pale unhealthy abnormal little creatures that they were.

The sheykh hurried on through the old town with its towering fort-like houses to newer Siwa. Here the dwellings were only of two or three stories with open roofs that looked like great stone boxes shoved hastily together in irregular blocks.

El Shabur looked at the sun, then turned to his companion with such malice in his black eyes that she shrank from him.

"He is here."

She looked up at the house-front with its tiny windows and fought back the premonition of horror that made her throat dry and her heart beat heavily. She despised her weakness. Inside this sinister house, behind one of those dark slits of windows, Gunnar was waiting for her.

Why he'd not come to her, why she must visit him secretly with El Shabur, she refused to ask herself. She loved him. She was going to be with him. The rest did not count at all.

She followed her guide through a low entrance door, stumbled up a narrow dark stairway, caught glimpses of bare, untenanted, low-ceilinged rooms. El Shabur opened a door at the top of the house, drew back with a flash of white teeth. She stooped to enter the low doorway.

"Gunnar!"

There was no answer in words, but from the shadows a figure limped, his face and head cut and bleeding, so gaunt, so shadow-like too, that she cried out again.

"Oh! Oh, my dear!"

He took her in his arms. She clasped him, drew his head down to hers, kissed the grey tortured face with passionate love and pity.

"Gunnar, I am here with you! Look at me! What is it? - tell me, darling, let me help you!"

His eyes met hers in such bitter despair and longing that she clutched him to her again, pressing her face against his shoulder. With gentle touch he put her from him.

"Listen to me, Merle, my darling. My beloved! Listen carefully. This is the last time I shall see you - touch you - for ever. I am lost - lost and damned. In a moment you will see for yourself. That is why he brought you here. Remember that I love you more than the soul I have lost – always - always, Merle!"

He pushed her from him, retreated to the shadows, stood there with head flung up and back pressed to the grey mud wall. Even as she would have gone to him, he changed, swiftly, dreadfully! Down - down in the dust - torn rough head and yellow wolf's eyes at her feet.

Merle sat up on the broad divan. Dale had returned to find her walking up and down, up and down the long main room of the Rest-House. For long he had been unable to distract her mind from the terrible inner picture that tormented her. She would answer his anxious questions with an impatient glance of wild distracted eyes, then begin her endless restless pacing again.

She had drunk the strong sedative he gave her as if her body were acting independently of her mind, but the drug had acted. She had slept. Now she was awake and turned to the man who watched beside her - large, protecting, compassionate. She tried to tell him, but her voice refused to put the thing into words.

"My dear child, don't! Don't! I know what you saw."

"You know! You've seen him when - when -" She covered her face, then slipped from the divan and stood erect before him.

"Dale! I'm all right now. It was so inhuman, such a monstrous unbelievable thing! But he has to bear it - live through it. And we must talk about it. We have to help him. Dale! Dale! Surely there is a way to free him?"

He took her hands in his, swallowed hard before he could command his voice. "My chi-" He broke off abruptly.

There was nothing left of the child! It was a very resolute woman whose white face and anguished eyes confronted him. She looked, she was in effect, ten years older. He could not insult her by anything but the whole unvarnished truth now. She must make the final decision herself. He must not, he dare not withhold his knowledge. It would be a betrayal. Of her. Of Gunnar. Of himself.

"Merle!"

At the tightening of his clasp, the new note in his voice, she looked up with a passion of renewed hope.

"There is - there is a way?"

He nodded, and drew her down beside him on the divan. He looked ill and shaken all at once. His tongue felt stiff, as if it would not frame words. It was like pushing her over a precipice, or into a blazing fire. How cruel love was! Hers for Gunnar. His for Merle. Love that counted - it was always a sharp sword in the heart.

"There is a way," his hoarse voice made effort. "It's a way

that depends on your love and courage. Those two things alone - love and courage! It's a test of both, a most devilish test, so dangerous that the chances are you will not survive it. And if you don't -"

For a moment he bowed his head, put a hand up to shield his face from her wide eager gaze.

"Dear! It's a test, a trial of your will against that fiend, El Shabur. There are ancient records. It has been done. Only one or two survived the ordeal. The others perished – damned - lost as Gunnar is!"

"No." The low, softly breathed word was more impressive than a defiant blare of trumpets. "He is not lost, for I shall save him. Tell me what to do."

El Shabur listened in silence, looked from Merle's white worn face to Dale's maddening smile. He had not expected resistance. He had not thought this lovesick girl would try to win back her lover. The man was at the back of it, of course. Had taught her the formula, no doubt. Should he stoop to take up the gage to battle - with a woman?

"First time your bluff's ever been called, eh, Sheykh of the Mist? Are you meditating one of your famous disappearances? Am I trying you a peg too high? It is, of course, a perilous experiment - this trial of will between you and my little cousin!"

The Arab's white teeth gleamed in a mocking, mirthless smile. His eyes showed two dark flames that flared up hotly at the taunt.

"You cannot save him. He is mine, my creature, my slave."

"Not for long, Sheykh El Shabur," the girl spoke softly.

"For ever," he suavely corrected her. "And you also put yourself in my hands by this foolish test - which is no test!"

Dale stood watching near the door of the Rest-House. Could this be the child he had known so well, this resolute stern little figure, whose steadfast look never wavered from the Arab's face? - who spoke to him with authority on which his evil sneering contempt broke like waves on a rock?

"You think that you - a woman, can withstand me? A vain trifling woman, and one, moreover, who is overburdened by lust for my servant as a frail craft by heavy cargo. I will destroy you with your lover."

"I don't take your gloomy view of the situation," Dale interrupted. He watched the other intently from under drooped eyelids, saw that Merle's fearlessness and his own refusal to be serious were piercing the man's colossal self-esteem, goading him to accept the challenge to his power. El Shabur felt himself a god on earth. In so far as he was master of himself, he was a god! Dale had never met so disciplined and powerful a will. Few could boast so controlled and obedient an intellect. But he was proud, as the fallen Lucifer was proud!

It was the ultimate weakness of all who dabbled in occult powers. They were forced to take themselves with such profound seriousness that in the end the fine balance of sanity was lost.

Dale continued as if they were discussing a trifling matter that began to bore him. His mouth was so dry that he found difficulty in speaking at all. It was like stroking an asp.

"The point is that I have never seen our young friend take this extraordinary semblance of a - a werewolf. My cousin is, as you remark so emphatically, a woman. Not her fault, and all that, of course! But no doubt she was over-sensitive, imaginative, conjured up that peculiar vision of our absent Gunnar by reason of excessive anxiety."

"She saw my disobedient servant," the sheykh's deep voice rang like steel on an anvil, "undergoing punishment. It was no delusion of the senses."

"Ah! Good! Excellent! You mean she was not so weak,

after all. That's one up to her, don't you think? I mean, seeing him as he really was. Rather penetrating, if you take me!"

"She saw what she saw, because it was my design that she should. She is no more than a woman because of it."

"Ah, I can't quite agree there." Dale was persuasive, anxious to prove his point politely. "I'll bet she didn't scream or faint. Just trotted home a bit wobbly at the knees, perhaps?"

"She is obstinate, as all women are obstinate." The sheykh's lean hands were hidden by flowing sleeves, to Dale's disgust; but a muscle twitched above the high cheek-bone, and the dark fire of his eyes glowed red.

"Since you desire to sacrifice yourself," the Arab turned to Merle, "Ilbrahaim shall bring you just before sundown to the house."

"Any objections to my coming along?" Dale spoke as if a supper-party were under discussion. "My interest in magic-ceremonial -"

El Shabur cut in. "You think to save her from me? Ah, do I not know of your learning, your researches, your study of occult mysteries! It will avail you nothing. No other cabalist has dared what I have dared. I - the High Priest of Melek Taos! Power is mine. No man clothed in flesh can stand against me."

He seemed, in the dim low-ceilinged room, to fill the place with wind and darkness and the sound of beating wings. Suddenly he was gone. Like a black cloud he was gone.

Dale looked after him for long tense minutes. "No man clothed in flesh," he quoted reflectively. "And there's quite a lot of clothing in my case, too."

Once more the grim stone house in the outskirts of the city. The cousins stood before it. Ilbrahaim, who had guided them, put a hand before his face in terror.

"Effendi, I go! This is an evil place." The whites of his eyes glinted between outspread fingers. "An abode of the shaitans!"

He turned, scuttled under a low archway. They heard the agitated clap-clap of his heelless slippers on hard-baked earth. Then silence closed round about them. They stood in the warm glow of approaching sunset.

Merle looked at the western sky and the great globe that was remorselessly bringing day to a close. Dale studied her grave, set face. He hoped against hope that she might even now turn back. Her eyes were on the round red sun as it sank.

He too stared as if hypnotized. If he could hold it - stop its slow fatal moving on... on.... It was drawing Merle's life with it. It was vanishing into darkness and night. Merle too would vanish into darkness... into awful night...

She turned and smiled at him. The glory of the sky touched her pale face with fire. Her eyes shone solemn and clear as altar lamps. He gave one last glance at the lovely earth and sky and glorious indifferent sun, then opened the low door for Merle to pass.

Gunnar, in the upper room, stood by the narrow slit of his solitary window, more gaunt, more shadowy than yesterday. He saw Merle, rushed across to her, pushed her violently back across the threshold.

"I will not have it! This monstrous sacrifice! Take her away - at once. Go! I refuse it. Take her away!"

He thrust her back into Dale's arms, tried to close the door in their faces. Once more a faint hope of rescuing Merle at the eleventh hour rose in Dale's mind. But the door was flung wide. El Shabur confronted them, led them into the room, imperiously motioned Gunnar aside.

"Ya! Now is it too late to turn back. My hour is come. My power is upon me. Let Melek Taos claim his own!"

Merle went over to Gunnar, took his hand in hers, looked

up into his grey face with the same look of shining inner exaltation Dale had seen as they lingered at the outer door.

"Yes, it is too late now to turn back," she affirmed. "For this last time you must endure your agony. The last time, Gunnar - my beloved. It shall swiftly pass to me. Can I not bear for a brief moment what you have borne so long? Through my soul and body this devil that possesses you shall pass to El Shabur, who created it. Endure for my sake, as I for yours."

"No! No! You cannot guess the agony - the torture -"

Dale sprang forward at her gesture, and drew about them a circle with oil poured from a long-necked phial. Instantly the two were shut within a barrier of fire, blue as wood-hyacinths, that rose in curving, swaying, lovely pillars to the ceiling, transforming the grey salt mud to a night-sky lit with stars.

"Ya gomâny! O mine enemy!" El Shabur's deep voice held sudden anguish. "Is it thou? Through all the years thy coming has been known to me, yet till now I knew thee not. Who taught thee such power as this?"

He strode to the fiery circle, put out a hand, drew it back scorched and blackened to the bone. He turned in savage menace. Dale's hand flashed, poured oil in a swift practised fling about El Shabur's feet and touched it to leaping flame.

Within this second ring the Arab stood upright. His voice boomed out like a great metal gong.

"Melek Taos! Melek Taos! Have I not served thee truly? Give aid - give aid! Ruler of Wind and Stars and Fire! I am held in chains!"

Dale breathed in suffocating gasps. He was cold to the marrow of his bones. He lost all sense of time - of space. He was hanging somewhere in the vast gulf of eternity. Hell battled for dominion in earth and sea and sky.

"To me, Abeor! Aberer! Chavajoth! Aid - give aid!" Again the great voice called upon his demon-gods.

A sudden shock made the room quiver. Dale saw that the fires grew pale. "Was I too soon? Too soon?" he asked himself in agony. "If the oil burns out before sundown -"

There was a crash. On every hand the solid ancient walls were riven. Up - up leaped the blue fiery pillars.

A shout of awful appeal. "Melek Taos! Master! Give aid!"

With almost blinded eyes, Dale saw Gunnar drop at Merle's feet, saw in his stead a wolf-shape crouching, saw her stoop to it, kneel, kiss the great beast between the eyes, heard her clear, steady voice repeat the words of power, saw the flames sink and leap again.

The issue was joined. Now! Now! God or Demon! The Arab, devil-possessed, calling on his gods. Merle, fearless before the onrush of his malice. Hate, cruel as the grave. Love, stronger than death.

Dale's breath tore him. Cold! Cold! Cold to the blood in his veins! God! it was upon her!

Gunnar stood in his own body, staring with wild eyes at the beast which brushed against his knee. He collapsed beside it, blind and deaf to further agony.

And still El Shabur's will was undefeated. Still beside the unconscious Gunnar stood a wolf, its head flung up, its yellow lambent eyes fixed, remote, suffering.

Again Dale felt himself a tiny point of conscious life swung in the womb of time. Again the forces that bear up the earth, sun, moon, and stars were caught in chaos and destruction. Again he heard the roar of fire and flood and winds that drive the seas before them. Through all the tumult there rang a voice, rallying hell's legions, waking old dark gods, calling from planet to planet, from star to star, calling for aid!

Dale knew himself on earth again. Stillness was about him.

In a dim and dusty room he saw Merle and Gunnar, handfast, looking into each other's eyes. About their feet a little trail of fire ran - blue as a border of gentian.

Another circle showed, its fires dead, black ash upon the dusty ground. Across it sprawled a body, its burnoose charred and smouldering. Servant of Melek Taos. Victim of his own dark spells. El Shabur destroyed by the demon that had tormented Gunnar. Driven forth, homeless, it returned to him who had created it.

THE DEVIL OF THE MARSH
Henry Brereton Marriott Watson

It was nigh upon dusk when I drew close to the Great Marsh, and already the white vapours were about, riding across the sunken levels like ghosts in a churchyard. Though I had set forth in a mood of wild delight, I had sobered in the lonely ride across the moor and was now uneasily alert. As my horse jerked down the grassy slopes that fell away to the jaws of the swamp I could see thin streams of mist rise slowly, hover like wraiths above the long rushes, and then, turning gradually more material, go blowing heavily away across the flat. The appearance of the place at this desolate hour, so remote from human society and so darkly significant of evil presences, struck me with a certain wonder that she should have chosen this spot for our meeting. She was a familiar of the moors, where I had invariably encountered her; but it was like her arrogant caprice to test my devotion by some such dreary assignation. The wide and horrid prospect depressed me beyond reason, but the fact of her neighbourhood drew me on, and my spirits mounted at the thought that at last she was to put me in possession of herself. Tethering my horse upon the verge of the swamp, I soon discovered the path that crossed it, and entering struck out boldly for the heart. The track could have been little used, for the reeds, which stood high above the level of my eyes upon either side, straggled everywhere across in low arches, through which I dodged, and broke my way with some inconvenience and much impatience. A full half hour I was solitary in that wilderness, and when at last a sound other than my own footsteps broke the silence the dusk had fallen.

I was moving very slowly at the time, with a mind half disposed to turn from the melancholy expedition, which it seemed to me now must surely be a cruel jest she had played upon me. While some such reluctance held me, I was suddenly arrested by a hoarse croaking which broke out upon my left, sounding somewhere from the reeds in the black mire. A little further it came again from close at hand, and when I had passed on a few more steps in wonder and perplexity, I heard it for the third time. I stopped and listened, but the marsh was as a grave, and so taking the noise for the signal of some raucous frog, I resumed my way. But in a little the croaking was repeated, and coming quickly to a stand I pushed the reeds aside and peered into the darkness. I could see nothing, but at the immediate moment of my pause I thought I detected the sound of some body trailing through the rushes. My distaste for the adventure grew with this suspicion, and had it not been for my delirious infatuation I had assuredly turned back and ridden home. The ghastly sound pursued me at intervals along the track, until at last, irritated beyond endurance by the sense of this persistent and invisible company, I broke into a sort of run. This, it seemed, the creature (whatever it was) could not achieve, for I heard no more of it, and continued my way in peace. My path at length ran out from among the reeds upon the smooth flat of which she had spoken, and here my heart quickened, and the gloom of the dreadful place lifted. The flat lay in the very centre of the marsh, and here and there in it a gaunt bush or withered tree rose like a spectre against the white mists. At the further end I fancied some kind of building loomed up; but the fog which had been gathering ever since my entrance upon the passage sailed down upon me at that moment and the prospect went out with suddenness. As I stood waiting for the clouds to pass, a voice cried to me out of its centre, and I saw her next second with bands of mist swirling about her body, come rushing to me from the darkness. She put her long arms about me, and, drawing her close, I looked into her deep eyes. Far down in them, it seemed to me, I could discern a mystic laughter dancing in the wells of light, and I had that ecstatic sense of nearness to some spirit of fire which was wont to possess me at her contact.

"At last," she said, "at last, my beloved!" I caressed her.

"Why," said I, tingling at the nerves, "why have you put this dolorous journey between us? And what mad freak is your presence in this swamp?" She uttered her silver laugh, and nestled to me again.

"I am the creature of this place," she answered. "This is my home. I have sworn you should behold me in my native sin ere you ravished me away."

"Come, then," said I; "I have seen; let there be an end of this. I know you, what you are. This marsh chokes up my heart. God forbid you should spend more of your days here. Come."

"You are in haste," she cried. "There is yet much to learn. Look, my friend," she said, "you who know me, what I am. This is my prison, and I have inherited its properties. Have you no fear?"

For answer I pulled her to me, and her warm lips drove out the horrid humours of the night; but the swift passage of a flickering mockery over her eyes struck me as a flash of lightning, and I grew chill again.

"I have the marsh in my blood," she whispered: "the marsh and the fog of it. Think ere you vow to me, for I am the cloud in a starry night."

A lithe and lovely creature, palpable of warm flesh, she lifted her magic face to mine and besought me plaintively with these words. The dews of the nightfall hung on her lashes, and seemed to plead with me for her forlorn and solitary plight.

"Behold!" I cried, "witch or devil of the marsh, you shall come with me! I have known you on the moors, a roving apparition of beauty; nothing more I know, nothing more I ask. I care not what this dismal haunt means; not what these strange and mystic eyes. You have powers and senses above me; your sphere and habits are as mysterious and incomprehensible as your beauty. But that," I said, "is mine, and the world that is mine shall be yours also."

She moved her head nearer to me with an antic gesture, and her gleaming eyes glanced up at me with a sudden flash, the similitude (great heavens!) of a hooded snake. Starting, I fell away, but at that moment she turned her face and set it fast towards the fog that came rolling in thick volumes over the flat. Noiselessly the great cloud crept down upon us, and all dazed and troubled I watched her watching it in silence. It was as if she awaited some omen of horror, and I too trembled in the fear of its coming.

Then suddenly out of the night issued the hoarse and hideous croaking I had heard upon my passage. I reached out my arm to take her hand, but in an instant the mists broke over us, and I was groping in the vacancy. Something like panic took hold of me, and, beating through the blind obscurity, I rushed over the flat, calling upon her. In a little the swirl went by, and I perceived her upon the margin of the swamp, her arm raised as in imperious command. I ran to her, but stopped, amazed and shaken by a fearful sight. Low by the dripping reeds crouched a small squat thing, in the likeness of a monstrous frog, coughing and choking in its throat. As I stared, the creature rose upon its legs and disclosed a horrid human resemblance. Its face was white and thin, with long black hair; its body gnarled and twisted as with the ague of a thousand years. Shaking, it whined in a breathless voice, pointing a skeleton finger at the woman by my side.

"Your eyes were my guide," it quavered. "Do you think that after all these years I have no knowledge of your eyes? Lo, is there aught of evil in you I am not instructed in? This is the Hell you designed for me, and now you would leave me to a greater."

The wretch paused, and panting leaned upon a bush, while she stood silent, mocking him with her eyes, and soothing my terror with her soft touch.

"Hear!" he cried, turning to me, "hear the tale of this woman that you may know her as she is. She is the Presence of the marshes. Woman or Devil I know not, but only that the accursed marsh has crept into her soul and she herself is become its Evil Spirit; she herself, that lives and grows young and beautiful by it, has its full power to blight and chill and slay. I, who was once as you are, have this knowledge. What bones lie deep in this black swamp who can say but she? She has drained of health, she has drained of mind and of soul; what is between her and her desire that she should not drain also of life? She has made me a devil in her Hell, and now she would leave me to my solitary pain, and go search for another victim. But she shall not!" he screamed through his chattering teeth; "she shall not! My Hell is also hers! She shall not!"

Her smiling untroubled eyes left his face and turned to me: she put out her arms, swaying towards me, and so fervid and so great a light glowed in her face that, as one distraught of superhuman means, I took her into my embrace. And then the madness seized me.

"Woman or devil," I said, "I will go with you! Of what account this pitiful past? Blight me even as that wretch, so be only you are with me."

She laughed, and, disengaging herself, leaned, half-clinging to me, towards the coughing creature by the mire.

"Come," I cried, catching her by the waist. "Come!" She laughed again a silver-ringing laugh. She moved with me slowly across the flat to where the track started for the portals of the marsh. She laughed and clung to me.

But at the edge of the track I was startled by a shrill, hoarse screaming; and behold, from my very feet, that loathsome creature rose up and wound his long black arms about her shrieking and crying in his pain. Stooping I pushed him from her skirts, and with one sweep of my arm drew her across the pathway; as her face passed mine her eyes were wide and smiling. Then of a sudden the still mist enveloped us once more; but ere it descended I had a glimpse of that contorted figure trembling on the margin, the white face drawn and full of desolate pain. At the sight an icy shiver ran through me. And then through the yellow gloom the shadow of her darted past me to the further side. I heard the hoarse cough, the dim noise of a struggle, a swishing sound, a thin cry, and then the sucking of the slime over something in the rushes. I leapt forward: and once again the fog thinned, and I beheld her, woman or devil, standing upon the verge, and peering with smiling eyes into the foul and sickly bog. With a sharp cry wrung from my nerveless soul, I turned and fled down the narrow way from that accursed spot; and as I ran the thickening fog closed round me, and I heard far off and lessening still the silver sound of her mocking laughter.

FISHHEAD
Irvin S. Cobb

It goes past the powers of my pen to try to describe Reelfoot Lake for you so that you, reading this, will get the picture of it in your mind as I have it in mine.

For Reelfoot Lake is like no other lake that I know anything about. It is an after-thought of Creation.

The rest of this continent was made and had dried in the sun for thousands of years - millions of years, for all I know - before Reelfoot came to be. It's the newest big thing in nature on this hemisphere, probably, for it was formed by the great earthquake of 1811.

That earthquake of 1811 surely altered the face of the earth on the then far frontier of this country.

It changed the course of rivers, it converted hills into what are now the sunk lands of three states, and it turned the solid ground to jelly and made it roll in waves like the sea.

And in the midst of the retching of the land and the vomiting of the waters it depressed to varying depths a section of the earth crust sixty miles long, taking it down - trees, hills, hollows, and all, and a crack broke through to the Mississippi River so that for three days the river ran up stream, filling the hole.

The result was the largest lake south of the Ohio, lying mostly in Tennessee, but extending up across what is now the Kentucky line, and taking its name from a fancied resemblance in its outline to the splay, reeled foot of a cornfield negro. Niggerwool Swamp, not so far away, may have got its name from the same man who christened Reelfoot: at least so it sounds.

Reelfoot is, and has always been, a lake of mystery.

In places it is bottomless. Other places the skeletons of the cypress-trees that went down when the earth sank, still stand upright so that if the sun shines from the right quarter, and the water is less muddy than common, a man, peering face downward into its depths, sees, or thinks he sees, down below him the bare top-limbs upstretching like drowned men's fingers, all coated with the mud of years and bandaged with pennons of the green lake slime.

In still other places the lake is shallow for long stretches, no deeper than breast high to a man, but dangerous because of the weed growths and the sunken drifts which entangle a swimmer's limbs. Its banks are mainly mud, its waters are muddled, too, being a rich coffee colour in the spring and a copperish yellow in the summer, and the trees along its shore are mud coloured clear up their lower limbs after the spring floods, when the dried sediment covers their trunks with a thick, scrofulous-looking coat.

There are stretches of unbroken woodland around it, and slashes where the cypress knees rise countlessly like headstones and footstones for the dead snags that rot in the soft ooze.

There are deadenings with the lowland corn growing high and rank below and the bleached, fire-blackened girdled trees rising above, barren of leaf and limb.

There are long, dismal flats where in the spring the clotted frog-spawn cling like patches of white mucus among the weed-stalks, and at night the turtles crawl out to lay clutches of perfectly, round, white eggs with tough, rubbery shells in the sand.

There are bayous leading off to nowhere, and sloughs that wind aimlessly, like great, blind worms, to finally join the big river that rolls its semi-liquid torrents a few miles to the westward.

So Reelfoot lies there, flat in the bottoms, freezing lightly in the winter, steaming torridly in the summer, swollen in the spring when the woods have turned a vivid green and the buffalo-gnats by the million and the billion fill the flooded hollows with their pestilential buzzing, and in the fall, ringed about gloriously with all the colours which the first frost brings - gold of hickory, yellow-russet of sycamore, red of dogwood and ash, and purple-black of sweet-gum.

But the Reelfoot country has its uses. It is the best game and fish country, natural or artificial, that is left in the South today.

In their appointed seasons the duck and the geese flock in, and even semi-tropical birds, like the brown pelican and the Florida snake-bird, have been known to come there to nest.

Pigs, gone back to wildness, range the ridges, each razor-backed drove captained by a gaunt, savage, slab-sided old boar. By night the bullfrogs, inconceivably big and tremendously vocal, bellow under the banks.

It is a wonderful place for fish - bass and crappie, and perch, and the snouted buffalo fish.

How these edible sorts live to spawn, and how their spawn in turn live to spawn again is a marvel, seeing how many of the big fish-eating cannibal-fish there are in Reelfoot.

Here, bigger than anywhere else, you find the garfish, all bones and appetite and horny plates, with a snout like an alligator, the nearest link, naturalists say, between the animal life of today and the animal life of the Reptilian Period.

The shovel-nose cat, really a deformed kind of fresh-water sturgeon, with a great fan-shaped membranous plate jutting out from his nose like a bowsprit, jumps all day in the quiet places with mighty splashing sounds, as though a horse had fallen into the water.

On every stranded log the huge snapping turtles lie on sunny days in groups of four and six, baking their shells black in the sun, with their little snaky heads raised watchfully, ready to slip noiselessly off at the first sound of oars grating in the row-locks. But the biggest of them all are the catfish!

These are monstrous creatures, these catfish of Reelfoot - scaleless, slick things, with corpsy, dead eyes and poisonous fins, like javelins, and huge whiskers dangling from the sides of their cavernous heads.

Six and seven feet long they grow to be, and weigh 200 pounds or more, and they have mouths wide enough to take in a man's foot or a man's fist, and strong enough to break any hook save the strongest, and greedy enough to eat anything, living or dead or putrid, that the horny jaws can master.

Oh, but they are wicked things, and they tell wicked tales of them down there. They call them man-eaters, and compare them, in certain of their habits, to sharks.

Fishhead was of a piece with this setting.

He fitted into it as an acorn fits its cup. All his life he had lived on Reelfoot, always in the one place, at the mouth of a certain slough.

He had been born there, of a negro father and a half-breed Indian mother, both of them now dead, and the story was that before his birth his mother was frightened by one of the big fish, so that the child came into the world most hideously marked.

Anyhow, Fishhead was a human monstrosity, the veritable embodiment of nightmare!

He had the body of a man - a short, stocky sinewy body - but his face was as near to being the face of a great fish as any face could be and yet retain some trace of human aspect.

His skull sloped back so abruptly that he could hardly be said to have a have a forehead at all; his chin slanted off right into nothing. His eyes were small and round with shallow, glazed, pale-yellow pupils, and they were set wide apart in his head, and they were unwinking and staring, like a fish's eyes.

His nose was no more than a pair of tiny slits in the middle of the yellow mask. His mouth was the worst of all. It was the awful mouth of a catfish, lipless and almost inconceivably wide, stretching from side to side.

Also when Fishhead became a man grown his likeness to a fish increased, for the hair upon his face grew out into two tightly kinked slender pendants that drooped down either side of the mouth like the beards of a fish!

If he had another name than Fishhead, none excepting he knew it. As Fishhead he was known, and as Fishhead he answered. Because he knew the waters and the woods of Reelfoot better than any other man there, he was valued as a guide by the city men who came every year to hunt or fish; but there were few such jobs that Fishhead would take.

Mainly he kept to himself, tending his corn patch, netting the lake, trapping a little, and in season pot hunting for the city markets. His neighbours, ague-bitten whites and malaria-proof negroes alike, left him to himself

Indeed, for the most part they had a superstitious fear of him. So he lived alone, with no kith nor kin, nor even a friend, shunning his kind and shunned by them.

His cabin stood just below the State line, where Mud Slough runs into the lake. It was a shack of logs, the only human habitation for four miles up or down.

Behind it the thick timber came shouldering right up to the edge of Fishhead's small truck patch, enclosing it in thick shade except when the sun stood just overhead.

He cooked his food in a primitive fashion, outdoors, over a hole in the soggy earth or upon the rusted red ruin of an old cookstove, and he drank the saffron water of the lake out of a dipper made of a gourd, faring and fending for himself, a master hand at skiff and net, competent with duck gun and fishspear, yet a creature of affliction and loneliness, part savage, almost amphibious, set apart from his fellows, silent and suspicious.

In front of his cabin jutted out a long fallen cottonwood trunk, lying half in and half out of the water, its top side burnt by the sun and worn by the friction of Fishhead's bare feet until it showed countless patterns of tiny scrolled lines, its underside black and rotted, and lapped at unceasingly by little waves like tiny licking tongues.

Its farther end reached deep water. And it was a part of Fishhead, for no matter how far his fishing and trapping might take him in the daytime, sunset would find him back there, his boat drawn up on the bank, and he on the other end of this log.

From a distance men had seen him there many times, sometimes squatted motionless as the big turtles that would crawl upon its dipping tip in his absence, sometimes erect and motionless like a creek crane, his misshapen yellow form outlined against the yellow sun, the yellow water, the yellow banks - all of them yellow together.

If the Reelfooters shunned Fishhead by day they feared him by night and avoided him as a plague, dreading even the chance of a casual meeting. For there were ugly stories about Fishhead - stories which all the negroes and some of the whites believed.

They said that a cry which had been heard just before dusk and just after, skittering across the darkened waters, was his calling cry to the big cats, and at his bidding they came trooping in, and that in their company he swam in the lake on moonlight nights, sporting with them, diving with them, even feeding with them on what manner of unclean things they fed.

The cry had been heard many times, that much was certain, and it was certain also that the big fish were noticeably thick at the mouth of Fishhead's slough. No native Reelfooter, white or black, would willingly wet a leg or an arm there.

Here Fishhead had lived, and here he was going to die. The Baxters were going to kill him, and this day in late summer was to be the time of the killing.

The two Baxters - Jake and Joel - were coming in their dugout to do it!

This murder had been a long time in the making. The Baxters had to brew their hate over a slow fire for months before it reached the pitch of action.

They were poor whites, poor in everything, repute, and worldly goods, and standing - a pair of fever-ridden squatters who lived on whiskey and tobacco when they could get it, and on fish and cornbread when they couldn't.

The feud itself was of months' standing. Meeting Fishhead one day, in the spring on the spindly scaffolding of the skiff landing at Walnut Log, and being themselves far overtaken in liquor and vainglorious with a bogus alcoholic substitute for courage, the brothers had accused him, wantonly and without proof, of running their trout-line and stripping it of the hooked catch - an unforgivable sin among the water dwellers and the shanty boaters of the South.

Seeing that he bore this accusation in silence, only eyeing them steadfastly, they had been emboldened then to slap his face, whereupon he turned and gave them both the beating of their lives - bloodying their noses and bruising their lips with hard blows against their front teeth, and finally leaving them, mauled and prone, in the dirt.

Moreover, in the onlookers a sense of the everlasting fitness of things had triumphed over race prejudice and allowed them - two freeborn, sovereign whites - to be licked by, a nigger! Therefore they were going to get the nigger!

The whole thing had been planned out amply. They were going to kill him on his log at sundown. There would be no witnesses to see it, no retribution to follow after it. The very ease of the undertaking made them forget even their inborn fear of the place of Fishhead's habitation.

For more than an hour they had been coming from their shack across a deeply indented arm of the lake.

Their dugout, fashioned by fire and adz and draw-knife from the bole of a gum-tree, moved through the water as noiselessly as a swimming mallard, leaving behind it a long, wavy trail on the stilled waters.

Jake, the better oarsman, sat flat in the stern of the round-bottomed craft, paddling with quick, splashless strokes, Joel, the better shot, was squatted forward. There was a heavy, rusted duck gun between his knees.

Though their spying upon the victim had made them certain sure he would not be about the shore for hours, a doubled sense of caution led them to hug closely the weedy banks. They slid along the shore like shadows, moving so swiftly and in such silence that the watchful mudturtles barely turned their snaky heads as they passed.

So, a full hour before the time, they came slipping around the mouth of the slough and made for a natural ambuscade which the mixed-breed had left within a stone's jerk of his cabin to his own undoing.

Where the slough's flow joined deeper water a partly uprooted tree was stretched, prone from shore, at the top still thick and green with leaves that drew nourishment from the earth in which the half uncovered roots yet held, and twined about with an exuberance of trumpet vines and wild fox-grapes. All about was a huddle of drift - last year's cornstalks, shreddy strips of bark, chunks of rotted weed, all the riffle and dunnage of a quiet eddy.

Straight into this green clump glided the dugout and swung, broadside on, against the protecting trunk of the tree, hidden from the inner side by the intervening curtains of rank growth, just as the Baxters had intended it should be hidden when days before in their scouting they marked this masked place of waiting and included it, then and there, in the scope of their plans.

There had been no hitch or mishap. No one had been abroad in the late afternoon to mark their movements - and in a little while Fishhead ought to be due. Jake's woodman's eye followed the downward swing of the sun speculatively.

The shadows, thrown shoreward, lengthened and slithered on the small ripples. The small noises of the day died out; the small noises of the coming night began to multiply.

The green-bodied flies went away and big mosquitoes with speckled grey legs came to take the places of the flies.

The sleepy lake sucked at the mud banks with small mouthing sounds, as though it found the taste of the raw mud agreeable. A monster crawfish, big as a chicken lobster, crawled out of the top of his dried mud chimney and perched himself there, an armoured sentinel on the watchtower.

Bull bats began to flitter back and forth, above the tops of the trees. A pudgy muskrat, swimming with head up, was moved to sidle off briskly as he met a cotton-mouth moccasin snake, so fat and swollen with summer poison that it looked almost like a legless lizard as it moved along the surface of the water in a series of slow torpid S's. Directly above the head of either of the waiting assassins a compact little swarm of midges hung, holding to a sort of kite-shaped formation.

A little more time passed and Fishhead came out of the woods at the back, walking swiftly, with a sack over his shoulder.

For a few seconds his deformities showed in the clearing, then the black inside of the cabin swallowed him up.

By now the sun was almost down. Only the red nub of it showed above the timber line across the lake, and the shadows lay inland a long way. Out beyond, the big cats were stirring, and the great smacking sounds as their twisting bodies leaped clear and fell back in the water, came shoreward in a chorus.

But the two brothers, in their green covert, gave heed to nothing except the one thing upon which their hearts were set and their nerves tensed. Joel gently shoved his gun barrels across the log, cuddling the stock to his shoulder and slipping two fingers caressingly back and forth upon the triggers. Jake held the narrow dugout steady by a grip upon a fox-grape tendril.

A little wait and then the finish came!

Fishhead emerged from the cabin door and came down the narrow footpath to the water and out upon the water on his log.

He was barefooted and bareheaded, his cotton shirt open down the front to show his yellow neck and breast, his dungaree trousers held about his waist by a twisted tow string.

His broad splay feet, with the prehensile toes outspread, gripped the polished curve of the log as he moved along its swaying, dipping surface until he came to its outer end, and stood there erect, his chest filling, his chinless face lifted up, and something of mastership and dominion in his poise.

And then - his eye caught what another's eyes might have missed - the round, twin ends of the gun barrels, the fixed gleam of Joel's eyes, aimed at him through the green tracery! In that swift passage of time, too swift almost to be measured by seconds, realization flashed all through him, and he threw his head still higher and opened wide his shapeless trap of a mouth, and out across the lake he sent skittering and rolling his cry.

And in his cry was the laugh of a loon, and the croaking bellow of a frog, and the bay of a hound, all the compounded night noises of the lake. And in it, too, was a farewell, and a defiance, and an appeal!

The heavy roar of the duck gun came!

At twenty yards the double charge tore the throat out of him. He came down, face forward, upon the log and clung there, his trunk twisting distortedly, his legs twitching and kicking like the legs of a speared frog; his shoulders hunching and lifting spasmodically as the life ran out of him all in one swift coursing flow.

His head canted up between the heaving shoulders, his eyes looked full on the staring face of his murderer, and then the blood came out of his mouth, and Fishhead, in death still as much fish as man, slid, flopping, head first, off the end of the log, and sank, face downward slowly, his limbs all extended out.

One after another a string of big bubbles came up to burst in the middle of a widening reddish stain on the coffee-coloured water.

The brothers watched this, held by the horror of the thing they had done, and the cranky dugout, having been tipped far over by the recoil of the gun, took water steadily across its gunwale; and now there was a sudden stroke from below upon its careening bottom and it went over and they were in the lake.

But shore was only twenty feet away, the trunk of the uprooted tree only five. Joel, still holding fast to his shot gun, made for the log, gaining it with one stroke. He threw his free arm over it and clung there, treading water, as he shook his eyes free.

Something gripped him - some great, sinewy, unseen thing gripped him fast by the thigh, crushing down on his flesh!

He uttered no cry, but his eyes popped out, and his mouth set in a square shape of agony, and his fingers gripped into the bark of the tree like grapples. He was pulled down and down, by steady jerks, not rapidly but steadily, so steadily, and as he went his fingernails tore four little white strips in the tree-bark. His mouth went under, next his popping eyes, then his erect hair, and finally his clawing, clutching hand, and that was the end of him.

Jake's fate was harder still, for he lived longer - long enough to see Joel's finish. He saw it through the water that ran down his face, and with a great surge of his whole body, he literally flung himself across the log and jerked his legs up high into the air to save them. He flung himself too far, though, for his face and chest hit the water on the far side.

And out of this water rose the head of a great fish, with the lake slime of years on its flat, black head, its whiskers bristling, its corpsy eyes alight. Its horny jaws closed and clamped in the front of Jake's flannel shirt. His hand struck out wildly and was speared on a poisoned fin, and, unlike Joel, he went from sight with a great yell, and a whirling and churning of the water that made the cornstalks circle on the edges of a small whirlpool.

But the whirlpool soon thinned away, into widening rings of ripples, and the corn stalks quit circling and became still again, and only the multiplying night noises sounded about the mouth of the slough.

The bodies of all three came ashore on the same day near the same place. Except for the gaping gunshot wound where the neck met the chest, Fishhead's body was unmarked.

But the bodies of the two Baxters were so marred and mauled that the Reelfooters buried them together on the bank without ever knowing which might be Jake's and which might be Joel's.

THE BLACK STATUE: THE STORY OF A DOCTOR'S GRUESOME DISCOVERY
Huan Mee

"I always sed no good could come of it," the woman cries with a choke, and then the little group edges back to the kerb, and gazes open-mouthed at the shuttered windows.

"And you ain't seen your Jim since last Monday, eh?"

"No, I ain't set eyes on 'im. It's just a week to-day, I sed as 'e left in the mornin', 'It would be better for you, Jim, if you slung up your job at Doctor Hazard's, 'cos no good can come of it; and he gives me the creeps every time I looks at 'im.'"

"Wot did Jim say?"

"He says, 'Beggars can't be choosers,' and the doctor paid 'im well."

"And you ain't seen 'im since?"

"No, I ain't, and I b'leve he's a bein' 'sperimented on."

"Well, why don't you tell the pleece?"

"I 'ave, and they're comin' round this mornin'."

The group comes forward again as a man, accompanied by a couple of constables, enters the square and pauses before the gloomy house.

"Clear this gaping lot away, Jackson," he says; and the crowd, by dint of physical persuasion, and repeated injunctions to "pass along," is hustled to the corner, where it awaits events. "Now, Smith, just knock a rat-tat."

Neither the first, second, nor third knock has the slightest effect, except to bring back the crowd, strongly reinforced, until it hangs around the railings.

"Force it," the man quietly remarks; and in a few minutes the door is open, and the excited idlers almost encroach on to the doorstep, "Jackson, clear this mob out of the square; Smith, follow me."

The door is pulled to behind the men; the crowd again retreats in disorder to the corner, and the constable walks to and fro in front of the house.

The two who have entered glance into the front room; it is empty, while the back room and the upper part of the house are the same.

"Try the basement, Smith."

They descend the stairs, and come to a sudden stop as they are met by an unexpected door.

"Sounds like iron," the chief exclaims, as he raps his knuckles against it.

"That's what it is," the constable agrees.

"Knock on it with that bar, and see if anyone's alive in the house or not."

As soon as the first blow has fallen the door is thrown open, and a man clad in his shirt and trousers confronts them; a man tall and dark, with his face clean shaven, his hair cut closely to his head, and his shirt-sleeves rolled tightly to his shoulders.

"Well, what is it, eh?" he asks. "Come in"; and as they enter he closes the door behind them.

The whole place seems weird and uncanny. The further end is draped by a long curtain, hanging from the ceiling to the floor; the walls are covered with shelves and cases, filled with glass vessels and polished instruments that vividly suggest their own uses, while in a corner alcove stands a life-sized statue, a Greek god, in black marble.

"What is the meaning of this intrusion? What do you want? Am I in London, or is this some part of the world where men's homes can be broken into, their scientific researches disturbed by strangers?"

"This house has been without a sign of life for a week, and your servant, who entered then, has never left it."

"You mean the man who used to do odd jobs for me. I discharged him ten days ago, and have not seen him since."

"He came here on Monday."

"He did not. I see you don't believe me - maybe you go so far as to think I have murdered him, eh? Of course, you've searched the house. This is my laboratory, and there's only the room through the curtains, there."

The officers step forward; the man draws back the curtains.

"Now, then, look! You see there's no one there, and if you're quite satisfied, I prefer to be left alone. You found your way in, so now you can find it out."

For three years the gloomy house in the square has been vacant - not to let, but simply vacant, for Dr. Hazard is touring on the Continent. The missing servant has not been seen in London since the day he so suddenly and mysteriously disappeared, and the little gossiping group which once took such a morbid interest in his whereabouts has forgotten him in the excitement of other nine-day wonders, which have flourished and withered in their turn.

But now a change has suddenly come about; for the master is returning.

Brisk, business-like men measure floors and windows, energetic British workmen sit on planks and smoke, and all is ostentatious bustle and activity. At last the day comes when the final workman grudgingly and reluctantly takes his leave. Pantechnicons arrive and disgorge their contents, which shall transform the dismal dwelling into a habitation fit for a man and woman - for it is rumoured that Dr. Hazard is bringing home a wife.

That she is beautiful, the few loungers who are privileged to see the couple descend from the carriage cannot but admit; but still there is something chilling and repellent in that beauty. There is so much of the doctor's cold, insolent sneer reflected in her face, that it seems to them that like has chosen like.

Dr. Hazard assists his wife to alight, and she passes up the steps, and then turns and glances back in icy astonishment, as a young woman darts across the road, and lays a detaining arm upon her husband's sleeve.

"'Ave you found 'im, doctor?"

"Found whom?"

"My brother - Jim, you know - 'im as used to work for you."

"No, no, my good woman. Go away. How should I have found him?"

"You do know, 'cos you knows as I knows 'e's in there," and she points to the house.

Without further parley, he thrusts her on one side and passes in.

His wife, moving from the window, turns towards him as he enters.

"Some of your friends seem to have good memories for you," she says.

"Yes. It's nonsense. Her brother disappeared three years ago, and she thinks I had something to do with it."

"And had you?"

"You're jesting."

"I never jest; I know life is nothing to you."

"On the contrary, life is a great deal to me. I have studied it; it interests me. I shall be able to show you some remarkable experiments, now we are home. I have everything to my hand in my laboratory - everything to aid me in my study of life and death."

"And I, to my horror, have found how little you think of either."

"You speak truly," the doctor answers. "I think nothing of either; but it is your home-coming. Forget these trifles, and let me show you the house."

"I wonder why I married you," she says, as she glares into his eyes.

"Out of gratitude for my service to your father."

"I wonder why I did not sooner kill myself."

"Tush! You talk like a child."

"The first time I saw you I shuddered, for you were as a blight in the very air; and then, slowly and viciously, you plotted in silence, until you had broken my heart and bought me from my father - until you held him bound hand and foot, and I was the price of your silence."

"You have said this so many times before," he mockingly interjects.

"And I say it for the last time now," she cried; "for in this house I see death written, and it is yours. A death worthy of such a devil."

"Loud applause from the gallery," the man cynically interjects; "now for the tour of inspection."

"My laboratory," Dr. Hazard exclaims, as they pause at length before the iron door, "or what you would perhaps call my torture chamber. Do you care to see it before science resumes her researches?"

She inclines her head, enters as he switches on the light, and gazes coldly round the room, aware that her husband's eye is upon her to catch a tremor of the lips that would show a spark of fear, and then with a gasp she falls back, and points with a trembling hand to the corner, where a curtain on a brass rod cuts off a portion of the room.

"Who is behind there?" she cries. "Who is behind there?"

He crosses the room, pulls back the curtain, and faces her.

"You are frightened at nothing," he chuckles. "A statue in black marble is sufficient to set you trembling; come nearer and examine it. Come and see with what marvellous accuracy every vein, every muscle and tendon is carved upon the stone."

"Who did it?"

"I, from life. You did not know I excelled in sculpture as well as other arts."

"It's a wonderful piece of work," she whispers, attracted in spite of herself, struggling to regain her composure, and not knowing why an icy fear still seems to grip her heart. "Very true to life."

"Very true indeed. Give me your hand."

He takes her hand, and places it upon the arm of the statue.

"There," he says, quietly, "you can almost fancy you feel the muscles beneath the skin, almost fancy that arm once moved. It is, as you say, very true to life."

With a cry of terror she drags her hand away, and, clutching the table for support, leans back against it, utterly unnerved, a nameless horror in her eyes.

"Is he – it - like the missing man?" she gasps at last.

Dr. Hazard purses his lips, and eyes the statue critically.

"Hum! it is strange," he answers, after a moment of silence. "But now you mention it, there is a likeness."

He offers her his arm.

"Don't come near me."

"As you please."

"Do you experiment with that in the room?"

"Certainly; for that is the result of my greatest experiment. You heard of the missing man they're still worrying me about?" He jerked his head meaningly towards the statue.

"It is not true; you are trying to drive me mad."

"Nonsense! It's true enough. That's the man, and I defy the world to find it out!"

His face flushes with a dull blaze of passion, and he catches her by the wrist and twists her round until her eyes look into his. "And remember this, Beatrice: let there be no more of this childish folly and foolish threats, or as sure as you stand before me I'll kill you, and you shall be the companion statue on the opposite pedestal."

"What do you think of the port, Hertz?"

"Splendid wine; '47, eh?" the man replies, holding his glass to the light.

"No, quite a modern vintage. Treated by my own process."

"What a wonderful chap you are, Hazard - always doing something to astound people; always inventing something."

"Pooh? You can't call an artificial manufacturing of wine an invention; but I have one or two inventions with which I mean to surprise the world. The illumination of this room is one of my secrets; those electric lights will burn for years without renewal or attention. Electricity as men understand it now is nothing. As I know it, it is a power that can control the world, that can prolong man's life beyond his wildest dreams, and then preserve his body unalterable for all time. The height of the ambition of the ancients was embalming.

"What progress! They embalmed their departed dead, that they might keep them even at their feasts. Death at their feasts," repeats Dr. Hazard, frowning under his eyebrows at his wife, who sits opposite to him at the table.

Throughout the dinner, the doctor's scorn of his wife has been so obvious that his guests gladly seize upon the new tenor of the conversation for relief.

"Then you have invented a process to arrest decay?" Dr. Hertz asks.

"Yes."

The doctor's wife rests her arms upon the table and leans towards her husband.

"You own you have invented a process to arrest decay in a body?" she says, coldly. "You own it, before your friends?"

"Certainly," he exclaims, carelessly flicking the ash from his cigar.

"It is wonderful!" Dr. Hertz remarks.

"Mrs. Hazard, your husband is a remarkable man. You must be proud of him."

"Proud of him!" she exclaims, twisting her fingers in the tablecloth, and bending towards the visitor. "Proud of him! I hate him. I loathe him. He is right; he speaks truly; he has invented such a process - a process that permits him to slay men with impunity, and change them into black and shining marble. He is, as you say, a remarkable man."

The two guests gaze in astonishment at the woman who has risen from her seat, and with dilated eyes points at her husband, who sits back in his chair smoking his cigar.

"My dear Beatrice," he coldly exclaims it last, "you have another of your hysterical fits coming on. I am afraid I have erred in allowing you to hear so much of my discoveries. You are overwrought and excited. If you would rather retire, we will excuse you."

"I denounce you," she cries, "denounce you before your guests as a murderer - the murderer of the man who was in your employ three years ago. They searched London for him, and he was never found, and why? Because he never left this house; because he is here now. I dare you, I defy you, to take your friends, scientists like yourself, to your laboratory and show them the black statue - the body of the man you murdered, as you would murder me - if you dared."

The doctor frowns and looks perplexedly at his guests.

"I am sorry, my dear friends," he exclaims, rising and

laying a hand on the shoulder of each. "It is very unfortunate, poor girl. You understand, of course. You mind humouring her? Will you come and see the statue that frightens her? It's a magnificent piece of work, a Greek god I bought in Florence."

The doctor and his colleagues descend to the laboratory, and his wife follows.

With eyes that keenly appreciate, the two men glance around the room at the various appliances and delicate instruments that fill the cases lining the walls, at the strange-looking coils and other apparatus that even they cannot give names to.

"Here," cries the doctor, walking to the alcove screened by the curtain, "is the statue. Life-like I confess, startingly life-like; but that is all. Behold!"

With a flourish almost melodramatic, he flings back the curtain, and the lights gleam upon the polished figure - the Greek god with his arms folded upon his breast. The men stand rooted to the spot in admiration.

"Well, what do you think of my statue?"

"Your victim!"

"Hush, Beatrice. You alarm my friends."

"It is magnificent!"

"Yes," the doctor continues, "it is life itself. Look how the muscles stand out upon the arms, the veins in the hands and temples. Observe the folds of the girdle. Is it not superb?"

"Perfection!"

"And yet it is marble. Only marble, Beatrice," he continues, picking up a tiny pestle from the table. "Test it. Hertz."

"My dear Hazard -"

"To gratify her. Perhaps it will soothe her."

Dr. Hertz places his hand upon the smooth, cold surface of the statue, and then lightly taps it.

"It's a body," the woman cries. "Can't you see it is a body, or are you fools?"

"My dear Mrs. Hazard, no. You must forget all about that; it's only a beautiful piece of work in marble."

"You fool!"

"Beatrice, how dare you?"

"Now, my dear Hazard, don't excite her. It's very unfortunate."

"It's marble, Beatrice, don't you understand? Marble! marble! marble!" and the doctor strikes the figure with his fist as he shouts and glares at his wife. "I'm expecting a companion to it, Beatrice - a Venus. I've waited too long for it. I've been too lenient, but I will have it within a week."

There are hidden meanings, for his wife alone, in all that Dr. Hazard says during the remainder of the evening, and she answers back, scorn for scorn, hate for hate, and contempt for his contempt.

He has received the half-suggested, half-expressed commiserations of his friends with the quiet dignity suitable to the circumstances, and now he bolts the door and descends direct to the laboratory.

"It's a good thing for me that some scientists are fools, or I should have been in a bad way to-night," he mutters. "Curse the spitfire, she's too dangerous."

He passes into the inner room, there is a sound of basket work creaking as a big jar is dragged across the room, and then a running and splashing as liquid pours into the bath. The furnace throws out a ruddy glow, and the doctor takes off his coat and vest, and works in a red light as the heat of the room increases.

Then wires are attached to one of the strange instruments at which his guests had marvelled, the opposite ends to plates of metal which are cast into the bath, and, lighting a cigar, he starts the battery and waits.

In a quarter of an hour he dips a rod into the liquid, and, withdrawing it, gazes with a sigh of satisfaction at the black, shining glaze with which it has become coated. Then, placing it on one side, he re-enters the outer room.

For a moment he stands listening at the door of the laboratory, and then stealthily moves up the stairs. The house is silent. Through the long, oval fanlight over the hall door a struggling moonbeam throws a narrow ribbon of light upon the polished floor. Outside, a distant footstep approaches, passes, and fades away. The clock strikes two.

Slowly he ascends towards his wife's room. No doubt she is sleeping, and the task will be easier. And then, in the blackness of the staircase, he becomes conscious of another person, hears the faint suppressed breathing of someone hiding, lurking in the darkest corner and fearful of discovery.

He takes a phial from his pocket, and holding it well away from his face, pours the contents upon a handkerchief and listens again. Yes, there is someone. It is Beatrice. Perhaps creeping down to him as he is creeping up to her; coming by stealth to kill him as he works.

Suddenly he springs forward, and grips her by the throat. There is an instant's struggle as he holds the handkerchief over her mouth - a moan, stifled in its birth, and she drops limply to the floor - dead.

Half carrying, half dragging the body, he descends to the laboratory. The light has gone out.

"Curse it," he mutters; "at this time, above all others - and I boasted it was infallible."

He passes into the inner room, where the crimson glow from the furnace gives just sufficient light to enable him to discern the outline of the bath, and then gradually and carefully he lowers his burden, until it lies full length upon the bottom and the liquid rises almost to the edge.

He returns to the outer chamber, and by the flare of a spirit-lamp sets himself to remedy the defect in the light. As he works in the shadow, a woman glides round the half-open door, glances at him, then at the knife she carries; but, as he slightly shifts his position, passes swiftly across the room and conceals herself behind the curtain of the empty alcove.

The doctor holds the lamp above his head, and looks anxiously around. The curtains sway as though someone moved behind them, and he holds his breath and takes a step backwards; then the half-open door catches his eye, and with a sneer at his own nerves he pushes it to and turns again to his work.

A little longer, and the rooms blaze with light once more, and he walks into the inner chamber and gazes into the bath.

At the bottom there lies a figure seemingly cut from black polished marble. There is a long-drawn sigh behind him, and he turns with an involuntary cry of terror.

"Beatrice!"

He must be mad, haunted; he grips the side of the bath and stares down into it.

Yes, there lies the woman - not Beatrice, but the sister of the man standing behind that curtain - the two now turned to everlasting stone.

He knows that his wife is walking towards him, and yet he cannot move; his limbs seem paralysed. In a moment she will clutch him, and force him down beside his victim.

He must break the spell of horror that roots him to the spot, and with a supreme effort he takes a step towards her; but the gleam of frenzy in her eyes unnerves him. He blindly retreats, then stumbles against the bath, and, falling backwards, meets the doom he had prepared for her.

The Pool of the Stone God
Abraham Merritt

This is Professor James Marston's story. A score of learned bodies have courteously heard him tell it, and then among themselves have lamented that so brilliant a man should have such an obsession.

Professor Marston told it to me in San Francisco, just before he started to find the island that holds his pool of the stone god and the wings that guard it. He seemed to me very sane. It is true that the equipment of his expedition was unusual, and not the least curious part of it are the suits of fine chain mail and masks and gauntlets with which each man of the party is provided.

The five of us, said Professor Marston, sat side by side on the beach.

There was Wilkinson the first officer, Bates and Cassidy the two seamen, Waters the pearler and myself. We had all been on our way to New Guinea, I to study the fossils for the Smithsonian. The Moranus had struck the hidden reef the night before and had sunk swiftly. We were then, roughly, about five hundred miles northeast of the Guinea coast. The five of us had managed to drop a lifeboat and get away. The boat was well stocked with water and provisions. Whether the rest of the crew had escaped we did not know. We had sighted the island at dawn and had made for her. The lifeboat was drawn safely up on the sands.

"We'd better explore a bit, anyway," said Waters. "This may be a perfect place for us to wait rescue. At least until the typhoon season is over. We've our pistols. Let's start by following this brook to its source, look over the place and then decide what we'll do."

The trees began to thin out. We saw ahead an open space. We reached it and stopped in sheer amazement. The clearing was perfectly square and about five hundred feet wide. The trees stopped abruptly at its edges as though held back by something unseen.

But it was not this singular impression that held us. At the far end of the square were a dozen stone huts clustered about one slightly larger. They reminded me powerfully of those prehistoric structures you see in parts of England and France. I approach now the most singular thing about this whole singular and sinister place. In the centre of the space was a pool walled about with huge blocks of cut stone. At the side of the pool rose a great stone figure, carved in the semblance of a man with outstretched hands. It was at least twenty feet high and was extremely well executed. At the distance the statue seemed nude and yet it had a peculiar effect of drapery about it. As we drew nearer we saw that it was covered from ankles to neck with the most extraordinary carved wings. They looked exactly like bat wings when they were folded.

There was something extremely disquieting about this figure. The face was inexpressibly ugly and malignant. The eyes, Mongol-shaped, slanted evil. It was not from the face, though, that this feeling seemed to emanate. It was from the body covered with wings - and especially from the wings. They were part of the idol and yet they gave one the idea that they were clinging to it.

Cassidy, a big brute of a man, swaggered up to the idol and laid his hand on it. He drew it away quickly, his face white, his mouth twitching. I followed him and conquering my unscientific repugnance, examined the stone. It, like the huts and in fact the whole place, was clearly the work of that forgotten race whose monuments are scattered over the Southern Pacific. The carving of the wings was wonderful.

They were batlike, as I have said, folded and each ended in a little ring of conventionalised feathers. They ranged in size from four to ten inches. I ran my fingers over one. Never have I felt the equal of the nausea that sent me to my knees before the idol. The wing had felt like smooth, cold stone, but I had the sensation of having touched back of the stone some monstrous obscene creature of a lower world.

The sensation came of course, I reasoned, only from the temperature and texture of the stone - and yet this did not really satisfy me.

Dusk was soon due. We decided to return to the beach and examine the clearing further on the morrow. I desired greatly to explore the stone huts.

We started back through the forest. We walked some distance and then night fell. We lost the brook. After a half hour's wandering we heard it again. We started for it. The trees began to thin out and we thought we were approaching the beach. Then Waters clutched my arm. I stopped. Directly in front of us was the open space with the stone god leering under the moon and the green water shining at his feet!

We had made a circle. Bates and Wilkinson were exhausted. Cassidy swore that devils or no devils he was going to camp that night beside the pool!

The moon was very bright. And it was so very quiet. My scientific curiosity got the better of me and I thought I would examine the huts.

I left Bates on guard and walked over to the largest. There was only one room and the moonlight shining through the chinks in the wall illuminated it clearly. At the back were two small basins set in the stone. I looked in one and saw a faint reddish gleam reflected from a number of globular objects. I drew a half dozen of them out. They were pearls, very wonderful pearls of a peculiarly rosy hue. I ran toward the door to call Bates - and stopped!

My eyes had been drawn to the stone idol. Was it an effect of the moonlight or did it move? No, it was the wings! They stood out from the stone and waved - they waved, I say, from the ankles to the neck of that monstrous statue.

Bates had seen them, too. He was standing with his pistol raised. Then there was a shot. And after that the air was filled with a rushing sound like that of a thousand fans. I saw the wings loose themselves from the stone god and sweep down in a cloud upon the four men.

Another cloud raced up from the pool and joined them. I could not move. The wings circled swiftly around and about the four. All were now on their feet and I never saw such horror as was in their faces.

Then the wings closed in. They clung to my companions as they had clung to the stone.

I fell back into the hut. I lay there through the night insane with terror. Many times I heard the fan-like rushing about the enclosure, but nothing entered my hut. Dawn came, and silence, and I dragged myself to the door. There stood the stone god with the wings carved upon him as we had seen him ten hours before!

I ran over to the four lying on the grass. I thought that perhaps I had had a nightmare. But they were dead. That was not the worst of it.

Each man was shrunken to his bones! They looked like collapsed white balloons. There was not a drop of blood in them. They were nothing but bones wrapped around in thin skin!

Mastering myself, I went close to the idol. There was something different about it. It seemed larger - as though, the thought went through my mind, as though it had eaten. Then

I saw that it was covered with tiny drops of blood that had dropped from the ends of the wings that clothed it!

I do not remember what happened afterward. I awoke on the pearling schooner Luana which had picked me up, crazed with thirst as they supposed in the boat of the Moranus.

THE SEA-WITCH
Nictzin Dyalhis

Heldra Helstrom entered my life in a manner peculiarly her own. And while she was the most utterly damnable woman in all the world, at the same time, in my opinion, she was the sweetest and the most superbly lovely woman who ever lived. A three-day northeast gale was hammering at the coast. It was late in the fall of the year, and cold as only our North Atlantic coast can very well be, but in the very midst of the tempest I became afflicted with a mild form of claustrophobia. So I donned sea-boots, oilskins and sou'wester hat, and sallied forth for a walk along the shore. My little cottage stood at the top of a high cliff. There was a broad, safe path running down to the beach, and down it I hurried. The short winter day was even then drawing to a close, and after I'd trudged a quarter of a mile along the shore, I decided I'd best return to my comfortable fireside. The walk had at least given me a good appetite. There was none of the usual lingering twilight of a clear winter evening. Darkness fell so abruptly I was glad I'd brought along a powerful flashlight. I'd almost reached the foot of my path up the cliff when I halted, incredulous, yet desiring to make sure.

I turned the ray of the flashlight on the great comber just curling to break on the shore, and held the light steady, my breath gasping in my throat. Such a thing as I thought I'd seen couldn't be - yet it was!

I started to run to the rescue, and could not move a foot. A power stronger than my own will held me immovable. I could only watch, spellbound. And even as I stared, that gigantic comber gently subsided, depositing its precious living burden on the sands as softly as any nurse laying a babe into a cradle.

Waist-deep in a smother of foam she stood for a brief second, then calmly waded ashore and walked with free swinging stride straight up the beam of my flashlight to where I stood. Regardless of the hellish din and turmoil of the tempest, I thrilled, old as I am, at the superb loveliness of this most amazing specimen of flotsam ever a raging sea cast ashore within memory of man. Never a shred of clothing masked her matchless body, yet her flesh glowed rosy-white, when by all natural laws it should have been blue-white from the icy chill of wintry seas. "Well!" I exclaimed. "Where did you come from? Are you real - or am I seeing that which is not?"

"I am real," replied a clear, silvery voice. "And I came from out there." An exquisitely moulded arm flung a gesture toward the raging ocean. "The ship I was on was sinking, so I stripped off my garb, flung myself on Ran's bosom, and Ran's horses gave me a most magnificent ride! But well for you that you stood still as I bade you, while I walked ashore. Ran is an angry god, and seldom well-disposed toward mortals."

"Ran?" The sea-god of the old Norse Vikings! What strange woman was this, who talked of "Ran" and his "horses," the white-maned waves of old ocean? But then I bethought me of her naked state in that unholy tempest. "Surely you must be Ran's daughter," I said. "That reef is ten miles off land! Come - I have a house near by, and comforts - you cannot stand here."

"Lead, and I will follow," she replied simply.

She went up that path with greater ease than I, and walked companionably beside me from path-top to house, although she made no talk. Oddly, I felt that she was reading me, and that what she read gave her comfort.

When I opened the door, it seemed as if she held back for a merest moment.

"Enter," I bade her, a bit testily. "I should think you'd had enough of this weather by now!"

She bowed her head with a natural stateliness which convinced me that she was no common person, and murmured something too low for me to catch, but the accents had a distinct Scandinavian trend. "What did you say?" I queried, for I supposed she'd spoken to me.

"I invoked the favour of the old gods on the hospitable of heart, and on the sheltering rooftree," she replied. Then she crossed my threshold, but she reached out her arm and rested her shapely white hand lightly yet firmly on my left forearm as she stepped within.

She went direct to the big stove, which was glowing dull-red, and stood there, smiling slightly, calm, serene, wholly ignoring her nakedness, obviously enjoying the warmth, and not by a single shiver betraying that she had any chill as result of exposure.

"I think you need this," I said, proffering a glass of brandy. "There's time enough for exchanging names and giving explanations, later," I added. "But right now, I'll try and find something for you to put on. I have no women's things in the house, as I live alone, but will do the best I can."

I passed into my bedroom, laid out a suit of pyjamas and a heavily quilted bathrobe, and returned to the living-room where she stood.

"You are a most disconcertingly beautiful young woman," I stated bluntly; "which you know quite well without being told. But doubtless you will feel more at ease if you go in there and don some things I've laid out for you. When you come out, I'll get some supper ready."

She was back instantly, still unclad. I stared, wonderingly.

"Those things did not fit," she shrugged. "And that heavy robe - in this warm house?"

"But -" I began.

"But - this," she smiled, catching up a crimson silk spread embroidered in gold, which covered a sandalwood table I'd brought from the orient many years before. A couple of swift motions and the gorgeous thing became a wondrous robe adorning her lovely figure, clinging, and in some subtle manner hinting at the flawless splendour of her incomparable body. A long narrow scarf of black silk whereon twisted a silver dragon was whipped from its place on a shelf and transposed into a sash from her swelling breasts to her sloping hips, bringing out more fully every exquisite curve of her slender waist and torso - and she smiled again.

"Now," she laughed softly, "am I still a picture for your eyes? I hope so, for you have befriended me this night - I who sorely need a friend; and it is such a little thing I can do - making myself pleasing in your sight.

"And because you have holpen me" - I stared at the archaic form she used - "and will continue to aid and befriend (for so my spirit tells me), I will love you always, love you as Ragnar Wave-Flame loved Jarl Wulf Red-Brand, as a younger sister, or a dutiful niece."

"Yet of her it is told," I interrupted, deliberately speaking Swedish and watching keenly to see the effect, "that the love given by the foam-born Sea-Witch brought old Earl Wulf of the Red-Sword but little luck, and that not of a sort desired by most men!"

"That is ill said," she retorted. "His fate was from the Norns, as is the fate of all. Not hers the fault of his doom, and when his carles within the hour captured his three slayers, she took red vengeance. With her own foam-white hands she flayed them alive, and covered their twitching bodies with salt ere she placed the old Jarl in his long-ship and set it afire. And she sailed with that old man on his last seafaring, steering his blazing dragon-ship out of the stead, singing of his great deeds in life, that the heroes in Valhalla might know who honoured them by his coming."

She paused, her superb bosom heaving tumultuously. Then with a visible effort she calmed herself.

"But you speak my tongue, and know the old tales of the Skalds. Are you, then, a Swede?"

"I speak the tongue, and the old tales of the Skalds, the ancient minstrels, I learned from my grandmother, who was of your race."

"Of my race?" her tone held a curious inflection. "Ah, yes! All women are of one race... perhaps."

"But I spoke of supper," I said, moving toward the kitchen.

"But - no!" She barred my progress with one of her lovely hands laid flat against my chest. "It is not meet and fitting, Jarl Wulf, that you should cook for me, like any common house-carle! Rather, let your niece, Heldra, prepare for you a repast."

"'Heldra'? That, then, is your name?"

"Heldra Helstrom, and your loving niece," she nodded.

"But why call me Jarl Wulf?" I demanded, curious to understand. She had bestowed the name seriously, rather than in playful banter.

"Jarl Wulf you were, in a former life," she asserted flatly. "I knew you on the shore, even before Ran's horse stood me on my feet!"

"Surely, then, you must be Ragnar Wave-Flame born again," I countered.

"How may that be?" she retorted. "Ragnar Wave-Flame never died; and surely I do not look that old! The sea-born witch returned to the sea-caves whence she came, when the dragon-ship burned out... But ask me not of myself, now.

"Yet one thing more I will say: The warp and woof of this strange pattern wherein we both are depicted was woven of the Norns ere the world began. We have met before - we meet again, here and now - we shall meet yet again; but how, and when, and where, I may not say."

"Of a truth, you are 'fey'," I muttered.

"At times - I am," she assented. Then her wondrous sapphire eyes gleamed softly into my own hard grey eyes, her smile was tender, wistful, womanly, and my doubts were dissipated like wisps of smoke. Yet I shook an admonitory forefinger at her:

"Witch at least I know you to be," I said in mock harshness. "Casting glamyr on an old man."

"No need for witchery," she laughed. "All women possess that power!"

During the "repast" she spread before me, I told her that regardless of who I might have been in a dim and remote past of which I had no memory, in this present life I was plain John Craig, retired professor of anthropology, ethnology and archaeology, and living on a very modest income. I explained that while I personally admired her, and she was welcome to remain in my home for ever, yet in the village near by were curious minds, and gossiping tongues, and evil thoughts a-plenty, and if I were to tell the truth of her arrival -

"But I have nowhere to go, and none save you to befriend me; all I loved or owned is out there." Again she indicated the general direction of the reef. "And you say that I may remain here, indefinitely? I will be known as your niece, Heldra, no? Surely, considering the differences in our age and appearance, there can be no slander."

Her eyes said a thousand things no words could convey. There was eagerness, sadness, and a strange tenderness... I came to an abrupt decision. After all, whose business was it?

"I am alone in the world, as you are," I said gravely. "As my niece, Heldra, you shall remain. If you will write out a list of a woman's total requirements in wearing-apparel, I will send away as soon as possible and have them shipped here in haste. I am old, as all can see, and I do not think any sensible persons will suspect aught untoward in your making your home with me. And I will think up a plausible story which will satisfy the minds of fools without telling, in reality, anything."

Our repast ended, we arose from the table and returned to the living-room. I filled and lighted a nargilyeh, a three-stemmed water-pipe, and settled myself in my armchair. She helped herself to a cigarette from a box on the table, then stretched her long, slender body at full length on my divan, in full relaxation of comfort.

I told her enough of myself and my forebears to insure her being able to carry out the fiction of being my niece. And in return I learned mighty little about her. But what she did tell me was sufficient. I never was unduly curious about other people's business.

Unexpectedly, and most impolitely, I yawned. Yet it was natural enough, and it struck me that she needed a rest, if anyone ever did. But before I could speak, she forestalled me. With a single graceful movement she rose from her reclining posture and came and stood before me within easy arm's-reach. Two swift motions, and her superb body flashed rosy-white, as nude as when she waded ashore.

The crimson silken spread she'd worn as regally as any robe was laid at my feet with a single gesture, the black scarf went across my knees, and the glorious creature was kneeling before me in attitude of absolute humility. Before I could remonstrate or bid her arise, her silvery voice rang softly, solemnly, like a muted trumpet:

"Thus, naked and with empty hands, out of the wintry seas in a twilight grey and cold, on a night of storm I came. And you lighted a beacon for my tired eyes, that I might see my way ashore. You led me up the cliff and to your hospitable hearth, and in your kindly heart you had already given the homeless a home.

"And now, kneeling naked before you, as I came, I place my hands between your hands – thus - and all that I am, and such service as I can render, are yours, hand-fasted."

I stared, well-nigh incredulous. In effect, in the old Norse manner, she was declaring herself to all intents and purposes my slave! But her silvery voice went on: "And now, I rise and cover myself again with the mantle of your bounty, that you may know me, indeed your niece, as Jarl Wulf knew Ragnar Wave-Flame!"

"Truly," I gasped in amazement when I could catch my breath, "you are a strange mixture of the ancient days and this modern period. I have known you but for a few hours, yet I feel toward you as that old Jarl must have felt toward that other sea-witch, unless indeed you and she are one!"

"Almost," she replied a trifle sombrely. "At least, she was my ancestress!" Then she added swiftly: "Do not misunderstand. Leman to the old Jarl she never was. But later, after he went to Valhalla, in the sea-girt isle where she dwelt she mated with a young Viking whom Ran had cast ashore sorely wounded and insensible. She nursed him back to life for sake of his beauty, and he made love to her. "But he soon tired of her and her witch ways; wherefore, in wrath she gave him back to Ran - and he was seen no more. Of that mating was born a daughter, also given to Ran, who pitied her and bore her to an old man and his wife whose steading was nigh to the mouth of a fjord; and they, being childless, called her Ranhild, and reared her as their daughter. In course of time, she wed, and bore three tall sons and a daughter...

"That was long and long ago - yet I have dived into Ragnar's hidden sea-cave and talked with Ragnar Wave-Flame face to face. All one night I lay in her arms, and in the dawning she breathed her breath on my brow, lips, and bosom; and all that following day she talked and I listened, and much I learned of the wisdom that an elder world termed witchcraft."

For a moment she lapsed into silence. Then she leaned forward, laid her shapely, cool hands on my temples and kissed me on my furrowed old forehead, very solemnly, yet with ineffable gentleness. "And now," she murmured, "ask me never again aught concerning myself, I pray you; for I have told all I may, and further questioning will drive me back to the sea. And I would not have that happen - yet!" Without another word she turned, flung herself at full length again on the divan, and, like any tired child, went instantly to sleep. Decidedly, I thought, this "niece" of mine was not as are other women; and later I found that she possessed certain abilities it is well for the world that few indeed can wield. She gave me another proof of that belief, by demonstrating her unholy powers, on the night of the next full moon after her arrival.

It was her custom of an evening to array herself as she had done on her first night - in crimson robe and black sash and naught else, despite the fact that her wardrobe which I had ordered from the great city forty miles away contained all any woman's heart could wish for. But I admit I enjoyed seeing her in that semi-barbaric attire. At times she would sit on the arm of my chair, often with her smooth cool cheek laid against my rough old face, and her exquisitely modelled arm curved about my leathery old neck. The first time she had done that, I had demanded ironically:

"Witch, are you making love to me?"

But her sighing, wistful reply had disarmed me, and likewise had brought a lump into my throat.

"Nay! Not that, 0 Jarl from of old! But - I never knew a father."

"Nor I a fair daughter," I choked. And thereafter, when that mood was upon her I indulged in no more ironies, and we'd sit for hours, neither speaking, engrossed in thoughts for which there are no words. But on the night whereof I write, she pressed her scarlet lips to my cheek, and I asked jestingly:

"Is there something you want, Heldra?"

"There is," she replied gravely. "Will you get a boat - one with oars and a sail, but no engine? Ran hates those."

"But surely you do not want it now, tonight, do you?"

"Yes, if you will be so kind to me."

"You must have a very good reason, or you'd not ask," I said. "I'll go and get a centre board dory and bring it to the beach at the foot of the cliff path. It's clear weather, and the sea is calm, with but a moderate breeze blowing; yet it is colder on the water than you imagine, so you'd best bundle up warmly."

"You will hasten," she implored anxiously.

"Surely," I nodded.

I went out and down to the wharves in the village, where I kept the boat I said I'd get. But when I beached the dory at foot of the path I stared, swearing softly under my breath. Not one stitch of apparel did that witch have on, save the crimson silk robe and black sash she'd worn when I left the cottage!

"Do you want to freeze?" I was provoked, I admit. "The very sight of you dressed like that gives me the shivers!"

"Neither you nor I will be cold this night," she laughed. "Isn't it glorious? And this is a good boat you brought. Please, let me sail it, and ask me no questions."

She took the tiller, hauled in on the sheet; the sail filled, and she began singing, with a queer, wild strain running through her song. That dory fairly flew - and I swear there was not enough wind to drive us at such speed.

Finally I saw something I didn't admire. No one does, who dwells on that part of the coast.

"Are you crazy, girl?" I demanded sharply. "That reef is dead ahead! Can't you see the breakers?"

"Why, so it is - the reef! And am I to be affrighted by a few puny breakers? Nay, it is in the heart of those breakers that I wish to be! But you - have you fear, O Jarl Wulf?"

I suspected from her tone that the witch was laughing at me; so I subsided, but fervently wished that I'd not been so indulgent of her whim for a moonlight sail on a cold winter's night. Then we hit those breakers - or rather, we didn't! For they seemed to part as the racing dory sped into them, making a smooth clear lane of silvery glinting water over which we glided as easily as if on a calm inland mill-pond!

"Drop the sail and unstep the mast," she called suddenly.

I was beyond argument, and obeyed dumbly, like any boat-carle of the olden days.

"Now, take to the oars," she directed, "and hold the boat just hereabouts for a while," and even as I slid the oars into the oarlocks she made that swift movement of hers and stood nude, the loveliest sight that grim, ship-shattering, life-destroying reef had ever beheld.

Suddenly she flung up both shapely white arms with a shrill, piercing cry, thrice repeated. Then without a word she went overside in a long clean dive, with never a splash to show where she'd hit the water. "Hold the boat about here for a while," she'd bidden me! All I'd ever loved in this world was somewhere down below, in the hellish cross-currents of that icy water! I'd hold that boat there, if need were, in the teeth of a worse tempest than raged the night she came to me. She'd find me waiting. And if she never came up, I'd hold that boat there till its planks rotted and I joined her in the frigid depths. It seemed an eternity, and I know that it was an hour ere a glimmer of white appeared beneath the surface. Then her shapely arm emerged and her hand grasped the gunwale, her regal head broke water, she blew like a porpoise; then she laughed in clear ringing triumph.

"You old dearling!" she cried in her archaic Norse. "Did I seem long gone? The boat has not moved a foot from where I dove. Come, bear a hand and lift my burden; it is heavy, and I am near spent. There are handles by which to grasp it."

The burden proved to be a greenish metal coffer - bronze, I judged - which I estimated to measure some twenty inches long by twelve wide and nine inches deep. And how she rose to the surface weighted with that, passes my understanding. But how she knew it was down there passes my comprehension, too. But then, Heldra Helstrom herself was an enigma.

She re-wrapped herself in her flimsy silken robe of crimson and smiled happily, when she should have been shivering almost to pieces.

"If you'll ship the mast and spread the sail again, Uncle John," she said, surprisingly matter-of-fact now that her errand was successfully accomplished, "we'll go home. I'd like a glass of brandy and a smoke, myself; and I read in your mind that such is your chief desire, at present."

Back at the cottage again, and comfortable once more, Heldra requested me to bear the coffer into her room, which I did. For over an hour she remained in there, then returned to the living-room where I sat, and I stared at the picture she presented. If she had always been beautiful, now she was surpassingly glorious.

Instead of the usual crimson robe, her lovely body was sheathed in a sleeveless, sheer, tightly fitting silken slip, cut at the throat in a long sloping V reaching nearly to her waist. The garment was palest sea-green, so flimsy in texture that it might as well have been compounded of mingled moon-mist and cobwebs. Her rosy-pearl flesh gleamed through the fabric with an alluring shimmer which thrilled anew my jaded old senses at the artistic wonder of her.

A gold collar, gem-studded, unmistakably of ancient Egyptian workmanship, was resting on her superb shoulders - loot of some Viking foray into the far South-lands, doubtless. A broad girdle of gold plates, squared, and also gem-studded, was about her sloping hips, and was clasped in front by a broader plate with a sun-emblem in jewelled sets; from which plate or buckle it fell in two broad bands nearly to her white slender feet.

Broad torques of gold on upper arms and about her wrists, and an intricately wrought golden tiara with disks of engraved gold pendent by chains and hanging over her ears, set off her loveliness as never before. Even her red-gold hair, braided in two thick ropes, falling over her breasts to below her waist, were clasped by gem-set brooches of gold. "Ragnar Wave-Flame's gift to me, O Jarl Wulf," she breathed softly. "Do you like your niece thus arrayed?"

Norse princess out of an elder day, or Norse witch from an even older and wickeder period of the world - whichever this Heldra Helstrom was, of one thing I was certain, no lovelier woman ever lived than this superb being who styled herself my "niece." And so I told her, and was amply rewarded by the radiance of her smile, and the ecstatic kiss she implanted on my cheek. Despite her splendid array, she perched on the arm of my chair, and began toying with my left hand. Presently she lifted it to the level of my eyes, laughing softly. I'd felt nothing, yet she'd slipped a broad tarnished silver ring of antique design on my third finger.

"It was yours in the ancient days, O Jarl Wulf," she whispered in her favourite tongue - the archaic form of the Norsk language. "Yours again is the ancient ring, now! Ragnar herself carved the mystic runes upon it. Shall I read them, O Jarl, or will you?"

"They are beyond my skill," I confessed. "The words are in the 'secret' language that only the Rime-Kanaars' understood. Nor was it well for others than witches and warlocks to seek to understand them."

"Ragnar took that ring from Jarl Wulf's finger ere she set fire to the dragon-ship," Heldra murmured. "Had those runes been on the ring when your foes set upon you - they, not you, would have perished in the sword-play, Jarl Red-Sword!

"But the sea-born witch knew that you would weary of Valhalla in a day to come, and would return to this world of strife and slaying, of loss and grief, of hate and the glutting of vengeance - and, knowing, she carved the runes, that in time the charmed ring would return to its proper owner.

"It is her express command that I read them to you, for knowing the runes, never shall water drown or fire burn; nor sword or spear or axe ever wound you, so be it that in time of danger you speak the weird words!

"And for my sake - you who are my 'Uncle John' to all the rest of the world, but to me are dearer than old Jarl Wulf was to Ragnar the sea-witch - I implore you to learn the runic charm, and use it if ever danger menaces. Promise me! Promise me, I say!"

Her silvery voice was vibrant with fierce intensity. She caught my right hand and pressed it against her palpitant body, just beneath her proudly swelling left breast. "Promise!" she reiterated. "I beg your promise! With your right hand on my heart I adjure you to learn the rune."

"No fool like an old fool," I grumbled, adding a trifle maliciously, "particularly when in the hands of a lovely woman. But such a fuss you make over a few words of outlandish gibberish! Read me the rune, then, witch-maid! I'd learn words worse than those can be to please you and set your mind at rest."

With her scarlet lips close to my ear, with bated breath, and in a tone so low I could barely catch her carefully enunciated syllables, she whispered the words. And although her whisper was softer than the sighing of gentlest summer breeze, the tones rang on my inner hearing like strokes of a great war-hammer smiting on a shield of bronze. There was no need to repeat them - either on her part or mine. There was no likelihood of my ever forgetting that runic charm. I could not, even if I would.

"Surely," I muttered, "you are an adept in the ancient magic. Well for me that you love me, else your witcheries might

Most amazingly she laughed, a clear, ringing merriment with no trace of the mystic about it.

"Let me show you something - a game, a play; one that will amuse me and entertain you."

She fairly danced across the room and into her own room, emerging with an antique mirror of some burnished, silver-like metal. This she held out to me. I grasped it by its handle obediently enough, humouring this new whim.

"Look into it and say if it is a good mirror," she bade, her sapphire eyes a-dance with elfin mirth.

I looked. All I could see was my same old face, tanned and wrinkled, which I daily saw whenever I shaved or combed my hair, and I told her so. She perched again on the arm of my chair, laid her cheek against mine, and curved her cool arm about my neck.

"Now look again!"

Again the mirror told truth. I saw my face the same as ever, and hers as well, "Like a rose beside a granite boulder," as I assured her.

"You do but see yourself as you think of yourself," she murmured softly, "and me you behold as you believe me to be."

She brought her lips close to the mirror and breathed upon its surface with her warm breath. It clouded over, then cleared. Her voice came, more murmurous than before, but with a definite note of sadness: "Once more, look! Behold yourself as I see you always; and behold me as I know myself to be! And when I am gone beyond your ken, remember the witch-maid, Heldra, as one woman who loved you so truly that she showed you herself as she actually was!"

The man's face was still my own, but mine as it was in the days of early manhood, ere life's thunders had graven their scars on brow and cheeks and lips, and before the snows of many winters had whitened my hair.

Her features were no less beautiful, but in her reflected eyes I saw ages and ages of life, and bitter experience, and terrible wisdom that was far more wicked than holy; and it came to me with conviction irrefutable that beside this young-appearing girl, maid, or woman, all my years were but as the span of a puling babe compared to the ageless age of an immortal.

"That, at least, is no glamyr," her voice sighed drearily, heavy with the burden of her own knowledge of herself.

I laid my thick, heavy old arm across her smooth satiny white shoulders, and I turned her head until her sapphire eyes met mine fairly. Very gently I kissed her on her brow.

"Heldra Helstrom," I said, and my voice sounded husky with emotion, "you may be all you have just shown me, or worse! You may be Ragnar Wave-Flame herself, the sea-witch who never dies. You may be even what I sometimes suspect, the empress of Hell, come amongst mortals for no good purpose! But be you what you may, old or young, maid or woman, good or evil, witch, spirit, angel or she-devil, such as you are, you are you and I am I, and for some weird reason we seem to love each other in our own way; so let there be an end to what you are or have been, or who I was in other lives, and content ourselves with what is!"

Were those bright glitters in her sapphire eyes tear-drops ready to fall? If so, I was not sure, for with a cry like that of a lost soul who has found sanctuary, she buried her face on my shoulder... After a long silence, she slipped from the arm of my chair, and wordlessly, her face averted, she passed into her room. After an hour or so, I went to my own room - but I could not sleep... Time passed, and I dwelt in a "fool's paradise," dreaming that it would last for ever. The summer colony began to arrive. There were cottages all along the shore, but there were likewise big estates, whose owners were rated as "somebodies," to put it mildly.

A governor of a great and sovereign state; an ex-president of our nation; several foreign diplomats and some of their legation attaches - but why enumerate, when one man only concerns this narrative? Michael Commnenus, tall, slight, dapper, inclined to swarthiness, with black eyes under crescent-curved black eyebrows; with supercilious smiling lips, a trifle too red for a man; with suave Old World manners, and a most amazingly conceited opinion of himself as a "Lady-charmer."

It was not his first summer in our midst; and although when he was in Washington at his legation I never gave him a thought, when I saw his too handsome face on the beach, I felt a trifle sick! I knew, positively, that the minute he set eyes on Heldra... Of course I knew, too, that my witch-niece could take care of herself; but just the same, I sensed annoyance, and perhaps, tragedy. Well, I was in nowise mistaken.

Heldra and I were just about to shove off in my dory for a sail. It was her chief delight, and mine too, for that matter.

Casually, along strolled Michael Commnenus, twirling a slender stick, caressing a slender black thread he styled a moustache, smiling his approbation of himself. I'd seen that variety of casual approach before. As our flippant young moderns say: It was "old stuff."

Out of the corner of my eye I watched. The Don Juan smirk faded when his calculating, appraising eyes met her sapphire orbs, now shining like the never-melting polar ice. An expression of bewilderment spread over his features. His swarthy skin went a sickly greenish-bronze. Involuntarily he crossed himself and passed on. The man was afraid, actually fear-struck!

"Ever see him before, Heldra?" I queried. "He looked at you as if the devil would be a pleasanter sight. That's one man who failed to fall for your vivid beauty, you sea-witch!"

"Who is he?" she asked in a peculiar tone. "I liked his looks even less than he liked mine."

"Michael Commnenus," I informed her, and was about to give her his pedigree as we local people knew him, but was interrupted by her violently explosive:

"Who?"

"Michael Commnenus," I stated again, a trifle testily. "And you needn't shout! What's he done but again she interrupted, speaking her archaic Norsk:

"Ho! Varang Chiefs of the Guard Imperial! Thorfinn! Arvid! Sven! And ye who followed them - Gudrun! Randvar! Haakon! Smid! And all ye Varangs in Valhalla, give ear! And ye, 0 fiends, witches, warlocks, trolls, vampyrs, and all the dark gods who dwell in Hel's halls where the eternal frozen fires blaze without heat, give ear to my voice, and cherish my words, for I give ye all joyous tidings.

"He lives! After all these long centuries Michael Commnenus dwells again on the bosom of fair Earth! In a body of flesh and blood and bone, of nerve and tissue and muscle he lives! He lives, I say! And I have found him!

"Oh, now I know why the Norns who rule all fate sent me to this place. And I shall not fail ye, heroes! Content ye, one and all, I shall not fail!"

Was this the gorgeous beauty I'd learned to love for her gentleness? Hers was the face of a furious female demon for a moment; but then her normal expression returned and she sighed heavily.

"Heed me not, Uncle John," she said drearily. "I did but recall an ancient tale of foul treachery perpetrated on sundry Norsemen in the Varangian Guard of a Byzantine emperor ages agone.

"The niddering - worse than 'coward' - who wrought the bane of some thirty-odd Vikings, was a Commnenus, nephew to the Emperor Alexander Commnenus... I live too much in memories of the past, I fear, and for the moment somewhat forgot myself in the hate all good Norse maids should hold toward any who bear the accursed name of the Commneni.

"Still, even as I know you to be old Jarl Wulf Red-Brand returned to this world through the gateway of birth - it would be nothing surprising if this spawn of the Commneni were in truth that same Michael Commnenus of whom the tale is told."

"The belief in reincarnation is age-old," I said reflectively. "And in several parts of the world it is a fundamental tenet of religion. If there be truth in the idea, there is, as you say, nothing surprising if anybody now living should have been anybody else in some former life... And that sample of the Commneni appears quite capable of any treachery that might serve a purpose at the moment! But, Heldra," I implored her, struck by a sudden intuition, "I beg of you not to indulge in any of your devilries, witcheries, or Norse magic. If this Michael is that other Michael, yet that was long ago; and if he has not already atoned for his sin, you may be very sure that somewhere, sometime, somehow he will atone; so do not worry your regal head about him."

"Spoken like a right Saga-man," she smiled as I finished my brief homily. "I thank you for your words of wisdom. And now, Jarl Wulf Red-Brand, I know you to be fey as well as I am. 'Surely he will atone for his sin'... oh! a most comforting thought! So let us think no more about the matter."

I glanced sharply at her. Her too instant acquiescence was suspicious. But her sapphire eyes met mine fairly, smilingly, sending as always a warm glow of contentment through me. So I accepted her assurance as it sounded, and gave myself up to the enjoyment of the sail and the sound of her silvery voice as she sang an old English love ballad I'd known as a young man. And under the spell of her magnetic personality gradually the episode of Michael Commnenus faded into nothingness - for a while.

A couple of days later, just about dark, Heldra came down the stairs from the attic, where she'd been rummaging. In her hand she carried an old violin-case. I looked and grinned ruefully. "You are a bad old Uncle John," she scolded. "Why did you not tell me you played the 'fidel,' even as Jarl Wulf played one in his time? Think of all the sweet music you might have made in the past winter nights, and think of the dances I might have danced for your delight while you played - even as Ragnar danced for her old Jarl."

"But I did not tell you that I played a fiddle - because I don't," I stated flatly. "That is a memento of an absurd ambition I once cherished, but which died a-borning. I tried to learn the thing, but the noises I extracted were so abominable that I quit before I'd fairly got started."

"You are teasing," she retorted, her eyes sparkling with mischief. "But I am not to be put off thus easily. Tonight you will play, and I will dance - such a dance as you have never beheld even when you were Jarl Wulf."

"If I try to play that thing," I assured her seriously, "you'll have a time dancing to my discords, you gorgeous tease!"

"We'll see," she nodded. "But even as my magic revealed to me the whereabouts of the 'fidel,' so my spirit tells me that you play splendidly."

"Your 'magic' may be all right, but your 'spirit' has certainly misinformed you," I growled.

"My spirit has never yet lied to me - nor has it done so this time." Her tone was grave, yet therein was a lurking mockery; and I became a trifle provoked.

"All right," I assented grouchily. "Whenever you feel like hearing me 'play,' I'll do it. And you'll never want to listen to such noises again."

She went into her room laughing sweetly, and took the fiddle with her.

After supper she said nothing about me playing that old fiddle, and I fatuously thought she'd let the matter drop. But about ten o'clock she went to her room without a word. She emerged after a bit, wearing naught but a sheer loose palest blue silk robe, held at the waist only by a tiny jewelled gold filigree clasp. Loose as the robe was, it clung lovingly to her every curve as if caressing the beauteous, statuesque body it could not and would not conceal.

She was totally devoid of all ornament save that tiny brooch, and her wondrous fiery-gold hair was wholly unconfined, falling below her waist in a cascade of shimmering sunset hues, against which her rose-pearl body gleamed through the filmy gossamer-like robe.

Again she sat and talked for a while. But along toward midnight she broke a short silence with:

"I'll be back in a minute. I wish to prepare for my dancing."

From her room she brought four antique bronze lamps and a strangely shaped urn of oil. She filled the lamps and placed one at each corner of the living-room, on the floor.

Back into her room she went, and out again with an octagonal-shaped stone, flat on both sides, about an inch thick, and some four inches across. This she placed on the low taboret whereon I usually kept my nargilyeh. She propped up that slab of stone as if placing a mirror - which I decided it couldn't very well be, as it did not even reflect light but seemed as dull as a slab of slate.

As a final touch, she brought out that confounded old fiddle! And on her scarlet lips was a smile that a seraph might have envied, so innocent and devoid of guile it seemed.

"What's this?" I demanded - as if I didn't know!

"Your little 'fidel' with which you will make for your Heldra such rapturous music," she smiled caressingly.

"Um-m-m-m!" I grunted. "And what are those lamps for - and that ugly slab of black rock?"

"That black slab is a 'Hel-stone,' having the property of reflecting whatever is directly before it, if illumined by those four lamps placed at certain angles; and later it will give off those same reflections - even as the stuff called luminous calcium sulphide absorbs light-rays until surcharged, and then emits them, when properly exposed. So, you see, we can preserve the picture of my dance."

"Heldra," I demanded sharply, "are you up to some devilishness? All this looks amazingly like the stage-setting for witch-working!"

"I have sung for you, on different nights," she replied in gentlest reproach, "and have told old tales, and have attired myself again and again for your pleasure in beholding me. Have all these things ever bewitched you, or harmed anyone? How, then, can the fact of my dancing for my own satisfaction, before the mystic Hel-stone, do any harm?"

As ever, she won. Her sapphire orbs did queer things to me whenever they looked into my own grey, faded old eyes - trusting me to understand and approve whatever she did, simply because she was she and I was I.

"All right," I said. "But you're making a fool of me - insisting that I play this old fiddle. Well - I'll teach you a lesson!" And I drew the bow over the strings with a most appalling wail.

And with the unexpected swiftness of a steel trap closing on its victim, icy fingers locked about my wrist, and I knew very definitely that another and alien personality was guiding my arm and fingers! But there came likewise a swift certitude that if I behaved, no harm would ensue - to me, at least. So I let the thing have its way - and listened to such music as I had not believed could be played on any instrument devised by a mortal.

I wish that I could describe that music, but I do not know the right words. I doubt if they have been invented. It was wild, barbaric, savage, but likewise it was alluring, seductive, stealing away all inhibitions - too much of it would have corrupted the angels in heaven. I was almost in a stupor, intoxicated, like a hasheesh-eater in a drugged dream, spellbound, unable to break from the thralldom holding my will, drowning in rapture well-nigh unbearable.

Heldra suddenly blew out the big kerosene lamp standing on the table, leaving as sole illumination the rays from those four bronze lights standing in the corners.

Her superb body moved gracefully, slowly at first, then faster, into the intricate figure and pattern of a dance that was old when the world was young...

With inward horror I knew the why and wherefore of that entire ceremonial; knew I'd been be-cozened and be-japed; yet knew, likewise, that it was too late for interference. I could not even speak. I could but watch, while some personality alien to my body played maddeningly on my fiddle, and the 'niece' I loved danced a dance deliberately planned to seduce a man who hated and feared the dancer - and for what devilish purpose I could well guess!

I saw the light-rays converge on her alluring, statuesque body, saw them apparently pass through her and impinge on the surface of that black, sullen, octagonal Hel-stone, and be greedily swallowed up, until the dull, black surface glowed like a rare black Australian opal; and ever the dancing of the witch-girl grew more alluring, more seductive, more abandoned. And I knew why Heldra was thus shamefully - shamelessly, rather - conducting! She had read Michael Commnenus his character very accurately; knew that his soul had recognized her hatred for him, and feared her - and that her one chance to get him in her clutches lay in inflaming his senses... and she'd even told me the properties of that most damnable Hel-stone!

Wilder and faster came the music, and swifter and still more alluring grew the rhythmic response as Heldra's lovely body swayed and spun and swooped and postured; until ultimately her waving arms brought her fluttering hands, in the briefest of touches, into contact with the tiny brooch at her waist and the filmy robe was swept away in a single gesture that was faithfully recorded on the sullen surface of the Hel-stone.

Instantly the dancer stopped as if petrified, her arms outstretched as in invitation, her regal head thrown back, showing the long smooth white column of her throat, her clear, half-closed, sapphire-blue eyes agleam with subtle challenge...

The uncanny music died in a single sighing, sobbing whisper, poison-sweet... the clutching, icy fingers were gone from my wrist... my first coherent thought was: Had that spell been directed at me, the old adage anent "old fools" would have been swiftly justified!

And I knew that to all intents and purposes, Michael Commnenus was sunk!

Just the same, I was furious. Heldra had gone too far, and I told her so, flatly. I pointed out in terms unmistakable that what she planned was murder, or worse; and that this was modern America wherein witchcraft had neither place nor sanction, and that I'd be no accessory to any such devilishness as she was contriving. Oh, I made myself and my meaning plain.

And she stood and looked at me with a most injured expression. She made me feel as if I'd wantonly struck a child across the face in the midst of its innocent diversions!

"I don't actually care if the devil flies off with Michael Commnenus," I concluded wrathfully, "but I won't have him murdered by you while you're living here, posing as my niece! No doubt it's quite possible for you to evade any legal consequences by disappearing, but what of me? As accessory, I'd be liable to life imprisonment, at the least!"

Her face lightened as by magic, and her voice was genuinely regretful, and in her eyes was a light of sincere love. She came to me and wrapped her white arms about my neck, murmuring terms of affectionate consolation.

"Poor dear Uncle John! Heldra was thoughtless - wicked me! And I might have involved you in serious trouble? I am ashamed! But the fate laid upon me by the Norns is heavy, and I may not evade it, even for you, whom I love. Tell me," she demanded suddenly, "if I should destroy the vile earthworm without any suspicion attaching to you, or to me, would you love me as before, even knowing what I had done?"

"No!" I fairly snarled the denial. I wanted it to be emphatic.

She smiled serenely, and kissed me full on my lips.

"I never thought to thank a mortal for lying to me, but now I do! Deep in your heart I can read your true feeling, and I am glad! But now" - and her tone took on a sadness most desolate - "I regret to say that on the morrow I leave you. The lovely garments you gave me, and the trunks containing them, I take with me, as you would not wish that I go empty-handed. Nor will I insult you, 0 Jarl Wulf, by talk of payment.

"When I am gone, you will just casually mention that I have returned to my home, and the local gossips will not suspect aught untoward. And soon I shall be forgotten, and no one will suspect, or possibly connect you, or me, with what inevitably must happen to that spawn of the Commneni.

"But of this be very sure: Somewhere, sometime, you and I shall be together again..." Her voice broke, she kissed me fiercely on the lips, then tenderly on both cheeks, then lastly, with a queer reverence, on my furrowed old brow. Then she turned, went straight to her room, shut the door, and I heard the click of the key as she locked herself in, for the first time during her stay in my house... Next morning, as she'd planned, she departed on the first train cityward. I'd given her money enough for all her requirements - more, indeed, than she was willing to take at first, declaring that she intended selling some few of her jewels.

And with her departure went all which made life worth living...

Heavily I dragged my reluctant feet back to the empty shell of a cottage which until then had been an earthly paradise to an old man - and the very first thing I laid eyes on was that accursed Hel-stone, lying on the living-room table.

I picked it up, half minded to shatter it to fragments, but an idea seized me. I bore it down-cellar, where semi-darkness prevailed, and the Hel-stone glowed softly with its witch-light, showing me the loveliness of her who had departed from me. And I pressed the cold octagon to my lips, thankful that she'd left me the thing as a feeble substitute for her presence. Then I turned and went back upstairs, found an old ivory box of Chinese workmanship, and placed the Hel-stone therein, very carefully, as a thing priceless.

I went to bed early that night. There was no reason to sit up. But I could not sleep. I lay there in my bed, cursing the entire line of Commneni, root, trunk and branch, from the first of that ilk whom history records to this latest scion, or "spawn," as Heldra had termed him.

Around midnight, being still wakeful, I arose, got the Hel-stone and sat in the darkness - and gradually became aware that I was not alone! Looking up, I saw her I'd lost standing in a witch-glow of phosphorescent light. I knew at once that it was not Heldra in person, but her "scin-loecca" or "shining double," a "sending," and that it was another of her witcheries.

"But even this is welcome," I thought. Then I felt her thought expressed through that phantasmal semblance of her own gorgeous self - and promptly strove, angrily, to resist her command. Much good it did me! Utterly helpless, yet fully cognizant of my actions, but oddly assured that about me was a cloak of invisibility - the "glamyr" of the ancient Alrunas - I dressed, took the Hel-stone, and passed out into the night.

Straight to the cottage of Commnenus I went, pawed about under the door-step, and planted there the Hel-stone; then, still secure in the mystic glamour, I returned to my own abode. And no sooner had I seated myself in my chair for a smoke, than I realized fully the utter devilishness of that witch from out the wintry seas whom I had taken into my home and had sponsored as my "niece" in the eyes of the world.

Right then I decided to go back and get that Hel-stone, and smash it - and couldn't do it! I got sleepy so suddenly that

I awoke to find that it was broad daylight, and nine-thirty a.m. And from then on, as regularly as twilight came, I could only stay awake so long as I kept my thoughts away from that accursed Hel-stone; wherefore I determined that the thing could stay where it was until it rotted, for all me! Then Commnenus came along the beach late one afternoon. He raised his hat in his Old World, courtly fashion, and tried to make some small talk. I grunted churlishly and ignored him. But finally he came out bluntly with:

"Professor Craig, I know your opinion of me, and admit it is to some extent justifiable. I seem to have acquired the reputation of being a Don Juan. But I ask you to believe that I bitterly regret that - now! Yet, despite that reputation, I'd like to ask you a most natural question, if I may."

I nodded assent, unprepared for what was coming, yet somehow assured it would concern Heldra. Nor was I at all disappointed, for he fairly blurted out:

"When do you expect Miss Helstrom to return, if at all?"

I was flabbergasted! That is the only word adequate. I glared at him in a black fury. When I could catch my breath I demanded:

"How did even you summon up the infernal gall to ask me that?"

His reply finished flattening me out.

"Because I love her! Wait" - he begged - "and hear me out, please! Even a criminal is allowed that courtesy." Then as I nodded grudgingly, he resumed:

"The first time I saw her, something deep within me shrank away from her with repulsion. Still, I admired her matchless beauty. But of late, since her departure, there is not a night I do not see her in my mind's eye, and I know that I love her, and hope that she will return; hence my query.

"I will be frank - I even hope that she noticed me and read my admiration without dislike. Perhaps two minds can reach

each other - sometimes. For invariably I see her with head thrown back, her eyes half closed, and her arms held out as if calling me to come to her. And if I knew her whereabouts I'd most certainly go, nor would I be 'trifling,' where she is concerned. I want to win her, if possible, as my wife; and an emperor should be proud to call her that."

"Very romantic," I sneered. "But, Mr. Woman-Chaser, I cut my eye-teeth a long while before you were born, and I'm not so easily taken in. The whereabouts of my niece are no concern of yours. So get away from me before I lose my temper, or I'll not be answerable for my actions. Get!"

He went! The expression of my face and the rage in my eyes must have warned him that I was in a killing humour. Well, I was. But likewise, I was sick with fear. What he'd just told me was sufficient to sicken me - the Helstone had gotten in its damnable work. My very soul was aghast as it envisioned the inevitable consequences...

An idea obsessed me, and I needed the shades of night to cloak my purpose.

Aimlessly I wandered from room to room in my cottage, and finally drifted into the room which had been Heldra's. Still aimlessly I pulled open drawer after drawer in the dresser, and in the lowest one I heard a faint metallic clink.

The four antique bronze lamps were there. I shrewdly suspected she had left them there as means of establishing contact with her, should need arise. I examined them, and found, as I'd hoped, that they were filled.

Around ten o'clock I placed those lamps in the four corners of the living-room, and lighted them, precisely as I'd seen Heldra do. Then I tried my talents at making an invocation.

"Heldra! Heldra! Heldra!" I called. "I, John Craig, who gave you shelter at your need, call to you now, wheresoever you be, to come to me at my need!"

The four lights went out, yet not a breath of air stirred in the room. A faintly luminous glow, the witch-light, ensued; and there she stood, or rather, the scin-loecca, her shining double! But I knew that anything I might say to it would be the same as if she were there in the flesh.

"Heldra," I beseeched that witch-lighted simulacrum, "by the love you gave me, as Ragnar loved Jarl Wulf Red –

"Sword, I ask that you again enshroud me with the mantle of invisibility, the glamyr,' and allow me to lift that accursed Hel-stone from where you compelled me to conceal it. Let me return it to you, at any place you may appoint, so that it can do no more harm.

"Already that poor bewitched fool is madly in love with you, because the radiations of that enchanted stone have saturated him every time he put foot on the door-step beneath which I buried it! Heldra, grant me this one kindness, and I will condone all sins you ever did in all your witch-life."

The shining wraith nodded slowly, unmistakably assenting to my request. As from a far distance I heard a faint whisper:

"Since it is your desire, get the Helstone, and bear it yourself to the sea-cave at the foot of the great cliff guarding the north passage into the harbour. Once you have borne it there, its work, and yours, are done.

"And I thank you for saying that you will condone all I have ever done, for the burden of the past is heavy, and your words have made it easier to bear."

The shining wraith vanished, and I went forth into the darkness. Straight to the house where I'd hidden the Hel-stone I betook myself, felt under the step, found what I sought, took it with an inward prayer of gratitude that because of Heldra's 'glamyr' I had not been caught at something questionable in appearance, and started up the beach.

The tide was nearly out; so I walked rapidly, as I had some distance to go, and the sea-cave Heldra had designated could not be entered at high tide, although once within, one was safe enough and could leave when the entrance was once more exposed.

I entered the cave believing that I'd promptly be rid of the entire mess, once and for all. But there was no one there, and the interior of the cave was as dark as Erebus. I lit a match, and saw nothing. The match burned out. I fumbled for another - a dazzling ray from a flashlight blinded me for a moment, then left my face and swept the cave. A hated voice, suave yet menacing, said:

"Well, Professor Craig, you may now hand me whatever it was that you purloined from under my door-step!"

An extremely business-like automatic pistol was aimed in the exact direction of my solar plexus - and the speaker was none other than Michael Commnenus!

Very evidently the mystic 'glamyr' had failed to work that time. And I was in a rather nasty predicament.

Then, abruptly, Heldra came! She looked like an avenging fury, emerging out of nowhere, apparently, and the tables were turned. She wore a dark cloak or long mantle draped over her head and falling to her feet.

Her right hand was outstretched, and with her left hand she seized the Helstone from my grasp. She pointed one finger at Commnenus, and did not even touch him; yet had she smote with an ancient war-hammer the effect would have been the same.

"You dog, and son of a long line of dogs!" her icy voice rang with excoriating virulence. "Drop that silly pistol! Drop it, I say!"

A faint blue flicker snapped from her extended finger - the pistol fell from a flaccid hand. Commnenus seemed totally paralysed. Heldra's magic held him completely in thralldom... I snapped into activity and scooped up the gun.

"Followed me, did you?" I snarled.

"Wait, Jarl Wulf!" Heldra's tone was frankly amused. "No need for you to do aught! Mine is the blood-feud, mine the blood-right! And ere I finish with yon Michael Commnenus, an ancient hate will be surfeited, and an ancient vengeance, too long delayed, will be consummated."

"Heldra," I began, for dread seized me at the ominous quality of her words, "I will not stand for this affair going any farther! I -"

"Be silent! Seat yourself over there against the wall and watch and hear, but move not nor speak again, lest I silence you for ever!"

A force irresistible hurled me across the cave and set me down, hard, on a flat rock. I realized fully that I was obeying her mandate - I couldn't speak, couldn't even move my eyelids, so thoroughly had she inhibited any further interference on my part.

Paying no further attention to Commnenus for the moment, she crossed over to me, bent and kissed me on my lips, her sapphire eyes laughing into my own blazing, wrathful eyes. "Poor dear! It is too bad, but you made me do it. I wanted you to help me all the way through this tangled coil - but you have been so difficult to manage! Yet in some ways you have played into my hands splendidly. Yes, even to bringing the Hel-stone back to me - and I would not care to lose that for a king's ransom. And I put it into yon fool's head to be wakeful tonight, and see you regain the Hel-stone, and follow you - and thus walk into my nice little trap.

"And now!"

She whirled and faced Commnenus. And for all that he was spellbound, in his eyes I read fear and a ghastly foreknowledge of some dreadful fate about to be meted out to him at her hands. She picked up the flashlight he had dropped and extinguished it with the dry comment:

"We need a different light here - the Hel-light from Hela's halls!" And at her word, a most peculiar light pervaded the cave, and there was that about its luminance that actually affrighted. Again she spoke: "Michael Commnenus, you utterly vile worm of the earth! You know that your doom is upon you - but as yet you know not why. 0 beast lower than the swine! Harken and remember my words even after eternity is swallowed up in the Twilight of the Gods! You are a modern, and know not that the self, the soul, is eternal, undying, changing its body and name in every clime and period, yet ever the same soul, responsible for the deeds of its bodies. You have even prated of your soul - when in fact, you are the property of the soul!

"Watch, now!" She pointed to the cave entrance. "Behold there the wisps of sea-fog gathering; and gradually will come the rising tide. And on the curtain of that cold, swirling mist, behold the pictures of the past - a past centuries old; a past wherein your craven, treacherous soul sinned beyond all pardon!

"Look you, too, Jarl Wulf Red-Brand, so that in all the days remaining to you upon Earth, you may know that his doom was just, and that Heldra is but executing a merited penalty!

"And while the shuttles of the Norns weave the tapestry of the sin of this Commnenus, I will tell all the tale of his crimes.

"In Byzantium reigned the emperor, Alexander Commnenus. Secure his throne, guarded by the ponderous axes and the long swords of the Varangians, the splendid sons of the Norse-lands, who had gone a-viking. Trusted and loved were the Varangs by the emperor, and oft he boasted of their fidelity, swearing on the cross of Constantine that to the last man would his Varangs perish ere one would flinch a step from over-whelming foes, citing in proof their battle-cry:

"'Valhalla! Valhalla! Victory or Valhalla!'

"Into the harbour of the Golden Horn sailed the Viking long-ship, the Grettir. Three noble brothers owned her - Thorfinn, Arvid, Sven. With them sailed their sister... her fame as an Alrunamaid, prophetess and priestess, was sung throughout the Norse-lands. No man so low but bore her reverence. Sin it was to cast eyes of desire on any Alruna, and the sister of the three brothers was held especially holy.

"Between the hands of the Emperor Alexander Commnenus, the three brethren placed their hands, swearing fealty for a year and a day. Thirty fighting-men, their crew, followed wherever the three brothers led. And the great emperor, hearing of their war-fame from others of the Varangian guard, gave the brothers high place in his esteem, and held them nigh his own person.

"Their sister, the Alruna-maid, was treated as became her rank and holy repute. Aye! Even in Christian Byzantium respect and honour were shown her by the priests of an alien belief. But one man in Byzantium aspired more greatly than any other, Norseman or Byzantine, had ever dared.

"A Commnenus he, grand admiral of Byzantium's war fleet, nephew to the emperor, enjoying to the full the confidence and love of his imperial uncle. Notorious for his profligacy, he cast his libertine eyes on the Norse Alruna-maid, but with no thought of making her his wife. Nay! 'Twas only as his Leman he desired her... So, he plotted...

"The three brothers, Thorfinn, Arvid, Sven, with their full crew, in the long-ship Grettir were ordered to sea to cruise against certain pirates harrying a portion of the emperor's coasts.

"Every man of the Grettir's crew died the deaths of rats - poison in the water-casks!... They died as no Norseman should die, brutes' deaths, unfit for Valhalla and the company of heroes who had passed in battle! And their splendid bodies, warped and distorted by pangs of the poison, were cast overside as prey for sharks, by two creatures of this grand admiral, whom he had sent with the three brothers as pilots knowing the coast. They placed the drug in the casks, they flung over the dead and dying, they ran the Grettir aground and set fire to her - but his was the command - and his the crime!"

And as Heldra told the tale, in a voice whose dreary tones made the recital seem even worse - the watching Commnenus and I saw clearly depicted on the curtain of the mist, each separate incident... Heldra turned to the wildly glaring Michael.

"There was but one person in all Byzantium who knew the truth," she screamed in sudden frenzy. "I give back for a moment your power of speech. Say, O fool! Coward! Niddering! Who am I?" Abruptly she tore off the sombre cloak and stood in all her loveliness, enhanced by every ornament she once had worn for my pleasure in beholding her thus arrayed.

A cry of unearthly terror broke from the staring Commnenus. His voice was a strangled croak as he gasped:

"The Alruna-maid, Heldra! The red-haired sea-witch - sister to the three brothers, Thorfinn, Arvid, Sven!"

"Aye, you foul dog! And me you took at night, after they sailed away, and me you shut up where my cries for aid could not be heard; and me you would have despoiled - me, the Alruna-maid, sworn to chastity! Me you jeered at and reviled, boasting of your recent crimes against all that the Norse-folk hold most sacred!

"Yet I escaped from that last dreadful dungeon wherein you immured me - how?

"By that magic known to such as I, I called upon the empress of the Underworld, Hela herself, and pledged her my service in return for indefinitely continued life, until I could repay you and avenge the heroes denied the joys of Valhalla - by you!

"And now - comes swiftly the doom I have planned for you... you who now remember!"

Heldra spoke truly. Swiftly it came! Sitting where I was, I saw it plainly, a great dragon-ship with round shields displayed along her gunwales, with a big square sail of crimson embroidered in gold, with long oars dipping and lifting in unison - in faint ghostly tones I could hear the deep-sea rowers chanting, "Duch! Hey! Sa-sa-sa! Hey-sa, Hey-sa, Hey-sa, Hey-sa!" and knew it for the time-beat rowing-song of the ancient Vikings!

The whole picture was limned in the cold sea-fires from whence that terrible Viking ghost-ship had risen with its crew of long-dead Norsemen who were not dead - the men too good for Hel, and denied Valhalla...

Straight to the mouth of the cave came the ghost-ship, and its crew disembarked and entered. Heldra cried out in joyous welcome:

"Even from out of the deeps, ye heroes, one and all, have ye heard my silent summons, and obeyed the voice of your Alruna from old time! Now your waiting is at an end!

"Yonder stands the Commnenus. That other concerns ye not - but mark him well, for in a former life he was Jarl Wulf Red-Brand! See, on his left hand is still the old silver ring with its runes of Ragnar Wave-Flame!"

The ghost-Vikings turned their dead eyes on me with a curious fixity. One and all, they saluted. Evidently, Jarl Wulf must have been somebody, in his time. Then ignoring me, they turned to Heldra, awaiting her further commands. Commnenus they looked at, fiercely, avidly.

Heldra's voice came, heavily, solemnly, with a curious bell-like tone sounding the knell of doom incarnate:

"Michael Commnenus! This your present body has never wrought me harm, nor has it harmed any of these. It is not with your body that we hold our feud. Wherefore, your body shall go forth from this cave as it entered - as handsome as ever, bearing no mark of scathe.

"But your niddering soul, O most accursed, shall be drawn from out its earthly tenement this night and given over to these souls you wronged, who now await their victim and their vengeance! And I tell you, Michael Commnenus, that what they have in store for you will make the Hades of your religion seem as a devoutly-to-be-desired paradise!" Heldra stepped directly before Commnenus. Her shapely white arms were outstretched, palms down, fingers stiffly extended. A queer, violet-tinged radiance streamed from her fingers, gradually enveloping Commnenus - he began to glow, as if he had been immersed and had absorbed all his body could take up...

Heldra's voice took on the tone of finality:

"Michael Commnenus! Thou accursed soul, by the power I hold, given me by Hela's self, I call you forth from your hiding-place of flesh - come ye out!"

The living body never moved, but from out its mouth emerged a faint silvery-tinted vapour flowing toward the A!runa-maid, and as it came, the violet glow diminished. The accumulating silvery mist swirled and writhed, perceptibly taking on the semblance of the body from whence it was being extracted. There remained finally but a merest thread of silvery shimmer connecting soul and body. Heldra spoke beneath her breath:

"One of you hew that cord asunder!"

A double-bladed Norse battle-axe whirled and a ghostly voice croaked: "Thor Hulf!"

Thor, the old Norse war-god, must have helped, for the great ghost-axe evidently encountered a solid cable well-nigh as strong as tempered steel. Thrice the axe rose and fell, driven by the swelling thews of the towering giant wielding it, ere the silver cord was broken by the blade.

A tittering giggle burst from the lips of the present-day Michael Commnenus.

I realized with a sudden sickness at the pit of my stomach that an utterly mindless imbecile stood there, grinning vacuously!

"That Thing," Heldra said, coldly scornful as she pointed to the silvery shining soul, "is yours, heroes! Do with it as ye will!"

Two of the gigantic wraiths clamped their great hands on its shoulders. It turned a dull leaden-grey, the colour of abject fear. Cringing and squirming, it was hustled aboard the ghostly dragon-ship. The other ghost-Vikings went aboard, taking their places at the oars yet they waited. Heldra turned to me.

"Be free of the spell I laid upon you!" Her tone was as gentle as it had been in her sweetest moments while she dwelt in my home as my niece.

I gasped, rose and stretched. I wanted to be angry - and dared not. I'd seen too much of her hellish powers to risk incurring her displeasure. And reading my mind, she laughed merrily.

Then her cool, soft, white arms went about my neck, her wondrous sapphire eyes looked long and tenderly into mine -

and I will not write the message I read in those softly shining orbs. Once again her silvery voice spoke:

"Jarl Wulf Red-Brand! John Craig! I am the granddaughter of Ragnar Wave-Flame! And once I went a-viking with my three brothers, to far Byzantium. You know that tale. Now, once I said that Ragnar Wave-Flame never died. Also, I said that I had dived into her sea-cave and lain in her arms - and now I tell you the rest of that mystery: with her breath she entered this my body where ever since we have dwelt as one soul. I needed aid in seeking my vengeance, for it was after I'd escaped the clutches of the Commnenus, and had passed through adventures incredible while making my way back to the Norse-lands - and my spirit was very bitter. And when I sought her council, Ragnar helped

"This now do I ask of you: Do you, as I have sometimes thought, love me as a man loves a maid? Reflect well, ere you answer, and recall what I once showed you in a mirror - I am older than you! So, knowing that, despite my witcheries of the long, bitter past, and those of tonight, would you take me, were you and I young once more?"

"By all the gods in Valhalla, and by all the devils in Hela's halls: yes!" My reply was given without need of reflecting, or counting cost.

"Then, in a day to come, you shall take me - I swear it!"

Full upon my mouth she pressed her scarlet lips, and a surging flame suffused my entire body. Yet it was life - not death. Against my chest I felt the pressure of her swelling breasts, and fires undreamable streamed from her heart to mine. Time itself stood still. After an eon or so she unwound her clinging arms from about my neck and turned away, and with never a backward glance she entered that waiting, ghostly dragon-ship. The oars dipped...

"Juch! Hey! Sa-sa-sa! Hey-sa! Hey-sa! Hey-sal Hey-sa!" and repeated... and again... until the faint, ghostly chant was swallowed by distance...

I left the cave.

The drivelling idiot who had been Michael Commnenus was already gone. Later, the gossip ran that he'd "lost his mind," and that his embassy had returned him to his own land. None ever suspected, or coupled me or my "niece" with his affliction. And he himself had absolutely no memory - had lost even his own name when his soul departed! But within a month, I sold my cottage, packed and stored all my belongings until I could find a new location, where I'd be totally unknown; and then I went away from where I had dwelt for years - and with urgent reason.

The fire with which Heldra had imbued me from her breath and breast was renewing my youth! My hair was shades darker, my wrinkles almost gone; my step was brisker, I looked to be nearer forty than almost sixty. So marked was the change that the villagers stared openly at what seemed at least a miracle... tongues were wagging... old superstitions were being revived and dark hints were being bandied about... So I finally decided to leave, and go where my altered appearance would cause no comment.

I wonder if -

THE LADY'S MAID'S BELL
Edith Wharton

I

It was the autumn after I had the typhoid. I'd been three months in hospital, and when I came out I looked so weak and tottery that the two or three ladies I applied to were afraid to engage me. Most of my money was gone, and after I'd boarded for two months, hanging about the employment agencies, and answering any advertisement that looked any way respectable, I pretty nearly lost heart, for fretting hadn't made me fatter, and I didn't see why my luck should ever turn. It did though - or I thought so at the time. A Mrs. Railton, a friend of the lady that first brought me out to the States, met me one day and stopped to speak to me: she was one that had always a friendly way with her. She asked me what ailed me to look so white, and when I told her, "Why, Hartley," says she, "I believe I've got the very place for you. Come in to-morrow and we'll talk about it."

The next day, when I called, she told me the lady she'd in mind was a niece of hers, a Mrs. Brympton, a youngish lady, but something of an invalid, who lived all the year round at her country-place on the Hudson, owing to not being able to stand the fatigue of town life.

"Now, Hartley," Mrs. Railton said, in that cheery way that always made me feel things must be going to take a turn for the better - "now understand me; it's not a cheerful place I'm sending you to. The house is big and gloomy; my niece is nervous, vaporish; her husband - well, he's generally away; and the two children are dead. A year ago I would as soon have thought of shutting a rosy active girl like you into a vault; but you're not particularly brisk yourself just now, are you? And a quiet place, with country air and wholesome food and early hours, ought to be the very thing for you. Don't mistake me," she added, for I suppose I looked a trifle downcast; "you may find it dull but you won't be unhappy. My niece is an angel. Her former maid, who died last spring, had been with her twenty years and worshiped the ground she walked on. She's a kind mistress to all, and where the mistress is kind, as you know, the servants are generally good-humoured, so you'll probably get on well enough with the rest of the household. And you're the very woman I want for my niece: quiet, well-mannered, and educated above your station. You read aloud well, I think? That's a good thing; my niece likes to be read to. She wants a maid that can be something of a companion: her last was, and I can't say how she misses her. It's a lonely life... Well, have you decided?"

"Why, ma'am," I said, "I'm not afraid of solitude."

"Well, then, go; my niece will take you on my recommendation. I'll telegraph her at once and you can take the afternoon train. She has no one to wait on her at present, and I don't want you to lose any time."

I was ready enough to start, yet something in me hung back; and to gain time I asked, "And the gentleman, ma'am?"

"The gentleman's almost always away, I tell you," said Mrs. Railton, quick-like, "and when he's there," says she suddenly, "you've only to keep out of his way."

I took the afternoon train and got out at D---- station at about four o'clock. A groom in a dog-cart was waiting, and we drove off at a smart pace. It was a dull October day, with rain hanging close overhead, and by the time we turned into Brympton Place woods the daylight was almost gone. The drive wound through the woods for a mile or two, and came out on a gravel court shut in with thickets of tall black-looking shrubs. There were no lights in the windows, and the house did look a bit gloomy.

I had asked no questions of the groom, for I never was one to get my notion of new masters from their other servants: I prefer to wait and see for myself. But I could tell by the look of everything that I had got into the right kind of house, and that things were done handsomely. A pleasant-faced cook met me at the back door and called the house-maid to show me up to my room. "You'll see madam later," she said. "Mrs. Brympton has a visitor. "

I hadn't fancied Mrs. Brympton was a lady to have many visitors, and somehow the words cheered me. I followed the house-maid upstairs, and saw, through a door on the upper landing, that the main part of the house seemed well-furnished, with dark panelling and a number of old portraits. Another flight of stairs led up to the servants' wing. It was almost dark now, and the house-maid excused herself for not having brought a light. "But there's matches in your room," she said, "and if you go careful you'll be all right. Mind the step at the end of the passage. Your room is just beyond."

I looked ahead as she spoke, and half-way down the passage I saw a woman standing. She drew back into a doorway as we passed and the house-maid didn't appear to notice her. She was a thin woman with a white face, and a darkish stuff gown and apron. I took her for the housekeeper and thought it odd that she didn't speak, but just gave me a long look as she went by. My room opened into a square hall at the end of the passage. Facing my door was another which stood open: the house-maid exclaimed when she saw it:

"There - Mrs. Blinder's left that door open again!" said she, closing it.

"Is Mrs. Blinder the housekeeper?"

"There's no housekeeper: Mrs. Blinder's the cook."

"And is that her room?"

"Laws, no," said the house-maid, crosslike. "That's nobody's room. It's empty, I mean, and the door hadn't ought to be open. Mrs. Brympton wants it kept locked."

She opened my door and led me into a neat room, nicely furnished, with a picture or two on the walls; and having lit a candle she took leave, telling me that the servants'-hall tea was at six, and that Mrs. Brympton would see me afterward.

I found them a pleasant-spoken set in the servants' hall, and by what they let fall I gathered that, as Mrs. Railton had said, Mrs. Brympton was the kindest of ladies; but I didn't take much notice of their talk, for I was watching to see the pale woman in the dark gown come in. She didn't show herself, however, and I wondered if she ate apart; but if she wasn't the housekeeper, why should she? Suddenly it struck me that she might be a trained nurse, and in that case her meals would of course be served in her room. If Mrs. Brympton was an invalid it was likely enough she had a nurse. The idea annoyed me, I own, for they're not always the easiest to get on with, and if I'd known I shouldn't have taken the place. But there I was and there was no use pulling a long face over it; and not being one to ask questions I waited to see what would turn up.

When tea was over the house-maid said to the footman: "Has Mr. Ranford gone?" and when he said yes, she told me to come up with her to Mrs. Brympton.

Mrs. Brympton was lying down in her bedroom. Her lounge stood near the fire and beside it was a shaded lamp. She was a delicate-looking lady, but when she smiled I felt there was nothing I wouldn't do for her. She spoke very pleasantly, in a low voice, asking me my name and age and so on, and if I had everything I wanted, and if I wasn't afraid of feeling lonely in the country.

"Not with you I wouldn't be, madam," I said, and the words surprised me when I'd spoken them, for I'm not an impulsive person; but it was just as if I'd thought aloud.

She seemed pleased at that, and said she hoped I'd continue in the same mind; then she gave me a few directions about her toilet, and said Agnes the house-maid would show me next morning where things were kept.

"I am tired to-night, and shall dine upstairs," she said. "Agnes will bring me my tray, that you may have time to unpack and settle yourself; and later you may come and undress me."

"Very well, ma'am," I said. "You'll ring, I suppose?"

I thought she looked odd.

"No - Agnes will fetch you," says she quickly, and took up her book again.

Well - that was certainly strange: a lady's-maid having to be fetched by the house-maid whenever her lady wanted her! I wondered if there were no bells in the house; but the next day I satisfied myself that there was one in every room, and a special one ringing from my mistress's room to mine; and after that it did strike me as queer that, whenever Mrs. Brympton wanted anything, she rang for Agnes, who had to walk the whole length of the servants' wing to call me.

But that wasn't the only queer thing in the house. The very next day I found out that Mrs. Brympton had no nurse; and then I asked Agnes about the woman I had seen in the passage the afternoon before. Agnes said she had seen no one, and I saw that she thought I was dreaming. To be sure, it was dusk when we went down the passage, and she had excused herself for not bringing a light; but I had seen the woman plain enough to know her again if we should meet. I decided that she must have been a friend of the cook's, or of one of the other women servants: perhaps she had come down from town for a night's visit, and the servants wanted it kept secret.

Some ladies are very stiff about having their servants' friends in the house overnight. At any rate, I made up my mind to ask no more questions.

In a day or two another odd thing happened. I was chatting one afternoon with Mrs. Blinder, who was a friendly disposed woman, and had been longer in the house than the other servants, and she asked me if I was quite comfortable and had everything I needed. I said I had no fault to find with my place or with my mistress, but I thought it odd that in so large a house there was no sewing-room for the lady's maid.

"Why," says she, "there is one: the room you're in is the old sewing-room. "

"Oh," said I; "and where did the other lady's maid sleep?"

At that she grew confused, and said hurriedly that the servants' rooms had all been changed about last year, and she didn't rightly remember.

That struck me as peculiar, but I went on as if I hadn't noticed: "Well, there's a vacant room opposite mine, and I mean to ask Mrs. Brympton if I mayn't use that as a sewing-room."

To my astonishment, Mrs. Blinder went white, and gave my hand a kind of squeeze. "Don't do that, my dear," said she, trembling-like. "To tell you the truth, that was Emma Saxon's room, and my mistress has kept it closed ever since her death."

"And who was Emma Saxon?"

"Mrs. Brympton's former maid."

"The one that was with her so many years?" said I, remembering what Mrs. Railton had told me.

Mrs. Blinder nodded.

"What sort of woman was she?"

"No better walked the earth," said Mrs. Blinder. "My mistress loved her like a sister."

"But I mean - what did she look like?"

Mrs. Blinder got up and gave me a kind of angry stare. "I'm no great hand at describing," she said; "and I believe my pastry's rising." And she walked off into the kitchen and shut the door after her.

II

I had been near a week at Brympton before I saw my master. Word came that he was arriving one afternoon, and a change passed over the whole household. It was plain that nobody loved him below stairs. Mrs. Blinder took uncommon care with the dinner that night, but she snapped at the kitchen-maid in a way quite unusual with her; and Mr. Wace, the butler, a serious, slow-spoken man, went about his duties as if he'd been getting ready for a funeral. He was a great Bible-reader, Mr. Wace was, and had a beautiful assortment of texts at his command; but that day he used such dreadful language, that I was about to leave the table, when he assured me it was all out of Isaiah; and I noticed that whenever the master came Mr. Wace took to the prophets.

About seven, Agnes called me to my mistress's room; and there I found Mr. Brympton. He was standing on the hearth; a big fair bull-necked man, with a red face and little bad-tempered blue eyes: the kind of man a young simpleton might have thought handsome, and would have been like to pay dear for thinking it.

He swung about when I came in, and looked me over in a trice. I knew what the look meant, from having experienced it once or twice in my former places. Then he turned his back on me, and went on talking to his wife; and I knew what that meant, too. I was not the kind of morsel he was after. The typhoid had served me well enough in one way: it kept that kind of gentleman at arm's length.

"This is my new maid, Hartley," says Mrs. Brympton in her kind voice; and he nodded and went on with what he was saying.

In a minute or two he went off, and left my mistress to dress for dinner, and I noticed as I waited on her that she was white, and chill to the touch.

Mr. Brympton took himself off the next morning, and the whole house drew a long breath when he drove away. As for my mistress, she put on her hat and furs (for it was a fine winter morning) and went out for a walk in the gardens, coming back quite fresh and rosy, so that for a minute, before her colour faded, I could guess what a pretty young lady she must have been, and not so long ago, either.

She had met Mr. Ranford in the grounds, and the two came back together, I remember, smiling and talking as they walked along the terrace under my window. That was the first time I saw Mr. Ranford, though I had often heard his name mentioned in the hall. He was a neighbour, it appeared, living a mile or two beyond Brympton, at the end of the village; and as he was in the habit of spending his winters in the country he was almost the only company my mistress had at that season. He was a slight tall gentleman of about thirty, and I thought him rather melancholy-looking till I saw his smile, which had a kind of surprise in it, like the first warm day in spring. He was a great reader, I heard, like my mistress, and the two were forever borrowing books of one another, and sometimes (Mr. Wace told me) he would read aloud to Mrs. Brympton by the hour, in the big dark library where she sat in the winter afternoons. The servants all liked him, and perhaps that's more of a compliment than the masters' suspect. He had a friendly word for every one of us, and we were all glad to think that Mrs. Brympton had a pleasant companionable gentleman like that to keep her company when the master was away. Mr. Ranford seemed on excellent terms with Mr. Brympton too; though I couldn't but wonder that two gentlemen so unlike each other should be so friendly. But then I knew how the real quality can keep their feelings to themselves.

As for Mr. Brympton, he came and went, never staying more than a day or two, cursing the dullness and the solitude, grumbling at everything, and (as I soon found out) drinking a deal more than was good for him. After Mrs. Brympton left the table he would sit half the night over the old Brympton port and Madeira, and once, as I was leaving my mistress's room rather later than usual, I met him coming up the stairs in such a state that I turned sick to think of what some ladies have to endure and hold their tongues about.

The servants said very little about their master; but from what they let drop I could see it had been an unhappy match from the beginning. Mr. Brympton was coarse, loud and pleasure-loving; my mistress quiet, retiring, and perhaps a trifle cold. Not that she was not always pleasant-spoken to him: I thought her wonderfully forbearing; but to a gentleman as free as Mr. Brympton I dare say she seemed a little offish.

Well, things went on quietly for several weeks. My mistress was kind, my duties were light, and I got on well with the other servants. In short, I had nothing to complain of; yet there was always a weight on me. I can't say why it was so, but I know it was not the loneliness that I felt. I soon got used to that; and being still languid from the fever, I was thankful for the quiet and the good country air. Nevertheless, I was never quite easy in my mind. My mistress, knowing I had been ill, insisted that I should take my walk regularly, and often invented errands for me: a yard of ribbon to be fetched from the village, a letter posted, or a book returned to Mr. Ranford. As soon as I was out of doors my spirits rose, and I looked forward to my walks through the bare moist-smelling woods; but the moment I caught sight of the house again my heart dropped down like a stone in a well. It was not a gloomy house exactly, yet I never entered it but a feeling of gloom came over me.

Mrs. Brympton seldom went out in winter; only on the finest days did she walk an hour at noon on the south terrace. Excepting Mr. Ranford, we had no visitors but the doctor, who, drove over from D---- about once a week. He sent for me once or twice to give me some trifling direction about my mistress, and though he never told me what her illness was, I thought, from a waxy look she had now and then of a morning, that it might be the heart that ailed her. The season was soft and unwholesome, and in January we had a long spell of rain. That was a sore trial to me, I own, for I couldn't go out, and sitting over my sewing all day, listening to the drip, drip of the eaves, I grew so nervous that the least sound made me jump. Somehow, the thought of that locked room across the passage began to weigh on me. Once or twice, in the long rainy nights, I fancied I heard noises there; but that was nonsense, of course, and the daylight drove such notions out of my head. Well, one morning Mrs. Brympton gave me quite a start of pleasure by telling me she wished me to go to town for some shopping. I hadn't known till then how low my spirits had fallen. I set off in high glee, and my first sight of the crowded streets and the cheerful-looking shops quite took me out of myself. Toward afternoon, however, the noise and confusion began to tire me, and I was actually looking forward to the quiet of Brympton, and thinking how I should enjoy the drive home through the dark woods, when I ran across an old acquaintance, a maid I had once been in service with. We had lost sight of each other for a number of years, and I had to stop and tell her what had happened to me in the interval. When I mentioned where I was living she rolled up her eyes and pulled a long face.

"What! The Mrs. Brympton that lives all the year at her place on the Hudson? My dear, you won't stay there three months."

"Oh, but I don't mind the country," says I, offended somehow at her tone. "Since the fever I'm glad to be quiet."

She shook her head. "It's not the country I'm thinking of. All I know is she's had four maids in the last six months, and the last one, who was friend of mine, told me nobody could stay in the house."

"Did she say why?" I asked.

"No - she wouldn't give me her reason. But she says to me, Mrs. Ansey, she says, if ever a young woman as you know of thinks of going there, you tell her it's not worth while to unpack her boxes.'"

"Is she young and handsome?" said I, thinking of Mr. Brympton.

"Not her! She's the kind that mothers engage when they've gay young gentlemen at college."

Well, though I knew the woman was an idle gossip, the words stuck in my head, and my heart sank lower than ever as I drove up to Brympton in the dusk. There was something about the house - I was sure of it now...

When I went in to tea I heard that Mr. Brympton had arrived, and I saw at a glance that there had been a disturbance of some kind. Mrs. Blinder's hand shook so that she could hardly pour the tea, and Mr. Wace quoted the most dreadful texts full of brimstone. Nobody said a word to me then, but when I went up to my room Mrs. Blinder followed me.

"Oh, my dear," says she, taking my hand, "I'm so glad and thankful you've come back to us!"

That struck me, as you may imagine. "Why," said I, "did you think I was leaving for good?"

"No, no, to be sure," said she, a little confused, "but I can't a-bear to have madam left alone for a day even." She pressed my hand hard, and, "Oh, Miss Hartley," says she, "be good to your mistress, as you're a Christian woman." And with that she hurried away, and left me staring.

A moment later Agnes called me to Mrs. Brympton. Hearing Mr. Brympton's voice in her room, I went round by the dressing-room, thinking I would lay out her dinner-gown before going in. The dressing-room is a large room with a window over the portico that looks toward the gardens. Mr. Brympton's apartments are beyond. When I went in, the door into the bedroom was ajar, and I heard Mr. Brympton saying angrily: "One would suppose he was the only person fit for you to talk to."

"I don't have many visitors in winter," Mrs. Brympton answered quietly.

"You have me!" he flung at her, sneeringly.

"You are here so seldom," said she.

"Well - whose fault is that? You make the place about as lively as the family vault -"

With that I rattled the toilet things, to give my mistress warning, and she rose and called me in.

The two dined alone, as usual, and I knew by Mr. Wace's manner at supper that things must be going badly. He quoted the prophets something terrible, and worked on the kitchen-maid so that she declared she wouldn't go down alone to put the cold meat in the icebox. I felt nervous myself, and after I had put my mistress to bed I was half tempted to go down again and persuade Mrs. Blinder to sit up awhile over a game of cards. But I heard her door closing for the night and so I went on to my own room. The rain had begun again, and the drip, drip, drip seemed to be dropping into my brain. I lay awake listening to it, and turning over what my friend in town had said. What puzzled me was that it was always the maids who left...

After a while I slept; but suddenly a loud noise wakened me. My bell had rung. I sat up, terrified by the unusual sound, which seemed to go on jangling through the darkness. My hands shook so that I couldn't find the matches. At length I struck a light and jumped out of bed. I began to think I must have been dreaming; but I looked at the bell against the wall, and there was the little hammer still quivering.

I was just beginning to huddle on my clothes when I heard another sound. This time it was the door of the locked room opposite mine softly opening and closing. I heard the sound distinctly, and it frightened me so that I stood stock still. Then I heard a footstep hurrying down the passage toward the main house. The floor being carpeted, the sound was very faint, but I was quite sure it was a woman's step. I turned cold with the thought of it, and for a minute or two I dursn't breathe or move. Then I came to my senses.

"Alice Hartley," says I to myself, "someone left that room just now and ran down the passage ahead of you. The idea isn't pleasant, but you may as well face it. Your mistress has rung for you, and to answer her bell you've got to go the way that other woman has gone."

Well - I did it. I never walked faster in my life, yet I thought I should never get to the end of the passage or reach Mrs. Brympton's room. On the way I heard nothing and saw nothing: all was dark and quiet as the grave. When I reached my mistress's door the silence was so deep that I began to think I must be dreaming, and was half minded to turn back. Then a panic seized me, and I knocked.

There was no answer, and I knocked again, loudly. To my astonishment the door was opened by Mr. Brympton. He started back when he saw me, and in the light of my candle his face looked red and savage.

"You?" he said, in a queer voice. "How many of you are there, in God's name?"

At that I felt the ground give under me; but I said to myself that he had been drinking, and answered as steadily as I could: "May I go in, sir? Mrs. Brympton has rung for me."

"You may all go in, for what I care," says he, and, pushing by me, walked down the hall to his own bedroom. I looked after him as he went, and to my surprise I saw that he walked as straight as a sober man.

I found my mistress lying very weak and still, but she forced a smile when she saw me, and signed to me to pour out some drops for her. After that she lay without speaking, her breath coming quick, and her eyes closed. Suddenly she groped out with her hand, and "Emma," says she, faintly.

"It's Hartley, madam," I said. "Do you want anything?"

She opened her eyes wide and gave me a startled look.

"I was dreaming," she said. "You may go, now, Hartley, and thank you kindly. I'm quite well again, you see." And she turned her face away from me.

III

There was no more sleep for me that night, and I was thankful when daylight came.

Soon afterward, Agnes called me to Mrs. Brympton. I was afraid she was ill again, for she seldom sent for me before nine, but I found her sitting up in bed, pale and drawn-looking, but quite herself.

"Hartley," says she quickly, "will you put on your things at once and go down to the village for me? I want this prescription made up -" here she hesitated a minute and blushed -"and I should like you to be back again before Mr. Brympton is up."

"Certainly, madam," I said.

"And - stay a moment -" she called me back as if an idea had just struck her -"while you're waiting for the mixture, you'll have time to go on to Mr. Ranford's with this note."

It was a two-mile walk to the village, and on my way I had time to turn things over in my mind. It struck me as peculiar that my mistress should wish the prescription made up without Mr. Brympton's knowledge; and, putting this together with the scene of the night before, and with much else that I had noticed and suspected, I began to wonder if the poor lady was weary of her life, and had come to the mad resolve of ending it. The idea took such hold on me that I reached the village on a run, and dropped breathless into a chair before the chemist's counter. The good man, who was just taking down his shutters, stared at me so hard that it brought me to myself.

"Mr. Limmel," I says, trying to speak indifferently, "will you run your eye over this, and tell me if it's quite right?"

He put on his spectacles and studied the prescription.

"Why, it's one of Dr. Walton's," says he. "What should be wrong with it?"

"Well - is it dangerous to take?"

"Dangerous - how do you mean?"

I could have shaken the man for his stupidity.

"I mean - if a person was to take too much of it - by mistake of course -" says I, my heart in my throat.

"Lord bless you, no. It's only lime-water. You might feed it to a baby by the bottleful."

I gave a great sigh of relief and hurried on to Mr. Ranford's. But on the way another thought struck me. If there was nothing to conceal about my visit to the chemist's, was it my other errand that Mrs. Brympton wished me to keep private? Somehow, that thought frightened me worse than the other. Yet the two gentlemen seemed fast friends, and I would have staked my head on my mistress' goodness. I felt ashamed of my suspicions, and concluded that I was still disturbed by the strange events of the night. I left the note at Mr. Ranford's, and hurrying back to Brympton, slipped in by a side door without being seen, as I thought.

An hour later, however, as I was carrying in my mistress's breakfast, I was stopped in the hall by Mr. Brympton.

"What were you doing out so early?" he says, looking hard at me.

"Early - me, sir?" I said, in a tremble.

"Come, come," he says, an angry red spot coming out on his forehead, "didn't I see you scuttling home through the shrubbery an hour or more ago?"

I'm a truthful woman by nature, but at that a lie popped out ready-made. "No, sir, you didn't," said I and looked straight back at him.

He shrugged his shoulders and gave a sullen laugh. "I suppose you think I was drunk last night?" he asked suddenly.

"No, sir, I don't," I answered, this time truthfully enough.

He turned away with another shrug. "A pretty notion my servants have of me!" I heard him mutter as he walked off.

Not till I had settled down to my afternoon's sewing did I realize how the events of the night had shaken me. I couldn't pass that locked door without a shiver. I knew I had heard someone come out of it, and walk down the passage ahead of me. I thought of speaking to Mrs. Blinder or to Mr. Wace, the only two in the house who appeared to have an inkling of what was going on, but I had a feeling that if I questioned them they would deny everything, and that I might learn more by holding my tongue and keeping my eyes open. The idea of spending another night opposite the locked room sickened me, and once I was seized with the notion of packing my trunk and taking the first train to town; but it wasn't in me to throw over a kind mistress in that manner, and I tried to go on with my sewing as if nothing had happened.

I hadn't worked ten minutes before the sewing machine broke down. It was one I had found in the house, a good machine but a trifle out of order: Mrs. Blinder said it had never been used since Emma Saxon's death. I stopped to see what was wrong, and as I was working at the machine a drawer which I had never been able to open slid forward and a photograph fell out. I picked it up and sat looking at it in a maze. It was a woman's likeness, and I knew I had seen the face somewhere - the eyes had an asking look that I had felt on me before. And suddenly I remembered the pale woman in the passage.

I stood up, cold all over, and ran out of the room. My heart seemed to be thumping in the top of my head, and I felt as if I should never get away from the look in those eyes. I went straight to Mrs. Blinder. She was taking her afternoon nap, and sat up with a jump when I came in.

"Mrs. Blinder," said I, "who is that?" And I held out the photograph.

She rubbed her eyes and stared.

"Why, Emma Saxon," says she. "Where did you find it?"

I looked hard at her for a minute. "Mrs. Blinder," I said, "I've seen that face before."

Mrs. Blinder got up and walked over to the looking-glass. "Dear me! I must have been asleep," she says. "My front is all over one ear. And now do run along, Miss Hartley, dear, for I hear the clock striking four, and I must go down this very minute and put on the Virginia ham for Mr. Brympton's dinner."

IV

To all appearances, things went on as usual for a week or two. The only difference was that Mr. Brympton stayed on, instead of going off as he usually did, and that Mr. Ranford never showed himself. I heard Mr. Brympton remark on this one afternoon when he was sitting in my mistress's room before dinner:

"Where's Ranford?" says he. "He hasn't been near the house for a week. Does he keep away because I'm here?"

Mrs. Brympton spoke so low that I couldn't catch her answer.

"Well," he went on, "two's company and three's trumpery; I'm sorry to be in Ranford's way, and I suppose I shall have to take myself off again in a day or two and give him a show." And he laughed at his own joke.

The very next day, as it happened, Mr. Ranford called. The footman said the three were very merry over their tea in the library, and Mr. Brympton strolled down to the gate with Mr. Ranford when he left.

I have said that things went on as usual; and so they did with the rest of the household; but as for myself, I had never been the same since the night my bell had rung. Night after night I used to lie awake, listening for it to ring again, and for the door of the locked room to open stealthily. But the bell never rang, and I heard no sound across the passage. At last the silence began to be more dreadful to me than the most mysterious sounds. I felt that someone was cowering there, behind the locked door, watching and listening as I watched and listened, and I could almost have cried out, "Whoever you are, come out and let me see you face to face, but don't lurk there and spy on me in the darkness!"

Feeling as I did, you may wonder I didn't give warning. Once I very nearly did so; but at the last moment something held me back. Whether it was compassion for my mistress, who had grown more and more dependent on me, or unwillingness to try a new place, or some other feeling that I couldn't put a name to, I lingered on as if spell-bound, though every night was dreadful to me, and the days but little better.

For one thing, I didn't like Mrs. Brympton's looks. She had never been the same since that night, no more than I had. I thought she would brighten up after Mr. Brympton left, but though she seemed easier in her mind, her spirits didn't revive, nor her strength either. She had grown attached to me, and seemed to like to have me about; and Agnes told me one day that, since Emma Saxon's death, I was the only maid her mistress had taken to. This gave me a warm feeling for the poor lady, though after all there was little I could do to help her.

After Mr. Brympton's departure, Mr. Ranford took to coming again, though less often than formerly. I met him once or twice in the grounds, or in the village, and I couldn't but think there was a change in him too; but I set it down to my disordered fancy.

The weeks passed, and Mr. Brympton had now been a month absent. We heard he was cruising with a friend in the West Indies, and Mr. Wace said that was a long way off, but though you had the wings of a dove and went to the uttermost parts of the earth, you couldn't get away from the Almighty. Agnes said that as long as he stayed away from Brympton the Almighty might have him and welcome; and this raised a laugh, though Mrs. Blinder tried to look shocked, and Mr. Wace said the bears would eat us.

We were all glad to hear that the West Indies were a long way off, and I remember that, in spite of Mr. Wace's solemn looks, we had a very merry dinner that day in the hall. I don't know if it was because of my being in better spirits, but I fancied Mrs. Brympton looked better too, and seemed more cheerful in her manner. She had been for a walk in the morning, and after luncheon she lay down in her room, and I read aloud to her. When she dismissed me I went to my own room feeling quite bright and happy, and for the first time in weeks walked past the locked door without thinking of it. As I sat down to my work I looked out and saw a few snowflakes falling. The sight was pleasanter than the eternal rain, and I pictured to myself how pretty the bare gardens would look in their white mantle. It seemed to me as if the snow would cover up all the dreariness, indoors as well as out.

The fancy had hardly crossed my mind when I heard a step at my side. I looked up, thinking it was Agnes.

"Well, Agnes -" said I, and the words froze on my tongue; for there, in the door, stood Emma Saxon.

I don't know how long she stood there. I only know I couldn't stir or take my eyes from her. Afterward I was terribly frightened, but at the time it wasn't fear I felt, but something deeper and quieter. She looked at me long and hard, and her face was just one dumb prayer to me - but how in the world was I to help her? Suddenly she turned, and I heard her walk down the passage. This time I wasn't afraid to follow - I felt that I must know what she wanted. I sprang up and ran out. She was at the other end of the passage, and I expected her to take the turn toward my mistress's room; but instead of that she pushed open the door that led to the backstairs. I followed her down the stairs, and across the passageway to the back door. The kitchen and hall were empty at that hour, the servants being off duty, except for the footman, who was in the pantry. At the door she stood still a moment, with another look at me; then she turned the handle, and stepped out. For a minute I hesitated. Where was she leading me to? The door had closed softly after her, and I opened it and looked out, half-expecting to find that she had disappeared. But I saw her a few yards off hurrying across the courtyard to the path through the woods. Her figure looked black and lonely in the snow, and for a second my heart failed me and I thought of turning back. But all the while she was drawing me after her; and catching up an old shawl of Mrs. Blinder's I ran out into the open.

Emma Saxon was in the wood path now. She walked on steadily, and I followed at the same pace, till we passed out of the gates and reached the high-road. Then she struck across the open fields to the village. By this time the ground was white, and as she climbed the slope of a bare hill ahead of me I noticed that she left no footprints behind her. At sight of that my heart shrivelled up within me, and my knees were water. Somehow, it was worse here than indoors. She made the whole countryside seem lonely as the grave, with none but us two in it, and no help in the wide world.

Once I tried to go back; but she turned and looked at me, and it was as if she had dragged me with ropes. After that I followed her like a dog. We came to the village and she led me through it, past the church and the blacksmith's shop, and down the lane to Mr. Ranford's. Mr. Ranford's house stands close to the road: a plain old-fashioned building, with a flagged path leading to the door between box-borders. The lane was deserted, and as I turned into it I saw Emma Saxon pause under the old elm by the gate. And now another fear came over me. I saw that we had reached the end of our journey, and that it was my turn to act. All the way from Brympton I had been asking myself what she wanted of me, but I had followed in a trance, as it were, and not till I saw her stop at Mr. Ranford's gate did my brain begin to clear itself. I stood a little way off in the snow, my heart beating fit to strangle me, and my feet frozen to the ground; and she stood under the elm and watched me.

I knew well enough that she hadn't led me there for nothing. I felt there was something I ought to say or do - but how was I to guess what it was? I had never thought harm of my mistress and Mr. Ranford, but I was sure now that, from one cause or another, some dreadful thing hung over them. She knew what it was; she would tell me if she could; perhaps she would answer if I questioned her.

It turned me faint to think of speaking to her; but I plucked up heart and dragged myself across the few yards between us. As I did so, I heard the house door open and saw Mr. Ranford approaching. He looked handsome and cheerful, as my mistress had looked that morning, and at sight of him the blood began to flow again in my veins.

"Why, Hartley," said he, "what's the matter? I saw you coming down the lane just now, and came out to see if you had taken root in the snow." He stopped and stared at me. "What are you looking at?" he says.

I turned toward the elm as he spoke, and his eyes followed me; but there was no one there. The lane was empty as far as the eye could reach.

A sense of helplessness came over me. She was gone, and I had not been able to guess what she wanted. Her last look had pierced me to the marrow; and yet it had not told me! All at once, I felt more desolate than when she had stood there watching me. It seemed as if she had left me all alone to carry the weight of the secret I couldn't guess. The snow went round me in great circles, and the ground fell away from me...

A drop of brandy and the warmth of Mr. Ranford's fire soon brought me to, and I insisted on being driven back at once to Brympton. It was nearly dark, and I was afraid my mistress might be wanting me. I explained to Mr. Ranford that I had been out for a walk and had been taken with a fit of giddiness as I passed his gate. This was true enough; yet I never felt more like a liar than when I said it.

When I dressed Mrs. Brympton for dinner she remarked on my pale looks and asked what ailed me. I told her I had a headache, and she said she would not require me again that evening, and advised me to go to bed.

It was a fact that I could scarcely keep on my feet; yet I had no fancy to spend a solitary evening in my room. I sat downstairs in the hall as long as I could hold my head up; but by nine I crept upstairs, too weary to care what happened if I could but get my head on a pillow. The rest of the household went to bed soon afterward; they kept early hours when the master was away, and before ten I heard Mrs. Blinder's door close, and Mr. Wace's soon after.

It was a very still night, earth and air all muffled in snow. Once in bed I felt easier, and lay quiet, listening to the strange noises that come out in a house after dark. Once I thought I heard a door open and close again below: it might have been the glass door that led to the gardens. I got up and peered out of the window; but it was in the dark of the moon, and nothing visible outside but the streaking of snow against the panes.

I went back to bed and must have dozed, for I jumped awake to the furious ringing of my bell. Before my head was clear I had sprung out of bed, and was dragging on my clothes. It is going to happen now, I heard myself saying; but what I meant I had no notion. My hands seemed to be covered with glue - I thought I should never get into my clothes. At last I opened my door and peered down the passage. As far as my candle flame carried, I could see nothing unusual ahead of me. I hurried on, breathless; but as I pushed open the baize door leading to the main hall my heart stood still, for there at the head of the stairs was Emma Saxon, peering dreadfully down into the darkness.

For a second I couldn't stir; but my hand slipped from the door, and as it swung shut the figure vanished. At the same instant there came another sound from below stairs - a stealthy mysterious sound, as of a latchkey turning in the house door. I ran to Mrs. Brympton's room and knocked.

There was no answer, and I knocked again. This time I heard someone moving in the room; the bolt slipped back and my mistress stood before me. To my surprise I saw that she had not undressed for the night. She gave me a startled look.

"What is this, Hartley?" she says in a whisper. "Are you ill? What are you doing here at this hour?"

"I am not ill, madam; but my bell rang."

At that she turned pale, and seemed about to fall.

"You are mistaken," she said harshly; "I didn't ring. You must have been dreaming." I had never heard her speak in such a tone. "Go back to bed," she said, closing the door on me.

But as she spoke I heard sounds again in the hall below: a man's step this time; and the truth leaped out on me.

"Madam," I said, pushing past her, "there is someone in the house -"

"Someone?"

"Mr. Brympton, I think - I hear his step below -"

A dreadful look came over her, and without a word, she dropped flat at my feet. I fell on my knees and tried to lift her: by the way she breathed I saw it was no common faint. But as I raised her head there came quick steps on the stairs and across the hall: the door was flung open, and there stood Mr. Brympton, in his travelling clothes, the snow dripping from him. He drew back with a start as he saw me kneeling by my mistress.

"What the devil is this?" he shouted. He was less high-coloured than usual, and the red spot came out on his forehead.

"Mrs. Brympton has fainted, sir," said I.

He laughed unsteadily and pushed by me. "It's a pity she didn't choose a more convenient moment. I'm sorry to disturb her, but -"

I raised myself up aghast at the man's action.

"Sir," said I, "are you mad? What are you doing?"

"Going to meet a friend," said he, and seemed to make for the dressing-room.

At that my heart turned over. I don't know what I thought or feared; but I sprang up and caught him by the sleeve.

"Sir, sir," said I, "for pity's sake look at your wife!"

He shook me off furiously.

"It seems that's done for me," says he, and caught hold of the dressing-room door.

At that moment I heard a slight noise inside. Slight as it was, he heard it too, and tore the door open; but as he did so he dropped back. On the threshold stood Emma Saxon. All was dark behind her, but I saw her plainly, and so did he. He threw up his hands as if to hide his face from her; and when I looked again she was gone.

He stood motionless, as if the strength had run out of him; and in the stillness my mistress suddenly raised herself, and opening her eyes fixed a look on him. Then she fell back, and I saw the death-flutter pass over her...

We buried her on the third day, in a driving snow-storm. There were few people in the church, for it was bad weather to come from town, and I've a notion my mistress was one that hadn't many near friends. Mr. Ranford was among the last to come, just before they carried her up the aisle. He was in black, of course, being such a friend of the family, and I never saw a gentleman so pale. As he passed me, I noticed that he leaned a trifle on a stick he carried; and I fancy Mr. Brympton noticed it too, for the red spot came out sharp on his forehead, and all through the service he kept staring across the church at Mr. Ranford, instead of following the prayers as a mourner should.

When it was over and we went out to the graveyard, Mr. Ranford had disappeared, and as soon as my poor mistress's body was underground, Mr. Brympton jumped into the carriage nearest the gate and drove off without a word to any of us. I heard him call out, "To the station," and we servants went back alone to the house.

Also available from Parallel Universe Publications

BLACK CEREMONIES
by Charles Black
ISBN-10: 0957453558

THE HEAVEN MAKER AND OTHER GRUESOME TALES
by Craig Herbertson
ISBN-10: 0957453517

GOBLIN MIRE
by David A. Riley
ISBN-10: 095745354X

Check our website:
http://paralleluniversepublications.blogspot.co.uk/

Printed in Great Britain
by Amazon.co.uk, Ltd.,
Marston Gate.